Waterloo

The final book in the Napoleonic Horseman series
By Griff Hosker

Published by Sword Books Ltd 2021
Copyright © Griff Hosker Second Edition

A CIP catalogue record for this title is available from the British Library.

Contents

Waterloo i
Prologue 1
Chapter 1 4
Chapter 2 19
Chapter 3 31
Chapter 4 43
Chapter 5 60
Chapter 6 67
Chapter 7 80
Chapter 8 92
Chapter 9 101
Chapter 10 113
Chapter 11 125
Chapter 12 134
Chapter 13 142
Chapter 14 155
Chapter 15 168
Chapter 16 176
Chapter 17 188
Chapter 18 194
Chapter 19 204
Chapter 20 216
Epilogue 232
Glossary... 234
Historical note 235
Other books by Griff Hosker... 241

Prologue

Returning to winter quarters was depressing. Sergeant Major Sharp was still in England and he was enjoying not only his family, but he was getting to do that which I wished above all things, to see my wife, Emily, and my newly born son, Charles. I could not. I had been sent by General Wellesley to rescue Colonel Selkirk. That I had done so successfully and been praised by both the Colonel, a rare event in itself, and the General was cold comfort. The battles of St Pierre and the Nivelle had taken their toll on the General's officers and many of them, indeed most of them had been allowed to travel back to England. Even the service with which I felt most comfortable, the cavalrymen were also in winter cantonments and were far from the lines where the Spanish and English infantry faced each other.

The Marquess of Wellington was also distracted; this time it was a woman. He was very discreet and his servant, John, facilitated the relationship. I discovered it by accident and, to be frank, I did not care except that I rattled around my rooms knowing that I would not now have time to take a ship back to England. I spent the time riding and exploring the ground over which I knew we would be fighting.

It was with great relief that I welcomed back Sergeant Major Alan Sharp. I barely gave him time to take off his cloak before I began bombarding him with questions. "How are my wife and son?"

He grinned, "They are both well. He has a set of lungs on him, that son of yours. Mind, my son Robert is almost as loud. The ladies are happy." He hung his cloak up and said, "I was sad to leave, sir, but I knew that you would need me. How did the mission go?"

"Better than I expected. They gave Colonel Selkirk a hard time, but I got him out."

"Good, but I hope we are done with him, sir. Whenever he is around it normally means our lives are in danger!"

We chatted about the estate, Rafe Jenkins and Troop Sergeant Fenwick as well as details about our families which would have bored any other. I sent for food to a local bar. We could have cooked but I did not want to waste a moment of the time. I needed to know everything. The more Alan spoke the more I realised that as soon as this was over, I would resign my commission. Emily had never seen Sicily and I had an idea to send to my cousin there and ask if we might spend an extended working holiday. Cesar was always keen to involve me in the running of the estate and now that I had a son, he would be even happier to accommodate me. I was aware that Alan looked a little uncomfortable and that was not like him. We had always been open and honest with each other. I respected his privacy, but I had drunk enough of the local red wine to broach the subject.

"Alan, what is amiss? Is there something you have not told me?"

He gave a weak smile, "You can see right through me, sir, well as it happens there is something, but I am not sure how to tell you."

My heart sank for it sounded serious, but I forced a smile, "Just do as we have always done with each other, Alan, and tell me honestly."

He took a deep breath and a draught of wine, "It is like this sir. You know I took back the treasure and coins we had accumulated?" I nodded. We had managed to acquire, in the grand scheme of things, a small part of King Joseph's treasure. Wellington knew of it and had not asked for it back. Perhaps he had thought it was due to us. "Well when I gave it to Mrs Matthews, she said we ought to go with it to Mr Hudson, your agent." I began to smile. This was not something to be concerned about. It was just business. Alan saw my smile and spoke more hurriedly. "Your wife has a fine head for business. She said we ought to go into partnership and buy another ship." He looked at me and I saw genuine fear on his face. This was Alan Sharp who had endured French torture but the thought of upsetting me appeared to terrify him.

"That is a good idea, go on."

He drank some more wine, "Mrs Matthews and Maria they get on well. They always have done, and I think that it was Maria who suggested the idea, sorry sir!"

"Nothing to be sorry about, Alan. I cannot think of a better arrangement. And what did Mr Hudson say?"

"He said it was a capital idea and had been going to suggest something similar. He said that the war was almost over and the trade between the Mediterranean and England would increase. He sent for Captain Dinsdale and before I knew where we were there was a contract and we had bought a ship. Captain Dinsdale said he would find a captain for it. This has nothing to do with your d'Alpini estates, sir, just the transporting of goods. Mr Hudson said that I will be a rich man!"

I laughed and the laughter was loud because of the relief. "This is great news for I was loath to lose your company once we left the service. I am delighted."

"We leave the service, sir?"

"As soon as the war is over, I shall resign but, of course, you could go now. Even though you are a Sergeant Major you are on the regimental books as my servant. If you wished to go back to Matthew's Farm, I would not blame you."

He shook his head, "No, sir, we shall finish it together. You were the one who saved me when I was a trooper, and I swore then that the only time I would leave your side was when you stopped being a soldier. We are almost at the end now, sir. We will stick it out together."

Chapter 1

It was February when we were called back to Sir Arthur and given our orders. Bayonne was still a thorn in our side and to get around that problem and force Marshal Soult to fall back Sir Arthur had his engineers build a bridge of boats across the Adour. It did not go either as easily or quickly as we had expected but we managed it. I confess that my heart was no longer in this. It seemed to me to be a party that was almost over and the guests were beginning to leave. I suppose that it was also the number of new faces too. Many regiments had already been sent to America to fight in that war. Somerset and Ponsonby were there and they were both cavalrymen but building a bridge of boats across a river was not my idea of war. However, once it was in place then Sharp and I were given the chance to ride once more, I did not have to sit on a riverbank with Sir Arthur while engineers attached cables and hawsers to boats!

On the 24th of February, Sir Arthur sent for me. Unusually he took me into his confidence. Perhaps the favour I had done rescuing Colonel Selkirk helped. He gave me his rough plans for the campaign. He wanted to bring Soult to battle, defeat him and end the war in this part of France! "Matthews, I believe that Soult is at Orthez and I would have you and your fellow accompany the 3rd Division for I intend to end this war and capture the only army which can provide us with opposition. I shall stay with General Beresford and the 4th. The other aides can stay with me. I hope that we can force the crossing of the Adour, but I need you with the 3rd and General Picton."

I smiled, "In my experience sir, General Picton does not require a nursemaid!"

He said, quietly, "He has still not recovered totally from the wounds he received. You appear to be able to recover almost overnight but others are not so lucky. Besides, he asked for you. He seems to think you are a reliable sort of fellow. Use your judgement, eh?"

Both Lieutenant Fortescue and Lieutenant Winterton were back from a brief leave and I told them before I left what Sharp and I would be doing. Both had grown into the role and while I knew they wished to be in a regiment where there would be more opportunities for action the fact that the war's end was so close meant that they were realists and would learn as much as they could from Sir Arthur.

"I don't envy you, sir, General Picton has a tongue on him like a dock labourer!"

I smiled, General Picton stood out amongst Wellington's generals. He had the foulest mouth of any officer I had ever met and did not wear a uniform. "Aye, but his men will follow him anywhere and he has the beating of the French. Do not judge an officer by his uniform, gentlemen. Watch him in action and both of you, try to keep your heads down!"

We took our horses and headed east to join the 3rd division. The irascible general look pleased to see us as we rode in, "If you fellows are here then it means his lordship will be moving soon. I take it our orders have not changed?"

"No, Sir Thomas, we still support the Fourth."

"Good fellows I do not doubt but not the equal of my chaps. Still…"

"Any orders for me, sir?"

"Somerset and his light cavalry are to the east of us. Find yourself a billet and then find them and make sure that Major General Somerset knows to keep close to my flanks."

"Sir."

The orders I had been given suited me well. It would give Sharp and me the opportunity to get the lay of the land. We had not scouted out this area yet. The brigade of light cavalry consisted of the 7th, 10th and 15th Hussars. Sir Arthur's cavalry had improved over the last few years and the Hussars were now less likely to regard battle as an extended fox hunt. I did not know the 7th and the 15th that well but I had served with the 10th and knew them to be good soldiers. I had been with them at Vittoria on the chase after the French. I did not know General Somerset.

As I rode into their encampment, which they must have only recently set up judging by the work still going on, I saw that the General had gathered his senior officers in a tent. I reined in and handed my reins to Alan, "We shall not be spending the night here. Let them graze and get some water."

As I walked in, I was surprised that I was recognised. Colonel Grant of the 10th knew me, but the others were strangers. Sir Edward smiled, "Have you come from Sir Arthur, Colonel?"

"No, sir. I have been detached to serve with Sir Thomas."

He laughed, "And what does our commander wish of us?"

"Why, sir, to keep close to his flank."

Nodding he pointed to the map, "As you can see, Matthews, this is not cavalry country! It will be the devil's own job to keep close and my scouts tell me that French skirmishers could hold my chaps up."

"Yes sir. Sir Arthur is hoping to cross the river further west and we will be in support. I think he believes that the light horse will be more useful once the enemy is broken."

"Aye, well we are ready and eager. You may tell Sir Thomas that we will be there to protect his flanks when he advances."

I nodded, "And that will not be until the left flank is secure. I shall keep you informed." I saluted and turned to leave. I saw Colonel Grant waiting to speak with me, "How are Aitkens and Hargreaves, Colonel?"

The bugler and trooper had been wounded at Vittoria. "Good of you to ask. Both are back in the saddle although I am not sure they should be. You are a cavalryman, Matthews, and know that these chaps hate to be idle, but I do not think that this time we will be as lucky as we were when we chased King Joseph!"

I laughed for the treasure taken that day would guarantee that when the regiments came to recruit again, they would have a tale to tell to entice many more men.

On the way back to headquarters, riding along an increasingly dark road Sharp's words reflected the opinion of the rank and file. That the next battle would be the last one. "On the ship back, sir, the captain was telling us that Boney can't last above a month more. Is this battle necessary?"

"Napoleon Bonaparte is a survivor, Alan. The only part of France which he has lost is the part captured by us, here in the south. He will believe that he can turn his enemies to fight each other. You should know that we take one battle at a time. Until we are told the war is over, we assume it is the same as when we waited behind the Portuguese border. That was less than two years ago." I paused for I knew why he thought this way. He had been home and that changed him. Alan was no longer a soldier with heart in the job. I had not had that delight and my adventure in Antibes had kept me sharp. I would have to watch Alan.

For two days we cooled our heels in the encampment. We heard distant guns but that was all and then Lieutenant Fortescue rode in with orders. I followed him in to speak with Sir Thomas, "Sir, the general requests that you bring the 3rd Division to the River Gave d'Oloron and pin the French centre. General Hill has secured a bridgehead on the far bank." He paused, "The French are dug in on two spurs, sir."

Sir Thomas was studying the map, "Aye, well sir, you bugger off down the road and tell General Somerset what we are about eh?"

I smiled as the Lieutenant hurriedly saluted and let us as quickly as he could.

Turning to his aide Sir Thomas said, "Send in my officers. We have action at last!"

I did not recognise most of the colonels and brigadiers who entered as the last months in Spain and southern France had resulted in many changes. I would have to get to know them.

Sir Thomas did not bother with preliminaries, he just went to the map and pointed to the spur beyond the river, "There, gentlemen, is your goal. You will take the spur. Major General Brisbane will lead the assault with his brigade, the Sixth Division will support you. As soon as you have a foothold then we will spread out to the south and east and trap the bastard Soult in Orthez!" He glowered at his officers and sucked on his cigar, "Any questions?"

Major Brisbane asked, "And if they are hard to dislodge sir?"

"Then, General, you go in with the bayonet yourself and shift them! You have a division to support you and if that does not suffice then I suggest you go back to England and write your memoirs! It will be a short volume!"

The General visibly shrank and they all left before they, too, had to endure Picton's ire.

"Keep an eye on that one, he thinks he is better than he is!"

"Then why send him in first, General?"

"Simple, he has the Highlanders and the Connaught Rangers. Those mad buggers can storm anything! Besides which he has the largest brigade in my Division."

I suppose that had I not bumped into the Major General outside then things might have been different, but my mind was elsewhere. Sharp's words had set in motion a train of thoughts that distracted me. The war was almost over and there was a rosy prospect awaiting me. I would have done what I intended when I joined the British Army and, in my own small way, helped to defeat Bonaparte.

Major General Brisbane was speaking with his aides as I emerged. "Dammit, the man is no gentleman. He should not be commanding a home depot let alone a division. I shall do this my way and he can be damned!"

I should have walked on, but I did not, "Major General Brisbane, Sir Thomas Picton is one of the most highly regarded men in this army. He knows his business, sir."

"And who the hell are you? I do not recognise your uniform."

One of his aides did and tried to avoid his superior putting his foot in it again, "Sir, this is Lieutenant Colonel Matthews, and he is one of General Wellesley's aides."

"Hmph, well when I want the opinion of a glorified messenger boy, I shall ask for it!"

I smiled, "I am sure that Sir Arthur would appreciate that... sir!" I turned on my heels and I was seething but I kept my temper under control and went to find Sharp and the horses,

Sharp had not used Donna for she was getting a little old but one of the French horses we had captured. I did not take my Baker rifle, but I did ensure that I had four pistols. "We are to advance with Brisbane's Brigade. Let us get ahead of them so that we can anticipate any problems. I fear that Sir Thomas has sent the wrong man."

As we neared the spur and heard the French Divisional cannons pounding away, we saw streams of wounded soldiers head back to the dressing stations. This was Anson's Brigade and even before they began the attack they had less than half the numbers of General Brisbane's. General Anson recognised me and rode over to me. Even as he came a French sharpshooter sent a bullet to pluck at his hat. As he took it off to examine it I saw a Portuguese officer order his Caçadores to direct their fire at the Voltigeur.

"Damn, this was almost a new hat!" He replaced it and smiled at me, "Damned hot here, Matthews. I take it the marquess has orders for us?"

I nodded, "The Third is on its way here to relieve you. Once they arrive you can pull back."

"The chaps aren't afraid you know but Foy has a good position up there. Near as we can make out, he has almost four thousand men, light and heavy as well as well sited guns. They will take some shifting."

"General Brisbane has almost that and the Sixth Division. I think General Wellington wants this flank turning."

It always takes time to withdraw one unit and replace it with another. So it proved and time was wasted during which more men fell. Eventually, however, Colonel Lister arrived with the 45th. I saw that the Highlanders and the Connaught Rangers had been assigned to protect the guns which were quickly deployed. I had met Captain Turner and knew him to be a good gunner. He deployed his nine pounders and they began to pound the French positions. The 45th waited. I wondered why General Brisbane had not used the Connaughts and Highlanders for the initial attack. The two regiments were both renowned as indomitable fighters. One was his regiment.

The artillery battered away, and I rode over to Colonel Lister, "Why are you not attacking?"

He sniffed, "We would, Colonel, but the General wants the French weakening further."

I whipped my horse's head around and galloped the five hundred yards back to the General, "General Brisbane, Sir Thomas wishes you to attack! Why are you not doing so?"

"I am using my judgement, Colonel, and do not be insubordinate. You are here as a messenger and that is all!"

I was just about to say something else when I saw Sir Edward Pakenham gallop up. I liked Sir Edward who just happened to be Sir Arthur's brother in law. He was, like me, a cavalryman, and he galloped up to me, "Sir Thomas sent me, Matthews. The rest of the Sixth are backed up on the road. Why are we not attacking?"

I smiled, "General Brisbane knows best, or so he says."

"We shall see!" Sir Edward galloped up and waved his hat in the direction of the French, "Good God! General Brisbane. Why stand here while the brigade gets cut up? Form line and send out the 45th skirmishing!"

I saw the General glare at me as though I had told tales on him, he waved to me, "Go then, sir, and ask Colonel Lister to advance!"

Sir Edward shook his head, "I pray you do it, Colonel!"

I spurred my horse. The inactivity had encouraged the French and musket balls were sent in my direction. I reined in and dismounted. Sharp was behind me and he took my horse's reins, "Colonel, General Brisbane orders you to advance with a skirmish line."

"Thank you, Colonel. We are not cowards, but we need order, don't you know?"

We stayed there as the light companies of the Nottinghamshire Regiment formed up and behind them the rest of the companies in skirmish order. General Keane's men were to the west of us and between the two advancing lines was a muddy valley which both battalions had avoided.

"Sharp, you had better dismount. Take the horses to Captain Turner's Batteries."

"Sir!"

I did not bother with my pistols; the enemy were too far away but I followed the grenadier company a little way up the spur. A ball plucked at my hat and I saw a grenadier fall wounded. This would be slow going. The skirmishers advanced like the rifles. One fired while the other advanced and reloaded. That way they kept up a steady rate of fire. The French light infantry had been good opposition, but the war had weakened them. The 45th were progressing albeit slowly. I had been a Chasseur in the French cavalry and I knew all the bugle calls. It was the sort of thing that was ingrained in your memory. In the distance, I heard the call to form line. Looking along the line I saw the only place that the French could use cavalry was down the muddy valley. They were going for the Connaughts and the guns. I ran, shouting as I did, "Ware cavalry!"

My voice carried to the General who turned his telescope. Of course, he would see nothing for the spur hid the advancing cavalrymen. The 45th were making progress and the Sixth Division, led by General Pack were already forming up to exploit the advances made by the now much depleted Nottinghamshire regiment. Even before I reached the Connaught Rangers, I was shouting, "Connaughts, prepare to receive cavalry! I had fought with the regiment twice before, most notably in Oporto and enough officers recognised both me and my voice to obey.

As I ran towards Sharp, who had now dismounted, I heard Captain Turner rattling out his orders to the gunners. I also heard the bugle ordering the charge! I made it to the line of nine-pound guns just as I saw the Chasseurs appear. They were the 21st and there were two squadrons of them. The days when the French could be profligate were long gone! I drew my sword and pistol. The Connaughts were good. Considered by Sir Arthur to be wild men I had found them courageous and able to stand and take seemingly endless punishment without breaking. Sharp had tied off the horses and he ran to me with his own sword and pistol.

He shook his head, "Be careful sir, Mrs Matthews would not like you to suffer another wound!"

The Major of the Connaughts shouted, "Present! Fire!" The smoke from the belching artillery, added to the smoke from the muskets, shrank the view to a few yards. The Connaught Rangers continued to do what they had been taught. They fired, reloaded, fired again and kept doing so until they could not do so. The Chasseur who appeared from the fog was just twenty yards from me when I saw him, The gunners had just fired and, seeing the horsemen, wisely took shelter beneath the artillery pieces. I raised my left hand and fired. I was never as accurate as when I used my right hand, but I was so close and the pistol so relatively accurate that I scored a wound along the neck of the horse. The Connaughts were firing to their front and that meant it was just Sharp and I who were protecting the gun. The Chasseur had intended to make his horse rear but the wound made it veer to the horseman's left and I stepped from behind the gun and backhanded my sword into the thigh of the Chasseur. His sword hovered above my head, but I saw that he was young. It was hard to control the wounded horse and although his sword came down mine drew blood and ripped across his breeches. It was not a fatal wound but as the sword also raked his horse it made his horse turn from the torment.

"Sergeant, load your gun!"

As the crew leapt from hiding, I holstered one pistol and drew my second, stepping back behind the barrel. Sharp stood next to me and raised his piece as two more horsemen appeared, and I could see two more shadows behind. We both fired at once but before we could see the effect the cannon roared and sent grapeshot at the horsemen. The two before us were swept from their saddles and I saw the shadow of the one I had wounded spread his arms and fall.

The Major allowed one more volley and then shouted, "Cease fire!"

As the smoke cleared, I saw that there were at least six dead horses and more than fifteen dead troopers. More would have been wounded. Captain Turner shouted, "Clean out the guns and reload." Turning to me he said, "Thank you, sir! It is good to know that your reputation is well deserved."

Before I could answer I heard the French bugle once more. There would be a second attack, "Face your front! Here they come again."

I saw wounded men being dragged away for the French guns had begun to fire again as soon as their cavalry had withdrawn, and fresh Rangers took the place of those wounded or injured. We would not have time to reload and so Sharp ran the two hundred yards to the horses to fetch the saddle pistols. The gunners fired ball, not at the horsemen but the Frenchmen on the spur of land. I could see that they were almost at the summit of the ridge. The second attack was with a fresh squadron of Chasseurs. Perhaps the French thought we had been weakened, we had not. Sharp arrived back just as the Chasseurs put spurs to their horses for the charge. They were brave and they were young. Their bravery meant that they were happy to risk death for France, but their youth meant they lacked experience. It was the latter that counted. Even so, they were fresh and their artillery had knocked the red-coated defenders about a little. The cannons belched and the gunners took shelter. This time more of the Chasseurs made it through to the guns and the front ranks. They slashed and stabbed at the bayonets of the Rangers but when they saw the guns some were young enough and fearless enough to jump them. I was pleased that I had elected to stay behind one. I fired up at the Chasseur who, as he was leaping the gun was slashing down at me. My ball caught his shoulder and my slashing sword ripped across his horse's chest. In his falling and his steed's attempt to move to the side, he crashed into the next gun, which would need to be realigned. I holstered my pistol.

"You bastard!" One of the gunners leapt from under his gun and hacked into the horseman's neck.

I had no time to see his fate for two others jumped. Sharp's shot was more accurate than mine for he was using his right hand and his ball scored a line along the horse's neck and then drove into the skull of the rider who was dead before his wounded horse landed. I was without a loaded pistol and so I took off my hat and waved it at the next horse which baulked. The rider turned to his right and, using the gun's carriage I leapt into the air. I took not only the Frenchman but the gunners and the Connaughts by surprise. I was lucky and my feet knocked him from his saddle and provided a soft landing. The weight of my body drove the air from him and I was on my feet in an instant. I put my sword to his throat and said, "Surrender, my friend, it is over!"

At that moment the French cavalry began to withdraw and there was a cheer as the 48th took the ridge. The Frenchman nodded and handed me his sabre.

Sharp grabbed the horse's reins and shaking his head led it to the others, "Sir that would definitely not have pleased your good lady."

I nodded, shocked by my own actions, "You are right, but we appear to have succeeded here. Let us visit with Sir Thomas before we report back to Sir Arthur."

We mounted our horses and, leading the captured Chasseurs, we were greeted by cheers from red coats and gunners alike. I believe it was because we contrasted with General Brisbane and his staff who had merely watched us. The French Chasseur shook his head as he was led off with the other prisoners. As I passed the General, I said,

"Congratulations, sir. Your men have succeeded. All that they needed was the command."

It was close to insubordination, but I knew he would say nothing. I had made an enemy but then again, it was a habit that was hard to break. We finally caught up with General Wellesley as he was about to enter Orthez. Soult and his army had fallen back and were heading for Tarbes. The General was with Somerset's Hussars and as we rode east, we collected many hundreds of National Guardsmen who had deserted. For me, it highlighted the lack of spirit amongst the French. These were men defending their homes and I had expected that they would have fought harder. Even Sir Arthur was in an ebullient mood, believing as we all did that the end of the war might be days away. We began the pursuit of Soult at the end of February. So confident was I that I did not even send a letter to Emily as I believed I had a better chance of delivering the letter myself!

Napoleon had other ideas!

The Royalists also muddied the water. Two representatives from Bordeaux were admitted to our camp promising that Bordeaux would rise and welcome King Louis back to France. The Duc Angoulême had returned from exile. I was privileged to be there when Sir Arthur spoke to them. Sir Edward and Lord Beresford were also present, but I was the only aide. I saw from their faces that they expected a happier reaction from the general. He sent them for refreshments and then spoke to his two confederates, "This may either be a ploy or, at best a distraction, gentlemen. We gain nothing from this. I have no idea what our superiors have planned for Bonaparte. I cannot entertain welcoming the King back to France!"

"Nor, my lord, can we afford to ignore this offer."

"Quite, you are right Beresford, but I can ill afford to detach a large number of men. Take the 4th and the 7th, along with Vivian and his Hussars. Go to Bordeaux but go there in my name! Neither of us has the authority to offer the crown to King Louis!"

I saw a different side to Wellington that day. He was a politician as well as a great general. I could never be a politician. I saw that he was also hampered by a wound which he had suffered in the battle of Orthez. A musket ball had struck his sword hilt and driven it into his body. He continued to work but I saw the pain on his face. It made him seem more human in my eyes.

Fourteen thousand men were detached and that, along with the losses we had incurred, seemed to encourage Soult who showed no signs of defeat. We had taken many losses winkling him from his ridge and now, as we headed to Toulouse, he used his cavalry to keep us at bay. For my part, I dreaded taking a walled town. The Spanish and Portuguese ones were bad enough but as I had seen at Antibes, the French had taken the constructions of forts and strongholds to a completely different level.

It all began with two disastrous attempts to ford the river with pontoons and with bridges made of boats. Both were failures and both were down to Sir Arthur. He became irritable for he knew it was his fault. He had been advised his pontoon equipment was not long enough and that he had not enough boats. Time was wasted and that aided Soult who was able to prepare his defences. This type of mistake permeated down through the generals and commanders beneath Wellington. It was as though everyone expected the French to surrender. We looked for Imperial messengers to ride from Paris with news that the Emperor had capitulated. It did not happen.

Sharp and I were kept with Sir Arthur as we headed to Toulouse over roads which were soaked by heavy rain. With General Stewart attacking through the suburb of St Etienne we probed without cavalry up towards the walls of Toulouse. It was the irascible Sir Thomas who made the first mistake. He was asked to probe the French defences. I had been with Sir Arthur when he had specifically ordered him not to try to force the Ponts Jumeaux. It may have been General Brisbane's early failures at Orthez, I know not but Sir Thomas tried to force the crossing and many of his men were lost.

When Lieutenant Fortescue brought the news Sir Arthur turned to me and shook his head, "You know, Matthews, we have been at this too long! Sir Thomas would not have made such a mistake two years ago! We need this war ending now!"

Marshal Beresford was one of the few, that day, who did not make a mistake. He was never brilliant, as Crauford had been, but he was reliable and obeyed his orders. He would be the punch that would render the French confused but as he deployed his guns, General Freire, commanding our Spanish allies, mistook the preliminaries for the actual attack and ordered his men to storm the Great Redoubt. They were thrown back with huge losses. Once again Sir Arthur was enraged but he knew not to lose his temper. His plan was a sound one but already we had lost thousands of men and the medieval walls of Toulouse had yet to be attacked. "Matthews, I have a long ride for you and your fellow. Ride to Marshal Beresford. I want you to be my eyes and ears there. I shall stay here and ensure that Generals Picton and Freire do not mistake my orders again"

"Sir."

"The Marshal is a sound fellow and I do not doubt for an instant that he will do anything less than obey my orders but…" He shrugged. Sir Arthur was not himself. I wonder if the musket ball to his sword hilt had damaged his confidence. Sharp and I wheeled our horses and followed Marshal Beresford's two divisions. I could see them deploying as we reached them. The delay in crossing the river had resulted in the French constructing huge redoubts. Although the artillery was having an effect the only way that they would be taken would be by British infantry. That in itself gave me hope for with equal numbers the sheer firepower of the British soldier was so superior to the French that the outcome would not be in doubt for long.

I saluted to the Marshal as I reined in, "Matthews, come to keep your eye on me for Sir Arthur?"

I smiled although that was what I was doing, "No sir, I am merely here to report to him when the redoubts are taken."

I could see he was not convinced but he nodded, "Well sir, we have a good seat here, do we not? Let us see what the fine fellows of Anson's Brigade can do!"

The brigades were echeloned, and they advanced in a three-deep line. Sir Arthur had been right, the Marshal was reliable, and he did not panic as the whole front became enveloped in white smoke as the two forces met. One of his aides had a telescope and he suddenly shouted, "Marshal, the French cavalry are forming up to attack General Pack and his men!"

"Calm down Anderson. General Pack will form square!" He turned to me, "You do not panic so easily, Matthews, be so good as to ask General Somerset to bring his brigade and deal with those French horsemen."

"Sir!"

My old friends the 10th Hussars were with General Somerset as well as the 7th and the 15th. They were all reliable and Sharp and I galloped to the brigade which was just half a mile away guarding the left flank. Reining in I said, "The Marshal's compliments and would you be so good as to chase away those Hussars and Chasseurs, sir?"

The General smiled, "Action at last. Of course, Colonel and would you be so good as to join us? I know the 10th would like you to ride with them again."

"I would be delighted, sir."

We rode to the regiment as the bugles sounded the command to form lines. Some of the troopers cheered as we approached. I knew not if this was because we were joining them or at the thought of action. The cavalry, since the chase from Vittoria, had played a secondary role.

Colonel Grant nodded, "Glad you are joining us, Matthews. Good to be reunited at the end, eh?"

"Yes, Colonel, but this day is far from over."

I saw that the bugler, Aitkens, had returned to duty and he nodded to me as he spat and put the bugle to his lips. "The regiment will advance!"

As the bugle sounded, I saw Pack's brigade form square. They had been in Spain for virtually the whole war and they would not be put out by having to form square. Even so, General Somerset wasted no time in advancing. The 10th Hussars were the leading regiment with the other two echeloned behind us. A general and two colonels were leading this cavalry charge, but we were not the reckless and some might say feckless fellows from the early days of the war. We rode steadily with sabres sheathed. The French light horsemen were trying to get at the infantry squares, but these were cuirassiers riding huge horses and with breastplates. These were Chasseurs and Hussars. Their slashing sabres could cause terrible wounds but first, they had to penetrate the hedgehog of bayonets. Of course, a square would find it hard to reload and once they had fired an initial volley, they might have to endure the French swords.

We were less than three hundred paces from the French when the order was given to charge. Sabres were drawn and spurs put to horses. We did this further away than normal because we had the advantage over the French. They were not in lines and General Somerset wished to hit them hard. I was riding Donna. This would be her last battle, but she held her own with the fine horse ridden by General Somerset. It had been some time since I had charged, and I had forgotten the sheer exhilaration of a cavalry charge. My blade never wavered as I leaned over Donna's head. I knew that behind me Sergeant Major Sharp was next to Corporal Aitkens and his sword was as unwavering.

The French reacted when we were less than eighty yards from them. The smoke which enveloped their front and the noise of battle masked our attack. French cavalry never lacked courage and when we were seen I heard the bugle call which told me they were going to attempt a counter charge. It made sense for if they turned and fled our superior speed would catch them and none of them relished being sabred in the back. Better to face your foe where you had a chance!

I had used a Chasseur sword and knew that the longer straighter one I now used was better. I almost felt sorry for the Chasseur who faced me for he was a good soldier. He obeyed his orders instantly and turned his horse. He was a good rider with perfect control of a horse I could see was not the best. He saw that I was a senior officer and did not baulk at charging me. Despite that, I knew that I would win. His sword was a slashing sword, mine had a point and I could lunge. Added to that he had been fighting already and I could see that his overalls were cut and, no doubt, the edge had been taken off his blade. We both leaned forward, facing each other sword to sword. I held mine out and he took the decision to try to deflect mine. He did succeed in moving my blade, but he merely drove it towards his left side and the razor-sharp blade drove into his dolman and then his side. Worse, his momentum meant that the edge of the sword ripped across his stomach and he tumbled from his horse.

I withdrew the sword as he fell and had the time to see that some of the troops had turned to flee. Our charge had allowed General Pack's squares to reform and fire a volley. With musket fire on one side and sabres on the other many decided that flight was the better option. The few who continued to fight were soon overwhelmed and taken captive. The Light Cavalry did me proud for unlike six or seven years earlier, they heeded the bugle call and formed ranks. The threat to General Pack and his brigade was gone and they were able to continue their attack. That was the moment when Marshal Beresford and his two Divisions finally broke through the lines of the redoubts. The French fled back to the walls of Toulouse. That they made it was not the fault of the attackers. The slopes leading up to the fortifications were a testament to their courage and they were littered with bloodied corpses. We had Toulouse surrounded but the threat from Soult was not gone. He and the Army of Spain retreated to Carcassonne. We learned that the Emperor had abdicated ten days earlier and peace signed almost a week later. The eight thousand men who had died at Toulouse had not needed to. Worse was to follow when four days after Toulouse had fallen the garrison at Bayonne tried to sortie. The fact that they failed was immaterial for a thousand French men and a thousand coalition soldiers were either killed or wounded. I had expected joy when victory finally came but I was left with a sour taste in my mouth.

Chapter 2

Surprisingly, Sir Arthur seemed quite understanding when I said that I wished to resign my commission. We were in Bayonne and it may have been that the news of his new title had just arrived. He was now the Marquess of Wellington! He nodded when I told him, "I shall miss you, Robbie, for you are a good chap and do what you are ordered. That is rare. But I will not accept the resignation of your commission. You are too valuable to England. You shall go on half-pay as shall your fellow, Sharp."

"But, my lord, I do not wish to war again."

"And you may not be needed but as the colonial spat is still ongoing, I fear that Englishmen will be needed there."

"And that is why I wish to resign so that I will not be asked to go there."

He smiled, "Let me tell you something in confidence. I have no intention of becoming embroiled in a war that we should not be fighting and certainly can never win. If I do not request your presence, then no one shall!"

"Not even Colonel Selkirk?"

He laughed, "After Antibes, I think that the Colonel will be in your debt and you can say no to him any time you like." He saw that I was undecided. "Robbie, if you are asked to war again and do not wish to go then resign your commission then."

"And be seen as a coward?"

"That is the one thing that no one, even your enemies, can say of you. Your wounds are your medals."

I saw no reason to resign if there was no real need, "Then I will not resign my commission."

"Good and I have a fast packet waiting to take my reports to London. You might as well be the chap who takes them!"

And so in May 1814, I left Spain. We took the brig to London where I delivered the reports and then Alan and I rode directly to Matthew's Farm and my family. There had been no chance to warn them of our imminent arrival but the workers in my fields, some of the old soldiers who had served with us, must have recognised us for they waved and shouted. By the time we reached the farm, which had been derelict when I had bought it but now it looked like a small village, our wives and

19

children were waiting for us. I say children, the only child was Juan, Alan's stepson. Charles was held in his mother's arms. I had never seen my son and I was so excited that I thought I would burst. I saw Emily wipe what must have been a tear from her eye. I was just glad she had not seen me after my last wounds. At least now I was whole but when we were alone it would have to be in a darkened room for my body looked like a badly drawn map.

Jack Jones and Ned Fenwick looked fit to burst and they took the reins of the horses. As much as they both wished to speak with us they knew our wives were there and they would demand our attention first. As I dismounted and I answered their unspoken question, "The war is over, and Alan and I are done with the army!"

"That is great news, sir. We will see to the horses and mebbe we can have a chat later, eh sir?"

"Of course, Jack!"

I turned to Emily who burst into tears, and I opened my arms as she and a somewhat bemused Charles were thrown into them. "I thought this day would never come and although I promised I would not shed a tear the day has come, and I am weeping like a heroine at Drury Lane!"

I, too, felt overwhelmed but it was not just the sight of my wife and child which prompted the feeling. Seeing Jack and Ned brought back memories of all of those who would not be returning. The last unnecessary battles and deaths had affected me! I just hugged them and felt the tears soaking my shirt. I think we might have remained there longer had not Charles grabbed a hunk of my hair and pulled, squealing with delight as he did so!

It made Emily laugh and she said, "He is such a little monkey! Charles, this is your father!

I was not sure he would understand and, indeed, he just giggled and tried to grab my nose. I just laughed. This was a world away from the Marquess of Wellington and the world of war. "Come let us go inside. I would change from these clothes and wear others which have not seen the back of a horse nor war!"

The first few days were a whirlwind as I adjusted to life as a civilian. I still woke well before dawn and Emily groaned as I did so, "Charles was awake an hour since. Did you not hear him?"

I shook my head as I crawled back beneath the covers. I had not heard a baby cry but had I heard a footstep coming towards me then I would have been instantly awake. I was able to bathe and choose clothes that hung from a wardrobe rather than picked from a pile on a footlocker. It was also strange to have a hot cooked breakfast and good coffee. I even managed to play with Charles while Emily prepared his breakfast. The feeding process looked to me to be an experiment as more food flew through the air than entered his mouth. Emily seemed satisfied and, for his part, he was happy enough giggling as he blew some porridge down his nose. I spent time, those first days, walking my land and speaking with those who lived upon it. Often I did so with Charles upon my shoulders and Emily in close attendance. We did not wish to miss a moment together. I did not regard them as employees but rather as friends that I paid. Rafe, Jack and Ned all wished to know about the war, and I obliged but I told them that I would not repeat it.

I had been home a week when Emily broached the subject of the ship and the partnership with Alan. "You have had time to enjoy your son and your friends but now is the time to take the reins of the future. I know that Alan will have mentioned my plan." I nodded. I had seen Emily's firm hand all over it. "And?"

"And I think it is a good plan."

"Then you and Alan must do something about it. Mr Hudson has found a shipbuilder down at Tilbury and there is a ship which has been begun. The previous owner became bankrupt. He gambled on the French winning and lost. Mr Hudson says that he can buy the ship at a bargain price and you can fit it out the way you wish!"

I smiled, "I see motherhood has not mellowed you!"

She smiled back, "We have much time to make up and I am anxious to see your family home in Sicily. From the way you describe the place, it sounds like the garden of Eden and poor Maria has endured a winter in England. She, too, would like some sun!" I saw then that the two women had become almost as close as Alan and I. They could never have the same bond for we had saved each other's lives on more than one occasion and seen the other facing death. We were closer than brothers!

And so Alan and I took two horses and rode the short way to Mr Hudson's offices. The d'Alpini family and me, along with the merchants Fortnum and Mason, were his biggest clients. When I had first engaged him, he had been almost on his own and now they had a bevvy of clerks. He dropped everything and hired a hackney to go with us to the yard. As we rode, he filled us in on the background. With the end of the war the shipbuilder, who had built some small ships for the navy, did not know where his money was coming from. It explained the relatively low cost.

"Is Matthew Dinsdale in port?" Matthew was another partner of mine and as great a seaman as I had ever met.

"No, Colonel, he is due in port sometime next month."

"Well, my problem is that I need a seaman's views on the design. Still, we can begin the process and then Sharp and I will seek a suitable adviser."

William Harrington was a gnarled old man with a clay pipe perpetually in his mouth. I took to him immediately for he employed not only his sons but also ex sailors. He was as loyal an Englishman as I had ever met and once he discovered I was recently returned from serving Sir Arthur he could not do enough for us.

"Well, Colonel, the keel is sound, and we have begun to plank her. The hard work was done. She will be fast and yet have enough hold to give you a good profit from your cargo."

I smiled for I recognised the fine lines. She looked like a large brig such as Captain Jonathan Teer had commanded in the war. The last time I had seen *'Black Prince'* had been at the turn of the year when she had put into Barcelona for repairs. His advice would have been more than useful. "Captain, you have made the sail. I need to find a captain but until I find one would you be able to continue to work on her?"

"Of course. Have you a name, Colonel, only my men are superstitious about such things? A ship without a name is like a man without a soul. She should have been named months ago but…"

I looked at Alan. We had spoken of the name and I said, without hesitation, "She shall be named, *'Donna Maria'* after a real lady who died for her country."

He beamed, "Aye, that would suit."

"Mr Hudson here will deal with any requests for money. Tell me, Master William, are there any alehouses around here where old sailors gather?"

He nodded and pointed, "Aye, sir. Being so close to the Naval Dockyard the *'Ship'* attracts many seamen. It will be filled with them at the moment. The ink is barely dried on the peace and they are laying up ships in ordinary and their crews left to find jobs." He pointed to some of his men, "I took on six and that is two more than I needed. England always does this sir, uses them in war and then gets rid once it is over. Sorry, sir."

I shook my head, "No, I agree with you. Then I may well be able to find a skipper and a crew here?"

"Crew, aye sir, but skipper? You will be lucky!"

We bade farewell to Mr Hudson who hurried back to his office. Leaving our horses at the shipyard we strolled over to the alehouse. It was not the sort of inn which a gentleman would enter. Even as we were walking towards it three men rolled out of the front door and continued a fight that had begun inside. It became clear that two men were attacking the other man and the smaller man was held by one while the other assailant punched him. The one being beaten was a sailor and I saw from his tattoos that he had served in the navy. I could never abide bullying. That was how Alan and I had met, I had seen him bullied by some of his fellow troopers.

The officer in me came to the fore, "You there, whatever he has done that is enough, leave him alone."

I saw that the two men doing the beating were not sailors. They looked to me to be ex-soldiers. You learn to look at tattoos and style of dress. These two still had the remnants of an ancient uniform. I do not think that they recognised me, but they dropped the sailor, now unconscious, to the ground and, pulling old bayonets from their belts, turned to face me. Alan stood to one side and I think the two thought me alone. They might not have recognised me but the sword, cavalry boots and my tone told them enough.

"And what have we here, Cedric? It looks to me like it is an officer, well Mr lah di dah this is not the army so push off before we give the same to you. The boss said we had to give him a going over and we have! Now clear off!"

I nodded, "When I have ensured that this sailor is not injured then I will continue on into the inn."

"Over my dead body!"

I saw from the faded jacket of the one who spoke to me that he had been a corporal at one time for I could see where his stripes had been. He advanced towards me with a knife held before him. I could smell the ale on him. I did not reach for my weapon but I allowed him to stab at me. Using my left hand to deflect the wild stab and stepping to the side I punched him hard in the ribs. Even as the other tried to help his friend Alan had pulled his sap from his coat and laid out the man with one blow. Old habits die hard, and Alan had retained the green coat we had worn in Spain. He called it his riding out coat. I wore a new one and my only weapon was my sword. As the corporal doubled up, I brought up my knee to smash into his face. I cursed for the blood stained my breeches. Emily would see it! With the two laid on their backs, we took their bayonets and went to help up the sailor. He had come to.

"Thank 'ee sir. They sort of snuck up on me. Toby Taylor, topman. I am much obliged!"

"What happened?"

"These two work for Paddy the Mick. He owns the *'Ship'*. He doesn't like sailors which is daft as his inn is by the river, but I reckon he is a smuggler and just doesn't like the navy." He tapped his tattoo, "I am navy. Fifteen years I served on the *'Bellerophon'* and then they threw me on the beach!"

Alan asked, "Then why drink here?"

"Mr Harrington lets us sleep in the shipyard and his wife give us food and besides, it is where old sailors meet. Paddy the Mick reckoned I paid him with a counterfeit coin. Not true, sir, for if I did then I got it here."

I nodded, "Then come with us and we will buy you an ale and perhaps offer you work."

"You have a ship, sir?" He brightened up and forgot his beating.

"I have one which is being built and I seek a crew. Come let us enter."

The corporal was rising slowly and groggily to his feet. I did not see them as a threat. The men standing in the door saw us approaching and moved back inside. It was weird, for as we entered it was as though it was a church for the silence seemed to envelop you. We walked towards the bar and the sailors, I could see more than twenty of them, parted. I saw Paddy the Mick. He too looked like an ex-soldier. He was huge with a broken nose and a scar on his cheek. He looked beyond us to see if he could see his men.

"Where are Jack and Bill?"

I deliberately spoke in what the man would see as an officer's voice, "You mean those men who were attacking this fellow and then set about me? Why, they had an accident. I suppose they will be safe enough until I call for the constable."

"This is my inn! They work for me!"

"Then you are the one I need to deal with."

He suddenly became nervous, "Why, who are you? This is not the army!"

I leaned forward and spoke quietly, "No? But I bet you were in the army and I am also guessing that you have no discharge papers." I saw his tattoo. "The Connaughts? A fine regiment and I served with them at Oporto and Orthez. They would be embarrassed by you. Now, do you

24

serve me, or shall I send for the provosts?" He was a deserter and as his face had paled when I had said Oporto then I guessed that he had finally recognised me. I did not know him but then again I had seen so many soldiers.

He gave a false smile, "No need for that, sir. This is a simple misunderstanding that is all. You three can have a drink on the house before you go."

"Very generous but not only will we not be going, not anytime soon, anyway, but we will also be here regularly for I am having a ship built." I smiled and leaned forward, "In my case, it will be a legitimate trader and not a smuggler!"

Before he could answer a voice shouted, "Is that you Major Matthews?"

I turned and saw a man I recognised but could not put a name to his face. "It is Colonel Matthews now but as the war is over the point is moot. I am sorry, sir, but you have the advantage of me. I recognise your face but not your name."

He strode over with a huge grin on his face, "Jack Robinson, sir, I was Master's Mate on the *'Black Prince'* with Captain Teer. The worst day of my life was when I took the promotion to serve aboard *'Tiger'*. I have been laid off these six months."

The drinks had arrived and I turned to Paddy the Mick, "And a drink for my friend." I shoved over a coin. "I only accept drinks from friends or gentlemen, and you are neither."

He coloured but could do nothing about it. The four of us went to a table. It seemed most of the customers liked to stand at the bar. Jack's tale and Toby's were remarkably similar. Both were specialists and when the navy decided that they did not need such a large fleet they were both unlucky enough to be laid off. I knew, from Rafe at my farm, that work in England was hard enough to come by at the best of times and for a master's mate and a topman, it was almost impossible.

While Alan went to fetch more beer, I laid out my proposition to the two of them. "Jack, how would you like to be the captain of the new ship we are having built at the yard?"

Alan came back with the beer and Jack looked at him, "I thought you were just a sergeant?"

It sounded insulting but Alan and I knew that the sailor did not mean it to be. He nodded, "Sergeant Major but you are right. Colonel Matthews here invited me to be his partner in this ship. You do not have to be what you were born, Jack. You can change your own destiny."

Jack nodded.

I looked at Toby, "And we need a crew. Subject to Jack's approval and if he accepts the position then we would like you to be the first."

They both nodded and almost spoke at the same time as they hurriedly agreed. I waved a hand around the bar, "I am guessing that you two know the lads in here better than any and both being sailors then you should be able to choose a good crew."

Jack nodded, "Aye, sir, but what will the ship be doing? You told Paddy the Mick it was legitimate but what exactly will we be doing?"

"I have contacts in Sicily, and you will be bringing goods from Sicily here to London. I am happy for you, should you be empty on the outward leg, negotiating your own cargo."

He looked happy at that. It was the same arrangement I had with Captain Dinsdale and was mutually beneficial. "The ship, how close is it to completion, sir?"

"That is the urgency, Jack. The keel is laid and the hull almost complete, but you are a sailor and I want you to work with Mr Harrington." I took out a bag of coins. There were about forty guineas in it. I slipped it over to Jack. "Here is money for you to hire a crew and for expenses."

Toby said, "Make sure the Mick's hard men don't see it, Jack, or you could end up floating in the Thames."

Jack nodded, "Don't worry, Toby. We shall arm ourselves. We can continue to sleep in the shipyard but now we can pay Mr Harrington for the privilege and we can arm ourselves."

I looked over and saw the two men we had laid out were at the bar speaking with Paddy the Mick. "We will leave you now and head back to our home. If you need anything then send a message to Matthew's Farm. You will find it on the road out of London to the north. One of us will be back every week or so to speak with you and to provide more funds if you need them. We will have a word with these deserters before we leave."

"Thank you, Colonel, you have given us a chance of a better life."

I nodded, "It is nothing less than you deserve having served your country for so long."

We walked over to the bar and saw Jack and Bill bunch their fists. I laughed and spoke to Paddy the Mick, "Did you not explain to these buffoons what the consequences of violence will be?" He just shrugged and I turned to the two men, "Let me explain a few facts of life. I have contacts in Whitehall, and I know that the three of you deserted from the army. You may think with the war over that you can't be punished. You may be right but if you cause any more trouble to the sailors who come here to drink then I will make certain that you are arrested and punished for desertion. If you heed my advice, then you can have a new start." I looked at Paddy the Mick, "I may even overlook your smuggling activities. So think about it."

Paddy the Mick was an evil man, but he was no fool and he nodded, "Your lads will be alright now...?"

"Matthews, Colonel Matthews."

It was clear then that they recognised my name and confirmed that they had served in Spain and Portugal. I saw in their eyes. There would be no further trouble.

Emily had meant what she had said about visiting and perhaps even living in Sicily. A week after we had returned from the shipyard and after another meal dominated by a conversation concerning a move, I asked her, "Emily, do you not like the farm? I thought you were happy here?"

"I am and I think your people are the kindest and most hard-working ones I have ever met. It is not that." She took my hands. Charles was abed and he was a good sleeper. We were alone now that the servants had cleared the table and we could speak, "My father is moving to Canada. He has remarried and wishes for a new start. He told me when Charles was born, and he made arrangements for a trust to be set up in both our names." She shrugged, "He knew that you lived a dangerous life and did not want me destitute. He has given up Parliament for he says that the politicians there are all corrupt and self-serving; they think nothing of the country except how they can profit from it. He sees hope in the new land of Canada. I remembered how fondly you spoke of your time in Sicily."

I nodded, "I was happy there and I confess that I always thought to return but..."

"But then you took on me. I confess that it was Maria who made the idea grow and Alan nurtured it but if you think it is a bad idea..."

I kissed her, "No. I think it is a fine idea, but I wanted to be sure."

Like Emily, once the idea was planted then I could not wait to make a start.

Sometimes there is a convergence of forces and they combine as though directed by a hand unseen. William Harrington was keen to finish the ship and start on his next project. Jack and my newly assembled crew were desperate to get back to sea and doing what they loved, and Emily and Maria were forces of nature who pushed us on apace. It was early August when we launched *'Donna Maria'* and fitted her out. The letters I had sent to Cesar assured us of a fine welcome and he even had an estate in mind for us to purchase. We planned on a September departure.

That was the easy part. The hard part was telling Rafe, Jack, Ned, and the others that we were leaving. I was not sure it would be a permanent move, but Jack's age meant that it was unlikely that I would see him again. The old Sergeant Major made it easy for me, "Sir, I had no future after the army. In fact, I was dreading it, but you gave me a new home and a new life. Aye, I will miss you, but it is just the same as missing the other lads from the regiment." He waved a hand, "This is a good home and, God willing, I shall see a few more years here. Ned and I like working with the horses and this is like the regiment was after you got rid of the bad apples, it is a family and you will visit, won't you sir?"

I nodded, "I will but you must realise that although I fought for my mother's land, I was not born here. To you, England is home but to me, it is just one of my homes."

The day we left and headed to Tilbury was a sad one. The partings were hard. Emily's father had left at the end of August and she had shed tears then but parting from those who had been with her while I was in Spain was just as hard. Charles was too young to really know what was going on but he had a voice now and he wept when Ned and Jack said farewell. They had spoiled the babe and the toddler would remember that. Mr Hudson came to see us off. He had a chest of coins for us as we would have to buy the things we needed when we reached Sicily.

"This is a drop in the ocean Colonel Matthews. The profits you have made and the money we invested is paying healthy dividends. I see you becoming richer."

And so we left England. I had no regrets as we headed through the cold waters of the Channel, now safe for ships. Even though it was late summer we were wrapped up well but anticipating a better clime once we passed Gibraltar. Jack had been a good choice as captain. The crew, all single men, worked hard and were grateful for legal employment. We had fitted the ship with guns as the waters, whilst much safer than in times of war still had pirates and those who might wish to take cargo from us. When Captain Dinsdale had seen the ship it was his suggestion that we fit four pounders. Charles loved the crew who spoiled him. Emily had her hands full as did Maria for the two toddlers regarded the ship as a huge playground. Juan helped too but each time we put into a port the two mothers breathed a sigh of relief.

It had been some years since I had seen Cesar and Sicily. The land had not changed but Cesar was now a little older and looked it. He was a sentimental man and he burst into tears when he saw Emily and Charles. His tears embarrassed Emily, but I understood them. To Cesar, the family was all.

The estate he had found for us had belonged to one of Murat's supporters. When the former French cavalryman had fallen from power and had been executed his supporters also fled. We had picked up the huge estate for less than I had paid for the farm in England. With fifteen rooms there was space for us all. By the time Christmas came we had settled in and Emily told me that she was expecting our second child. I would have the first peaceful Christmas since before the Revolution. My life was perfect and I looked forward to the lazy life of a rich merchant.

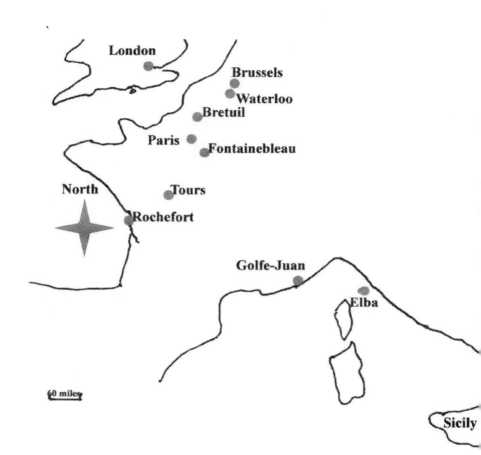

Chapter 3

That all changed when Alan and I were required to pay a visit to London. We had been in Sicily for less than six months, but things had changed. The new baby was due in a couple of months and the one thing which Sicily lacked was somewhere we could buy decent furniture for a nursery. I had a shopping list. Alan and I would also be able to talk to Mr Hudson, our agent for we wanted another ship. Our trade had blossomed, and we now exported more goods to England than ever before. We had contacts in North Africa as well as Italy and Greece. Our first ship was a good one, a fast trading ship that ensured that our lemons and olives reached the markets of Europe as fresh as possible. Emily and Maria were quite happy to stay on the estate. Both were pregnant and, to be truthful, enjoyed the lifestyle. Why trade Sicily's sun for London, which, even in early spring could be cold and damp? Of course, my son Charles, as well as Juan and Robert, wished to come with us, but Alan and I were adamant. There was peace but there were still pirates and privateers who might risk attacking one of the best-armed merchant ships afloat.

As we headed north towards the French coast, for we had cargo to land at Marseille, I reflected on the changes peace had wrought. Not far away was Napoleon Bonaparte's new kingdom, a little rock with eleven thousand subjects. For the man who had ruled Europe from Russia to the English Channel, it was something of a come down. I had served both the Emperor and the Marquess of Wellington. I believed I knew them both; I liked neither of them, but I respected them as leaders and generals.

The General, whom I had served and admired more than any other leader, General Moore, had been killed at Corunna. I wondered how events would have turned out had he not died on the lonely hillside. That thought had haunted me for the last seven years. As I watched the coast of Italy in the distance I wondered if the loss of so many fine soldiers had been worth it.

My reverie was ended by a lookout shouting, "Sails to port."

Jack Robinson was the captain of our ship, the *"Donna Maria"*. He had been in the Royal Navy but, after the war ended, was left on the beach like so many others who had served their country and then been discarded. This was the ship that Alan and I jointly owned. We had helped with her design and in the selection of her crew as had Jack. She was a smart new ship and he was the perfect captain for her. He ran a tight ship and our shared past made us almost family. He took out his telescope.

Turning to me he said, "That is strange. The leading ship is painted like a British brig."

"What is strange about that?"

"She has no flag from her jackstaff. If she was Royal Navy, then she would have and she looks a little lubberly to be Royal Navy. And her lines... if I didn't know better, I would swear that she was French."

I had learned to trust my captain in the six months that he had served me. I also trusted my instincts and when the hairs on the back of my neck began to prickle, I said, "Go a little closer, Captain Robinson. It is peacetime, and we shall be civil. We will chat with these captains and ask about the weather." I turned to Alan Sharp who had served with me since I had joined the British army, "Fetch my telescope, Alan."

As my ship changed course, I wondered at the ships sailing in convoy. It was unusual for three ships to sail together. In the war, it had been commonplace but now that there was peace, captains preferred to move at a pace not dictated by the vagaries of war. *'Donna Maria'* was a fast ship. When we had commissioned her we had chosen a ship that could make fast voyages. We wanted our ships to sail quickly not least because in the Mediterranean there were still pirates. My ship could outrun them all. Alan returned with my telescope. It had been a rare present from Sir Arthur after the battle of Salamanca.

I could now see the three ships with the naked eye. The two larger vessels could have come from anywhere in the Mediterranean, but Jack was correct, the smallest of them did have the look of a Frenchman about her. When I looked with the telescope, I could see what Jack had meant. There was something not quite right about them. I saw that they changed course to avoid us. That, too, was unusual, for we flew the flag of Naples and had none of our gun ports open. It was normal for ship's captains to exchange pleasantries and news. It was only in war that strange ships avoided each other. Not that we would have been any kind of threat to them. We only carried ten four pounders. They were more than enough to discourage Barbary pirates.

I lifted the glass again to my eye. I examined the brig painted in English colours. I do not know what I expected to see but the hairs on the back of my neck stood on end when I saw the distinctive uniform of a Polish Lancer walking on the poop deck. They were the personal bodyguard of Napoleon Bonaparte and could mean only one thing...the

32

beast was loose again! Emperor Napoleon Bonaparte had left his island and was heading for France. That did not bode well for France and Europe.

Jack confirmed it when he said, "I recognise her and she's a French brig. I can't remember her name, but I saw her in Toulon towards the end of the war."

Sailors could easily discern between seemingly identical ships. It was a mystery to me. Despite owning ships I was still a landsman. I nodded, "I am guessing that Boney is not supposed to leave his island home. Captain, resume your normal course. There is little point in chasing three of them. You had better put on all sail and make for Antibes." I knew the port for I had rescued Colonel Selkirk from there after the battle of Vittoria.

As he left to give his orders I turned to Sharp. "I think our little holiday just ended and we have come out of retirement."

Alan had been with me for as long as I had served His Majesty the King and nothing ruffled him. "What do you plan to do, sir?" He could never get out of the habit of calling me 'sir', even though he was now a wealthy man and a junior partner in all of my enterprises. He seemed more than happy to still play the role of aide.

"We must get to Paris and warn the ambassador there."

"The Ambassador?"

"I believe it is the Marquess of Wellington; not the most sensible of appointments but handy for us."

"But how do you know what Boney intends?"

"I do not know what he intends but I can guess. It will involve mischief of that you can be sure. I know that his Guard and those who followed him to Russia still yearn for his return. The Bourbons are not popular. Good God, the King of France has spent twenty-three years in England! He is not French any more than I am." I had been born in France, the illegitimate son of a French Count and a Scottish lady fallen on hard times. I spoke French but I felt English. It was bizarre.

I looked up as the sails began to fill and we overtook the two transports and the brig as though they were standing still. The Polish Lancer had disappeared, and the decks and sails were filled with sailors; he was maintaining the illusion that they were a peaceful trio of commercial ships. "He has to get his army first which gives us time. Perhaps the French army can stop him."

"But you do not believe so."

"No, Alan. For the French Army, Bonaparte is almost a God. In him, they see success and victory. In Russia, he was defeated by the weather and the land and in the last days, it took four armies to finally crush him and even then, he almost grasped victory from the jaws of defeat. Our only hope is Wellington. Thank God that he was appointed Ambassador to France. I know he was not a popular choice, but he is the only man to take on Bonaparte and beat him."

We went below with the captain to study the maps. I knew the area for I had served there with the French army when Bonaparte had conquered Italy and I had served further north. I had been there more recently rescuing Colonel Selkirk and that had given me a better picture of the land. I worked out the fastest route to Paris. We gathered what we would need for the journey. My sword and four pistols were obvious choices. Sharp packed two cloaks for me. One was an oilskin cloak that was lined. I had bought it some years ago and it was invaluable. I took just one change of clothes; we would need to travel light. Force of habit made us pack the mould for musket balls. Our two leather bags were well scuffed, but they were hard-wearing. I had purchased them in London, and they had been expensive. Finally, I packed gold coins in the money belts we would wear. We always carried gold on the ship. We could have used credit, but gold had a way of smoothing our passage in the most difficult of waters.

We reached the French coast by nightfall. I knew that there was a consulate at Genoa, but I knew that Bonaparte would land as close as he could to the main road to Paris. As we disembarked, I handed the letters to Captain Robinson. "Hand this letter to the most senior official in Gibraltar and then make the *"Donna Maria"* fly to England and deliver this to Colonel Selkirk at Horse Guards." I handed him the second letter, "And give this to my wife when you return to Sicily."

"All will be safely delivered, sir," He nodded, "And then what, sir?"

That had me stumped briefly, I smiled, "Well, I daresay Mr Fortnum will be delighted to get his lemons and his wines so promptly. If you tell him that I think Napoleon is on the loose again he may throw a lucrative cargo your way. If not see what you can pick up. Sharp and I may be away some time."

He nodded, "I can give you a couple of hands for protection, Mr Matthews. I have some tough lads here."

I laughed, "Despite our increasing grey hairs, Mr Sharp and I are more than capable of looking after ourselves." I nodded to Alan who was strapping his sword onto his waist. "We can handle whatever comes our way. I have money and we know this land. Take care, Captain Robinson and look after my ship. You may tell Captain Dinsdale and the Count what we are about when you return to Sicily. I am confident they will conduct my business for me in my absence."

Alan said, "What about the nursery furniture for the new baby, sir?"

I sighed, "Captain Robinson, if you can, ask Mr Fortnum to source the nursery furniture."

He smiled, "Of course, Colonel!"

We were experienced travellers, and we would only need two riding horses and a packhorse. Our clothes were well made and extremely functional. We could deal with whatever the weather and the land threw at us. We entered the walled town of Antibes through the gate the fishermen used when they landed and then sold their catches. They had all gone but the detritus of fish gutting and the smell of fish remained along with the puddles of water they had used to sluice down the dock. I turned and watched as my ship turned and headed south-west. We were alone in France once more.

I had a dilemma, as we hurried towards the French walled town. When I had been there the last time I had pretended to be one of Joseph Fouché's men and now I did not need to play a part. I could be what I was, a businessman. We had gained time on the Emperor, as I still thought of him, but I needed to find out where he was and what were his plans. He had the whole coast of France on which to land. We would need to find out what we could about the defences now that the Bourbons had taken charge once more.

The sentries who were on guard at the gate told me that there was a garrison here. Would the Emperor risk all from the moment he landed? I did not think he would land anywhere which had a garrison. Not only did Antibes have a garrison it had a fort that commanded the entrance. If the commander was loyal to the new king, then Bonaparte's dreams of Empire would be shattered before he even landed.

We approached them and they regarded us with curiosity rather than suspicion. "What is your business here?"

"We are Italian businessmen, and we are keen to export our produce to France."

The senior of the two nodded towards my sword; our pistols were packed in our cases. "You come armed, sir. We are at peace."

"True but we both know that there are bandits, and a man needs to protect himself." Seemingly satisfied he waved us through the gate into the narrow streets of Antibes.

I stopped by the small fountain and regarded the street which ran next to the wall of the town. "Sharp, let us find a room and horses. We may end up not using the room but we need as much intelligence as we can gather." I would not use the inn I had used last time for they might remember me and I did not want that. We hurried past the one I had used, *'The Grapes'*, and found one close to the market hall.

I had spied for the French and both Sharp and I had both been agents for Colonel Selkirk, Sir John Moore and the Marquess of Wellington. We knew how to gather information. Somewhere small and inconspicuous was always the best choice. I knew that we were in France legally and were now allies with our former foes but old habits die hard. We settled upon the small inn whose owner was pleased for the business. The Bourbons were not ruling as well as one might have hoped. They had a stagnant economy. I could see why the return of Bonaparte might seem an attractive prospect. While Sharp went to buy three horses I began to question the owner. My payment for the room in advance with a gold coin loosened his tongue.

I kept my hand hovering over the coin as I spoke, "Tell me, sir, what other ports are there along this coast?" He looked at me suspiciously. I smiled. "I own many ships in Sicily and I transport wine, lemons and olive oil from my estates. Now that the war is over, and commerce has begun again I am looking for new markets."

He looked relieved. I had painted a picture of a businessman. My newly acquired paunch helped the illusion. A few days living on the road would make me look more like my old self. "You do not look Italian and you sound French."

I smiled, "A French father."

That seemed to satisfy him. He laughed, "Then already I like you. I can forgive your Italian half." He stroked his moustache and glanced at the old map which stood behind the desk. "Ah let me think, there is Juan le Pins and Cannes just along the coast but neither have a harbour. You would not want to land your cargo on a beach, would you?" I shook my head. "I thought not. Golfe Juan might suit. It is small and has a harbour. Yes, Golfe Juan would do. But what is wrong with Antibes? We are a good port, and our harbour is safe."

"Nothing, my friend but I need to get my goods to Paris as quickly as I can, and I need a fast road to do so."

"Then Toulon or Marseille might be better."

I knew that Napoleon would have to avoid those two places as there would be regiments in both and they would probably be loyal to King Louis. I leaned forward and tapped my nose, "I am guessing that there are fewer customs officers at Golfe Juan than there would be at Toulon or Marseille?"

He grinned; now he thought he understood my motives. My story was more believable. He deduced that I was trying to avoid paying duty by choosing a smaller port where the officials might be corrupt. "Ah, I see. You are right. There are just a couple of old soldiers there and they spend more time in the bar near to the harbour rather than checking manifests." He rubbed the small gold piece I had finally given him between his fingers. "I can see why you are so successful." He closed the register. "It is not a bad port I must confess. Although smaller than Antibes it has a stone jetty and harbour."

"We will be leaving early tomorrow morning."

"Breakfast may not be ready."

I nodded, "There is a boulangerie just along the street. I think we will make do with some fresh bread."

"Albert makes good bread. We use it here. Will you be eating tonight?"

"What is on the menu?"

"Cassoulet."

"Then a bottle of your Provencal wine and two bowls of Cassoulet when my companion returns." I stayed at the entrance while he went to place the order. When he returned I asked, "Has Antibes and the land around here changed much since the war?"

"There is a little more business but it is slow. We have not enjoyed the same business we did in the past. Unfortunately, there are many old soldiers returning and they have little money and few job opportunities. Here it is not so bad for many of those who went to war served in the navy and there are always ships that need sailors. It is the villages and the towns further inland where there is more discontent. Old soldiers would rather march and fight than tend vines and herd animals." He shook his head. "Such is life. I will go and bring your food. The tables are in there."

Sharp arrived and nodded "I have bought three horses." He smiled, "I had plenty to choose from. I think two of them are old cavalry mounts. They are sound. I suspect that when," he looked around to see if the innkeeper was close by, "*he* lands, the price of horseflesh may go up. I bought two good saddles for a song. I managed to get two with holsters for our pistols. They have a night man and we can take them whenever we choose." He smiled, "A sous or two goes a long way here."

We went into the dining room and the steaming bowls of food were on the table. A day at sea always made me hungry. It looked appetising and was totally different from the food we ate at home. This was the food of my youth and reminded me of happier times when my mother was still alive and the servants at the big house made such a fuss of me. They were all dead now. I ate in silence and the taste brought pictures of them into my head. I sipped the wine. I knew that here in Provence you drank rosé or you didn't drink wine.

After a few minutes, the innkeeper returned. "How is your food, gentlemen?"

"Good. The stew is tasty but this rosé is a little light for my taste."

He nodded, "You are Italian. I know that you all prefer reds. Each to his own."

We ate in silence for a while. Eating local food and drinking local wine helped us both to get into the role. We were speaking Italian, but we could lapse into French just as easily. We had had many years of practice. This part of France was so close to Italy that both languages were used with facility by most people. It was why the innkeeper had questioned me so closely. I realised that we could actually speak English if we chose but the spy in me made us keep to Italian.

"We will travel tomorrow to Golfe Juan and keep an eye open for the three ships."

"Do you think you might be wrong about it being… you know who?"

"Unless the Polish Lancers have deserted him then I think not. Besides, Jack was adamant that they were trying to deceive other ships with the disguise." I shrugged, "One last adventure, eh Alan?"

He pushed his empty plate away. "Oh, I am happy for a short adventure, after all, we have had many months of a normal life. It is good to have one last fling. Just so long as it is short. We both have wives and families we wish to return to."

I need not have worried, Alan was as happy as I was to be back in the saddle again. "I fear we are getting a little old for this but I cannot leave this business unfinished. My life and that of Bonaparte have been bound together since Italy. When it is finished then I shall hang up my sword." Sharp gave me a sceptical look. He would follow me come what may. He was as loyal as a brother.

We rose before dawn. It was not a long ride to Golfe Juan; the innkeeper thought it would take little more than an hour to ride along the coast road. A small coin to the groom meant we had a prompt departure. We waited at the gates of Antibes for them to be opened.

It was a punctilious young officer who stood there pointedly looking at the clock on the church while an '*old moustache*' shook his head. There was no reason why he could not open the gates, but it was a display of power. I doubted if the young officer had even fought in a single battle while the old soldier reminded me of the men, I had served alongside in my first regiment. He looked to be older than I was. As the gates were finally opened, I flipped a silver coin to the old soldier. "Have a drink on me, sergeant."

He saluted, "Thank you, sir!" His ramrod-straight back showed his pride in his uniform. He looked at me, "Did you serve, sir?"

"The Chasseurs."

He laughed, "A donkey walloper!"

I laughed, "And you?" I saw that the officer did not enjoy this interchange from which he was excluded.

"The 18th Grenadiers. A fine set of lads. They were good days."

"Aye well, when you have that drink toast your old comrades for me and all those who lie on the battlefields of Europe."

"Amen to that. I will do that, sir. You have a safe journey."

I wondered if he would flock to the eagles when Bonaparte returned. I hoped not. There had been too much waste already. I would like to think he could spend his days remembering the good old days and reminiscing with old comrades.

The fort across from the walled town had been hidden when we arrived. I had seen it from the sea but now, as we headed west, I saw it rising, menacingly, to the east. Napoleon would not risk his ships being fired upon. It covered both the town and the main road as well as the sea. It confirmed my view that he would not land at Antibes. He would head further west. We would wait at Golfe Juan for a day or two and if he did not land then head further west. St. Tropez looked to be small enough for him to use and it had a harbour, but it was a longer journey north. It had to be Golfe Juan.

We passed Juan le Pins not long after we rode over the small hill to the west of Antibes. Juan le Pins was a tiny fishing village with a dozen small fishing boats drawn up on the beach. There was, as my informant had told me, little chance of him landing there. I could have told him that as I had spent some nights there on the beach with Colonel Selkirk as we had awaited the arrival of the British brig which had taken us off the beach. We rode along a track rather than a road towards the small port of Golfe Juan. We saw it looming ahead as we approached. It was much bigger than Juan le Pins but there was no wall to protect it and I could not see a military presence. It would be a good place to land.

I saw beyond it, in the bay, the shape of the Ils de Marguerite. There was a fort there too but it was too far away to prevent someone from arriving at Golfe Juan. The closer I came to the small port the more I was convinced that Bonaparte would be arriving here.

I saw three old soldiers having their breakfast of bread and wine at the bar I had been told about. I assumed them to be the customs officials. While our horses drank from the trough I looked out to sea. It was devoid of either sails or ships. We had landed late on the previous day and I knew we would have beaten the slower transports to the coast. However, if they were coming to Golfe Juan then they would reach us some time that day, February twenty-eighth. The King had reverted to the old calendar which made it easier for me to work out the dates. We would wait and watch. We would drink and listen.

"Alan, you had better get us some food for our journey. I intend to ride as fast as possible once we leave here. I shall go to the bar and order a drink." I nodded to the old soldiers and he smiled. He knew the game I would play.

"Then I had better buy two more horses, sir. These are good mounts, but they will need resting." He grinned, "Besides, they are still cheap here. Wait until he arrives, and the prices will go through the roof." He rode off towards the interior of the town. He was good at haggling.

I sat at the bar and ordered a large pichet of wine which I shared with the old soldiers. "Do you get many ships through here?" Like the innkeeper, they had a suspicious look at my question. I went into my familiar story. "I am a shipowner looking for new ports. Now that the war is over there are many business opportunities in France. I never had the opportunity to visit this part of France before."

They nodded and relaxed. It was a reasonable excuse for questions. "We get two or three small ships a week. Not many for such a fine port.

However, I am sure that peace will bring more prosperity. At least I hope so."

The one who had the faded sergeant's stripes added, with a sly grin, "Should you wish your goods to speed through the port with the minimum of fuss then I am the man to see, Sergeant Jacques Leblanc."

"Excellent." I waved over the waiter, "Another pichet of wine for my new friends." He waited and I put a silver coin on the table. It was enough to keep them there all day.

My chat with the three soldiers proved useful. I discovered that King Louis had done nothing to ingratiate himself with his people. It seemed that only the Vendee had welcomed him. There were many unhappy soldiers who felt they had been let down by their king. Besides, there were many others who were not as lucky as these three. They had returned to a France without the prospect of employment. These were soldiers who had spent the last twenty years or more fighting for France. Their only skill was in fighting and marching. Those skills were not valued during peace. There was a great deal of discontent.

It took Alan longer than I had expected to buy the spare horses and the food. He joined me and the old soldiers for wine and a baguette. "Why do you need so many horses, sir?" The older of the soldiers was suspicious.

"We have far to travel." I waved west, "I intend to visit San Raphael, Toulon and Marseille too."

"If you have a ship then that would be easier." He was persistent. However, this was all useful for it prepared us for questions to come.

"True but I need to see what the land is like between the ports. There is little point in shipping goods if there is no one to buy them."

They nodded sagely at that. Two of them stood when a small lugger approached from the west. Jacques said, "They are supposed to be fishermen, but they may be smuggling. We need to stamp that sort of thing out." He sounded a little hypocritical to me. He waved his two men towards the harbour while he finished off his wine. Suddenly he stood and peered south. "That is strange, we were not expecting larger ships."

I looked and saw more sails approaching from the south-east. These were bigger than the lugger which was now almost in the harbour. I knew who they were before they became visible. It was Bonaparte.

I stood and left a tip for the waiter. "Well, if you are becoming busy then we will leave you. Thank you for your help, sergeant, and I will call again when we have made our decision."

41

He waved distractedly at me and wandered to the harbour wall, constantly watching the three ships as they approached. We were ignored. It would take some time for them to reach the harbour. "Alan, get the horses ready." I pointed to the road which led north. "We will watch from the shelter of that house and confirm that it is Bonaparte and then we shall leave by that road; for it is the road north."

By the time the horses were tied together and we had mounted, the small brig, we could see her name, *'Inconstant'*, was almost at the harbour entrance. I recognised the green uniform and the distinctive hat watching the land from the gunwale. I stared at Napoleon Bonaparte and he stared back. I saw his frown as he tried to place me. The three old soldiers cheered; it was a cheer taken up by the men on the ship and the others who had come to see what the three ships contained. The cheer was repeated on the other ships which I saw were lined with the Old Guard. The Emperor smiled and waved at them. The whole harbour was filled with the joyful sound of the Emperor returning. He was welcomed. Far from being in danger, the Emperor was embraced. This was a triumphant return for the Emperor. People thronged around him when he stepped onto the jetty. They were all pleased to see him returned.

I jerked my horse's head around and headed north. I needed to warn Wellington that the Emperor was back. The only man who could stop him was Sir Arthur Wellesley.

Chapter 4

It took ten days of hard riding to complete our journey. By the time we reached Auxerre, there were rumours of Bonaparte's landing, but they were just that, rumours. I wondered if Bonaparte had his spies and messengers riding to Paris. I would not underestimate Napoleon for I knew him well enough to know that he had been a clever man who planned meticulously. I could not see the short time since he had been exiled diminishing his powers. Perhaps his riders were ahead of us. Certainly, we entered many bars where the sole topic of conversation was either when would Bonaparte arrive or what would he do when he did return. Our journey might be wasted for the Marquess of Wellington would hear of Bonaparte's return long before we reached Paris. There was hope amongst the majority of people that we met and spoke with but those who had done well out of the royal return were both sceptical and fearful at the same time. It was a time of great unrest and unease.

What I did not know was that the news had gone from Genoa to Vienna and, even as we approached Paris, all of Europe knew that Bonaparte had returned. It was no longer a rumour. It was a fact. And for many an unpalatable fact. The city was in chaos as the King and his court fled north to Belgium. Each time we stopped envious looks were cast in the direction of our horses. Sharp had been correct; they were worth ten times what he had paid for them and the wisdom of buying five had been justified. It was like riding through a disturbed ant's nest. One of us had to stand guard over the five animals every time we halted.

Once we reached Paris we rode directly to the embassy and, while Sharp secured us rooms nearby, I went to speak with Sir Arthur. To my dismay, I discovered that he was at the peace talks in Vienna. My journey had been wasted. The official knew that Bonaparte had returned and seemed remarkably sanguine about it. He had never been a soldier, I could tell that. He was a diplomat!

"Emperor Napoleon Bonaparte can do nothing, Colonel Matthews. The king rules now and the people have welcomed him with open arms. He has no support in the country. Of that, you can be certain."

The official confirmed my view of both diplomats and politicians; neither knew anything! "We have travelled the length of France and there is a great deal of support for him." I waved my hand at the street outside, "How do you explain this panic?"

He smiled at me in a patronising manner, "They are French and very excitable. Do not worry yourself, Colonel. I shall tell Sir Arthur of your concern when he returns but there is no cause for alarm, I can assure you."

I left feeling frustrated. As I waited outside for Sharp I wondered if I had wasted my time. I could have stayed on the *'Donna Maria'* and not had to endure the uncomfortable journey riding for twelve hours a day and sleeping when I could. Why had I bothered? I had committed myself to another war. Had I forgotten Orthez and Toulouse so soon?

I decided that we would spend a night in Paris. The rooms and the stables had been paid for. In the cold light of a new day, I would make the decision about our future. I felt slightly depressed. I think I thought that my actions might have foiled Bonaparte's plans, but I was wrong. I was so distracted by my depressing thoughts that I almost bumped into the officer who came up the steps.

"Good God, but you have made a fortuitous visit to Paris, sir!"

I looked into the face of Colonel Selkirk, England's spymaster and the man who had sent Alan Sharp and me into danger more times than I cared to think of. I could not help laughing, "You have need to talk, Colonel Selkirk. When did you discover the news?"

"I was in Vienna with Sir Arthur. He sent me back as soon as we heard. He will appear calm and unflustered to calm our allies. But he will be arriving shortly."

So Captain Robinson's journey to Horse Guards and Whitehall had been in vain. I hoped that Mr Fortnum had profited from the news. Discovering that there would be a rush on military supplies ahead of one's rivals could make a man's fortune.

The Colonel put his arm around my shoulder and led me back inside. He waved imperiously to the diplomat who had just dismissed me. "I am pleased that you are here. It saves me having to send for you."

"I left the service. I am a shipowner and a successful businessman. I only came here to bring the news to the Marquess, and it seems that was an unnecessary journey. Remember, I am retired now."

He laughed, "But you are still a commissioned officer and I am recalling you to the colours, so to speak." He saw my frown and said in an almost pleading voice, "Come along Robbie, you didn't think this was over, did you? Surely you want to be there at the finish." I shrugged, "I know that Sir Arthur will want you."

"He is leading the allied armies?"

44

"The Czar himself has asked for him. The other heads of state know he is the only man to face Bonaparte." He smiled, "Let us say I am in your debt already for you saved my life in Antibes and this puts me more deeply into your debt. Do it for England!"

"I thought I had done my duty for England already." He had no answer to that and scurried along, like some sort of human crab.

We had reached a room with a marine sentry outside. "Here is the cubby hole they have given me." He suddenly stopped, "What brings you here so propitiously?"

"Sharp and I spotted Bonaparte when he left Elba. We followed him to Golfe Juan, and we have been one step ahead of him all the way north. We have been riding through France to bring the news." I shook my head, "A wasted journey."

He waved me to a seat. "Just the opposite, in fact, quite useful, especially to me. You came through France and you know the French people. You must have learned much as you travelled north. Will the Emperor be welcomed?"

"With open arms. At first, I thought it might be isolated pockets of old soldiers, but it is everyone who appeared to be eager for his return. Farmers, businessmen, everyone. They see Bonaparte as the hero who will come to rid them of the tyranny of this new king and equate him with success and prosperity. I am afraid the king did not endear himself to his people. He has brought the old aristocrats back with him and they have not learned their lesson. He has brought foreign businessmen and worst of all he has ignored the army. They do not forgive easily."

"Good. At least we know where we stand now. I want you and Sharp to find him and discover all that you can of his plans."

I shook my head, "Are you mad? He still has a price on my head, and I think that he will be even keener to have me dead than ever."

"Robbie, you and Sharp were the best two spies I ever had. You still are. You are like chameleons. You blend into the background. This is a perfect opportunity for you to do what you do best. There will be officers coming and going all the time. There will be confusion. Exploit it. Boney will be coming along the same route you just took." He went to a map. I could see that he thought he had persuaded me already. "Now I think that he will gather his generals and marshals here, at Fontainebleau. I am not certain how many will return to the colours. The ordinary soldiers will flock to be at his side but his generals and marshals? I am not so sure. Sir Arthur will need to know who is coming up against him. You need to find that out. You know yourself, Robbie, the more information Sir Arthur has the more chance he has of success."

"Supposing I do find out who is joining his army, how does that help us?" I went to the map. "He could go anywhere in Europe."

"Aye well, I want you to find out what he intends there too."

"Not asking for much are you, sir?"

"It is for your country."

"That might work with some bright-eyed lieutenant, but I have been doing this for more than twenty years. I have a nice life in Sicily now as well as a family as does Sergeant Major Sharp and you forget it is not my country. I was born in France and I live in Italy. I have spent less than three hundred days actually living in England!"

He gave me an evil grin. "And if Boney wins then all that might end. He came damned close the last time. We have to beat him once and for all."

He had me and he knew it.

"If I do as you ask where will you be? I know it will be somewhere safe." He frowned at the obvious insult, but I cared not. I was past being polite and diplomatic. "I am guessing Paris will be Imperial once more as soon as the Emperor comes closer."

"You are right. I am going to Brussels. I think Sir Arthur will be heading there too. The Dutch are keen to keep their kingdom independent of France and they will provide soldiers for our army. Remember our best troops are all in America fighting the colonials again. In addition, we have to keep our lines of communication with the Prussians open. It will take the Russians a long time to reach us and the Austrians are still calling their men to the colours." His face softened into what passed as a sympathetic smile. "You take care of yourself, Robbie." He smiled in an almost paternal manner which disconcerted me. "This puts me even deeper in your debt but the work you do will be vital and this time your speed will be crucial. Find out what you can as soon as you can. By April, I want you in Brussels!"

I nodded, "Then we will make a deal. For myself I need nothing, but poor Sharp has been a sergeant all these years. I want him made up to an officer, a Captain, with back pay for the last year."

"No. I cannot agree to that." He smiled. It was like haggling in the market. "But he can be promoted to lieutenant with back pay for six months as part of the agreement." I nodded my assent. He threw me a bag of gold coins. "You will need this for expenses and such. You will need to buy horses and I daresay they will be expensive in the current climate." He wagged an admonishing finger at me. "I would like some of it back!"

I found Alan waiting outside. I shook my head. "It looks like we will only have one night in the inn and then we have been recalled to the colours."

He nodded, "I signed on for twenty-five years, sir. I reckon I can give King George another two before my time is up."

It was soldiers like Sharp who would keep Great Britain both safe and great. "Well, at least you do it as a lieutenant and with a lieutenant's pay. Colonel Selkirk just promoted you."

"Thank you, sir. I appreciate it. The money means nothing, but it is nice to be an officer."

"Are the horses stabled?"

"Yes sir. I paid extra for some grain. They deserve it." Like me, Sharp was a horseman through and through.

"Right. We will have a little wander through some of the less popular parts of Paris and see what we can discover."

I still had a few contacts and friends from my days in the Chasseurs. Pierre was my closest friend and he lived close to the border with Belgium. There were others nearby, however, and I headed, with Alan walking just behind me as my protector, for the St Michel quarter. Pierre-Francois Gavroche had been invalided out of the 17th Chasseurs when he lost his left hand to an Austrian sword. He had been an engineer with a future. Now he worked as a scribe in the Sorbonne. He was literate and he transcribed some of the theses of the less diligent students. There were many of them and it paid a good wage. I had last met him when I had been in Paris on Colonel Selkirk's business. He lived amongst the more radical of the students and those with political ambition. He was a good listener and had many nuggets of information that would otherwise be lost.

"Your old comrade again then, sir?" was Sharp's only comment. I nodded and he trailed behind me as though he was visiting the city for the first time. He stared around in wonder when in fact he was watching the crowds for danger. In his hand, he held a razor-sharp knife, and a primed pistol was at his belt. He kept a good twenty yards behind me. He could become almost invisible.

I crossed the river by Notre Dame and headed up towards the Sorbonne and the University district. Pierre-Francois had a room in a large building just half a mile from the Sorbonne. There were many bars frequented by the students and it was a gay, cosmopolitan area. By its very nature, it was dangerous. The bars were all filled with people debating Napoleon's return. These were not the dangerous animals who would murder you for looking at them askance; these were the butterflies who took the nectar of gossip and redistributed it. Soon however I would have to leave the main thoroughfare and venture into the half-life who inhabited these dark sectors of Paris.

As soon as I took the side street, I became aware of the presence of danger. Two huge hulking brutes stepped out from the darkened shadows ahead of me. They looked to have a little of the Arab about them and that was confirmed when they spoke. Their accents reeked of North Africa.

"I think, sir, that your purse is too heavy for you. Allow us to relieve you of it. You will find walking much easier."

As soon as I had left the main street, I had slipped the Italian stiletto into my left hand. It had an edge with which you could shave, and it was a good weapon to use in a confined space. I saw that he was watching my right hand. It was nowhere near my sword; I was brushing a piece of imaginary fluff from my coat. He relaxed a little. There were hints of grey in my hair and my dress suggested a successful businessman rather than a cold-blooded killer. I had taken the stiletto from an Italian bandits' dead hand many years ago. He had been a tough man. These two were overweight and overconfident. I smiled and moved my right hand to the side. The eyes of the man who had spoken followed it. The stiletto in my left hand was at his throat before he had time to turn his head back.

"I do not think so, my friend. I am not here to be rooked by scum such as you."

He gulped and then smiled. "If there were only the two of us then I might agree but my other brother now has his sword at your back."

I felt pressure on my spine. I nodded. "Of course you would be dead long before your brother would have had his head blown off by my friend. Now drop your weapons."

The ominous click from Sharp's two pistols almost echoed down the narrow street. I saw the two before me stare towards the end of the alley. I knew what they would see; Sharp with two pistols which would look as big as blunderbusses. The weapons were dropped.

"Now stand against that wall. Spread your hands against it." As they did so I said, "Sharp, watch them." While he watched them, I removed their belts. "I will drop these at the end of the alley when I have

48

concluded our business. But if I see any of you when we come from that building then I will kill you. Do you understand?"

"Yes."

We left them ruing their misguided decision to rob me. The door to the apartments was open. I smelled the onion soup as we climbed the last stairs to Pierre-Francois' room. I knocked and waited. Eventually, it opened, and my old comrade greeted me. "Ah, Robbie, the English spy. Come in." I knew that he had a spy hole next to the door and had checked who we were before opening the door.

He was totally grey now, but his eyes still had the same sharpness they always had. He gestured towards the table where there was a jug of wine. It was not full.

He sought three glasses and he blew the dust from two of them; he was unaccustomed to company. After pouring the wine he raised his glass. We toasted him back. "And to what do I owe this honour? There is peace now!"

"The beast is back!"

He did not seem surprised. He shrugged, "I heard the news. He was defeated once before. Why should anyone worry about this time?"

"You and I know differently, my friend. He is dangerous. What do you know?"

"About what?"

"Who will serve with him?"

He sipped his wine as though it was a fine wine rather than the blackstrap it was. He looked at the ceiling as he ran through the various generals and marshals which were available to Bonaparte. "Bessières is dead. That is a shame. He was a good man. Berthier who is even better will hide away from this war and that is a shame for France. If he served Bonaparte, then I would fear for their enemies. Ney will be there hanging on to his master's coattails but he is a wild man and more of a hindrance to Napoleon than anything. Davout, Soult, Suchet, all of them will follow. They are the ones to worry about. The rest..." he waved his hands dismissively, "most are second rate and have been promoted far beyond their ability. "Your old friend from the Guards will be there, Lefebvre-Desnouettes. But you have no need to worry for your hooked nose General will command."

"True but he has never fought Bonaparte."

"It matters not, for he trounced every other French general. They all fear him. That is certain." He toasted me again and drank heavily.

"And what would you do if you were Bonaparte?"

"You mean if I was whole? If I had been promoted like so many men whom I served with?" The cynicism in his voice was unlike the young trooper with whom I had served. I nodded. He continued, "Then I would strike north towards Britain. Go through Belgium."

I was slightly taken aback. "But why?"

"As you know I hear much in the bars and we have students from all over Europe. That part of Europe is as far away from the Russians, Austrians, and Prussians as it is possible to get and Bonaparte gave the Belgians their freedom. The Dutch see them as subservient to them and many of the Belgians resent the attitude. The Dutch Crown Prince has been quite scathing about the new country of Belgium. They are less likely to fight for their old masters the Austrians and would be sympathetic to Bonaparte. From what I have heard three huge armies are heading west to defeat the Emperor. If Bonaparte can defeat your army it gives him the opportunity to build up his army and prepare to fight three tired armies one by one. Remember he has beaten them every time. It might also encourage the Irish to rise in revolt. You are already fighting one enemy who is tired of your colonialism. Two might just make you leave the coalition."

"But he has to go through the Netherlands, and they are our allies."

He laughed, "The Belgians are unhappy that they had their freedom and after the war, they were given to the fat Dutchman like a bonbon. Trust me, Robbie. There is much unrest in Belgium. They have exchanged Spanish and Austrian masters for Dutch ones. When Bonaparte ruled, he gave them some limited independence. Many of the Belgian students have headed home already. It was not to serve in the Young Frog's army believe me. Prince William is not popular. Your Marquess of Wellington will have to watch his back there."

"Thank you. That is useful. What of the royalists?"

"Most have already fled with the fat one and those in the Vendée will pose dramatically and then take ship as soon as they see a tricolour."

I laughed, "Nothing has changed there then."

"And you Robbie? What of you? I thought you had retired."

"I had but the thought of Bonaparte killing more Frenchmen appals me."

"True. I believe that Corsican has killed more Frenchmen than the Russian winter." I stood and slid a gold coin on the table. He scowled. "What is that for?" He did not like to be thought of as an informer.

"The wine and the company of an old friend. Business is good. If you ever tire of the intrigue of Paris come to Sicily. I can use a man with a mind as sharp as yours."

"If Bonaparte loses, I may take you up on that for the fat one is worse than his father as a king."

As we headed back to the hotel Sharp asked, "How does he know so much? He lives in a backwater."

"That is all you know. The Left Bank is a hive of intrigue and information. Old soldiers drink there, and students plot revolution. My old friend is a good listener and with only one hand, he is seen as harmless."

We returned to the hotel and prepared for an early start. We arranged to leave three of the horses there along with our baggage. People were leaving the city in their droves and the innkeeper was happy to take a handful of coins and hold our rooms for us. There would not be many new guests and if Bonaparte came then the rooms would be given for free to his officers. I was not certain we would return. We took the best two horses; both had been cavalry mounts. With our four pistols and our swords, we were as well-armed as any we might meet on the road. The main difference between us and the soldiers on whom we would be spying was that they would be in uniform.

Fontainebleau is a day's ride from Paris, and we reached the old royal palace before dark. It had a skeleton staff showing that Napoleon had yet to arrive. This might be a waste of time. We used the hours of darkness to spy out a refuge. I did not want to stay in a hotel or an inn. Fouché or whoever had taken over as spy catcher would have his men out looking for spies. We sought a house without smoke and a house without light.

After two hours we took what looked like a relatively well-worn trail into the forest. I thought it might just lead to an area they were felling lumber but eventually, we found a darkened cottage. Sharp held the horses whilst I approached the cottage. It appeared to be deserted but one never knew. "Hello, is anyone in? My friend has slipped from his horse and we need some assistance."

There was no noise at all, and I tried the door. It was not locked. As soon as I pushed open the creaking door, I smelled death. I whistled for Sharp. There was no moon and it was too dark to see well inside the small cottage but I guessed where the fireplace would be. Sharp gathered some kindling and, using a little powder and his flint, he soon had a fire going. There was a small pile of firewood next to the fireplace. He built up the fire. It illuminated the interior. One thing a good soldier learned how to do was to get a fire going quickly.

When the fire was going, I saw a tallow candle on an old, stained table. I lit it. The smell of the dead body was strong. I could not see it in the kitchen which also acted as a living room. I knew what I would find before I saw it. There were just two rooms in the small farm, a room for sitting and cooking and a bedroom. I pushed open the bedroom door and saw the corpse which lay there on the bed. It was an old man by the looks of his thinning, grey hair but the body was so decomposed that it was difficult to tell. It looked like he had gone to sleep one night and not woken up. It was not a soldier's death.

"Alan, in here."

A look of infinite sadness came over Sharp's face when he saw the body. Death was bad enough but to die without anyone there seemed even worse.

"We had better take him outside and bury him." We picked up the sheets and used them to carry him out through the back door. He did not weigh very much. There was an outhouse and when we searched, we found tools. We dug a grave and buried him. The two of us stood next to the freshly turned soil and looked at each other. I had no words for this. I did not know his name. I knew nothing, save that he had died alone.

"Go with God and may you be happy now." It was inadequate and it left me feeling a little sick.

We unsaddled and fed the horses and put them in the small, dilapidated barn we found. Sharp hobbled them. We could not afford to have them wander off. Neither of us wanted to sleep in the dead man's bed and so we wrapped ourselves in our cloaks and decided to sleep before the fire.

"I wonder where his family is."

"There have been so many soldiers who died it might be that he was the only one left from his family."

"It would be awful to die alone wouldn't it, sir?"

"I do not think we will have to worry about that, Alan. A ball or a blade will be our end and we will be on a battlefield surrounded by others suffering the same fate."

"What about our families, sir? What you said might have been right less than a year ago but not now." He was right but we had to survive first. On that sombre note, we both fell asleep. The dead could not hurt us; it was the living we had to fear.

When we awoke, we were able to see that the old man must have died some time ago. Weeds rampaged everywhere around the small farmstead. The only marks we could find on the ground were those made by our boots the night before. No one had visited for some time and we would be unlikely to be disturbed. We had a bolt hole.

We ate a cold breakfast; I did not wish to risk smoke until we had explored, and then we headed towards the palace. We reached the road. As we rode, we noted where we might hide if the necessity arose. It was just a habit with us. As with all such centres of royalty, houses had grown along the road providing a variety of services which might be needed by those visiting the chateau or, indeed, working there. There was a bar. I dare say it would normally be frequented by off duty soldiers. I hoped we would find some. Soldiers enjoyed talking. If the Emperor had returned, then some hints of his plans might emerge. Sharp and I approached the Chateau from the south. I wanted it to appear as though we were heading for Paris rather than fleeing from it. Those fleeing might be seen as the Emperor's enemies.

The inn had a groom who took our horses. I knew that the chateau was not large and the inn would have had a lucrative income providing rooms for lesser dignitaries and servants. As we entered, I said loudly, smiling as I did so, "I wish I had known this excellent establishment was so close, we could have pushed on last night and avoided a night in the woods."

The owner wiped the bar and, smiling, said, "Then you are not a local, sir. Everyone knows that Francois' Place serves the finest food and the best wine on the Paris road. And we have well-apportioned rooms too! You should have ridden further, sir and saved yourself an uncomfortable night."

I nodded and took in the room. There were half a dozen men drinking in the bar. From their clothes, they were all ex-soldiers. That made sense. They would want to hang around where their former leader lived.

The clothes we had slept in looked dishevelled. "And you are right. We have travelled from Italy and this is the best inn we have seen on the road. We will have some of your fine food and wine."

As we sat at a table he came over, "Italy?" He leaned in, "Are you with the Emperor?"

I feigned ignorance. "Emperor? Isn't he on Elba? We passed the island when we came north but…"

53

The landlord spoke conspiratorially, "There are Marshals of France in the Chateau and I have heard the Old Moustaches are marching in their thousands to join the eagles again. We have heard that the Emperor has returned. I wondered if you had travelled with him." He rubbed his hands. "The good times are returning. I will fetch your food."

Sharp and I did not need to comment. We had the information we sought. Now we just needed an idea of where and when the Emperor would strike.

Our food came. Its quality had been seriously exaggerated. We smiled and ate. We sipped the wine, and we watched all who came and went. Halfway through the meal, a lieutenant of the Imperial Guard entered with a sergeant. He was a Chasseur of the Middle Guard. "A pichet of wine! We bring great news. The Emperor will be here by nightfall. France's greatness will return!"

Everyone in the bar cheered. Sharp and I raised our beakers. It would not do to show as much enthusiasm as the majority of those in the bar as they were French; I had said we were Italian. We ate in silence but listened to the buzz of conversation around us. We learned a great deal. Marshal Ney had defected to the Emperor along with the army he commanded. Napoleon now had more than his personal guard. He had an army. We heard that many more troops had joined the Emperor as he marched north. By the time he reached the Chateau, he would have a sizeable army already. The lieutenant spoke of hundreds of thousands. I knew that was an exaggeration. Even so, it would be a bigger army than Colonel Selkirk was expecting.

The lieutenant and sergeant left as we finished the meal. I paid for it and, as we left the building, saw that they headed for Paris and not the Chateau of Fontainebleau. They were the messengers, Bonaparte's harbingers! Then I saw a squadron of Chasseurs. It was the 5th. They were trotting towards the gates of Fontainebleau. The colonel was right. They would be the members of Napoleon's Headquarters. I decided that we would not move and return to our deserted farmhouse until they had passed.

Suddenly the officer at the front halted and shouted, "Robbie, is that you?"

As I peered at the moustachioed face, I remembered him. It was Girod de l'Ain. We had been troopers together in Italy before I had been seconded to the Guides. Did he know of my past and was our mission about to end dramatically? I smiled and held out my hand, "Girod? Is that you? A colonel no less!"

He smiled back and I breathed a sigh of relief. He still remembered me as a trooper. We were safe, for a while at least. He turned to his second in command. "Major, take the men inside I will join you shortly." He nudged his horse towards mine. "I haven't seen you since Italy. That seems many years ago now when we were both young and foolish, full of piss and vinegar!" He dismounted and we shook hands.

A frown creased his face and I heard suspicion in his voice as he said, "Didn't I hear that you deserted in Egypt after killing a brother officer?"

I shook my head and adopted an outraged expression. "You heard wrong. Firstly, do you think I would desert and secondly it was a duel and he lost? I left Egypt with my honour intact! I was abandoned in Egypt when the Emperor returned to France. I had to find my own way out and I eventually landed up in Italy."

He stared at me for a moment and then a smile appeared upon his face. "I should have known that there was a good explanation. You were always a good soldier." He waved a hand at my dress. "You appear to have done well since you left the Emperor's service."

"I was lucky, and I am now a businessman who trades in wines."

"You should return to the colours. You would soon be promoted for I remember you as being a fine cavalryman. There are many opportunities for soldiers such as we. The Emperor is just behind me! I am certain that we can make peace between you. These will be great days again."

"Are you sure? It cost the country much the last time he led armies."

Girod shrugged, "I was on half-pay until he returned. For me, this is the only answer. There is a chance for glory and promotion. This time we will beat them all. We were so close the last time. Many of the men we served with are now promoted and are generals. Remember Ney? Even he is now a marshal of France!"

"He is brave enough."

"Yes, I grant you he has courage, but he has no sense on the battlefield. You should join us, Robbie. We already have sixty thousand men and many more are joining us in Paris. Once we are there we will strike north, and the Roast Beefs will scurry back across the Channel."

"I have business in Paris. When you reach Paris then look me up. I am staying close to the Champs de Mars. Perhaps if the Emperor is willing to overlook my past then…"

55

"I have no doubt. And now I must join my men." He shook my hand. "It is good to see you. I have no doubt that you would have been a general by now had you remained in the Emperor's service."

He mounted his horse and trotted off. I breathed a sigh of relief. I was about to mount when I saw, in the darkening lane, a document. It had not been there before the Chasseurs had passed. I picked it up and jammed it in my coat. I led Sharp and we headed north, to Paris. The moment we were out of sight of the palace I turned off the road and rode back along the track to the farmstead. We said nothing until we reached the deserted house.

"Did you get all of that, Alan?"

"Yes, sir. I had my pistol ready if it had turned ugly."

"I prefer to talk my way out of trouble. We need to see the size of this army. Colonel Selkirk will need more information than sixty thousand men and Marshal Ney. We need to ascertain accurate numbers and regiments. They will be arriving in the next day or so. We will hide out here and keep watch." I had no doubt that we would hear the arrival of sixty thousand men. The road was cobbled. "First we will examine this." I took the document I had picked up from my coat.

"Where did you get that?"

"I think the officer you were speaking with dropped it."

I opened it and saw that it was a map. It was northern France and southern Belgium. I saw that the Sambre river was circled as was Charleroi and Namur. "This is a bit of luck. It confirms what we heard in Paris and what the colonel said. Bonaparte will strike north."

"Won't your old friend miss it?"

"He might but he won't know where he dropped it. We will have to take that chance."

While we waited, we put snares down for rabbits and foraged for mushrooms. It would supplement the supplies we had brought with us.

We heard the army arrive two days later. The clatter of hooves on the road carried all the way to our hideaway. Soon we smelled the smoke of their fires. I knew it would take another day, at least, for them all to arrive. I wanted to ascertain numbers.

We had a problem now for Girod would recognise me if he saw me. He would wonder why we were still here. I had no choice; I had to rely on Alan. He would have to try to count the size of the army and the number of each arm. When we had seen the Chasseurs Alan had not been wearing his cloak and he had been wearing a hat. By adding a cloak and removing his hat I hoped he would look different. He headed south to pass the Chateau and then ride down the column. He would have to take a circuitous route back but that was preferable to capture. I knew he could do the job as well as I could. In the past I had had to rely on him when I had been wounded or incapacitated; ours was a dangerous business.

It was the job I always hated, waiting. I preferred to be in danger myself rather than having someone else put their life on the line. I always did the job myself rather than ordering one of my troopers to do it. It was the same with Alan. He was very good, but I always thought I could do it better.

To keep myself occupied I built a small fire using bone dry wood to avoid smoke and took two rabbits that had been trapped from the snares. I skinned and gutted them. Using some of the herbs and mushrooms we had found I put them in a pot with some water and the last of the wine we had brought. It filled the time until dark. The smell of cooking made me hungry. I was beginning to be worried. My worry escalated into fear when my horse neighed. I had my pistol out and cocked in an instant. I slipped out of the back door. It was more overgrown than the front and I could approach whoever it was from the side.

I walked along the path around what must have been a vegetable plot but was now a weed-infested mound. I crouched behind an old apple tree. Someone was moving through the woods towards the farm. I raised my pistol as I saw a shape appear.

"Sir, it is me!" I eased the hammer down. Alan appeared next to me. "I didn't want to make a noise; the French camp is bigger than we thought. There are some Voltigeurs half a mile to the east."

I immediately regretted the fire. The smell might alert them, especially as we were cooking game and I was certain that they would still be on hard rations. It was too late to do anything about it now. We would have to eat and run.

Sharp tied up his horse without unsaddling him and we both ate the rabbit as quickly as we could. There was little point in letting it go to waste. Between mouthfuls, Alan filled me in. "So far, there are mainly infantrymen who are camping, sir. At least forty thousand. It was hard to be accurate."

"What did you use as a measurement?"

"I counted the standards. I saw at least six hundred Old Guard. You can't mistake them with their bearskins. The Polish Lancers are there, a squadron and the Chasseur à Cheval of the Guard. He has four or five regiments of light cavalry too."

"Artillery?"

"Horse artillery."

"No twelve pounders then?"

"Not that I could see."

"Thank God. If the Emperor's daughters were there, then he would be ready to strike. We have some time. You have done well then Alan. Boney will not do anything until he has his artillery assembled and in place. When you have eaten, then we will leave."

We washed the food down with the last of our water. After feeding the horses we led them down the track towards the road. I wanted us to be able to move silently. It was as well that we did for at the road was a piquet of Chasseurs. We began to move north through the woods which lined the road. We almost made it but then my horse neighed. It was a French cavalry horse and recognised the smell and presence of the soldiers.

"Who goes there? Show yourself or we shoot!"

I mimed for Alan to mount. As I climbed on my horse I shouted, "I am Captain Leblanc of the 7th Chasseurs. Thank God we have found you. We have been wandering in these woods for hours." I wanted the soldiers off guard.

We had to move quickly. They would only take a moment or two to close with us and then they would discover our true identity. I dug my heels into the flanks of my mount. My horse leapt forward, followed by Alan and his mount. Both of us lay low across the saddle to make us a harder target to hit. We managed to get twenty yards before their musketoons fired at the trees we had just vacated. I knew that their view would now be obscured by both the dark and the smoke from their guns. I took the opportunity of leaping the ditch and rejoining the road to our left. I glanced over my shoulder and saw the five Chasseurs racing into the forest. They had not seen us leave. Their own shots had deceived them.

We rode hard and I was glad that we had fed our horses. They made good time. Although exhausted, we reached Paris by dawn and went directly to the stable of our hotel. I had decided when riding north, that I would need to get to Brussels sooner rather than later. The piquet would have reported to someone and they would be looking for us. Perhaps the soldiers would jog Girod's memory and he might remember where he dropped his map. They might question the owner of the inn. There was too much evidence of our presence. The other reason for flight was that the city was filled with uniforms as other soldiers, like Girod, flocked back to the colours. There were soldiers who might, like the colonel, recognise me. I had been around both armies for far too long.

While Alan changed saddles and horses, I went to settle our bill. The owner was disappointed that we were leaving. I gave him a wry smile as I collected my change. "I think, my friend, that the city will soon be filled with the Emperor and his army. I think you will be in profit again and soon. I have heard from a colleague that he is coming. This is no place for an Italian businessman."

He nodded, "This will not be a long war, sir. You will always be welcome here."

It was hard going, heading north through the city. There were still royalists who had been slow to leave and they were now flooding north with all their possessions. In the other direction was wave after wave of uniforms as Bonaparte's old soldiers flocked to their charismatic leader. The city was changing before my eyes; it had been Royalist and now it was becoming Imperial once more. The Emperor was coming back, and the city was buzzing with the thought of that prospect.

Chapter 5

I knew we could not make Brussels in one day. We would be lucky, with the way the roads were, to make it in two. The roads were thronged with refugees. There were the rich who worried that they would lose the treasures they had accumulated and their wagons, with guards, made progress difficult. There were others who just feared Bonaparte. They were taking family north to the safety of the Marquess of Wellington and his army. King Louis had already fled to Antwerp; that was not a surprise. It was a port after all, and he could flee to England once more and abandon his supporters.

I headed for Breteuil. It had been my home and I knew the area well. It was off the beaten track and not on the main road to Brussels. By taking a detour we could actually save time. Besides, our five horses were proving too great a temptation for those who were walking north. Riding was always easier than walking.

The last time we had been here Sharp had been close to death and we had had to kill the new owner of my former home. That had been long before we went to Denmark and the Iberian Peninsula. That was a lifetime ago. I prayed that Julian and Pierre would still be at the inn they had named *'Chasseur'*. They were both old comrades and I had helped them to buy their inn. I hoped they still lived there and had prospered. Pierre was a true friend and he had survived the war and made a new life for himself. I wanted him alive still. It would be proof that there was a god.

I had not wanted to embroil them in my activities. I could not risk them suffering. Until the war broke out again, I felt that I could risk it. We were still, technically, at peace. If soldiers came, I could explain us away as businessmen. In a few weeks, I would not be able to carry off that lie.

When I saw the sign of the horseman with the fading paint still swinging, I breathed a sigh of relief. It was still here and the smoke from the chimney showed that it was still occupied. As we reached the gate to the stables a stable boy came hurtling out. "Yes sir? Would you like a room?"

"We need stabling for five horses and rooms for the night." There was something about the boy which looked familiar and then it hit me; this was the son of Julian and Monique. I smiled. He had been a babe in arms when we had left. Now he was almost a youth. I felt a glow of warmth. There was hope. One of my comrades had sired a child. I smiled and it filled my face.

He grinned back at me with his hands on his hips. "You have come to the right place. If you would like to go into the inn, then I will see to your horses."

I took a silver coin out of my waistcoat pocket and flipped it in his direction. His eyes widened as he deftly caught and said, "Thank you, sir! I will look after these horses as though they were my own!"

Julian had his back to me and was poking the fire as I walked into the main room. He appeared to be standing easily on his wooden leg. I remembered when he had had to be carried up and down the stairs. Life had changed for my friends. Monique had her head down and was writing in a ledger at the table. She had begun to go grey and was a little heavier than she had been. She had been a stunning young woman. Julian had saved her from a life that had little future. I was pleased that they were still together. Of Pierre, there was no sign.

I wandered closer to Monique and took off my hat. She continued to write and did not lift her head as she said, "I will be with you in a minute, sir."

I said softly, "Take all the time you like, Monique."

She looked up and it took a moment for her to recognise me. "Robbie! It is you!"

Julian turned and stumped over to grab me in a bear hug. "My God, we thought you were dead! It is over ten years since we saw you! You are still alive!"

I hugged him back and then embraced Monique, "Longer my friend. Monique, remember Alan whom you nursed back to life. Do you not recognise him?"

"Of course, the wounded young trooper we tended!" She hugged him.

Alan said quietly, "I never got to thank you properly, Madame. My French was poor in those days; I hope it has improved."

"It has and you are welcome. You both are."

"Where is Pierre?"

They looked at each other and their faces clouded over. Monique shook her head. "He is not a well man, Robbie. The wound always pained him in the winter. He became worse year by year. This year was the worst yet and he has not left his bed since Christmas. When I go into his room I have to check if he is still breathing. I fear he is close to dying."

Suddenly Bonaparte and Wellington and the affairs of Europe seemed less important than they had been. Pierre was one of my oldest friends and the only one left from the regiment I had joined as a youth. "Alan, take our bags to our rooms." I looked at Monique. "Take me to him, please."

After the huge house in Sicily, the inn seemed narrow and tiny. The house was not the only thing that looked smaller. The stairs seemed barely large enough to accommodate me. As Monique opened the door, I could not believe that this was Pierre who lay in the bed. I had remembered him as a powerful Chasseur; full of life and with a confident happy go lucky attitude. He had been one of the best cavalrymen I had ever known. He had taken me under his wing when I had joined the Chasseurs. What I saw was a skeleton with skin thinly drawn over the bones. I swear I could almost see his blood trickling through his veins.

He was asleep and I was about to descend when Monique grabbed my arm and said, quietly, "Do not go down because he sleeps. I do not think he has long to live. Perhaps this is Fate, and he was waiting for you to return. Wait with him. He sleeps fitfully and I know that he will awake soon."

"How can that be? My return here is pure luck. The roads were crowded!"

She shrugged, "We do not understand everything in this world, Robbie. There are powers in the heavens who work their magic. You are here and that is all that is important. You have arrived in time. Speak with him. This was meant to be." Monique put her hand on mine and I nodded. Kissing me on the cheek she slipped out of the door and closed it behind her.

There was a chair next to the bed and I could see the half-eaten bowl of gruel on the table. Monique had looked after Pierre the way she had with Alan. She was one of the most caring people I had ever known. Monique and Julian had cared for my old friend and I would see that they were rewarded. When my life had been in danger and Alan's had hung in the balance, they had risked all to help us. I would not forget.

I sat on the chair and looked at him. His hair had almost gone, and I could see that he was just skin and bone held together by willpower. He was not yet ready to die. The warrior would choose his own moment for death. His breathing was laboured. The blade which had entered his lungs all those years ago had been weakening him gradually.

I must have sighed or made some sort of noise for his eyes flickered open. At first, his face was filled with incomprehension. I smiled and his face softened, "Robbie! Am I dead and seeing you in heaven or are you here before me? If so, then my prayers have been answered."

"I do not think that there is a place reserved for us in heaven, old friend."

He chuckled although I could see that it pained him. "You are probably right. What are you doing here?"

I held his hand in mind. "I have come to visit with an old friend."

He began coughing and I saw gobbets of blood spill forth. There was a cloth next to the bed and I dabbed his mouth. "You have come just in time then, Scotsman, for I am dying."

"Nonsense you are just suffering from a winter cold. The summer will bring the sun and with it your health."

He shook his head, and his eyes were sad, "Old friends do not lie to each other, Robbie. I can see death reflected in your eyes. Besides, I am ready to go. I think I only waited to speak with you, the last of my comrades. All the rest are gone although I see them each night when I close my eyes. They are in my head and my heart." He took in my clothes and my appearance as he tried to sit up. "You have done well for yourself. Are you still a soldier?"

He was right, old friends do not lie. "I am a Colonel and attached to the staff of the Marquess of Wellington."

"Good! And you are fighting still?"

"I was retired but Bonaparte has returned. I am recalled to the colours for one last battle against the beast."

He shook his head, "I did not know. Then more of my countrymen will die. You will fight against him?"

I nodded, "We were betrayed by him and his lust for glory. You were lucky when you were sent home. Egypt was soul-destroying. The regiment was wasted, and we were abandoned. It was a cruel way for our friends to die. We had peace ten years ago and he wanted more power. He took France down the slippery road to ruin. It was never for France and always for him."

He nodded, "How long will you stay?"

"A while, there is no rush." That was a lie but an understandable one. Monique was right. His eyes were closing even as we spoke. He was close to death and I could smell it in the room.

He nodded, "Then I will sleep a little more and speak with you again. I am tired and my eyes are heavy." His bony fingers gripped my hand. "I prayed to God that you would come, and he has granted my wish."

I waited until his eyes closed and his breathing became regular before I disentangled my hands and went downstairs. The four of them were watching me as I entered the room. "He is sleeping."

Monique and Julian both looked relieved.

I smiled, "I am guessing that this fine young man is your son?"

"He is. Julian, this is Robbie McGregor and he helped us to buy this inn."

He reached into his pocket and pulled out the coin I had given him. "Then I should return this to you."

I laughed and ruffled his head. "No, you earned the money." I waved my arm around the inn. I could see that it was faded and old. "Business has not been good, my friends?"

"No, the last years of the war saw great poverty. There were few travellers and the conscription meant that most men were fighting. The new king has not brought prosperity and we have not had the chance to recover. We need to spend money and make it as it once was but there are not enough customers."

I had seen that for myself. I nodded to Sharp. He knew my mind almost as well as I did. He smiled and went to our room.

"How long will you be staying, Robbie?"

"Two days, three at the most. I would have left tomorrow but Pierre... I have to get to Brussels." They deserved the truth too. "I am a Colonel on the staff of the Marquess of Wellington. I will be fighting Bonaparte."

Julian nodded, "I thought so."

Sharp returned with my leather valise. I reached in and took out the gold coins from the purse which the Colonel had given me. To Julian, they would be a small fortune. "Here take these."

Monique's eyes widened but Julian shook his head and said, "No, you have done enough already."

"Done enough? How can I repay the saving of Alan's life? Our survival? Looking after an old friend like Pierre? This money is from the army and I do not need it. You do and I will be insulted if you do not take it. You need them and if you ever require more then send a message to the Alpini family in Sicily. I want to be able to drink in the *'Chasseur'* long into my old age." I pressed the coins into his hand. I saw the doubt, the need for the money and the pride. "I am rich; Alan is rich, and we would not be had you not sheltered us. We would both like to share our bounty with you. Is that not right, Alan?"

"It is. If you ever need anything then we will provide it." There was sincerity in every syllable.

He nodded and his fingers grasped the coins and held them tightly. They might mean they would survive. I hoped so.

Monique came and kissed me on the cheek, "You were ever the gentleman and we are honoured to be your friends."

Alan and I then told them of our families and what we hoped to have in the future. I saw that they were genuinely pleased for us. Others might have been resentful at our good fortune.

The inn was quiet that night and we ate alone. There were just one or two villagers who came in for a brandy or a glass of wine early on and then they left. By eight o'clock all the customers had gone. Julian and I went up to Pierre. Monique had checked on him regularly and he still slept on. We sat on either side of his bed. Eventually, he opened his eyes. He smiled when he saw us both. "My two best friends. This is perfect. Robbie, you will look after the family when I am gone?" I nodded, "I know you will, but I needed to see it in your eyes. They are the only family I have and they are important to me. Young Julian is a good boy. He is the grandson I never had. Julian, your wife has been an angel to me. You are a lucky man as am I."

"I know, Pierre, but I have been lucky to have you as a friend too."

"To you both I say goodbye. I will watch over you both from…" He laughed, and more blood came out. I dabbed it away. "That depends upon St Peter I suppose. I hope that Albert and our other comrades are all there, for I have much to tell them."

He smiled and his eyes closed. It is bizarre but he looked better; he looked at peace. We sat for ten minutes and saw that his chest no longer rose and fell. "Monique!"

Monique came up and listened at his chest. "He is gone. Another brave soldier has passed away." She leaned over and kissed his forehead. "Goodbye, old friend."

We buried him the next day. I handed a pistol to Julian and another to his son. The four of us gave Pierre Boucher, Chasseur, a military salute and fired the pistols over his grave. We stood in silence as the smoke swirled around and rose heavenward. Monique nodded as though that was a good sign. I had seen too much battlefield smoke to regard it as a good sign.

"We will leave now. I would have stayed had he lived a little longer, but I have my duty to do and each day I stay here puts you and your family in greater danger. We will leave three horses for you. You may be able to rent them or sell them. We have not far to go and the two we have will suffice." I hugged Monique, "I meant what I said about money. I have more than enough." I scribbled my address on the back of a handbill left over from the war. "Here is my address, use it!" I grasped Julian's hand, "Thank you, old friend, and I will visit again in more peaceful times, that I swear." I ruffled his son's head, "And you, young man could do worse than be like your father."

The three of them were in each other's arms as we turned in the saddle and waved to them. We rode in silence for the first couple of miles and I knew we were both thinking of Pierre, Julian, and Monique. Then the thought came to me that we were now back to the land of war and my senses went on the alert. I was travelling through a familiar country and the ride north was comfortable. I sought landmarks I recognised and buildings I knew. It was as I was scanning the side of the road when a piece of white caught my eye. I halted, dismounted, and picked up the broadsheet.

"What is it, sir?"

I read it and my heart sank. It confirmed Pierre-Francois' intelligence. The heading and the first lines were enough confirmation.

Soldiers of Belgium
You have been betrayed and delivered into the hands of your enemies. The Emperor Napoleon returns and promises your country the freedom to rule yourselves........

Chapter 6

Brussels was like a disturbed wasps' nest. People scurried and buzzed around as though Napoleon was on our very heels. As far as I knew he was still at Fontainebleau. We forced our way through crowds of civilians searching for the Union Flag which would tell us we had reached the army headquarters on the Rue Royale. Sharp spied it and the two red coats who guarded the entrance. They lounged against the door jamb.

I left Sharp with the horses and mounted the steps.

"Where do you think you are going?" One of the guards put his musket across the door.

"I am Colonel Matthews, and I am looking for Colonel Selkirk," I said it quietly. I wanted no trouble. After all, I was not in uniform and I could have been anybody.

The belligerent sentry just stared at me. "Anybody can say that. How do I know you are an officer? You could be a French spy!"

The other sentry appeared to have some common sense. He tried to advise his comrade, "Colonel Selkirk is in charge of the Exploring Officers Old Nosey uses. I should let him in, Bert. He might be telling the truth." Bert still scowled at me. The other sentry said, quite quietly. "If he is a Colonel we could be in trouble."

Bert chewed his lip nervously then added, "Right but I have my gun trained on your man there."

I smiled, "And Lieutenant Sharp, if you will notice, has a brace of pistols aimed at you, Private. Your comrade has just saved your life." Sharp had a grin on his face and the private paled.

I found the Colonel on the top floor of the three-storied house. He seemed to enjoy confined spaces. It was a tiny room just like the one he used at Horse Guards. As there, he was surrounded by maps and reports. He liked collecting information. I think the last time he had acted like an ordinary soldier was when he had been a lieutenant. He was, however, a good spymaster.

"Ah, Matthews. Things have moved on apace since last we met. Sir Arthur will be here tomorrow, and the allies have declared Boney an outlaw. We will have him this time!"

He gestured to a seat and I sat down. I pushed over the paper with the numbers of men we had seen and the handbill we had found. He read as I

spoke. "I am not so sure, Colonel. I have found some disturbing news."
He leaned back and lit a cigar. "I only have rough numbers for his army,
but it is the news of his potential which is most worrying. Soldiers are
flocking to the eagles. All the old moustaches are unhappy with the
treatment they received from the king. The officers resented being on
half-pay and his men have spent their adult life at war. They have
nothing more in their lives and there are no jobs. They need the dignity
of employment. They are eager to fight for they fear the alternative.
There is an appetite for war."

"Four armies are coming for him."

"The only important ones are ours and the Prussians. By the time the
rest get here then the war will be over." I stood and walked over to a map
pinned to the wall. "The Belgians are unhappy about being given to the
Netherlands. They are not loyal." I pointed to the handbill we had found.
"I found this on the road to Brussels. If there are more…"

The Colonel took it and read it. "Damn! This puts the fox in the
henhouse. We will have to rely on the Dutch and the Belgians until we
can bring back the Peninsular veterans from America." He looked up at
me. "Your old regiment is over there, Robbie."

I nodded. "If you wanted some good news, it is that he has Marshal
Ney with him. He has changed sides."

"And how is that good news? Isn't he the bravest of the brave?"

"He might be brave but he cannot use soldiers well. And Bonaparte
has no Berthier to organise things for him. You know how much he likes
to have supplies and men in the right place at the right time. Bessières
did that for him and Berthier would be even better." I jabbed my finger at
the map. "The beast is coming here. Sir Arthur will not have to travel far
to fight him nor far to run if we lose. I would have a fast ship at
Dunkerque if I were Sir Arthur."

"This is not like you, Robbie. You are normally optimistic."

"We sent our best soldiers to fight in America and we will have to
fight with a polyglot army of dubious loyalty. How many British
regiments will he have?"

The Colonel stubbed out his cigar. "Not enough!" He smiled, "One
characteristic I like about you, Robbie, is that you will always give me
the truth. It might be unpalatable, but it will be the truth. Go and get
yourself a room. They will become scarce as soon as Sir Arthur arrives
and report back to me here in the morning."

I had decided to leave the best until last. "If you want confirmation of what Bonaparte intends, I managed to get this. It was dropped by a colonel of the Chasseurs who was accompanying Bonaparte." I dropped the map on the desk.

I thought he might explode. "My God but you have done well." He frowned. "Why the hell didn't you give this to me first?"

I smiled, "Perhaps I thought I would play games with you first, Colonel. You have been playing them with me since I first began serving. Call this payback. Besides this is the last job I do for you. Once I am with Sir Arthur again, I will be amongst proper soldiers."

He looked hurt, "Robbie, you can be cruel you know. I have always done the best I could for you."

I stood and laughed, "You have always done what is best for Colonel Selkirk and then Britain in that order. Any consideration given to me was purely accidental!"

When I reached the front door, I saw a sergeant talking to the two sentries and Sharp with a wry smile on his face. I recognised the sergeant. He normally served Colonel Selkirk at Horse Guards. "Sorry about the private, Colonel Matthews. It won't happen again."

"No problem, sergeant. We had the situation in hand."

After we had secured a room and stables for our two horses, we found a bar in the main square. We had learned, over the years, that sitting for a long period just sipping wine and listening was one of the best ways to gather intelligence. This might be friendly territory, but you could still pick up useful snippets. We became invisible as we sat this time and sipped Belgian beer and ate frites. As we did so I wondered about the friendly territory. The Belgians could be the knife that stabbed us in the back. Their resentment at being treated like a sweet to be given away as a reward could turn them against us and towards Bonaparte.

It was a depressing afternoon. The conversations we overheard did not fill me with confidence for the coming campaign. The good citizens of Brussels were torn. Those who had profited from Dutch rule feared for their lives whilst those who yearned for self-rule were excited at the prospect of the Emperor's return. This was neither a settled nor a united country. We went inside the restaurant where we ate a pleasant dinner and then retired early. Once we were briefed, we knew that we would not stop. Who knew when we would get another decent night's sleep in a soft bed?

We arrived at the Rue Royale early the next morning. Sharp joined me in the colonel's office. The colonel tried to second guess what the Marquess of Wellington would want to know. "His Exploring Officers are spread to the four winds. He usually relies on those for the intelligence he requires. I am afraid that you two will have to do the work of six men."

I nodded. "He had better get here quickly. We heard, yesterday, that Bonaparte has mobilised the National Guard."

The National Guard was a hundred and fifty thousand men all of whom had served in the army. "Where did you hear that?" The colonel was taken by surprise.

"We overheard a fellow and his wife who had fled France as he did not want to serve again. He was heading for England. I heard many such royalists expressing the desire to join their King, not to fight you understand, but just to be safe. There is talk of French conscription again."

"You may be correct then, Robbie. If the numbers you gave me yesterday and the map are accurate then he could come directly up the Brussels road today and capture Brussels before we even have any soldiers over here." He shook his head. "We had best prepare as much as we can before he gets here." The three of us pored over maps and measured distances. The Sambre would be vital and I spied some towns which would also be crucial if we were to stop Bonaparte.

It was late in the afternoon when Sir Arthur arrived. We heard the noise of his aides as they scurried around the headquarters; their boots clattering on the wooden stairs and floors. We peered out of the window and watched him dismount from his favourite horse, Copenhagen. As usual, he was dressed plainly without a uniform. It was his style. He needed no uniform. The soldiers knew who he was. He sent for Selkirk as soon as he arrived and a short while later Sharp and I were summoned to join them.

Sir Arthur Wellesley was ever the same. He had never changed in the eight years or so that I had known him. He showed no emotion and when he addressed you then you had an irresistible urge to check the bottom of your boots in case you had stepped in something unpleasant. "Ah, Matthews. Good of you to come." He smiled, "It seems I was wise not to let you resign your commission eh?" Of course, had I stayed in Sicily then by the time orders would have reached me the war would have been over, one way or the other.

That was as close to gushing as Sir Arthur ever got! We had known each other a long time and I believed I knew him as well as any other officer which meant I knew him not at all. His shell was never penetrated.

"It is not a problem, your lordship."

"I do not have all of my Exploring Officers so you and your fellow will have to do the work of six."

I gritted my teeth at his tone. He was talking as though Alan was not even in the office with us. Colonel Selkirk, who knew me well, gave a slight shake of his head. "Colonel Selkirk was kind enough to remedy an omission on your part Sir Arthur. Sergeant Major Sharp is now a lieutenant."

Sir Arthur seemed to see Sharp for the first time, "You are probably right. He is a good sort, I suppose."

I sighed. Sir Arthur was a snob but it was in his nature and he could not help the way he was, "When do you want us to start, sir?"

"Right away." He went to the map. "The route north has to take the French across the Sambre. I would expect them to come between Mons and Charleroi." We had already identified those as key towns. He held up the captured map I had given the colonel. "This suggests either Charleroi or Namur.

Colonel Selkirk nodded, "My money would be on Charleroi." He handed Sir Arthur the map I had taken.

The marquess nodded, "Useful and I am inclined to agree with your assessment, however, Mons is closer to our escape route west and Bonaparte is a cunning fellow."

That surprised me. He was thinking of deserting Belgium already. I had to hope that the populace would not discover that fact. It might tip the balance in favour of joining the French. I stood and went to the map. I had not been asked my opinion, but I would give it anyway. "Bonaparte will not cross the border until he is ready to attack, sir. There will be no sign of him north of the border. He will be in either Beaumont or Mauberge waiting on the other side of the border until he is ready to strike and then it will be like lightning."

"You seem to know the fellow well, Matthews."

"Let us just say that I have studied him. His Chasseurs can move very quickly as can his infantry. It is only twelve miles to Mons and twenty

71

miles to Charleroi from the border. His cavalry could be at either in an hour and his light infantry in three."

"Hm. So you are suggesting you go over the border and ascertain his numbers?"

"I am suggesting that someone ought to gather that intelligence."

He smiled a cold smile, "And as you two are the only ones available then it will be you two. You will leave as soon as it can be arranged and let me know when you see the French army gathering. It will take him some time to assemble his army and his supplies. Thank God that Berthier has decided not to join him. He was the best Chief of Staff Bonaparte ever had. I need to know as soon as they are at the border with your best estimate of the intended attack." He was asking a great deal but then he always did. I nodded. "I should have some cavalry in the next week so I can keep an eye on the roads on this side of the border. When you find out anything then let me know. I hate being blind!"

He went to his desk and I was dismissed. Colonel Selkirk followed me out. "He doesn't change does he, Robbie?"

"No. He is a hard man to like."

"You don't need to like him just follow his orders."

As I left, I thought that the two of them were as similar as two peas in a pod, but I was glad that they were on our side.

We spent the next days preparing for our journey. It was fortunate that it was not winter. I knew that we might have to sleep rough. We laid in a store of powder and ball. We each had four pistols and they had been the difference between life and death before now. The other thing we did was to rest. Once we left on our patrol, we had no idea what might lie in store for us. We left Brussels on the fifteenth of April.

As we headed south Alan asked, "Why did Sir Arthur not send us out immediately?"

"He knows how long it takes to gather an army. Bonaparte moves swiftly but even he needs to gather the supplies and the men he needs. I told Sir Arthur that Bonaparte has the ability to have the speed of a greyhound, but he can only do so when he has everything to hand. I suspect his lordship worried that the longer we were out the more chance we had of running into trouble and being spotted. As he said, we are the only spies he has at the moment. He does not wish to lose us... yet, having said that, I would be surprised if we saw much activity before the end of the month. Bonaparte must start gathering his army and bring them north. He cannot do that swiftly."

"Will we stay at Julian's?"

"No, it is too far from the Charleroi to Mons road and besides, I would not put their lives at risk. We will go to Mauberge. It is a big enough town to hide and yet we are close to the border."

We confirmed our story as we headed south. We had to know each other's minds. Talking in Italian we went over what we would say. The border guards would be more inquisitive, nervous and suspicious. This would not be easy.

The flood of refugees had diminished but we were still viewed with suspicion as we went, like migrating salmon, upstream, as it were. The traffic was all fleeing France. It was only fifty miles, but it took longer than it should have for there were now more guards at the border. My fluent French and credentials from my bankers were sufficient to get us into France. I suspected that our exit might prove to be a little harder than our entrance. They were stopping those with royalist sympathies from leaving. We would be closely scrutinised when we did try to escape.

The allies had besieged the town of Mauberge the year before and we saw the evidence of the shelling. There were some damaged walls and buildings on the outskirts. The centre of the town itself looked undamaged. That evening we ate in a small bar close to the main square where the innkeeper was happy to have businessmen who paid with coin rather than the military chits he would get from Napoleon and his officers. It was he who had directed us to the bar in which we drank. He assured us we would get good value for money. The fact that it was his brother's bar was, apparently, coincidental.

We struck gold the next day when a troop of Chasseurs arrived in the town. I was always wary of showing myself until I had seen the officers. It was many years since I had served and anyone who was still alive would have been promoted. We sat in our window seat and sipped our wine as we watched them clatter through. I breathed a sigh of relief when I did not recognise anyone for that told me that I would remain unrecognised. They set up camp at the northern end of the town. That was important as it meant they controlled the road and that they were there to prepare for the advance and that Mauberge was secure. When they set up their piquet on the road itself then I knew we had come to the right place.

It was in the afternoon when we saw the two French spies. We recognised them as spies for they behaved as we did. They scanned faces and kept watch for danger. We were less obvious for we had the advantage that we had been in the town for longer. We looked to be part of the town. They rode from the south, looking anxiously around them for escape routes. Their identity was confirmed when they were allowed north after a cursory look at their papers by the horsemen at the barricade. Everyone else had been subjected to rigorous interrogation. Fouché was an efficient spymaster. He provided his spies with documents. Colonel Selkirk left us to our own devices.

"Mark their faces and their mounts, Alan. When they return, we shall have to become better acquainted." Our job was not just to gather news from the south but to stop information leaking back south.

We had told the owner of the inn that we were seeking business opportunities here in the north. We were suitably vague about our business and the time we would be staying. He did not seem suspicious so long as we paid him well and drank in his brother's bar. We left more wine than we drank. A drunken spy was no use to anyone. Our search for business opportunities explained our twice-daily rides to the area surrounding Mauberge. We saw much on our rides. The army was clearly coming, admittedly they were in dribs and drabs, but camps were springing up in the fields around the border town.

We watched, over the next few days, the army as the soldiers began to gather. They came in battalions, regiments, and batteries. The rest of the cavalry regiment arrived followed by a horse battery which was unlimbered to cover the road north and then finally, the infantry began to arrive. The roadblock was now made much more formidable. We found it almost impossible to go south for the road was thronged with columns of blue-coated infantry. The cavalry used the fields in which to camp and the air was filled with the familiar smell of horses. I was happy that there were few cannon. Once the artillery arrived in numbers then it would herald an escalation. Even more important was the lack of Imperial Guards. Once I saw them then we would know that Bonaparte would be on his way. Due to the number of camps, we had to restrict our rides and exploration to the east and the west of the town. That stopped too when we saw light infantry battalions·setting up camp in both of those places.

The hardest part about this mission was the fact that we had no opportunity to write to our families. All that Maria and Emily would know of us was that we had left the *'Donna Maria'* at Antibes and disappeared into France. We had not had an opportunity to write to them. It caused me sleepless nights but there was nothing I could do about it.

We developed a routine of walking to the northern edge of the town each afternoon. It allowed us to check on the barricade, observe the practice of the guards and work out our escape route. While we would not be leaving by the road, we would have to pass close to it. I did not want the 1st Chasseurs to become suspicious. We had enough information to take back to Sir Arthur but there was little hurry. The French army was not arriving in numbers which suggested an attack was imminent. It was just two divisions of infantry, a regiment of cavalry and a horse battery. It was not enough to invade.

There was a small tobacconist at the edge of town, and we visited the old man who owned the shop. Our chats with the owner had no military value but they helped us for it allowed us to become friendly with him. Spies always needed friends. Jean was almost seventy and had lived in the town his whole life. His sons had died following the eagles and his shop was all that he had. He was passionate about tobacco. As with all such purveyors of specialist goods he had his own unique mix of tobacco and once we got him chatting, he became quite friendly. We talked, at first, of tobacco and what made a good pipe full. We both bought tobacco. We did not smoke it at the rate we bought it, but it allowed us the opportunity to stand outside his shop and watch the soldiers. Later we learned about the town itself.

After our first few visits, we learned much, not only from him but also from the Chasseurs. The troop sergeant enjoyed a clay pipe too and would often join us to chat about inconsequential matters such as the weather, the crops, the wine; normal chat which disappeared like the smoke from our pipes. It always began with a discussion about tobacco, the best type, the way to keep it moist and so on. As with all such chats a good spy can discern a great deal of information. It was from the sergeant that we learned of the date of the consolidation of the army. It would begin the first week in May. He bemoaned the fact that the politicians had delayed the muster by their debate. As with all soldiers he had little time for politicians. They talked and they did not fight. We also learned that the Emperor was still in Paris. That was the most crucial information we gleaned. No one would attack until he arrived. We discovered that vast quantities of powder, shell and ball were already on their way north; barns and warehouses were being commandeered. Bonaparte would be ready by early summer.

During the last week of April, we were chatting as usual when we heard gunfire. The sergeant ran back to the barricade and his men drew their carbines and musketoons. We saw two riders hurtling down the Mons road. Behind them, I saw Dutch Hussars with their sabres drawn. The barricade was opened to allow the two riders through. I saw that it was the two spies. The Hussars and the Chasseurs exchanged musket balls and, with honours even, the Dutch retired after filling the road with thick acrid smoke.

I nodded to Alan and we followed the two spies as they passed us. We shouted a cheery goodbye to Jean and the sergeant. The sergeant's wave back reassured the two spies that we were friends. They ignored us as they dismounted and led their horses down the street for their mounts were sweating and breathing heavily. The two men were no horsemen. They had ridden their horses almost to exhaustion. They stopped a few hundred yards down the road at a small inn. Taking their horses around the back was understandable. It allowed them to disguise their presence and leave discreetly.

When they had disappeared from view, I said to Alan. "Check their bags for any papers and maps. Make sure they cannot leave quickly." He grinned and left. We had learned many tricks over the years to delay an enemy. I had spoken in Italian in case anyone was eavesdropping.

I went into the smoky bar. It suited me as it hid me a little. The two men, who had entered from the rear entrance to the bar, bought a brandy each and downed it in one. They quickly ordered another. These men were not good at their job. A good spy drank when the job was finished not when he needed to calm his nerves as it slowed your reflexes. The Dutch horsemen must have come very close to catching them. I asked for a glass of beer, which I nursed while I studied them. Alan came in and shook his head. He walked to the bar and ordered a beer and stood well away from me. I covered the rear entrance and he the front.

After two more brandies and a pipe full each, the two spies paid their bill and left by the back door. I followed them. If they did not have the information in their saddlebags, then it was either on their person or in their heads. I slipped my stiletto into my left hand and took out my pistol. I kept them both behind my body. I knew that Sharp would be heading out of the front door to cut off any escape and I merely had to gain their attention.

I saw them approach their horses. I smiled as I shouted, cheerfully to them in French, "I saw your lucky escape from those Dutchmen! What on earth had you done?"

They turned around quickly and they both held a short sword in their hands which they pointed threateningly at me.

I feigned innocence and took a step back which invited them to move away from their horses and closer to me. "I am merely curious. I shall return to the bar. I do not need trouble."

They began to advance towards me just as Alan appeared around the corner from the street. The one at the back whipped around when he detected the movement, and I took the opportunity of using my stiletto to knock aside the sword of the other man and club him on the side of the head with the butt of my pistol. The other spy waved his sword ineffectually at Sharp to keep him away and then ran to his horse. As he put his foot in the stirrup the whole saddle slipped around. Sharp had loosened it. The surprised Frenchman fell to the floor and Sharp moved to go around the other side of the horse. The Frenchman lunged at Sharp with his short sword. Although Alan parried it successfully, he slipped on the slippery cobbled stones and fell. I saw the man raise his sword to finish off Sharp. I threw my stiletto and it plunged into his throat. It was a lucky throw, but it was fatal. I hit his artery and he died in a widening pool of blood.

"Search him, quickly."

I went to the man I had pistol-whipped. We only had one to question now. As I turned him over, I realised that I had hit him too hard and he was dead. Either that or he had hit his head when he struck the ground. Blood was coming from his ear. Either way, their knowledge had died with them.

I went through his pockets and found lists of regiments and a map. Alan had duplicates from the other. We had to work quickly. We grabbed the bodies, one by one, and hurled them into the stables. Covering them with hay would merely delay their discovery. They would be discovered and then we would be sought. However, the delay would buy us some time. The time had come to leave France.

We headed back to our inn and paid the bill. We explained that the presence of the Dutch horsemen had frightened us. The owner was disappointed, but he understood our dilemma. He wished us a safe journey. Within ten minutes we were heading through the back streets of the border town. I had planned on leaving in the dark, but the death of the spies had ended all chance of that. There were woods and fields to the east of the road, and we headed there.

Suddenly we heard a shout from our left. That was where the inn lay. The bodies had been discovered. We headed into the woods. They must have begun to search to the east of the stables quickly which meant it was the Chasseurs. They were mounted and could catch us quicker than the infantry. The sudden sound of a musket shot and its clatter as it rattled through the trees told us that we had been seen. We spurred our horses on through the thinly planted trees. I contemplated taking a chance and jumping the fences but that was too great a risk and we would have to find some other way to escape. We had to continue through the woods until we found a way to get to the road.

As we came out of the woods, I saw six troopers galloping across a field towards us. I led Alan diagonally to the road in the distance. It would bring us closer to the six Chasseurs, but we would make better time on the road. Another consideration was the Dutch cavalry. I hoped that they would be resting just on the other side of the border. If they were there, then we only had to reach them and we would be safe. It was a gamble. Such are the decisions you have to make when your life is in danger.

I drew a pistol as I galloped. Used at range it was worse than useless, but I knew that they would, inevitably, draw closer to us.

"Keep going, Alan!"

I dropped back a little. Looking over my shoulder I saw that they were just thirty yards behind us. I was taking a risk. I wanted them to fire their pistols and waste the ball. They would not be able to reload while riding and I did not think that they would have two pistols. I heard three cracks as the leading riders all fired at me. I felt nothing and knew that they had missed both me and my horse. In firing, they had also lost ground and their fellows were now bunching up behind them. They were just twenty yards behind me. I kicked hard as I turned around. I did not want my horse to slow up. I fired beneath my arm. I did not aim at anyone I just fired at the six of them. I wanted them to think that I, too, had used my only ball. I holstered my pistol and urged my horse on.

My shot had gained us yards as the horsemen ducked and took evasive action, but the Chasseurs had superior horses. They would begin to gain again. The only advantage we had was that ours were better fed and the Chasseurs were bunching up in the narrow lane. As we burst out on the road, I felt the wind of a pistol ball as another of them fired his pistol. I did not look around. My next move would need timing. I saw a crossroads ahead. "Alan, go right and then turn around and attack them! Let's end this here."

I saw him raise his hand in acknowledgement. I drew a second pistol. I watched as Alan went right at the crossroads. I veered left. I knew it would confuse the Chasseurs for an instant. We both turned together and, as the surprised Chasseurs came within twenty feet of us fired our first pistols almost simultaneously. I drew a second and fired as did Alan. The crossroads was now wreathed in smoke. Holstering one pistol I drew my last pistol and fired into the smoke.

I did not allow the Chasseurs to gain any composure. I drew my Austrian sword and galloped into the smoke. I saw that there was only one left in his saddle and unwounded. Some of the others had been wounded while rearing horses had unseated at least one rider. I slashed down at him before he could react. My sword sliced down his cheek and he tumbled from his horse. Grabbing his reins I led the Chasseur's horse from the fray. I heard Sharp's pistol as he fired his last gun into the smoke, and we headed north.

We did not stop until we were north of the border close to Mons. The horses needed a rest and so did we. We reloaded our pistols, but it was unnecessary. The road behind was clear. Our sudden attack had taken the Chasseurs by surprise. If we had been dressed as soldiers, then it might have been different. I was not certain how many we had killed but the saddles had all been empty when we had left.

Chapter 7

We reached Brussels and the Rue Royal on May Day. The Dutch Hussars had disappeared, perhaps they had returned to their camp for we did not find them. Colonel Selkirk was keen for our intelligence. He scribbled notes as we gave him our reports and then grabbed the maps and lists we had taken. "Well done, gentlemen, I'll take these to Sir Arthur. Report here in the morning when he has had time to digest them. I knew that Bonaparte might have spies in the town, but this is worse than I thought. You did well to eliminate that threat."

"Yes, Colonel, but how many others are there? We were lucky to happen to find two but how many are infiltrating the Belgian ranks?" His frown told me that he had not thought of that and he hurried along to Sir Arthur's quarters with the news.

We had paid for our rooms for a month and I was glad for the hotel was heaving. In the short time we had been away the city had filled with new arrivals. The army was here and I saw officers' wives begging for rooms. I had never understood the need to take a wife or woman on campaign. It was no place for a man let alone a woman and I was pleased that my wife was safe in Sicily, far from the war. Many followed their men wherever they went. Had we wished to, we could have sold our rooms for three times their value. The ones who could afford hotel rooms were the officers' wives. I knew that those who followed the privates and non-commissioned officers would be sleeping in fields and wherever they could find shelter. I still remembered the horror of passing dead women and babies on the retreat to Corunna. I wondered how the baby I had found all those years ago had fared. I know he made it back to England but the woman I had given him to had been the wife of a soldier. He could be here now.

That evening was pleasurable for the two of us. We could relax for the first time in a long time and we made the most of it. We enjoyed a leisurely bath, a fine meal and then too much wine. We had learned to take pleasure when we could. Unlike the two dead spies, we only drank to excess when there was little danger and until Bonaparte arrived, we would be safe and could indulge ourselves. The French army would be massing south of the Sambre and soon the battle would begin.

Sir Arthur was pleased with our report; he almost smiled. "Your fellow, Sharp, will not be needed yet but I shall want you with me today. You speak many languages and that may be more than useful."

Inside I sighed with disappointment, but I maintained my straight face. "Yes, your lordship." I was a man of action and I hated having to be diplomatic. I got on well with Sir Arthur's generals: men like Picton, Hill, Uxbridge and Clinton were fine fellows, and I could talk to them. Sadly, there were too many who played at being a soldier and those I could not bear. This time he had his normal coterie of aides. There was Sir William de Lancey, his Quarter Master; Fitzroy Somerset was his close friend and confidante. I also recognised, in the distance, General Paget, the Earl of Uxbridge, with whom I had served in the Corunna campaign. I knew that Sir Arthur would miss Sir George Murray whose hand had guided us through the Peninsula. He was in America and he would be sorely missed for he knew how to organise.

It proved to be a dull day for me although it was a necessary one as Sir Arthur discovered from his aides and generals the numbers and dispositions of the troops he would have available to fight the French. I had little translating to do as the few Dutch there spoke English as did the Hanoverian officers who had served with Wellington in Spain and Portugal. I could have had another lazy day.

The marquess turned to me. "You have a horse?" I nodded, "Good. Then tomorrow you and your fellow, Lieutenant Sharp, can accompany me while I have a look at the ground where we will fight Bonaparte."

I was not surprised that he knew where he would fight the battle despite the fact that Bonaparte had yet to cross the border. He was a meticulous planner.

"Come along De Lancey, Somerset, we have to meet our Prussian and Dutch friends. Today, gentlemen we smile at our allies and play the diplomat. We cannot beat Bonaparte with the few British and Hanoverian regiments at our disposal. Matthews, you may need to translate now."

I ventured a question, "Sir, will you be having any other aides this campaign?"

I had been one such aide in Spain. Wellington waved an irritated hand, "I daresay. I have granted a few favours and there should be three or four young hopefuls joining us soon. But I don't want them around me yet. They get under one's feet and ask ridiculous questions. There will be time enough when the fighting starts."

We headed for the palace where the meeting would take place. As soon as we entered my heart sank. There was Slender Billy, the Crown Prince of the Netherlands. He had served as an aide toSir Arthur in the latter years of the war and was, in my view, a disaster waiting to happen. He was only twenty-three years old but he fancied himself a general. He was not. He was incompetent. For some reason liked him. I suspect it was the snob in him. Sir Arthur had been a minor aristocrat from Ireland and royalty, even the Dutch, impressed him. At least I would not have to translate for him; he could speak English well having gone to Eton. That was another reason for my dislike of him. All the officers I had met who had come from public schools had a superior attitude which was totally unjustified. I had had to give him orders in northern Spain and he did not like me. Then he had been a lieutenant; now he commanded a corps.

The Prussian I did not recognise. He gave a slight bow, clicked his heels and held his hand out to Sir Arthur. "I am Baron von Muffling. I am the liaison with Field Marshal Blucher." I would be superfluous. Baron von Muffling spoke good English. However, I knew I would have to stay just in case Sir Arthur needed me.

As the day dragged on, I envied Sharp and his freedom. It was a boring meeting, but I confess a necessary one. The two armies had to act together if they were to defeat Bonaparte. It was agreed that the two armies would stay in communication and hold a line from Liege in the east as far as Ghent in the west. It was too large an area. I could see that immediately. The two armies would be spread over a hundred miles. Of course, the bulk of the two armies would be within twenty miles of each other and they would be touching just north of the Sambre close to the town of Mellet. The problem was that no one knew where Bonaparte would strike or when. The maps I had found suggested the Charleroi or Namur area but, having discovered the loss he could change his plans. Wellington had to remain flexible to counter the attack wherever it came. If he struck west, then he could outflank us and cut us off from the Channel ports. That was a very real threat.

Despite my reports, Sir Arthur was convinced that I had my numbers wrong and that the French would not be able to strike for some months. He was certain that the troops fighting in America would be able to return and fight in the final battle. He hoped for his friend and Quartermaster, Sir George to return. It was Sir George who made Sir Arthur more confident. The Crown Prince was keen for the war to start sooner rather than later. When I heard he was second in command for the allied army I feared the worst. My hope was von Muffling who seemed to know what he was about. I also knew that Blucher was a dependable general but no matter how good they were, the outcome of the battle might be decided by who was the better general: Wellington or Bonaparte. The Prussians might be the deciding factor but this would be a battle between two titans of their trade.

I was happier the next day when the three of us rode south to inspect the ground over which Sir Arthur was convinced the battle would be fought. Colonel Selkirk and Baron de Rebecque tried to persuade him to have an escort of cavalry but he was adamant he did not need them. "Good God man, I have two fine officers with me. I am only going down the road a short way. We will be well short of the border. If that causes me to come into danger, then we ought to go home now!"

I knew that he had garrisoned both Charleroi and Mons with small units. They were our early warning system. However, I still feared the rapid strike of the snake that was Bonaparte. We rode first to the area around Frasnes. As we passed Genappe he noticed the narrow streets. "This will slow up Bonaparte's artillery. He can only bring them through here a gun at a time."

We reached the tiny village of Frasnes. This was the nearest position to the Prussians and on the main road to Brussels. It would be the first place the French would be met if they came from Charleroi. We found that there was a Dutch battalion and some Dutch artillery already bivouacked there. Sir Arthur seemed happy with the position. He nodded approvingly. "Woods to the east and west. These fellows will hold them up." He spoke to the officer who commanded them and seemed satisfied with the replies.

We rode down to Charleroi so that he could look across the Sambre. This was the border. I kept my pistol cocked in case we had to leave in a hurry. However, the French seemed happy to let us observe them. They would just see three civilians watching them. On the other side, we could see the green uniformed Chasseurs and the blue infantry. Bonaparte had started massing his army.

It was when we rode north that Sharp and I noticed the greatest change in Sir Arthur. He would stop and peer all around him. Sometimes he would dismount and look around again. It happened every couple of hundred yards. As we approached the crossroads at Quatre Bras I plucked up the courage to ask him what he was doing. He sighed as though the question annoyed him and then he actually smiled, "I will answer you, Matthews, for I know that the question is not intended to be impertinent. I want to see what Boney will see when he comes north. I dismount because I wish to see what the infantry will see."

"Thank you, sir."

"I believe that he will come along this road. My purpose will be to slow him down and draw him on. I have chosen my battlefield already and if he attacks there then by God, we shall have him. Now come along we have far to go."

When we reached the crossroads at Mont St. Jean, he spent far longer looking at the landscape. Below us was a vast valley filled with rye which would cover the French and Allied skirmishers who were all small men. There was an inn on the other side, La Belle Alliance, and a ridge such as the one upon which we stood.

"This is where the battle will take place." He pointed with both hands to east and west. "This is where Boney will place his cannon and we will wait up there." He mounted Copenhagen and spurred him on. The road passed between fields of rye which came up to a man's chest. It was a strange battlefield. The distance between the two ridges was a little over half a mile. This would be the killing ground.

I saw two walled houses: a small one next to the west of the road, La Haie Sainte and a larger one to the south-west, Hougoumont. He seemed to ignore them. What I was aware of was the steady climb to the ridge and once we were there and turned around I saw the brilliance of the strategy. Sir Arthur loved hiding men on reverse slopes and here we had one finer than any I had ever seen in either Spain or Portugal. You could hide a whole army here and they would be safe from the Emperor's daughters, the deadly cannon which could cause carnage to regiments in line. As we headed through the village of Waterloo to Brussels I felt, for the first time, that we actually had a chance.

At the Rue Royale, he gave a curt, "Thank you, gentlemen. I shall see you in the morning." Then he headed back into his headquarters. We were dismissed.

The first two weeks in May were spent with Sharp. We set out early each day and rode either to the border or Sharp rode to the border while I sat in on meetings with generals whose English was not up to Sir Arthur's standard.

At one such meeting, I sat next to the Welsh general Sir Thomas Picton. I liked Sir Thomas. He was bluff and he was hard on his men, but they adored him and would follow him anywhere. His language was of the ordinary soldiers and not court! I knew that Sir Arthur disapproved of his dress. Like us, he did not wear a uniform, but he appeared to throw on whatever clothes came to hand. At the meetings with finely dressed officers, he stood out like a sore thumb. What you did know about Picton was that he would do the job he was given, and his men would never break no matter what the danger. He was one of the most dependable divisional commanders we had.

Sir Thomas gestured to the Dutch who hovered near Slender Billy, the rather disparaging name given to the Crown Prince by the British army, officers and enlisted men alike. He spoke quietly for, like me, he did not suffer fools gladly. "What do you make of these fellows? It seems I am to serve under Slender Billy and Sir Arthur is brigading his Dutchmen with my boys. He is a little young to be commanding a Corps. You know him better than I do. Is he reliable?"

"Brigading the two armies makes sense, Sir Thomas. At least the British soldiers have experience of fighting the French. The Belgians were fighting for Napoleon not long ago."

"Experience? Half of them have. The other half is made up of raw recruits. Mind you the French will have the same problem."

I shook my head. Sir Thomas was aware of my role behind enemy lines. "The old soldiers are coming back to the colours. The French want a war. They like the glory."

He shook his head, "Madness! War is a necessity that is all." He gave me a shrewd look. "Come along Colonel Matthews, we have served together long enough to trust each other's confidences, what do you make of the Crown Prince as a commander?"

I sighed. If this were not Sir Thomas, then my comments might be considered tittle-tattle, but the General deserved the truth. "If I was serving under him, I would develop a deaf ear and use my discretion. His only experience in war was being a messenger for Sir Arthur," I laughed, "I realise that I am being indiscreet, and I suspect that is another reason I have never been promoted!"

"Sometimes, Colonel Matthews, the better soldiers are not promoted. Incompetent ones, like scum, rise to the top. Remember Dalrymple and Burrard? Their incompetence cost us Portugal and Sir John Moore his life. Do not worry. Sir Arthur trusts you and I believe he will keep a sharp eye on the Prince."

As we listened to the various nationalities speaking, I realised that it was only the British who wanted this campaign for the right reasons. The

Prussians still rankled over the losses to their cities at the end of the war and wanted Bonaparte and the French punishing while Slender Billy and the Dutch saw the opportunity to make a name for their country and expand into French territory.

On the fifteenth Sharp and I were south of Charleroi. We were sent out most days to scout the road leading to the border. I was happy to be out in the fresh air, riding my horse and chatting to Sharp. It was preferable to the politically charged meetings in Brussels. My horse, whom I had named Pierre, had become a better horse than the others we had purchased. Alan had been correct, he had been a cavalry mount in a previous life. He had improved each day as he remembered his training. One just had to remember to give cavalry commands. Sharp and I pampered our mounts; we gave them grain when we could and apples as often as possible. They were plentiful at this time of year. Pierre didn't seem to mind that they were not quite ripe. He had become attuned to my riding style and commands. I gave him commands in French; after all, he was a French horse. The various skirmishes we had fought made him immune to gunfire and, bearing in mind the battle which was to come that would be useful.

We were used to seeing the French army and their vedettes. The sentries on both sides tactfully avoided shooting each other and a wary distance was kept. However, on that particular day whilst riding on the road to Beaumont I saw the unmistakable and distinctive uniforms of Polish Lancers and Chasseurs à Cheval. That meant that Bonaparte was close by; they were his personal Guards. They were led by a Major in a blue uniform.

I held up my hand to stop Sharp and we retreated into the trees. They were less than half a mile away. Taking out my telescope I confirmed what my sinking heart already knew, it was the Imperial Guard. Napoleon Bonaparte had joined his army and that could mean only one thing, the phoney war was over and the real thing would begin.

We watched them move up the road. Perhaps our recent escapades had made us complacent or maybe it was just bad luck; whatever the reason the Chasseurs who appeared behind us did so almost silently. Pierre was a good horse but he had not yet learned to detect the enemy. We were taken prisoner. Had they not levelled loaded musketoons then I might have tried something but an escape attempt would have been suicidal. I think that if we had been wearing uniforms they might have shot us first and asked questions of our corpses.

We were prodded down the road. The officer who was leading the patrol was not in the uniform of a Lancer. He was a major and he wore the blue uniform of a Grenadiers à Cheval. He frowned when he saw us. I knew enough to pretend I could not understand French as did Sharp.

"Where did you find these? Are they spies?"

The lancer sergeant said, "They were watching from the trees. They are not in uniform, but they are well armed."

The major reached over and took out one of my pistols. He examined it. "This is a well maintained and well-used weapon." He took out my sword. "And this is a fine Austrian weapon. I wonder if they are Prussian spies. You speak German do you not?" The sergeant nodded, "Then ask them their business."

I feigned ignorance of German and shrugged. The Major then said in poor English to the sergeant of lancers, "They must be English spies then. Prepare a firing squad and we will shoot them."

It was a trick and a stupid one. The lancers had no carbines. We maintained our puzzled expressions. He shook his head angrily and snapped, "Disarm them and we will take them to headquarters. There is something about them I do not like. If they attempt to flee then stick them!"

We were taken down the road towards Beaumont. The fields were filled with the soldiers of this new Grande Armée of the North. I saw row upon row of horses and there was the beginning of an artillery park. It seemed that I had the answers which Sir Arthur would want but not the means to deliver them. Sharp and I would be surrounded by the whole of the Army of the North. Escape would be unlikely.

The headquarters building was recognisable by the Tricolour and the Grenadiers of the Old Guard who stood guard outside. As we approached, I heard a cheer from down the road. Bearskins were placed on muskets and raised aloft. Muskets were fired and I heard a band strike up the Marseillaise. When I saw the Chasseur à Cheval of the Guard leading the column which approached then I knew it had to be Napoleon. He led the small column which approached us. Behind him were his marshals and generals. They made a fine sight in their extravagantly decorated uniforms. They contrasted with the plain green coat which the Emperor wore.

Bonaparte and his entourage had closed with us. As we approached, I saw that exile had not been kind to Napoleon. He was far portlier and his complexion was sallow. He did not look well, and he had aged somewhat. I knew I was a mere seven years younger than the Emperor, but I know he looked a great deal older than that.

He recognised me straight away. "Robbie!" His eyes narrowed. "I thought I recognised you in Golfe Juan!"

I nodded, "Yes, General."

"It is Emperor now!" He seemed to be vaguely irritated with my lack of respect. He gestured with his arm. "And you are a spy now unless you have come to join me again?"

There was little point in denying it. "So it would appear." I shrugged. "I was always a spy. I began spying for you, General, if you remember. And to answer your question, no, I will not serve you again."

I saw that those who were closest were outraged by my answers and I wondered if I had gone too far. He frowned and then burst out laughing. "And you were a damned good spy!" He turned to the men around him. "This man helped us to capture Malta for the loss of a handful of men." He turned back to me. "And now you spy again. Who for this time? Wellington?" I nodded.

He dismounted. I noticed that it was not easy for him. "Come we will talk." I dismounted too. One of the Chasseurs went to take my remaining pistols from me. Bonaparte laughed, "I think I am safe. He is a spy, but he is no assassin. You will not kill me will you, Robbie?"

I smiled back, "Not without orders."

He laughed, "I have missed your sense of humour. Some of these do not know how to laugh or even how to live. They are far too serious." He led me to a small walled garden that adjoined his headquarters. There was a bench there and a tree afforded some shade from the summer sun. We could not be overheard. "I know you said you would not serve me again. Reconsider now out of earshot of the others; would you come back and work for me, Robbie?"

I shook my head. I would not lie even to save my life and besides, I did not trust his word. "No. I cannot go back."

"You have served the English since you left me?"

"Mostly."

"Why?"

"My regiment was sacrificed in the desert and I was abandoned to my fate. When I was falsely accused of murder no one believed me. What else could I do?"

He was silent for a while. He picked up a piece of ivy from the side of the tree and began to twist it between his fingers. "I should have known that you were innocent of the charges brought against you. Always I worked for the glory of France."

We both knew that was a lie. He had done what he had done for the glory of Bonaparte.

He discarded the ivy, much as he had discarded me when I was of no further use to him. He looked at me. "What to do with you? Perhaps I should have you shot."

I nodded, "Most of my comrades are dead already. It might be good to see them all again."

"You are not afraid to die?"

"I served you, Emperor, as did my comrades. We lived life on the edge. But at least we had each other and the brotherhood of the regiment. You must remember that. We all knew that death was around the corner. We lived hard, fought hard and died hard."

"Aye, I have lost many good friends. Bessières is dead you know."

"I know; I heard. I am sad for I liked him."

"And I miss him more than you can know." He laughed, "You know he left huge debts and mistresses when he died. I had to clear them for my old friend. He knew how to live; as you do." He stood. "I will consider what to do about you." He waved over the Major. "Major Armand put our two guests somewhere safe. I would not have them harmed; not yet at least." The threat was obvious. "I will see you later, Robbie."

As we were marched to the room the Major suddenly pulled me around, "Now I know who you are! You are the man who murdered my cousin, Colonel Hougon!"

I sighed. How many times would I have to repeat the truth? "I killed him in a duel."

"Then you used a trick which is the same as murder for he was the finest swordsman in our family. I shall take great delight in ordering your death!"

I smiled, which I knew would enrage him further, "You will have to wait until the Emperor gives the order and he likes me!" The door rattled on its hinges as it was slammed shut.

The two of us were confined in a windowless antechamber in the old house they were using as headquarters. It must have been a pantry at some time. Alan said nothing as the door was closed. I began speaking in Italian. They would be listening for English.

"Well, Alan, it looks as though the jig is up."

"Don't worry, sir, you will think of something. You always do."

"This time, however, we are on the wrong side of the border and surrounded by the whole of the French Army. This will not be easy."

I examined the room for a means of escape. There was a candle and they had not taken our powder from us. Perhaps we could start a fire. I laughed at my own stupidity. We would be dead before we could escape. I had learned over the years that when there was nothing to do then rest and save your energy for when you could do something. I have no idea how long we were there, but, eventually, the door was flung open and the angry Major stood there. He spat out, in French, "Come! And do not try to deceive me, spy, I know you now. You speak English!"

I smiled, "And better German than your Poles too!"

His fingers clenched around his sword. We were taken to a large room. Sharp was detained by a guard and I was propelled unceremoniously into the room which was filled with senior officers.

He wagged a finger at the major. "It seems you have upset my men, Robbie. They wish me to have you shot as a spy." He reached up to put his arm around my back. I noticed that he was speaking Italian. "Listen to me. I have no desire to either kill you or slaughter your comrades and, believe me, I could slaughter them. All that I require is confirmation that I can rule France and keep my borders safe. That is not much to ask, is it? I have no territorial ambitions at all. France will suffice."

It was a lie. The smile was that of a Nile crocodile before he eats you. I shook my head. "I am afraid that the Prussians would not like that."

He spied hope in my words. "But perhaps the English might?"

"The Marquess of Wellington and Douro will do his duty. The Czar himself sees him as the man to lead the allied armies to success."

He nodded and considered my words. "We have never met in battle." We were at the window which looked north. His officers were on the other side of the room. "You know I have always admired the English. They are tenacious. They are like bulldogs. They never let go." That was a lie. He hated the English for they were riddled with royalty and aristocrats. It was why he had named himself Emperor rather than King. It seemed a greater title. "We are both undefeated in battle, perhaps it should stay that way."

That was not true. I knew that Bonaparte had suffered defeats. Not many but a few. I said nothing. He looked north and I knew that he was plotting. He must have made his mind up before I entered the room. He was using me and playing games with the Marquess of Wellington at the same time.

"Go back to your General and tell him that I am here to protect my borders. If he attacks me then I will defeat him. I have over a hundred thousand men gathered within a few miles of the border. However, if he stays in Brussels then he and his army will live." He chuckled. "They can live off the Dutch for a while eh, Robbie?" I smiled dutifully. "It has been good to see you. When this is over and we are at peace," he must have detected the cynicism in my face for he added, "Oh, peace will come. Soon they will all fight amongst themselves and France will be safe. When that day comes then return to Paris and we will reminisce about old friends eh?"

He led me outside and gestured that Sharp should accompany me. He said, loudly. "They may return north." There was surprise on the faces of his men. "Return them their weapons. They may need them." He smiled but there was no warmth in the smile. "But if you see either of them again after this day then shoot them on sight." I saw from his pinched face that he meant it.

Once mounted and with my weapons returned, I gave a half bow from my horse, "Thank you, Emperor Bonaparte. Your old spy says farewell."

We rode north not daring to look back. I did not trust Bonaparte and I expected a lance in my back at any time. The angry Major would seek revenge. That much I knew.

"I thought we were a goner then sir."

"Me too Alan."

"What did he want?"

"Oh, he was trying to use me to deceive Wellington. He told me he was defending his land with fewer than a hundred thousand men. He said he would only fight if attacked."

"So there will be no battle sir."

"There will be a battle and within the next month or so. He is trying to use me to tell a lie to Sir Arthur. I believe he has well in excess of a hundred thousand men."

"How do you know that sir?"

"Because he was happy to give me that number. He will attack with a far greater army, believe me, Alan, and I know that he will now attack quickly. He hopes his lie will allay Wellington's fears and make him complacent. We must get back to Brussels."

Chapter 8

Sir Arthur met with me and Colonel Selkirk alone. "He let you go?" Did I detect a hint of suspicion in the general's voice? Did he think I was dealing with Bonaparte behind his back?

"Yes sir. I think he wanted me to tell the lie to you. He wants you lulled into a sense of false security before he attacks."

"I do not think he can have raised an army of a hundred thousand yet. We believe that it will be the middle of July at the earliest before he attacks. In that, I believe that you are wrong."

Colonel Selkirk said, "I think he is correct, sir. Robbie reads situations well."

The marquess stared at me. He knew that I had served France and that I knew Bonaparte, but I did not think he knew the whole story. "And what did you tell him, Matthews?"

I ignored the implication. "Nothing directly but I did mention that the Prussians would not sue for peace."

He smiled, "And he may have the impression that we might. You are right Colonel. Colonel Matthews is clever. Was there anything else?"

"When he took me into his headquarters, I caught a glimpse of a map on the wall. I could not see numbers but he looked to have two armies. There were two blue arrows pinned to it. One appeared to be heading north-west and one northeast."

Wellington smacked one hand against the other. "He plans to defeat us piecemeal. He did it to the Austrians and the Russians. He keeps a small army occupying one force while he knocks out the other. By using the Charleroi road he maintains his lines of communication. Clever. You have done well, Colonel Matthews." He stared at his map before him. "Very well then have our outposts keep a close watch on the border and we will move the army towards Mont St. John. We will concentrate between Nivelles and Sombreffe. Bonaparte is not the only one who can keep his lines of communication open and his armies close together. I will inform Baron von Muffling."

I rested Pierre and the next day took the Chasseur's horse I had captured. He was a more spirited animal than Pierre and I had named him Wolf as it seemed to suit his wilder nature. When I arrived at the Rue Royale with Sharp, I discovered a troop of the Scots Greys waiting patiently outside. Some official in London had renamed them the Royal

North British Dragoons, a title assiduously avoided by all. It was all because of the Act of Union. Everyone called them the Scots Greys. They were big men on big grey horses. There was a captain commanding them. He saluted and said, "Morning, sir."

I returned his salute but before I could speak the Earl of Uxbridge came out. He had a grin on his face. "Good to see you again, Colonel Matthews. I didn't have an opportunity to speak the other day. I see you have been promoted. Damned good. You certainly deserve it."

"Good day, your lordship. I haven't seen you since the retreat to Corunna."

He looked a little shamefaced as he said, "Yes, well, Sir Arthur and I had a slight problem, a difference of opinion you might say. All sorted now. Best of friends once more!"

It was then that I remembered; one of the two greatest cavalry commanders of the war had had the effrontery to run off with Sir Arthur's sister-in-law. I guessed that bridges had been built since then. However, I doubted that they were the best of friends. Sir Arthur was not that kind of man. He did not forgive and forget.

"I want you to show me the battlefield. Sir Arthur says you went over it the other day. It will enable us to chat for I have lost touch somewhat. As I am to lead the cavalry you are the best fellow to tell me about the regiments. He has a very high opinion of you" He turned to the door and spoke to someone beyond it, "Come along, David. You are keeping us waiting." He shrugged, "My aide, and nephew, Ensign David York!" He rolled his eyes heavenward. I knew this was a common problem amongst senior officers. Soldiers whose regiments or battalions were still in England sought to send young officers as aides. I knew that Sir Arthur himself had three. They gained experience which might aid their careers. Slender Billy had been one such aide.

A harassed young man hurtled out of the door adjusting his jacket as he did so. "Sorry, Unc... sir!"

Shaking his head his lordship said, "Ready Captain Macgregor?"

The Scots Grey captain snapped his heels together, "Aye, sir."

I rode at the head of the column with the Earl of Uxbridge and Sharp tucked in behind us next to the harassed lieutenant. We were soon on the country lane leading to the ridge which was hard by Waterloo and the road to Charleroi. "The marquess says he has picked out his battlefield already before the blighters have even got here."

I laughed. "Yes sir. It can take some getting used to but I served with him for five years in Spain, Portugal and France. I know how he works. It is not the style of Sir John Moore, but it is effective and it saves soldiers' lives. He is not profligate with his men."

"You were a damned fine cavalryman. I am surprised you aren't a brigadier by now. The good ones like Marchant died young. You would have made a good commander." I had been at the battle where the charismatic Le Marchant had died after leading the greatest charge by heavy cavalry I had ever witnessed.

"I just seemed to be chosen by his lordship for lots of errands and my regiment was often in England."

"They are in America now I believe."

"Yes sir."

"Well if this goes on long enough they may be in time to join us."

"I think sir, that we will be in action sooner rather than later."

"Very cryptic but then again you always were the chap who rode behind the enemy lines."

We had reached the ridge and we halted beneath a huge elm tree. It afforded some shade. I pointed across the valley. "I fear, your lordship that this may be over in less than a month. Bonaparte is less than thirty miles in that direction, and he is not a patient man. You and I know that his horsemen could be here within a couple of hours at the most. I believe he has almost ten thousand horsemen at his disposal. The French light infantrymen are the fastest in the world. You have seen how few troops we have at the moment. If I were Bonaparte, I would be marching up the road now."

The Earl scanned the field before him. "This is where Sir Arthur intends to stand?"

"Yes sir. The guns will be placed here on the forward slope and the infantry in the shelter of the ridge." I pointed to the right. "The Chateau there can be used as a strong point and that farm by the road would be perfect for light infantry. Any enemy attacking up the slope would either have to take them both or risk being enfiladed from their walls."

"Captain Macgregor."

The dragoon rode next to us. "Sir!"

"What do you make of the field?"

"It depends on that field of rye. If we have to charge through it then it might be tricky."

94

The Earl laughed, "Typical dragoon! No man! It would be the French attacking up here. How do you think they would do?"

"Ah, sorry sir. Well in that case I reckon the guns would thin them out and the slope would tire them too," he pointed to the sunken lane which was hidden from the valley floor, "and that would catch them out. They would be disordered when they reached the top. If we were waiting, aye, then we could give them the sharp end of our swords!"

The Earl looked at me. "We have two fine brigades of heavy cavalry. For once we can match the French with their heavy cavalry. I agree with the captain here. This is a perfect country for horses." He took out his telescope and spied the inn on the other side of the valley.

"With respect sir, we have two brigades of heavy cavalry, I believe that the French have at least one Corps of heavy cavalry and two of light horse."

"Hmn, of course, they are only French; but I take your point." He peered through his telescope. "Come along. That appears to be a tavern. We shall have a look at the land from that side." He grinned at me, "And have a snifter of something, eh Colonel?"

When we reached La Belle Alliance, we all dismounted and the troopers watered their horses. After we had examined the ridge the Earl said, "Fancy a drink, Matthews?"

"No thank you, sir. A little early for me."

"Fine. Come along David; I hope you have brought some money!"

I stood with the captain. "You saluted me when I arrived, Captain Macgregor, yet I was not in uniform. Why?"

"We had been told to expect one of Sir Arthur's Exploring Officers who was a colonel and, well you and the other gentleman looked to be soldiers." He pointed to our pistols. I have never seen four pistols on a horseman before."

"They come in handy. I thought you chaps had them too."

He laughed, "We only need one in the troop and that is to put the horses out of their misery. We just need the sabre. Isn't that right Sergeant Ewart?"

A huge sergeant laughed, "Aye sir. A big man on a big horse with a bloody big sabre is all we need, sir."

The captain shook his head, "You will have to excuse Sergeant Ewart his language, but he is a damned good soldier."

"I am not offended. Lieutenant Sharp and I have heard and used worse." I noticed that the big greys were much bigger than the

Chasseur's horse I was riding. At the charge, they would be an imposing sight.

"My mother was a Macgregor you know, Captain."

"Really? Which part of Scotland?"

The spy in me made me be vague, "I am not sure. She and her family came to France after the forty-five."

"Jacobite eh? What was her name?"

"Marie."

"Seems I heard of a branch of the clan who left for France and didna return. That makes us cousins, Major." He held out his hand. "Welcome to the Clan Macgregor."

I shook it. I did not mention taking the seal of the clan back to the miserable old chief who lived alone and had shunned me. "Then I thank you, Captain. You may not know that you have relatives in Sicily."

"That is fantastic, sir. How?"

"One of the Macgregors became a knight of St. John on Malta. I met him and he told me of my connection to the family. I live in Sicily now."

"What a small world eh, sir?"

The Earl and his nephew came out. From the flushed cheeks of the nephew, I suspect he had had more than was good for him. As we mounted, I said quietly to Alan, "Keep your eye on the lieutenant eh? Wouldn't do to have him fall off his horse on his first day at work."

Grinning, Sharp said, "Sir."

I led the party down towards Frasnes. We passed the Nassau troops who looked to have made themselves comfortable. They had shelters rigged and a fire roasting rabbits. I hoped that they would not become too comfortable. They had to give us sufficient warning of the enemy.

Once we left them, we approached the Charleroi to Mons road and we found ourselves amongst the Prussian 1st Corps. After chatting to the commander, in German, of course, we turned to ride to Mons. I think it was reassuring for both forces to see the proximity of the others. Perhaps Bonaparte had got it wrong this time.

"Well, Matthews, we should have plenty of warning if Boney comes this way, eh?"

"I hope so, sir." What I did not confide to the Earl was that the troops I had seen did not appear to have the quality to stand against the French. I had no doubt that they would be brave, and they would stand but my former countrymen had been fighting for almost thirty years continuously. Their leaders knew their business, and all had a keen military mind. It was one reason why I had done so well in the British Army. Another worry for me was the number of trees we were encountering. They would provide excellent cover for the French light infantry. I had come to respect them when I had fought them in Italy. They were tenacious.

Perhaps I was distracted by the Earl's conversation about swords but whatever the reason I failed to spot the Chasseur patrol which was waiting in ambush for us. Their musketoons cracked from the trees. A notoriously inaccurate weapon, they merely succeeded in wounding one of the Scots Grey troopers and hitting a couple of horses.

The Earl's nephew's mount was one such horse. A ball scored a line along its rump. Unlike the troopers, he had no control over his recently acquired mount, and it galloped off down the lane. I reacted first. "Sharp! Get the lieutenant!" As Sharp galloped past me I drew a pistol and urged my horse into the woods. I saw a surprised Chasseur trying to reload his musketoon and I fired at him. He wheeled away clutching a bleeding arm. I holstered one pistol and drew a second as I rode parallel with the road. The Chasseurs, all eight of them, had not expected this and my sudden appearance made them panic. I fired my second pistol at point-blank range and a brigadier fell dead at my feet.

Suddenly I was surrounded by troopers from the Scots Greys. "Are you all right, sir?"

I turned to look into the concerned face of Sergeant Ewart, "Yes Sergeant. I have learned that offence is always the best defence." As I holstered my pistol I said wryly. "And a brace of pistols helps."

When we reached the road, leading the dead Chasseur's mount, the young lieutenant was being helped to his horse. "Good show, Matthews. I had forgotten what a madcap you are."

Captain Macgregor said, "I can see the value in a pistol now, sir."

"Hopefully, you will not need them if Sir Arthur has guessed correctly."

The young lieutenant had sobered up, but he was still shaken. "Thank you both. But for your prompt action..."

"I should spend the next few days learning to master your mount, lieutenant. The battlefield does not forgive such mistakes." I noticed as we rode back that he was more attentive and was definitely chastened.

I was given a couple of days off after my return. I would not be needed until after the fifteenth of June. It seemed that the Prussians and the Dutch were convinced that Napoleon was still gathering his army.

Consequently, Sir Arthur agreed to allow the Duchess of Richmond to hold her ball and he and his senior officers would attend.

It was unusual for me to be so inactive. It was not in my nature to sit and do nothing. Sharp knew my moods well. On the afternoon of the fifteenth of June, we were strolling around the main square. Around us was a sea of uniforms. Officers were busily preparing for the ball. The wives of the officers were in the most expensive shops buying adornments for their clothes. It was too much for me. It seemed a little like Nero fiddling while Rome burned.

After I had almost been barged over by a large and portly matron followed by a servant with several large boxes Sharp said, "Tell you what, sir. Let's have a little ride down to Charleroi. We can be there and back before dark."

"Charleroi? Why Sharp?"

He chuckled, "We have had interesting encounters the last two times we went down that road, it might stop you from becoming bored, sir."

I laughed, "You are right. If nothing else, it will stop these damned hairs from standing up on the back of my neck all the time!"

This time we halted at the crossroads at Quatre Bras. This was mainly because my girth needed tightening but also so that I could view this most important of junctions. As I tightened it, I noticed that the land to the north was open and here there were many trees. Dutch troops were digging in south of the crossroads and, after I had finished with my girth, we joined them for a brew. Unlike the British troops the Dutch preferred coffee. They gave us a generous mug each. I enjoyed coffee but I saw Sharp pulling a face. To him coffee was 'foreign muck' and he wanted his tea so strong that you could stand a spoon up in it. They were pleasant fellows. They spoke a little English and, with my knowledge of German, we were able to communicate. Suddenly Alan said, "Sir, is that thunder I can hear?"

I looked up at the wispy clouds and listened. I heard it. "I don't think so. That is cannon fire, and it is coming from the south or east. I cannot discern the direction yet." As I mounted, I said, "Ride to Brussels and tell Sir Arthur that I think the Prussians are being attacked."

"What will you do, sir?"

"Try to find them. Meet me back here, Sharp." I saw his disapproving look. "I will try to be careful."

"Where have I heard that before? Make sure you do, sir!"

As he rode away, I said to the officer commanding the company. "I would prepare for action. I think the French are coming."

I galloped south as fast as I could. Halfway to Frasnes where I reached the horse artillery battery, I saw that they had been alerted by the gunfire too. My frequent visits meant that they knew me to be the aide of Sir Arthur and my rank too.

I saw that Captain Bijleveld, who commanded the horse battery, had placed his guns on both sides of the road and built a crude roadblock. That was sound thinking. There were five companies of infantry there too. He nodded to the west. "Sounds like a battle. We thought they were the Prussians testing their guns..."

"I don't think so. Where is the colonel?"

The captain pointed towards Brussels. "He hurt his foot this morning and he has gone to Brussels for attention. Major Von Normann commands. He is on the other side of the village."

"I would load your guns, Captain, we will have visitors soon." I left him and his men loading their guns with carefully selected round shot. The first balls were inevitably the most accurate. The gun crews knew their business.

I kicked my horse on and found Major Von Normann. He took the cigar from his mouth. "Well Major, do you believe as I do that the guns are the start of an attack?"

"I do. I have sent word to Brussels and asked the captain to load his guns." I looked at his five companies. It seemed a little inadequate to me. "Do you have skirmishers in the woods yet?"

The Dutchman looked surprised at the question. "No, Major." He pointed to the end of the village. "But I have a sergeant and twelve men at the edge of the village."

It was too late to give him a lesson in tactics but a company in the woods would have been able to flank any attacker. I wondered if I should ride and find the Prussians or, at least, where the guns were firing. I was about to suggest sending his flank company there when my worst fears were confirmed. Thundering up the road were the horsemen who seemed destined to be wherever I was; it was the Red Lancers of the Imperial Guard. The French attack had begun without warning. Bonaparte had outwitted Sir Arthur who was busy at a dance while the Emperor was striking at Brussels!

Part 2: Quatre Bras

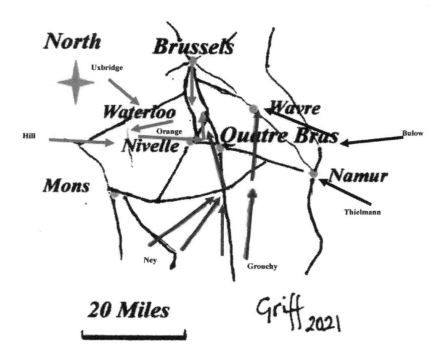

Chapter 9

To be fair to the Major he was a brave Dutchman. He was not discouraged by the lancers charging up the road, he simply said, "Lieutenant Muller, take your company forward and give those horsemen a volley or two."

The detachment in the outpost was firing ragged shots at the horsemen who were galloping towards the vital crossroads of Quatre Bras. I mounted my horse and drew my pistol. The thirteen men needed support immediately. Some of the lancers had passed the outpost. I saw one level his lance at me as he galloped towards what he thought was an easy victim; a civilian who had stumbled into a battle. I fired at a range of ten yards. His head disappeared and his body rolled backwards over his horse's back. I yelled to the Sergeant and twelve men of the isolated detachment, "Fall back!"

A second lancer rode at me from the side. I barely had enough time to pull a second pistol and fire. The flash from the muzzle, the smoke and the proximity of the gun made his horse rear and, as he fought to control it, he dropped his lance. The thirteen Dutchmen left the farmhouse and fled towards me. I heard the Lieutenant behind me order his men into ranks. I fired a third pistol at the advancing lancers and then turned to follow the detachment. The lines opened to allow us through, and I heard the volleys as they fired in ranks. Although not as fast as the British they cleared the road with three volleys, and I saw the Polish Lancers fall back out of musket range. We had a brief respite, but I knew that the horsemen would not be alone. Infantry would soon be joining the horsemen. The gaping error of an undefended wood might well come to haunt us.

"Well done, Lieutenant. Now I think you ought to take your men back to the major. They will reform and attack again. This time they will come in solid lines and not piecemeal." I pointed to the south where the lancers had split into two. Two squadrons of each were going to come along the side of the road. The eighty men would be isolated and cut to pieces.

The young lieutenant nodded and ordered another volley before leading the men back to the Major. As I reached the Major, I pulled out my telescope. "Major, I can see blue uniforms behind the lancers. That will be infantry. I would suggest you pull back up the road. There is a farm close to some woods not far from Quatre Bras. You will have shelter for your men and the artillery will discourage the French. At least there you will not be in danger of being outflanked. "

"You are right, Major." He turned to his Sergeant Major and rattled out orders. I took the opportunity of reloading my guns.

The lancers were not charging but they were trotting purposefully towards us. If these were ordinary cavalry then the Major might have a chance of extricating them easily. He could form a square and march north. A lancer could attack a square with impunity. These raw Nassau troops might be brave, but they would not stand an attack by lancers.

Our only chance lay with the artillery which was well placed to clear the road. Each company fired in turn and then retired behind the next company. They slowly headed up the road back to the safety of the guns. The captain leading the retreat had them alternate their fire and keep the lancers at bay. They did not cause many casualties amongst the Red Lancers, but they stopped them from coming too close. As the last company ran there was just the Major and myself left. Like me, he drew his pistol and as the lancers began to charge we both fired. The smoke from the muskets meant that it was hard to see if we hit anything, but it warned the lancers that there were still enemies ahead. As we rode the thousand yards to the guns, I heard the reassuring crack of the artillery pieces as they sent round shot towards the flanks and the advancing lancers.

We reached the guns at the same time as the last company. Major Von Normann reloaded his pistol. "Thank you, Colonel. I agree with you. This position is untenable. Sergeant Major, take the men to the farm at Gemincourt and dig in. Captain Bijleveld, hold them as long as you can but do not risk your guns." He turned to me, "Colonel?"

"I will stay with the guns." I shrugged, "I have done this before."

He smiled, "And I took you for a dandified staff officer!"

Smiling back I said, "Appearances can be deceptive."

When the infantry had left it felt lonely and isolated. The captain said, "Thank you for this, sir. It is my first action."

"And you are doing very well. If you don't mind some advice, have some canister ready and when they are a hundred yards away fire your guns with canister and ball. Then you can limber your guns and ride like the devil is after you."

He gave the orders and his men continued to send a round shot towards the lancers. They were now becoming more daring as they realised that the infantry was retiring. The gunners could not keep up as rapid a rate of fire as muskets and the lancers had the chance to dart in between shots. Their long lances would make short work of vulnerable gunners.

As they advanced towards us and reached a spot a hundred and fifty yards away the Captain looked at me and I nodded. He ordered the canister and the shot to be loaded together. I took out two pistols and cocked them. I gripped Pierre with my knees. I had confidence in my mount. At one hundred yards the two cannons spat out their deadly charges. The canister acted as a shotgun while the balls bounced and skipped south. The gunners needed no urging to limber their guns. Miraculously two lancers from the front ranks had survived the canister. I fired at both of them. One fell from his horse but the other came on at me. I holstered my pistols and drew my sword as I whipped my horse's head to the left. The lance came towards my chest and I saw the eager look on the face of the Pole. I hacked down at the lance and then quickly turned the blade sideways putting all my weight behind the blow. The lancer rode into the razor-sharp steel and I cut him almost through to his backbone.

The other lancers had seen the guns limber and they charged after me and the guns. I kicked hard and my horse obeyed both the reins and my knees and sprinted up the road. He was nimble and sure-footed. As we neared the farm, I saw the Dutchmen ready on either side of the road with their muskets levelled. Major von Normann had left the road free for the artillery to unlimber there. The rippling volleys sent the Red Lancers back to Frasnes. They fired until the crossroads was covered in smoke and dead horses. We had some respite. The battery was quickly unlimbered and readied to face the French. We had beaten off one attack, but I knew that it would not be the last.

I looked at my watch. The whole action had just taken an hour. I dismounted and turned to face the major and the captain of artillery. "Well done, gentlemen, and if you don't mind a suggestion from an old campaigner, I would let your men have a drink and a bite of something to eat." I pointed south. "There will be more soldiers coming up that road within the hour."

The major nodded and left to give orders. The captain shouted, "Albert, grab some food and water." He turned to me. "Are you always this cool, Colonel?"

"My heart was beating as fast as yours, Captain, but I have done this sort of thing before and know that you need to keep your head and deal with each problem as it arises."

I took my own advice and took a swig from my canteen. I remounted Pierre. He was tired but I knew that I could see further from his back than standing on the road. The men had taken advantage of the lull and were ready again with muskets levelled when I scanned the road to the south with my telescope. I saw the French advancing and this time I made out not only Chevau-Léger but also Chasseurs. This time a battery would not discourage them.

I turned to the Major. "I see cavalry and in some numbers. I would suggest you form square, Major."

"Your advice has been good up to now." He turned to his Nassauers and shouted, "Form square."

The square formed behind the guns. Once the cavalry attacked, the gunners would shelter beneath the guns of the front rank. The major and I took our horses inside the square. I had no confidence that two small Dutch battalions could hold out for long. We needed reinforcements and fast. I knew that Sharp would have only been in Brussels for a short time. He would need to find Colonel Selkirk or Sir Arthur, all of which would take time. Sir Arthur and most senior officers would be at the Duchess of Richmond's ball. It could prove to be a costly dance. We might only be twenty miles from Brussels but the French vanguard was less than a mile away. We would have to hold out, possibly until the middle of the night. Bonaparte had certainly outwitted both Wellington and Blucher.

Major von Normann nudged his horse next to mine. "My men have never done this before. Have you?"

I smiled, "I have charged a few squares but I have rarely been inside one. It is the Chevau-Léger who are the dangerous ones. They have a lance. But so long as your fellows show bristling bayonets and are resolute they will endure."

I looked at the sky. It was getting close to the longest day of the year. We would have daylight for some time yet. I watched the steady approach of the French. Their cavalry was using the open ground and fields to the east. I had no doubt that the light infantry would filter into the woods to the west once they closed with us. They could shelter in the trees and use sharpshooters to hit the gunners. If we had had more than two battalions then I would have suggested putting a couple of light companies there. It would be a total waste of the men with our paucity of numbers.

Captain Bijleveld fired a few rounds from his cannons. It was merely to discourage the enemy and give heart to the Dutch. One could sense the nervousness of the troops.

I turned to the major and spoke so that only he could hear me. "I am going to tell you an awful joke, sir. Pray laugh as though it is the funniest thing you have ever heard and then you tell me one." He gave me a strange look. "Please." He nodded. I loudly told him one of Sharp's jokes. It was not very good; it was more salacious than humorous. When he had finished laughing, he told me a joke which I did not understand although the men around did. I laughed out loud. When they smiled and laughed, I knew that my simple ploy had succeeded.

We both noticed a distinct relaxation in the men. He whispered to me. "Is this because we laughed?"

I nodded, "If the officers appear unconcerned then their men will believe they will survive. You were nervous and so were they. The Marquess of Wellington uses this all the time. He appears calm and in command. It makes the men believe there is nothing to fear. Even when, as now, were are in the direst of straits."

"Thank you, Colonel. This is a good lesson for me. We are new to such war."

Just then I heard the tramp of boots coming from behind us, from the village. My heart sank, briefly, had we been outflanked? If the French had taken the Nivelles road then they could get behind us. To my great relief, it was Prince Bernard von Sachsen-Weimar who had arrived with two more battalions. We had been reinforced.

He rode directly into the square. He was a good soldier and I saw him appraising the situation immediately. He turned and rattled off orders to his aide who galloped up the Brussels road. "Report, Major."

Major von Normann took him through our actions and the General nodded approvingly. He smiled at me. "Thank you, Colonel Matthews. I have heard of you." He pointed to the Bois de Bossu. "I think we will put our Jagers and Jager companies in there. Major von Normann, you will take your battalion and guard Quatre Bras." He lowered his voice. "There are two militia battalions there and they will need stiffening. Your men are now experienced. I would get some rest too for we have a long night ahead of us and tomorrow will be bloody."

As Major von Normann went to give his orders I said, "Where would you like me, General?"

"It would not do to lose the Commander's aide and besides you have done more than enough already. Go with Major von Normann. If things go awry then you can ride to Brussels and inform Sir Arthur and the Crown Prince of the situation."

I saluted and retired with the Dutch. I confess that I was tired but it was not in my nature to run from fighting. The militia did look nervous as we passed them but the confident strutting and demeanour of the 2nd Nassau-Usingen soldiers seemed to give them heart. These were different battalions from the ones I had met a few hours earlier. They had fought the Red Lancers and won.

Amazingly there were still people living in the houses at the crossroads. They spoke French and I explained that there would be a battle the next day. They seemed philosophical about it all. Jean-Claude, the owner of one of the houses said, "There will be no fighting tonight?"

"I don't think so."

"Then tonight we sleep in our beds and tomorrow morning we go to the cellar. It worked for my father twenty years ago."

I shook my head. I had been in the area twenty years earlier. The people had steel running through them. For a couple of coins, I secured food and the use of a settle in the living area. Having campaigned many times this was luxury, and I knew it.

I was up by three o'clock in the morning. Five hours of sleep was more than enough. Jean-Claude's wife, Eliane, was already up preparing food. She nodded approvingly when I emerged from the living room. "Good you are awake. The family will rise soon." She pointed to the south. "No guns yet. That is good."

After I had breakfasted, I emerged to the early morning light of the 16th of June. I did not know it yet but this would be a long day, more than that it would be an extremely hot day and I would be grateful for the five hours of sleep I had snatched and the food which I had managed to eat. I had learned that Major von Normann was called Philippe. I saw him striding amongst his men and joking with them. He was a quick learner.

I waved, "Morning Philippe. Did you sleep well?"

"Unlike you, my friend, my men and I had to sleep under the stars, but we slept and we ate. We are ready."

I laughed, "I have been campaigning for many years and I have fought and slept in snow and ice. You must forgive an old soldier if he grasps any opportunity for comfort." I looked south. "Tell me what happened in the night."

"There was a little skirmishing, but I think their general is waiting for dawn and then we will see his teeth."

"I will ride closer to the French."

I mounted my horse. There had been an orchard with some windfall apples. Pierre had enjoyed them although I knew they were still unripe. He was learning to be an old soldier too and to take whatever bounty came his way.

The Prince had used his resources well. He had placed one of his two batteries on the Namur road, but it could add its fire to that of Captain Bijleveld whose guns were the closest to the French. As I reached Gemincourt I saw that the French were just over fifteen hundred paces away from the Dutch front lines. However, I saw no sign of an imminent attack. Fires were burning and the French were breakfasting. The general rode over to me. He pointed to the French. "I cannot believe that they have not yet attacked. They have two Cavalry Divisions and two Infantry Divisions. They outnumber us hugely."

"I would leave them well alone, General. It does not do to poke a stick in a wasp's nest. They attack."

He laughed, "Believe me I will sit here until Hell freezes over if I have to. If they give the Crown Prince the chance to reinforce us then I shall be happy."

At that moment a small group of horsemen galloped up. It was Slender Billy himself; the Young Frog! I had never liked him and the feeling was reciprocated. He had been an aide to Wellington, and I had been responsible, oft times, for his orders. He did not take orders well. He greeted the Prince and then saw me. His lip curled.

"And just what are you doing here, Colonel Matthews?" It was the tone a master uses for a badly behaved servant.

I smiled, "I was in the area and decided to give your chaps a hand." I said it airily knowing it would annoy him as did my lack of deference.

Prince Bernard said, hurriedly, "The Colonel helped to turn back the Polish Lancers, sir."

He sniffed and then promptly ignored me. He rearranged the dispositions. I think he did so just to exert his authority. He waited for half an hour and then, as the heat took its toll, and the French showed no inclination to move he withdrew to the shade of the houses in Quatre Bras.

After he had gone the Prince said, "You do not like him?"

"The English learned long ago that the last place for the Royal family is the battlefield. They are of more use waving at soldiers when they parade after a victory. When the Duke of York commanded here in the seventeen nineties all he did was to march his men from one battlefield to another and then camp in a fever infested swamp. We lost. The French have the best idea. Let your armies be led by generals and we have now copied them."

"He means well." It was an apology for the Crown Prince.

"Tell that to the widows of the men who will die because of him."

He reflected on my words as we sweltered in the June heat. The temperature rose and the day became humid and oppressive. Water would be an issue before too long.

The second arrival on the battlefield was Sir Arthur himself. I saw the Earl of Uxbridge with him and Sharp who looked annoyed. I was, of course, ignored by Sir Arthur who spoke with the Prince. I saw the other aides with Sharp. They were also lieutenants, the difference was that they looked as though they had just left school. Those who survived might become good officers but most would remain upon the battlefield as corpses.

While Sir Arthur conferred with Slender Billy, Sharp rode to my side. "Sorry I didn't get back last night, sir. Sir Arthur wanted me with him. He said that you could look after yourself! And then we called at that farm near the ridge on the way here. He hasn't changed. How did you get on, sir?"

I smiled at his concern, "Oh, we had a little spat with the Red Lancers, but we sent them away with a flea in their ears."

Fifteen minutes later Sir Arthur rode over to me. He waved the other aides away from us. "Good to see you survived. The Dutch speak well of you." I inclined my head. "I am going to see Blucher. I would like you and your fellow to stay here. I have sent for reinforcements. If the French look like breaking through then send your fellow to let me know."

"Where is Marshal Blucher, sir?" He gave me a quizzical look. "Just so I know where to send Lieutenant Sharp, sir."

Nodding he said, "Brye, on the Namur road."

He turned and rode off. I was dismissed. I chatted to Prince Bernard who was interested in the Peninsular campaign. As I had been one of the few officers to serve right through that war he questioned me closely. We suddenly heard the pop of muskets coming from the outposts and skirmishers.

"It looks like it has begun, Colonel."

I pointed to the woods. "I think they are sending skirmishers into the woods to chase your chaps out. We could do with some rifles."

He turned to an aide, "Pop over and see if they need help. Tell them not to be shy of asking either for help or advice." When the aide had trotted off, he said, "They are good soldiers, but they fought alongside the French and they know how good they are." He looked over his shoulder in the direction of Brussels. "I shall be happier when Sir Thomas arrives."

"Oh, he will get here. He is a dependable leader. I would feel more confident if we had some cavalry." I pointed to the two divisions of Chasseurs and lancers. They were both formidable foes. I had recognised Ney when he had made a brief visit earlier. "I don't know what Marshal Ney is thinking. They outnumber us and their cavalry could sweep aside the horse batteries if they chose. Their attacks yesterday were half-hearted. Had they attacked with more conviction then they could be at Genappe already."

"Then let us thank God that Marshal Ney is delaying."

Away to the east, we could hear the crash of cannon. The Prussians were fighting too. We would know soon enough what the outcome was for Sir Arthur was there.

"Sharp, ride back to the crossroads at Quatre Bras. There is a house at the crossroads; it is the biggest one. The family will be sheltering in the cellar." I flipped him a coin. "Ask the lady for some food and wine, if she has it, for the English Colonel."

"Sir."

The General laughed, "Old soldiers."

I shrugged. "It is just noon and this battle has yet to begin. When it does then neither of us will have time to eat nor drink."

Sharp came back within half an hour. He had some freshly baked bread, cheese and a rough wine. I had seen the wife putting the bread in earlier that morning. They might have been sheltering in the cellar but life went on for these hardy people. We shared our food with the general. It is a strange thing about a full stomach; when it is empty then the world before you seems impossible and after you have eaten anything is possible. We began to believe we might survive until the 5th Division arrived. Even then we would still be outnumbered but with Picton's veterans, I would be happier.

It was as though the French had suddenly decided to do something about this arrogant little Dutch division that dared to stand in its way. The artillery which had remained silent began to fire at the defenders in Bois de Bossu. Then we saw the infantry column begin to move towards the woods.

"They will not be able to hold them for long." I felt sorry for the general. His Nassau brigade in the woods would soon be overwhelmed by the infantry. Already the effects of the artillery barrage could be seen as Jagers began to flee the woods. Soon the trickle became a flood as the infantry drove the skirmishers from Bois Bossu. The French Light Infantry knew their business. Our right flank was now in danger. The General sent a message back to the Crown Prince but before he arrived a second column of infantry with a cavalry division in support began to move along the ravine which divided Gemincourt from Piraumont. As that was close to the road to Namur it had to be held at all costs. If the road was severed then the two armies, ours and the Prussians would be separated and Bonaparte could destroy us individually.

Just at that moment, I spied some green jackets trudging down the road. It was the 95th. "They would do the job, General." I pointed to them.

It was only half a company, but they would have to do. "Take them, Colonel."

Sharp and I whipped our horses around. I saw the Crown Prince meandering down the Charleroi road. He might arrive in time to retreat. We ignored each other as we passed.

I reached the green jackets. It was a lieutenant leading the men. "Lieutenant, I am Colonel Matthews from Sir Arthur's staff, have your men follow me at the double." He looked at me as though I was speaking Dutch. The lieutenant might be new but some of the 95th remembered me from Spain. They grinned when they saw me. "Come along, Lieutenant. The road to the Prussians is in danger of being cut by the French. Until the rest of your division arrives you need to do the work of a battalion."

I turned Pierre's head around and headed east. The riflemen followed me. Already it was almost too late. I saw the Jagers being driven from the village of Piraumont. They gave a spirited volley and then raced back towards Gemincourt farm. I led the riflemen to the left of the Thyle stream. It proved to be the salvation of the Jagers. The lieutenant knew his job and the riflemen were deployed in pairs along the higher ground. They were able to fire over the heads of the retreating Jagers and they hit the cavalrymen with incredible accuracy. It was boggy ground and did not suit the horsemen. Their horses struggled and the ones who crossed the stream were picked off by the rifles. The cavalry began to fall back and the Jagers struggled up the slope to take up a position behind the green jackets.

Even so, the Chasseurs were not giving up easily and a few of them forced their mounts across the boggy ground and the stream. I took out my pistol and fired at them. I hit one in the arm and one of the rifles shouted, "Have you lost the rifle we gave you in Spain, sir?"

I laughed and answered before the lieutenant could reprimand the wag. "I didn't think I needed it with the finest riflemen in Europe to hand."

The sergeant, who was next to the lieutenant said, "With respect sir, the world!"

"And you are right, Sergeant." The men all cheered. It seemed to reassure the Jagers who added their fire to that of the rifles. We had held them. "Are you all right holding here lieutenant?"

"Yes sir."

"Then I will head back to the crossroads and assess the situation there."

We retraced our steps to the main road and saw that the Dutch I had seen there earlier were in danger of collapsing. They were in line and cavalry was coming. The Crown Prince was bellowing orders. There was cavalry close by and he needed to order his infantry into square. It did not help that some of the battalions were militia and they were facing lancers. I realised that the Crown Prince had ordered the two battalions to advance on cavalry, in line! I shouted as I approached the farm. "Form square!"

I was too far away from the 7th and the 5th to aid them but the nearest battalion to me began to form square. Other officers in nearby battalions must have seen the movement and the closest Dutch battalions managed to form a sort of square. The lancers, however, were upon the Crown Prince and his staff. Sharp and I had not slowed up as we headed west, and I took out a pistol and fired it at the lancer who was about to spear the Crown Prince. Later I wondered if I should have held my shot; I would have saved hundreds of lives.

Holstering my pistol I grew my sabre. Behind me, I heard Sharp's pistol as he also shot a lancer. Three of the Dutch staff lay dead or dying and Slender Billy was trying to get inside the 7th's defensive lines. These lancers were the 5th Chevau-Léger and they were not the Red Lancers. It showed. A lance is difficult to wield in a mêlée and this was a mêlée. As one tried to bring his lance around, I sliced at the arm holding the lance. I cut through, almost to the bone, and he wheeled away, trying to hold his severed arm together. I forced my horse between two of the lancers and hacked at the back of one whilst wrenching the lance from the hand of the one on my left. Pierre might not have been a trained warhorse, but he was learning and he snapped and bit at the French horses. Sharp finished off the last two lancers and we followed the Crown Prince inside the square.

I saw Prince Bernard. His face had been cut. He raised his sword. "Thank you, Colonel Matthews. A timely intervention."

Slender Billy just scowled.

As I entered the square my heart soared. Upon the Genappe road, I saw the Union flags and the red uniforms of Sir Thomas Picton's 5th Division and with them, The Marquess of Wellington mounted on Copenhagen. Relief was at hand. We were not out of the woods yet but there were five thousand men coming to our aid. Those five thousand men were the equal of anything the French could throw at us. I rode, with Sharp, out of the back of the square and headed up to Sir Arthur. I had been across the whole battlefield and I would be able to give him a dispassionate view of events. I knew that the one delivered by Slender Billy would annoy Sir Arthur for it would be filled with histrionics and an exaggerated account of his actions. Sir Arthur liked calm, clear reports.

Chapter 10

Sir Arthur was gesticulating to Sir Thomas when I reached the crossroads. Philippe waved as I approached. He and his soldiers had had an easier day.

"Quickly, Matthews, tell me what has happened."

I gave him the gist in four or five sentences. He nodded, "So there are rifles on the left flank?" I nodded. He turned to General Barnard who commanded the rifles. "Take your rifles to the south of the Namur Road. You must hold it. Your men have done well but things will get worse before they get better."

"Yes, Sir Arthur!"

"Sir Thomas take your men and have them shelter in the ditches along the Namur road. Our priority is to maintain our lines of communication with the Prussians. Bonaparte is trying to split us up. If he does that then all is lost. We must defend this road at all costs. Marshal Blucher is up against Bonaparte at Ligny and things are not going well."

I nudged Pierre close to Copenhagen, "Sir, the Crown Prince will get men killed!"

He frowned. He hated such criticism of his senior officers. I saw at that moment the respect he had for me. He sighed, "He is young, and he will make a good king. We must be patient with him." I saw the change in his demeanour as he went back to being the cold dispassionate leader. "Now then, be a good fellow and position yourself and Sharp at the crossroads. You have done well today, and you need a rest. Intervene where you think necessary." He allowed himself a rare smile. "I will go and see the Crown Prince and see if I can offer some sage advice eh?"

When I reached the crossroads, I saw that Major von Normann had taken the opportunity of cooking meat from one of the dead horses which had fallen. He waved me over. "Come Colonel. You look like you need feeding."

"I confess some food would not go amiss." As I ate, I watched Wellington speak with the Crown Prince and then he rode east to Sir Thomas Picton. The Leader of the Dutch then headed up the road in my direction. For the briefest of moments I wondered if it was to talk to me and then I heard the clatter of hooves behind me as Baron von Merlen arrived with the Dutch-Belgian cavalry. I felt the relief surge through my body. Now we had cavalry and when they had rested, we would be able to challenge the French. Down below it was difficult to make out what was going on. The whole front was covered in a pall of smoke. Occasionally there would be the flash of a volley or a cannon, but regiments could not be identified. Which French battalions were coming up the road?

Prince William had obviously not listened to Sir Arthur for he rode straight up to Baron von Merlen. As he turned, he pointed to the ground to the east of Gemincourt. I saw the 6th Chasseurs as they launched another attack. It could easily be defeated by the infantry but, to my horror, I saw the 6th Dutch Hussars and the 5th Belgian Light Dragoons ordered forward. I could see that the horses were lathered and exhausted, but their colonels led them forward in a ragged charge. Even though the Chasseurs were charging uphill they had fresh horses and they were riding knee to knee; a fatal combination. The Dutch-Belgian Brigade floundered against the Chasseurs. It was boys against men. It was novices against veterans. It could only end one way.

"Sharp, follow me!"

I saw, as we rode, the 92nd in line. They were our only hope. The Scotsmen were solid and dependable. I saw Sir John Cameron as we galloped by. Halting I said, "Sir John, we may need your assistance by and by. The Dutch cavalry is in some trouble."

"Aye laddie, I can see. Ready the 92nd!" He waved his sword and I saw the regiment as they moved down the slope. The Dutch and Belgians were being badly handled by the Chasseurs. The 6th was a fine regiment, and they knew their business. I put the reins in my teeth. I would need both hands. I drew my sword and a pistol. I was riding my horse using my knees now. I saw the Colonel of the 6th Dutch as he was struck by a sword. He retained his balance. I shouted, "Fall back to the ridge!"

I saw Colonel Boreel as he shouted something to his bugler and the retreat was sounded. Sharp and I did not slow down, and we ploughed into some Chasseurs. We had the slope on our side and fresh horses. We knocked aside some Chasseurs and I fired at an officer. I was rewarded by the sight of him plunging to the ground. I holstered my gun and, as I drew a second, guided my horse to the Colonel who, along with his bugler, was fighting off four Chasseurs. My pistol and Sharp's sounded at the same time. The smoke obscured the results, but I slashed down at the Chasseur who was before me. The Austrian sabre hacked into the left side of the horseman. I felt it bite into flesh. I saw the Colonel to my left, and I fired my pistol blindly ahead. I sensed, rather than saw the sword which sliced down at me and I barely deflected it. My momentum saved me for Pierre barged into my opponent's horse. He struggled to control it and I stabbed him in the stomach before he could recover.

"Sir! Fall back!"

Sharp's urgent call made me holster my pistol, grab my reins and whip my horse's head around. I headed for the kilted red line ahead. The Scotsmen parted to let us through and then a double volley ripped and tore French Chasseurs from their saddles.

As we made the Namur road I looked and saw that the crossroads had been overrun. Major Philippe von Normann was fighting for his life. On the left, the Dutch were broken and were streaming back through Picton's veterans. Sir Thomas himself was aiding Prince Bernard on the right flank as they tried to stem the attack through the Bois de Bossu.

I thought, at that moment, that the battle was lost. Major von Normann was engaged in hand to hand fighting at the crossroads. The French cavalry was threatening the Namur road and the Crown Prince and Sir Thomas Picton were falling back through the woods. I saw Sir Arthur close by the crossroads. Alarmingly, he was alone. Sharp and I galloped to his side.

"By God, Matthews, but Bonaparte has humbugged me. Damned if he hasn't got me."

Just then I saw the Hanoverians and the Guards as they appeared on the other side of Quatre Bras. Marching alongside them there were the black-uniformed soldiers of Brunswick. They were raw but they hated Bonaparte. I glimpsed a glimmer of hope. The French artillery had been brought forward and was doing terrible damage to the Brunswick troops who were trying to deploy. A Hanoverian battery unlimbered and began to lob shells at the French. Many would have said it was like spitting in the wind but, amazingly their proximity to the French and their courage meant that they began to turn the tide. Using canister, the French cavalry were cut down like the rye through which they rode. It was ferocious and uncompromising. Every soldier was fighting for his life. The French sensed victory and they were pushing home their advantage. Slender Billy had handed the battle to Ney!

The Brunswick cavalry formed on the ridge and prepared to charge the advancing French cavalry. French artillery scythed through them and gave their own cavalry hope. The Chasseurs and lancers charged the 5th Division. If this had not been commanded by Sir Thomas Picton and filled with Spanish veterans things might have gone awry. The bayonets bristled and the muskets rippled. I was with Sharp, close by Sir Thomas. I saw him wince. A spent cannonball had struck him. I rode next to him. "Just winded." He smiled. "Don't worry Matthews, we'll hold the buggers!"

It was then that I saw The Duke of Brunswick fall. He just plunged from his horse and the charismatic and popular leader died. It speaks well of his men that they renewed their attack with added vigour. He fell by the side of the road to Brussels, a road we were in danger of losing. I wished that it had been Crown Prince William.

Suddenly a regiment of French Dragoons appeared. The infantry who had marched in line down past the woods echeloned one flank and then fired. Although only a few of the dragoons were killed they all veered off and headed aimlessly along the ridge where the 95th took potshots at them as they passed. Had they continued their attack then Sir Arthur himself might have been lost. I heard a cheer from behind Quatre Bras. I later learned that it was General Alten with the 3rd Division. Their appearance made the French halt, and they began to readjust their lines. It was a mistake, for the Hanoverians chose that moment to launch an attack at Piraumont. They drove the defenders from the village and our left flank was more secure. The King's German Legion were tenacious fighters and they would hold that flank for us, of that, I had no doubt. I had fought with them through Portugal and Spain. There were no finer troops to have on your side.

The marquess said, "Matthews, ride to the edge of the wood. The damned smoke makes it hard to see anything. Tell me what you can see."

"Sir."

Sharp and I rode from the crossroads passing the 92nd which was waiting along the road to Nivelles. The farm, La Bergerie, was still held by the Dutch but I could see that the French infantry had begun to close to within a few yards of it. It was a whole regiment and it looked to me to be unscathed.

"Sharp, ride and tell the General he needs to send troops. The farm is about to be taken."

I joined the flank company of the 92nd. One of the Sergeants was chewing some rye. "It's a wee bit hot today sir."

"Aye it is, Sergeant, but I fear it will get hotter soon."

"You mean yon Frenchmen? We'll soon have them running back to Paris just as soon as Old Nosey lets us loose, eh lads?" The rest of the light infantry company began to whoop and cheer.

116

Colonel Cameron led his regiment from the ditch and on to the road. As they began to advance the French skirmishers began to fire at them. The colonel was hit almost immediately as was the ensign carrying the colours. Rather than deterring the Scotsmen, it acted as a spur and they marched resolutely towards the French. Although taking terrible losses they advanced. I was desperate to aid them but knew that my puny pistols could do little to help them.

They reached the edge of the farm, dressed ranks and then gave two volleys. They had taken many losses but the attack drove the French from the building. However, as soon as the French withdrew, the French cannon positioned at Gemincourt began to scythe them down. Wellington appeared at my shoulder, "Matthews, go and tell those fellows to head into the woods and withdraw to the Nivelles Road. They have done their duty."

I nudged Pierre forward. Sharp was about to join me, but I shook my head. "Stay here, the General may have more orders."

I kicked at Pierre's flanks and we left the safety of the crossroads to brave the maelstrom that lay in wait. Ball and shot zipped all around us but we seemed to bear a charmed life. I passed the dead and wounded Highlanders. They would have to wait for darkness for succour. When I reached the farm I saw the carnage of the victory. "Who commands here?"

"I do sir, Captain Peter Wilkie."

"You have done well, Captain. Extract your men." I pointed to the rear of the farm. "If you take them out of the back then you should have cover enough. Head for the woods and then make your way back to the Nivelles road."

"Sir."

I was about to leave when I saw the sergeant of the light company, his leg had been hit and I saw a reddened bandage around it.

"I told you it would get hot sir."

"Can you walk, sergeant?"

"I dinna think so. I'll just wait here for Johnny Frenchmen. I ken I might get a few."

I saw his company looking at me as the Captain ordered them out. "You lads help him up onto the back of my horse. I'll take him to the crossroads."

The delight on their faces was contrasted with the protests from the sergeant. "No sir, we'll be too heavy for your wee horsie."

117

I laughed. "Get on, man!" Once on the back, his huge hands gripped my waist. Like most infantry, he feared horses. "Don't worry sergeant, Pierre is a good horse. He will make it."

I heard the outrage in his voice, "You mean you have a bloody French horse!"

"It is all right Sergeant, he likes Scotsmen."

It was harder going back. We were heading up the slope, Pierre was carrying double and we were the only target for the French. When my hat was taken from my head by a musket ball I wondered if our time had come but we managed to make the crossroads safely. Sharp trotted over to us and he helped the sergeant to the ground.

"Thank you, sir. You have saved my life."

I pointed to the wagon which was loaded with wounded men. "Sharp, help him onto the wagon."

Sir Arthur lowered his telescope. "You are a strange fellow, Matthews. Did you know the sergeant?" I shook my head. "Extraordinary; you risk your life for a total stranger."

"No sir, no man who fights in the same army as I do is a stranger. He is just a friend I haven't met yet."

There was little respite. I dismounted and found a bucket of water to give to Pierre. While he drank, I looked at my watch. It was four-thirty. We had been fighting since early in the morning and the battle showed no signs of ending soon. We still had over four hours of daylight left. It seemed unlikely that we would hold. We had only retaken La Bergerie at the cost of a whole battalion.

As I remounted, I looked to the east and saw that the 42nd and the 28th had been attacked by lancers. They had barely formed square and the lancers were having their own way. Soldiers were being pierced by the long weapons and they had to endure it. The two regiments fought off the attack and the remnants of the lancers made their way south. We had held but it had been at a terrible cost. The two regiments were barely a battalion strong.

Then the last of the 3rd Division arrived. The Hanoverians were sent towards Namur to reinforce the men there while the British regiments were sent down to the road towards Gemincourt.

As I mounted Pierre, I began to feel that we might win. The thought was dashed from me when I saw Kellerman and his cuirassiers begin to line up. My heart sank. The armoured horsemen were even heavier than the Scots Greys. Your only chance was to hit them at point-blank range with as many musket balls as possible. They had a steel helmet and breastplate and they were good. We had little cavalry to oppose them, just six squadrons from the already battered Brunswick Hussars. We needed more cavalry for the seven hundred cuirassiers were dressing their lines. They were going to attack. It would be a slaughter.

The British regiments who had just arrived were hot and they were tired but they had yet to fight. My experience of the British soldier was that he was happiest when he was fighting. I saw the 30th and the 73rd regiments form square as the Cuirassiers approached. The slope did not favour heavy horses. Even from the crossroads, I heard the lead balls as they pinged off shiny steel breastplates. Not all in that particular regiment were lucky. I saw them withdraw back down the slope leaving horses and riders in their wake.

Closer to Gemincourt the 69th did not see the cuirassiers because of the corn. To my horror, I saw that the heavy horsemen had managed to get inside the incomplete square. It would be a massacre. I spurred Pierre down the slope. The gunners of the artillery pieces had taken shelter in the square and they were desperately using anything to hand to fight off the cuirassiers. I fired my pistol at the head of one cuirassier who was trying to tear the regimental colour from the wounded ensign. The young officer was bravely protecting it. The King's colour was being ripped from the hands of a second dying ensign. The dead colour party around his body showed the courage of the defence.

I fired a second pistol and hit another horseman. Drawing my sword I rode into the huddle of cuirassiers. Their mounts were much bigger than Pierre. He suddenly lifted up and his hooves clattered at the head of a cuirassier's horse. Mount and rider fell at my feet. I barely had time to hold on to my reins. As we landed, I swung my sword at the back of the nearest Frenchman. It slid down his helmet and ripped across the back of his neck. I looked around for the others and the colours but I saw them being carried back to the French lines.

A bloodied captain raised his sword in salute as the square was reformed and the angry soldiers fired volley after volley into the departing Frenchmen. When the survivors fled the square was ringed with dead Frenchman whilst the interior was a red sea. Inside the safety of the square, I was able to watch the other Cuirassier regiments as they tried to force the crossroads. Canister and volley fire drove them back. I shook my head. Ney was a fool. If he sent his horse artillery with the heavy horses, then this day would be his and he would have captured the crossroads. However, we had paid a price. I saw that a whole battalion of Landwehr had been ridden down and destroyed. They were not professional soldiers and this was no place for an amateur. As I watched the horsemen retreat, I left the security of the square and made my way back to the crossroads. I patted Pierre's head as we rode up the cobbled surface. He had probably saved my life by his impromptu action. I was glad that Sharp had chosen to buy him.

Suddenly I saw the flash of red to my right. The Guards Division had arrived. It was not before time. I did not know where they had come from but it was a miracle. They were the best that we had. Sir Arthur gave orders and Slender Billy rode off to give them their instructions. Sir Arthur turned to me. "Matthews, ride to La Bergerie, get the remnants of the regiments organised into a line of some description."

Although La Bergerie was just a couple of hundred yards from where we were it might as well have been a mile or more. The commanding general and his staff were sheltered behind buildings and the ridge. The shattered soldiers who were close to the farm just sheltered behind each other.

It was a terrifying ordeal to leave the relative safety of the crossroads and endure the shot and shell firing overhead and the musket balls flying up from the French lines. As I approached, I saw that many senior officers were already down. They had led by example and paid the ultimate price. I went to raise my hat in salute then realised that it had been blown from my head. I nodded to Sharp, "See if you can find me a hat, Alan. I feel naked without one."

"Yes sir." I saw him dismount and begin to examine the discarded officers' hats, French and Allied, which littered the road.

I saw a major of the 69th. He saluted me, "Thanks for your help before. You saved one colour."

I shrugged. There was little else to say. "General Wellesley would like you chaps to form line."

He shook his head, "We have lost too many to go forward, sir."

"I know." I pointed to the other side of the road. "The Guards are going in. We just have to stop them from being outflanked."

"Then we can do that."

I rode east giving orders as I went. "Form line on the 69th." I saw a lieutenant from the 30th looking dazed. "Come along lieutenant, your chaps have done well. Not long now. Just hang on a little longer." I pointed to the west. "The 1st Division is here."

A sergeant saluted, "Don't you worry, sir. The 30th won't let Old Nosey down. Come on lads. You heard the officer. Form line. Keep your ranks close eh boys?"

By the time I was returning east we had a two-deep line. It was a thin line, but the red coats were dependable. They would hold. One of the captains from the 73rd said, " Colonel Matthews we are short of ball and powder."

I saw a couple of slightly wounded soldiers and I waved them over. Sharp arrived with a hat. I noticed that it was a French one. He shrugged, "You have a big head, sir, it was the only one that would fit. I took off the cockade though."

"Thank you, lieutenant. Take these fellows to the crossroads and find some ball and powder. If you can find some water too then I am certain that they would appreciate it."

A voice from the line grumbled, "Rum would be better."

I laughed, "And I am sure there will be some when this little skirmish is over!"

They all laughed, and we waited. There was no longer volley fire, but the skirmishers fired when they could, and I saw odd men succumb to minor wounds as the balls flew around us. Sharp and the wounded men returned with some ball and a miniscule amount of powder, however, the resourceful Sharp had managed to get some water skins and that was invaluable. As they were drinking, I shouted, "See if the dead have ball and powder." The young shaken lieutenant gave me a look that showed how appalled he was at my suggestion 'Robbing the dead!' "Lieutenant, they have no use for it and it will save lives."

By the time the French began their approach most of the men were better supplied with ammunition. The smoke and the rye obscured our view and I saw the lancers late as they skirted the farm, I shouted, "Form square!" We formed two squares with the stragglers from the various regiments. I have never seen a square formed so quickly. I saw one light company racing back to the shelter of their regiment only to be cut down by the horsemen. Barely a handful crawled into our square. We were relatively secure, and a wall of bayonets bristled like a red hedgehog.

The major in my square shouted, "Front rank, fire."

Another voice shouted, "Second rank, fire.

Finally, an ensign shouted, "Third rank, fire." It was boys who now commanded men old enough to be their fathers.

Had this been Chasseurs then those three volleys would have been enough, but these were lancers and I saw a lance dart in and spear the shaken lieutenant in the shoulder. I fired my pistol, and the lancer flew backwards over his horse. On the western side of the square, the three ranks were firing at the horsemen as they charged up the road. The Hanoverian artillery began to clear the horsemen like a farmer with a scythe. We had to endure the attacks for another twenty minutes before the horsemen retired. We had no respite for the Tirailleurs began to pepper the huge target that was the square.

I saw that the major was being attended to and so I gave the orders, "Form line. Take the wounded to the rear! Skirmishers to the fore."

As we formed line Sir John Halkett appeared. He was the divisional commander. "Well done, Matthews. I believe that Sir Arthur has need of you. I shall take charge now."

"How is it going, sir?"

"It is a damned good job that the Guards arrived. At least we have some cavalry now, but my boys have suffered."

"They have, sir, but they were resolute and held their ground. I am proud to have served with them."

As I rode away I heard some tired cheers from the men I fought alongside.

Sir Arthur was consulting his map as I rode up. "How are the troops? Will they hold, Colonel Matthews?"

"I believe they will, sir."

"Good. They need not advance but I would have the stream held." He pointed to the woods, the Bois de Bossu. I could see it lined with red coats. "The Guards are in possession of the woods, but I would have you and Sharp ride to the east. The 1st Hanoverian brigade is there under the command of General Kielmansegge. I would like him to drive those infantry further south. If he can take Lairalle Farm, then so much the better." He hesitated, "I intend to secure Gemincourt farm once more and then we shall be secure. I have had word that General Dornberg is almost upon us with his cavalry. They are much needed."

I smiled, "Yes sir." It was unusual for Sir Arthur to give an explanation. I felt honoured.

"If I am not here when you return, I shall be in Genappe, the Hotel de le Roi d'Espagne."

"Yes sir."

"You are doing well, Matthews. We all are."

The Hanoverians were on the extreme left of the battlefield and we rode down the Namur road to reach them. There was a line of wounded soldiers limping and stumbling along the road. They were heading back to Brussels. There were many wagons and carts with the more seriously wounded. I shook my head. The French had realised that if you could attend to the wounded on the field then you saved the lives of valuable soldiers. The French ambulances were already darting across the valley bottom. We had yet to learn that lesson. When we had passed the last British battery, we headed off the road and down the valley. I could see the Hanoverian brigade as their light infantry duelled with the Tirailleurs. Here and there were pairs of green jackets as they picked off the officers and sergeants.

It was almost eight o'clock when I reached the Hanoverians. Pierre was stumbling now. He was exhausted. We dismounted and led our horses to the cluster of senior officers. The general turned as I approached. I saw his quizzical glance at my newly acquired French hat but he said nothing. "The marquess' compliments, sir, and could you push the French south of the farm?"

He smiled, "It is Colonel Matthews, is it not?"

"Yes sir."

"Is Sir Arthur aware that we have been engaged for six hours already?"

"I believe so sir, but he intends to take Gemincourt Farm. The pressure should decrease, and I believe that our cavalry is on their way."

He sighed, "You are a good fellow. We will try." He turned to give his orders and then, as he turned back saw that we were still there. "You are not returning to the safety of the crossroads?"

I pointed to the horses, "The horses need a rest sir, and I may be of assistance here."

He nodded, "Very well."

The soldiers of the King's German Legion were the equal of any British line regiment. They dressed and fought in the same way. But for the commands in German, of course, one would believe that they were British.

The four battalions set about their work with great efficiency. The company of rifles attached to the brigade darted forward in pairs followed by the light battalions. They soon began to drive the French light infantry back. I saw the rifles head towards the woods where they began to pick off the gunners. It enabled the Hanoverian line battalions to advance in column with few casualties from the artillery. The French horses were blown by continuous charges and the infantry found themselves outgunned. They gradually fell back to the shelter of the woods. Some of the light infantry managed to gain the eaves of the wood before being driven back.

When the recall was sounded the Hanoverians had done all that was asked of them. The general rode up to me and pointed west. "I can see Sir Arthur has regained the farm. Perhaps this little skirmish is over."

At that moment I caught sight of the helmets of the dragoons on the Namur to Nivelles road. The cavalry had arrived. "I believe it is sir. But I wonder what the morrow will bring."

"Indeed."

We mounted our horses and headed north to Genappe and a welcome bed.

Chapter 11

It was a vain hope. We reached the hotel at eleven p.m. Sir Arthur had retired and every room was taken. We had little option but to share the stable with our horses. Sharp was remarkably cheerful about the whole thing. "If a stable was good enough for the baby Jesus then it is good enough for me, sir."

We saw to our horses; we put them in the stall next to Copenhagen. Then we collapsed in the hayloft and I was asleep instantly. It is an old soldier's trick. I had first been taught how to utilise every opportunity to sleep by Old Albert in the Chasseurs. It came in handy. Especially when three hours of sleep a night was a luxury. The noise from below awoke me. I saw John, Sir Arthur's servant, saddling Copenhagen.

"I take it we are on duty again, John."

He looked up, temporarily startled, "Afraid so, Colonel. Sir Arthur wondered where you were."

"Any chance of breakfast?"

He laughed, "I daresay if you hurry you might get some."

"Come along, Alan. Duty calls."

Rubbing his head he said, "And just think sir, we could be in Sicily now! We could be smelling lemons and drinking fine wine. There would be freshly caught fish and a soft bed too."

"But would we be happy at missing all of this?"

"I think so."

I actually felt sorrier for Pierre than for me. He would have to bear me through another hot day which promised to be as sultry as the previous one. I threw some water on my face. I was acutely aware of my smell but I could do little about that. Sir Arthur was already poring over a map whilst eating, somewhat half-heartedly, what looked like a stale piece of bread.

He gave a half-smile. "Morning, Matthews. Should be another lively day eh?"

"Sir."

John grinned as he handed me half a loaf. As I expected it was stale but there was, at least, fresh butter. It was as good as it would get.

As I ate, he said, "Napoleon gave the Prussians a good hiding at Ligny. They had to head northeast." He gave me a smile, "Your little view of the map and Bonaparte's plans were correct. It seems that we faced the smaller corps yesterday while Marshal Blucher faced the full might of Bonaparte. I fear that today it is our turn to face Bonaparte's ire. What we must do is make sure that we hold on to the road to the east. If his plan succeeds then he can destroy us and finish off the Prussians before the Austrians and the Russians even leave home!"

I finished the bread and swilled it down with the hot sweet tea. "Ready sir."

"I shall need you and your fellow to have your wits about you today. We have not got the army I commanded in Spain, but do not say that outside these walls. I will need all of our people who command, and that includes you, to think on their feet and to solve problems. Eh Matthews?"

"Yes sir. We will do our best."

"Today your best may not be enough. You may need to be almost superhuman as I will. We must not show fear and we must never show panic. Always remember to deliver orders calmly and whenever possible walk rather than run." He laughed, "What am I telling you for? You were at Corunna!"

Sir Arthur mounted Copenhagen and Sharp and I followed him. There were three other junior aides who left the hotel with us. The rest had already been given their orders and were spread over Flanders. Wellington had had three hours of sleep. I remembered the Emperor was the same. They could both manage on ridiculously small amounts of sleep. It was strange how they were both so similar in so many ways.

We headed back to the crossroads. The land was now filled with small fires and soldiers sitting and sleeping around them. Sharp and I had a luxurious night in a hayloft in comparison to their sleeping arrangements. We dismounted and Sir Arthur wandered over to the fire of some highlanders.

"Ninety-Second I would be obliged for a little fire."

They dutifully made a small fire a little way away from their own and pulled some broken tree trunks for seats. Sir Arthur sat down. Sharp said, "I'll try and get us a little tea, eh sir?"

General Wellesley was preoccupied and I waved Sharp away saying, "I shall have a wander around, sir and ascertain the mood of the men."

I smiled at the three young aides who looked a little lost. They would learn, as I had, how to do this job. I walked around the camp of the 92nd and listened to the conversations. None of them seemed downhearted. I headed towards the camp of the 73rd and they, too seemed, despite their losses, to be confident. I knew why. We had not fled despite being outnumbered. They had driven the French away in spite of the overwhelming advantage the French had had in cavalry. And, most importantly, Old Nosey was leading them.

As I was heading back to the campfire of Sir Arthur, I saw a heavily pregnant woman and three young children. She looked distressed. "May I be of assistance, madam?"

"Oh sir, my husband, Ensign Deacon, was wounded and I cannot find him."

"I think, my dear, that he will have been taken away to Brussels. The only ones left on this field are the dead."

"Oh no sir, he is not dead. I have heard that he walked from the battle."

"Then I would head for Brussels. They will have taken him there. He will be cared for and besides, dear lady, I fear that a battle will take place tomorrow and this is no place for a woman in your condition. There should be wagons heading north." I reached into my waistcoat and found a silver coin. "This should expedite your journey."

"No sir, I could not take your money."

"I am afraid you have no choice. I outrank your husband and I insist that you take it."

"Thank you, sir." She looked at me fearfully. "He will not be upon the field?"

"If he could walk then he will be heading to Brussels. I beg of you to follow him."

"I will, sir, and God bless you."

I wandered back to the fire thinking about the courage of such women. I had seen, the previous day, poor young women lying dead by the side of the road. They had been killed by stray shots from the battle. They were not combatants but the eight-pound shot and the lead balls did not know that.

Sharp had produced the tea and we all drank the brew. Sir Arthur sent the three young lieutenants off to check on the numbers of soldiers who were fit to fight. He shook his head in irritation at me when they had gone. "I cannot abide these youngsters. They have never fought and I am supposed to be their nanny! I have more important things to do than teach them how to be officers." He sipped the hot sweet tea. "Tell me, Matthews, what do you think of our position and, more importantly, what do these chaps think of it?"

"They think as I do, that the French should have won already but they did not and that gives us hope. They have seen that the French and Bonaparte are not invincible. There is a chink in the armour of the old fox. In the past, he surrounded himself with good Marshals. Many have died and others are absent. Murat was not brilliant but he inspired men. Lannes is dead, Marmont and Massena are not here. It was Ney you fought and you outwitted him. All have taken heart. And the Dutch and Belgians did well. I was impressed with Prince Bernard and the way he defended the crossroads."

"But you do not like the Crown Prince of the Netherlands?"

This was no time to mince words. "The man is a poltroon and is not fit to command a platoon."

The allied commander burst out laughing. "You will never make a politician! That is for certain. He is a pleasant enough fellow and as I have said will make a good king. His chief of staff will manage him." I said nothing. Sir Arthur must have sensed that my silence was dangerous. "Do nothing to jeopardise our relationship with the Dutch! That is an order. I know you, Matthews, you have an inflated opinion of the rank and file. They serve their country and if they die then it is for the good of the country. Do not worry so much about them. You and I have to see the bigger picture."

I threw the dregs of the tea onto the fire where they sizzled and hissed, "Sir Arthur, I came back because Bonaparte needs stopping. The moment he is stopped then I return to Sicily and there I will see my picture, not a bigger picture and not a picture which denigrates ordinary soldiers."

He was not put out by my criticism of the army in which he fought. "You have a future in this army. I watched you yesterday. You inspired men and your decisions were all perfect ones. You could be a general."

I stood and stretched, watching dawn beginning to break. "But I do not want to be. I have had enough of useless and pointless slaughter. I will go home and grow lemons and grapes."

"It is a waste."

I smiled, "You have not tasted my lemons nor drunk my wine."

He laughed but our conversation was ended by the arrival of his other senior aide, Sir Alexander Gordon. He hurled himself from his saddle. "Your grace, bad news. Blucher has been driven from the field of Ligny by Bonaparte and he is retreating towards Wavre."

As Sir Arthur stood, he shook his head, "I knew that Marshal Blucher had been defeated but I hoped that he would still be able to hold up the

French. As he has gone back, we must go too. I suppose in England they will say we have been licked. I can't help it; as they are gone back, we must go too." He folded the map he had been studying. "Lieutenant Sharp go and find my lieutenants. They can actually start to do their jobs now. I want any wounded who remain collecting and sending back to Brussels. We may need them."

"Sir."

"Sir Alexander, Colonel. I want the army moving north to the ridge of Mont St. Jean. When the wounded have been collected, I want the infantry moving, surreptitiously and discreetly; then the artillery. If Ney will allow us we will then remove the cavalry and the horse artillery. I want you two to coordinate that movement. Today will decide who wins this battle. If the French advance early, then all is lost. We must maintain communication with the Prussians. They are our only hope."

Sir Alexander smiled, "Sir, so long as you lead us then there is hope."

Sharp and I, along with Sir Alexander spent an exhausting six hours liaising with the various commanders extricating the infantry and artillery. Each time I returned to the Charleroi road I expected to see blue uniforms marching north but all that I saw were the fires of their camps as they cooked their meals. By two o'clock we had just the rearguard of cavalry and horse artillery maintaining the illusion that the army was still guarding the crossroads. The reality was that the majority of the army was already approaching the ridge.

It seemed that Nature or if you were a believer, God, intervened. Just as Ney woke up to the situation black thunder clouds rolled in making the day night. The humid sultry weather had been a premonition of this storm, but it was one of Biblical proportions. Sir Arthur later said he had never endured worse in an Indian Monsoon.

Our horse batteries opened up as the French tried to pursue. Suddenly the sky was lightened by a roar as the Rocket battery used their rockets for the first time. They were a terrifying weapon as no one had any idea where they would go. Miraculously the first rocket flew directly at an artillery piece and destroyed it instantly. The effect was dramatic. The French limbered up their guns and fled south. It bought us time to retreat. I was exhausted and the torrential rain did not help. The explosions from the rockets and the shells mixed with the lightning and the thunder. It became difficult to work out what was the work of man and what the work of nature.

Sharp looked as tired as I was when he came to me at around five o'clock when we finally approached the bottleneck that was Genappe. I took the opportunity to send him back to Brussels. "Bring back our spare clothes and the spare horses. I fear we will need them both tomorrow. Sir Arthur is making his headquarters at a village called Waterloo. Meet me there."

Sharp knew me too well to argue. "You take care of yourself, sir!"

"You know I will." He shook his head as he turned. He did not believe me.

I felt a great sense of relief when Alan left. He had followed me in my pursuit of Bonaparte when he could have stayed in Sicily. I felt guilty. If anything happened to him then I would blame myself.

At Genappe I thought that we had escaped. I was wrong. I was with the 7th Hussars when French lancers attacked us. They came from nowhere. We were the rearguard and had no warning. My pistols were useless. The rain had seen to that but the poor Hussars with whom I fought had never fought against a lance before and many lost their lives because of it. I drew my sword as the Chevau-Léger attacked. I had fought lancers many times. They were not as intimidating as many thought they were.

I watched helplessly as a young lieutenant was speared by a lancer. The Frenchman pulled back his arm and punched with the spear. It almost came through the officer's chest. A second came at me, confident that I would suffer the same fate as the young lieutenant. I timed my blow so that the lance was close to Pierre's head. I deflected the lance with a sweep to the right. It was such a long weapon that a lancer had difficulty controlling the end. I quickly swung the sword back to disembowel the lancer. The Hussars seemed mesmerised by the lance and I saw them stuck like pigs. The light horsemen were brave boys and went at the lancers time and time again. The survivors learned the trick. Do not fight the lancer, fight the lance and get close. The lancers became discouraged. After I had despatched four lancers and others had also had their own success, I saw a gap. "7th! On me!" I led the troop with whom I had been fighting through the gap in the lancer's ranks.

It was not over and both cuirassiers and chasseurs pursued us. It would have gone ill for us had Sir Alexander not brought two squadrons of Life Guards to charge the French. They came just in time. The Hussars were exhausted and battered. The huge Life Guards tore through the lancers as though they were not even there. They showed the Hussars how to deal with the pig stickers!

We had done well despite the losses to the lancers. We had lost barely a hundred men in the retreat yet there was still an air of despondency as we trudged into the relative safety of our new camp. British soldiers, as I had discovered at Corunna, do not retreat well. They are obstinate and always believe that they can turn and bite at the animals who snap at their heels.

I saluted the Hussars. They raised tired hands in acknowledgement as I led Pierre, who looked as though he could keel over at any moment, to Wellington's headquarters. Every inch of me was wet. The rain had not stopped for hours. We were not to know it, but that rain probably saved the Marquess of Wellington's reputation. We did not discover that until the next day. What we did know was the roads and tracks were becoming impassable quagmires. Cannon wheels became embedded in the mud and everyone was soaked to the skin. Red jackets began to weep into white overalls making the redcoats look rusty from head to toe.

I followed Sir Arthur to the rooms he had secured. I knew we would be luckier than the men who would have to bivouac in the pouring rain. The lucky few would have tents, but the rest would have to shelter beneath hedges, wagons, guns, their limbers, indeed anything which kept a little of the pernicious and incessant rain at bay.

Sharp was in the stables with Wolf. We would, at least, have a spare horse the next day. That would be of some consolation. I actually smiled once we entered the stables. It was a relief to stand without rain driving into every orifice. Sharp held out some cheese and some bread. It seemed it was all that I had eaten for days and I was sick of it, but I ate it anyway.

"The roads are full of deserters and the wounded, sir. I had to leave the roads many times. If tomorrow does not go well for us, sir, then none of us will reach Brussels. The roads will be choked."

"I think Sir Arthur knows his business, Sharp, but one thing is certain. Tomorrow will decide the fate of Europe for the next few years."

"Do you think we might lose this time, sir? It was a little too close yesterday and today."

"I do not know. The despondency in the retreat was because we were falling back. It was not because we were beaten. The men who face Boney tomorrow are still undefeated and that is my hope. That and Sir Arthur."

When I had eaten, I donned my cloak as I headed for Sir Arthur's quarters.

"I'll sleep in the hayloft again, sir. It is warm, at least."

"I will join you when I have received my orders from the Marquess." I endured the rain in the short run to the house. Sir Arthur was alone and was seated, poring over a map. He acknowledged my presence with a nod. I hung my cloak close to the fire to allow it to dry. I saw the steam rising from it as the heat drove the damp away. I wondered about poor Martha Deacon. I hoped that she and her children had reached Brussels quickly. I dreaded to think of the four of them walking through this deluge.

"The rest have gone to bed, Matthews. I am afraid they left neither food nor drink for you."

"It matters not, sir. Sharp procured both for me."

He laughed, "Old soldiers. You always know how to campaign. Of course, it helps to have a good fellow like Sharp. He is loyal to you."

"He is more of a friend than anything."

The Marquess looked shocked, "'Pon my word you are a strange fellow. Isn't he your servant?"

I smiled, "He was, sir, but now he is an officer and besides, we are partners in our business."

Sir Arthur shook his head, "Trade, business, farming, they are all a mystery to me."

"What will you do when we have defeated Bonaparte then sir?"

Sir Arthur's hawk-like eyes bored into me, "You are confident that we can beat him then?"

I smiled, "I know that you think you can beat him and that is good enough for me."

He nodded and waved me around to his side of the table. He prodded the map. "This rain is a godsend. His balls will plough into the ground and not ricochet into our infantry. When he attacks, he will have to wade through mud to do so. What we need to do is stop him outflanking us. That is why I have put some strong forces to the west. Then we must hold on until Blucher comes. It will be a hard pounding. I believe our boys will stand the pounding, but the question is will the Dutch and the Belgians? He will outgun us and outnumber us. The Dutch and the Belgians have done well but they have been badly knocked about."

He yawned and shook his head and leaned back in his seat. I could see that he was close to exhaustion, yet he still kept going. He was quite remarkable. He had less sleep than his soldiers and that was something they would find hard to believe.

"We lost too many good men yesterday at Quatre Bras, Matthews, the 69th, 73rd, 44th; all of them suffered too many casualties. They lost many good officers and sergeants. Those three battalions were amongst the most experienced we had and now they have been halved. Even the Guards were hurt. Bonaparte still has his Old Guard. He did not use them today or yesterday." He looked at me keenly, "I know that you know about the Guard. Tell me about them."

"They are, as you know, the veterans of Bonaparte's army. Unlike the Guards that we have their officers do not come from privileged backgrounds. All began as ordinary soldiers and progressed through the ranks. They have done all the menial tasks that was asked of them. They have stood in columns and squares and suffered cannon fire. They know their business. They are all good soldiers. They are totally loyal to the Emperor. When they attack a few rounds of canister will not deter them, they will keep coming. They are like a savage fighting dog that will keep fighting even when all hope is gone. You have to not only kill them but also destroy every vestige of their existence. The good news is the Emperor will save them until the end. He will not be profligate with his Old Moustaches. He will only use them when victory is in sight or all is lost."

He rose and stretched. "Thank you for that. It confirms what I thought. I shall retire. We rise at six."

"Yes sir."

He left me there. It was typical of the man that he did not worry about me or my comfort. I decided to let my clothes dry out before I retired. I rested my head, briefly, on the table. I awoke stiff with my head over a numb arm and a dead fire. I had been so tired that my body had ordered me to sleep. At least my clothes were dry.

I pulled out my pocket watch. I was amazed that it was still working but then it was very expensive. The watchmaker had assured me that it would never let me down and so far he had been right. It was four o'clock in the morning. I raked out the fire and put more wood on the embers. I blew on the glowing embers and the flames began to grow; it soon flared up and started to take the chill from the room. I stood with my back to the fire and scanned the room. I was looking for sustenance. The locusts had finished everything off. There was no food whatsoever in the hotel. I donned my cloak and went outside.

133

Chapter 12

Dawn had broken and the skies were clearing. There were still a few clouds scudding along but there was enough blue to promise a better day. My boots were sucked into the mud as I stepped towards the stable. Then I stopped. Sharp needed his rest and I would let him sleep. I turned and headed to the edge of the village where I could view Mont St. Jean and the ridge. The smoke from the campfires mixed with the steam of drying clothes and the British camp looked as though it was wreathed in fog. It seemed to me that the soldiers had endured a bad enough night sleeping in mud and pounded by rain. I doubted that they had had much food either. It was no wonder that they often took to looting after a victory. After all those privations they would have to fight a battle! As I looked across the valley, I took heart from the fact that the French had had to endure the same conditions and, perforce, they would have reached their bivouac later than us. It was a thin glimmer of hope, but I clung to it.

I heard steps behind me, and I turned to see Sir Thomas Picton. His face was drawn. "Are you unwell, Sir Thomas?"

He drew me closer. He spoke confidentially to me. "Hit in the side yesterday by a damned cannonball and then fell off my horse when the French cavalry attacked. I think I have cracked a rib or two."

"Have you seen a surgeon, sir?"

He laughed, "See a damned sawbones, Matthews? I don't need blood-sucking leeches. I shall be better once we are sending Boney back to Paris. I shall grin and bear it. Besides, today is the day. We will either win or the Old Guard will be marching over our bones as they head for the Channel."

"This day is better than yesterday. Perhaps the outcome will be better too. We left the field in good order."

"Aye, Matthews, and the French will have the devil's own job to climb that ridge. But we were lucky the other day. Ney should have had us between two pieces of bread. I hope we haven't used up all our luck."

"The Dutch did well to hold them off. Prince Bernard is a sound general."

"Better than bloody Slender Billy! Ye Gods but the man is incompetent."

I was pleased that someone else shared my view. I nodded my agreement. "I had better go and see if Sir Arthur needs me. He said he would rise at six and it is close to that time already."

Sir Thomas nodded, "You watch yourself today, Matthews. It will get bloody and hot close to Sir Arthur. He always puts himself where the greatest danger is to be found."

"I will, sir, and make sure you have your ribs looked at."

"After the battle, after the day is won, then I will." He looked wistfully at the sky, "I think this will be my last battle, Matthews. I have been fighting long enough."

"Amen to that, sir, and it will be my last too."

"Then let us hope that we both manage to leave the battle using our own legs and not a stretcher."

I found that Sharp was up and about. He had already saddled Wolf. "I thought we could give Pierre a bit of a rest today."

"Good idea." I suddenly noticed he was not saddling his own horse but another. It was a French horse. "Where did you get that one?"

"When I was heading back to Brussels, I saw this one in a field. It is a lancer's horse. I think a few lads had tried to catch him and he was a little skittish. I spoke to him in French and he stayed still. He's a good 'un sir." I felt better already. It meant we both had remounts.

We led our horses out. Until we knew Sir Arthur's plans, we could leave our spare mounts in the stable. Sir Arthur's servant passed us as we left the stables. "Morning John, is Sir Arthur up and about?"

"Yes sir, complaining that his horse isn't ready." He chuckled. "The young gentlemen were woken rather rudely by his shouts, sir. I think it will be just you two who are ready to ride with him this morning."

General Wellesley strode into the stables. "Morning Matthews, Sharp." He pointed to the heavens. "Well, there is good news for it has stopped raining."

"Yes, sir, but the ground is still too muddy to move guns."

"Hmm, we shall see."

"Don't forget, sir, that Bonaparte likes his twelve pounders. They take some moving."

"You may be right." He looked up irritably. "Where is the fellow with my horse?"

John scurried out leading the grey from his stall. He put his hands out and Sir Arthur used them to step up into the saddle. I shook my head as he turned the horse and headed towards the ridge.

135

I leaned down to the servant who had been ignored. "Thank you, John."

The servant shrugged and gave a sad smile, "It is just his way, sir."

We rode to the ridge and I could see that almost all the soldiers were up and about. We headed for the forward positions. There was a sandpit by La Haie Sainte and it was filled with the familiar uniforms of the rifles. The three of us headed towards them. They were one of Sir Arthur's favourite regiments.

"Fancy a cuppa, sir?"

The cheery riflemen held out a mug of tea for Sir Arthur. "I don't mind if I do."

We dismounted and Sharp took out one of the loaves he had acquired in Brussels the previous day. He offered it to the green jackets. It was stale but the riflemen took it gratefully and handed us both a metal mug of tea.

I pointed across the valley. "Have the French been up to much?"

The sergeant rubbed the stubble on his chin, "A couple of officers rode forward and checked the ground. I think they were seeing if they could move their guns. Apart from that, they are just getting a brew on themselves." The rifleman looked at me, "Do the French drink tea, sir?"

"They are like you lot they will drink anything if they have to, but they prefer coffee. If they can't get coffee they roast acorns and grind them up."

He nodded sagely, "Funny that. They look like us but we are as different as chalk and cheese."

He did not know how wrong he was. I had fought in both armies and knew them to be cut from the same cloth.

The general handed back his mug. "What is the ground like then? You have been here all night."

"It is what we call claggy, at home sir."

"Claggy?"

"Yes sir. Very muddy but the kind of mud that clings to you and sucks you down. Not very nice. I wouldn't want to be Johnny Frenchman trying to move those cannons in this stuff, sir."

"Come along, Matthews. Thank you, gentlemen. I hope you will do your duty this day. I am counting on you."

"Don't you worry, sir, we'll cut old Boney down to size and that's no error."

We rode to the farmhouse and saw that the Hanoverians were trying their best to make the farmhouse defensible but there were no gates. Sir Arthur offered advice to the major who was in command. "Have water close by, not to drink you understand, but to put out fires. It is crucial that this is held as long as possible. If you can stop the French from taking it then they cannot bring their guns close to our lines. Do your best eh? There's a good fellow."

We headed towards the chateau. "Sir, if they cut loopholes in the walls then that might help them to defend it."

"Why the devil didn't you say something back there then? I can't think of everything. You are an aide, so aid me!"

I shook my head. This was not like the Marquess but I put it down to tiredness. In a way, it was a compliment as he rarely showed that he was irritated. I turned, "Alan, pop back and give them the advice eh?"

"Sir!"

As we neared the chateau we heard the pop of muskets. It began at the far side of the valley and rippled across towards us. It started on the French side too. There was another similarity; both sides cleared the old powder from their muskets before reloading with fresh. The first shot had to be perfect for who knew what the target might be. This was another sign that the soldiers on both sides knew that the battle was drawing closer. It was like the clearing of a throat before an actor spoke.

Alan soon caught up with us. The lancer's horse was, indeed, a good one. When we reached the chateau, I saw that there were Coldstream Guards within under the command of Lieutenant Colonel James Macdonell; they were in addition to the Nassauers. That immediately gave me hope. I also saw my old friend Major Philippe von Normann. While Sir Arthur spoke with the colonel I dismounted to chat to Philippe.

He smiled as he shook my hand, "I wondered if you had survived. Each time I saw you I watched as you charged into the fray recklessly. I did not think I would see you again. Have you a death wish, my friend?"

"No, Major, but I have learned, over the years, that he who hesitates is often lost. It is better to strike and be positive about the strike. "I nodded to the chateau. "At least you have nice strong walls about you here and support from the rear."

"Yes, we are not as exposed as we were at Quatre Bras." He leaned in, "Tell me, Colonel Matthews. How do you rate our chances today?" He pointed across to the other ridge. "Those are big guns. At that range, they cannot miss."

"True but, if you notice, they have not yet begun to fire. Had Bonaparte been able they would have been pounding us since early morning. He cannot fire them and the longer he waits the more chance we have of Blucher arriving."

Just then the Colonel of the Coldstreams appeared, "Major Von Normann, Sir Arthur would have loopholes cut. Be so good as to get your fellows to begin that work."

"Sir. I shall see you later, I hope."

"I am confident we shall. Good luck to you and your men."

Sir Arthur waved an irritated arm, "Come along, Matthews. We have much to see." Once again I heard the impatience in Sir Arthur's voice. Pleasantries were not for soldiers.

It was ten-thirty by the time we reached the elm tree on the top of the ridge at Mont St. Jean. This would be the unofficial headquarters for the rest of the day. The other aides were waiting on the ridge as we arrived. They were all late and Sir Arthur's face warned them that he would brook no more such tardiness. The lieutenants would be used as uniformed messenger pigeons as they rode back and forth to the Prussians so that Sir Arthur would have an accurate assessment of the time of their arrival. I knew he was becoming more nervous when he began to constantly ask for the time. The timing of the Prussian arrival was vital.

"Matthews, ride towards the French and see if you can spy any movement eh?"

I saluted and nodded to Sharp. It was a pointless exercise as the enemy's movements could be seen just as well from the top of the ridge but I did as asked. As I passed the sandpit, Captain John Kincaid hailed me. I had known him since Spain. "How is Old Nosey then, Colonel Matthews?"

"Irritable. He wants the battle to start but not yet. It is a dilemma for him."

"Where are you off to then?"

"Going to spy out the French and see what they are up to."

"We can see all that there is to see."

"I know but he wants me to go, Johnny, and go I shall."

He laughed, "They have those big buggers already in place. Twelve pounders." He pointed to the sandpit. "My lads and I will hide down there when they start. I would not want to be with you on the ridge. It is less than half a mile from those guns and I think that Old Nosey will be the target."

"I know. Still, the land helps us. If they try to bounce them then the balls will bury in the mud. Well, I better be off. I can feel his eyes upon my back even as we speak." I waved at the 95th. "You lads keep your heads down today. Don't try to win the battle all by yourselves."

I rode forward until I was barely four hundred yards from the Grand Battery. Surprisingly, I was safe for the artillery would not waste either powder or ball on a single rider. One of the sergeants shouted, in French, "Go home Englishman before we knock you off your horse."

His language, of course, was coarser. I answered. "I am just coming to see how far our men will have to come before they can capture those fine guns. I think I will have one melted down after the battle and made into a plaque for my home."

I think he was impressed by my French. "These ladies are not for the taking, Englishman. Why, I could hit your General now, with one shot if I chose."

All the time I was talking I was observing the mud around the wheels of the twelve-pounder gun. It had not fired yet and it had sunk into the mud already. They would not be able to fire until the ground dried out.

"I will go back then and tell the Marquess of Wellington that he ought to be careful."

He waved cheerily. "I will watch for you Englishman. You have balls, I will grant you that. Are you a soldier?"

"Yes, sergeant, a Colonel in the cavalry."

He nodded, "Good luck then Englishman. Perhaps we will let you live when all of this is over."

I rode back feeling very vulnerable. I had seen the lancers lined up behind the guns. If they chose to then they might want to gallop forward to pick off one of the general's aides. When I reached Johnny Kincaid, I breathed a sigh of relief. "They won't fire for a while. They are up to their rims in the mud."

"Thanks for that."

"But there are lancers up there so don't go wandering eh?"

"Not today, Colonel. We sit here and wait for them." He tapped his Baker rifle. We can hit them at over four hundred yards. If they get too close, my lads'll have them."

When I reached Sir Arthur, he was glowering at me. "You took your time, Matthews!"

"Sorry, sir. I wanted to be sure I saw as much as I could. They won't be able to fire for some time, your grace. There is too much mud and the ground is too wet. They have sunk to their rims in the mud. They have lancers just behind the guns though, sir, and I saw at least four large columns forming up."

"Hmn."

And so we waited until, at eleven o'clock, we saw one of the columns of men I had seen, head for the chateau of Hougoumont. The French artillery began to pound the trees and the walls of the chateau to soften them up. The battle proper was about to begin. The generals had postured, and the ground had dried out. Now it would be a test of who had the greatest nerve. Who would stand and who would run?

Part 3 Waterloo

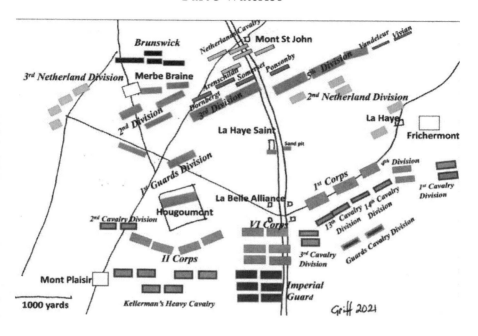

Chapter 13

I knew that the Marquess was nervous as he chewed his lip. I had come to know this stoic general. He tried to keep everything calm but inside he worried about everything. Soon we would be wherever the action was. That was the kind of general he was. We could do nothing more until Bonaparte had shown his hand. He was surrounded by his senior commanders and their aides. I wondered if the French gunner I had spoken to would choose that moment to send a ball our way. We were a very inviting and large target.

"This is a little clumsy of Bonaparte, Uxbridge. He is not even attempting to outflank the chateau. His column is marching right up to it."

"Yes, Sir Arthur. Perhaps he is hoping that his batteries will drive the defenders hence."

General Wellesley actually laughed, "I think it will take more than a few cannonballs to drive the guards from such a good vantage point."

The French column headed towards the chateau. The rifles and the skirmishers peppered away and gradually the attack slowed as the column hit the orchards and the woods. The first skirmishers fell back towards the column. The rifles and the light infantry in the small wood had done their job. Then the French cannon were brought closer and began to pound the walls in earnest. Over the next half hour, the skirmishers and rifles were forced from the woods into the shelter of the chateau. From the ridge, we saw the French begin to send more men towards the chateau.

"Who is their commander? Can you see Matthews?"

I held the telescope to my eye. "I am not certain, my lord, but I think it is Jerome Bonaparte. The Emperor's young brother."

He laughed. "If he is anything like Joseph then it bodes well for us. I thought I had it bad enough with my cousin's idiot sons as aides. At least I don't have incompetent relatives in command."

I glanced at the Earl of Uxbridge to see if he had taken offence at Sir Arthur's comments. He grinned and shrugged. He had thick skin.

General Wellesley stopped chewing his lip and he turned his attention to La Belle Alliance. The Guards and the Nassau battalion could hold the chateau. It was the first of many mistakes which the French would make that day. He wanted to see what Bonaparte would do next. It was obvious that the attack on the chateau was intended to draw reinforcements and weaken our centre. Sir Arthur would not oblige. Not yet anyway.

At twelve o'clock Napoleon's daughters began to belch out death and destruction. Normally ninety twelve pounders firing into a line would decimate regiments. This time they were hitting the slope and digging in. Instead of bouncing up and acting like a skimming stone, the mud was stopping them. Some did, by accident or poor gunnery, fly over the ridge but the casualties they caused were few. Napoleon was wasting his ammunition.

Slender Billy, however, decided to give Bonaparte a helping hand. While the British regiments were brought behind the reverse slope to protect them from the French fire, the Crown Prince decided to leave his Dutch Belgian regiments to be slaughtered by the balls which did not sink into the mud. Although they stuck it out longer than I would have, some of the regiments could not face the cannonade. They broke and they ran. I saw the look of annoyance on Sir Arthur's face. As another shower swept in, he hid his expression by pulling his cloak over his face.

There was a huddle of us together for most of that day: William de Lancey was the Quartermaster and was a dear friend of Sir Arthur's, Fitzroy Somerset was his friend and commanded the Household Cavalry and as stout a fellow as you could wish to meet and then there was the Earl of Uxbridge. Whilst not a close friend of Sir Arthur, the Earl was an invaluable cavalry commander. Had the French been more accurate with their cannon fire then the battle could have been ended there and then, for we were on the forward slope and a clear target. Baron von Muffling was also by his side as the Prussian received constant updates about the progress of the Prussians. All of us were aware of just how crucial the updates were. Miraculously both we and the tree were spared the cannonballs although we were spattered with mud and debris as the balls ploughed into the muddy ridge.

Suddenly we saw a huge column approaching. It rose from the other ridge like a wall of blue. We later found that there were eighteen thousand men in that column and they were heading towards our weaker left flank. Jerome Bonaparte was attacking our right and now D'Erlon was attacking our left. This was either very cunning or Bonaparte was losing his touch.

We heard the pas de charge as the drummer boys beat out the drumbeat. Sir Arthur had put all his strength in the right flank as the Prussians were coming from the east and would join our left flank.

Bonaparte had, somehow, seen that weakness and was trying to exploit it with D'Erlon's Corps. There would be just two brigades to face them: the 8th and the 9th. They were, however, largely English and Peninsular veterans. The only advantage the brigades had was the sunken lane before them and the fact that the French were advancing in four huge columns. We would be able to bring more muskets to bear, but, even so, we would be outnumbered. Our own batteries would be able to fire ball, canister, and Shrapnel. Sir Arthur had forbidden counter-battery fire. The French guns were safe but Bonaparte's infantrymen were in for a shock. The Grand Battery was, however, causing casualties. The ranks closed up as files were taken out by those balls which did not plough into the mud. I was just happy that these were Peninsular veterans who were standing so stoutly. Had they been the Dutch or the Belgians then they might have faltered.

It was almost two o'clock and this was the first serious attack from the French. It was obvious that the attack on Hougoumont was a diversion. We had almost forgotten it. Sir Arthur's young aides awaited their instructions as we watched the columns march relentlessly towards us. There looked to be twenty-four ranks, each with one hundred and sixty soldiers. It was like a blue, human battering ram.

They had skirmishers to the front but as the western column of the French advance passed the sandpit, they had to endure the fire of the 95th Rifles and the 2nd Light King's German Legion Battalion. Both were resolute and they were veterans. They began to thin, crucially, that western column. The artillery on the ridge was already thinning out the files and the attack on the flanks was sapping the power of the column of almost four thousand men. As they drew closer to the ridge so the gunners began to double shot the guns with canister and with ball. Coming closer to us then the Grand Battery had to stop firing and our artillery had some respite. The ranks were no longer thinned out and they prepared their muskets to unleash death upon the French column. The French drummers were bravely beating out the pas de charge. A glorious driving rhythm, but as they drew closer the effect of the cannon and the sandpit took its toll and the drumming diminished as drummer boys died; their bodies trampled by the men who followed.

The columns took twenty minutes to cross the eight hundred yards of death. As they neared the top of the ridge the gunners had to stop firing and race for the safety of the lines of redcoats which stoically stood with bayonets and muskets ready to unleash further death upon the brave French soldiers.

Of course, Slender Billy had to destroy this moment for when the King's German Legion and the 95th were, briefly, forced from the sandpit he sent a Hanoverian battalion to rescue them. Eight hundred cuirassiers were guarding the French flank and the Hanoverian battalion was destroyed for nothing; more deaths to be laid at the door of the Crown Prince. It was heartbreaking to watch their deaths and know that we could do nothing about them, save watch them die.

When the guns of the Grand Battery stopped firing the wind shifted the smoke and Bonaparte and Ney could see their chance of victory. My heart sank into my boots. We were less than one hundred yards from the enormous wall of blue and I wondered how we could stop it.

"Colonel Matthews, go and tell General Picton that it is almost time to charge. I will leave it to his judgement."

I was just pleased to be leaving the precarious position beneath the elm tree. It was attracting cannonballs like a magnet attracts metal.

I reached the general who was wearing a fine top hat, "General Picton, Sir Arthur's compliments and be prepared to charge."

Sir Thomas was still suffering from both the cannonball and the fall from his horse at Quatre Bras. I saw him wince as he mounted his horse. "Aye well, we have had long enough suffering these incursions." He raised his top hat and waved it so that his commanders could see him. "Forward. Give them a volley and then on!"

I watched as the meticulous red-coated infantry took a step forward, levelled their muskets and fired. The sergeants passed their orders along and three volleys later the front ranks of the French columns lay writhing beneath their feet. Sir Tomas judged it perfectly, "Fifth Division, charge! Charge, Hurrah!"

Poor Sir Thomas never saw the effect of his order. I watched in horror as a musket ball struck him between the eyes and he fell dead at my feet. Had he been on foot he would have survived for it was a stray shot. It mattered not. The gallant general fell dead as his beloved division marched forward with their bayonets glistening.

Initially, the division had success and they pushed the French from the ridge but there were French cavalrymen waiting to pounce. I kicked hard and headed back for Sir Arthur. "Sir Thomas is dead, your grace, and the French cavalry are threatening!"

Wellington nodded. When people say he was a defensive general and had no courage of conviction I think back to that moment. We had stalled the French attack, but the victory was within their grasp. The cavalry supporting D'Erlon and his men were ready to fall upon the flanks of the eager British infantry and it was at that moment that he turned to the quartermaster, Fitzroy Somerset. "It is time to turn the card and play the trump, gentlemen. Send in your heavies, Somerset! Drive them from the field."

The commander of the Heavy Brigade wheeled his horse and ordered his cavalry forward. In all the years I had fought with Sir Arthur this was the largest force of heavy cavalry I had ever seen gathered. The last heavy cavalry charge had been in Spain when the charismatic Le Marchant had died. The magnificent heavy cavalrymen forced their way between the redcoats. The French infantry was in the process of dressing their lines and then General Somerset yelled, "Charge!"

These were huge men on huge horses and they had spent years hearing of the charges and the glory of their light infantry cousins. They were desperate to show their worth. I knew that Captain Macgregor and Sergeant Ewart would be relishing the chance of showing what they could do. As they poured over the ridge the French appeared mesmerised. The 92nd and other allied regiments took the opportunity of racing forward with the cavalry and the effect was devastating. The French stood no chance. They were trampled and they were sabred; they were shot by musket and they were bayoneted. They fled down the slope up which they had trudged. They ran over the bodies of dead and dying comrades. I watched as pockets of brave Frenchmen tried to turn the tide. It was like Canute trying to turn back the tide.

Then the cavalry went to work with their sabres and swords. I watched the Scots Greys as they fell about the 45th regiment. It was a slaughter. I recognised Sergeant Ewart as he and his comrades attacked the French colour party. They were brave men defending the eagle but they were no match for those huge white horses and the enormous, fearless men in their bearskins. Superb horsemen all, Sergeant Ewart grabbed the eagle with one hand as he smashed down with his sabre to kill the last of the colour party. He held the eagle aloft for all to see. There was an audible wail from the French who were demoralised and a cheer from the gunners as they saw the eagle taken. I had seen precious few captured in all the years I had been fighting the French and I knew its import. The rest of the regiment crumbled, and the retreat became a rout.

146

I held my breath as nine hundred cuirassiers attempted to charge the heavy cavalry. It was brave and it was glorious but it was futile. The heavies had the slope in their favour and they had success in their heads. All that the cuirassiers had were breastplates and the heavy cavalry found groins, throats and faces. It was not swordsmanship; it was butchery. The cuirassiers were destroyed. I wondered if, at that moment, we had won the battle. I watched as hundreds of French prisoners were herded towards the rear preceded by Sergeant Ewart and the eagle. Surely, we had won. And then I heard the sigh of disappointment from Sir Arthur. "Colonel Matthews, would you be so good as to fetch back the heavies before they fall within the range of yonder cavalry and artillery!"

I looked to where he pointed. The heavy cavalrymen had lost all order and were charging through the fleeing French up the slope towards the French artillery. There I saw that the French were readying lancers and other cavalry regiments. Our finest cavalry were heading to their deaths. I knew, even though it was too far away to see, that the French gunners would be loading canister to cut down the reckless horsemen.

"Sir!" I turned to Alan, "Fetch our other mounts from the stables. I fear we shall need them soon enough!"

I kicked hard and plunged down into the sunken road. Wolf clambered over the other side and I began to ride after the cavalry. I could see the effect of their charge. Hundreds of infantry lay dead, dying or wounded. Disconsolate Frenchmen were being prodded to the rear by triumphant redcoats. The horses of the Heavy Brigade had done as much damage as the swords.

I watched in horror as the eager horsemen sought targets on the ridge, which was less than a mile away. The artillery did their terrible damage and I saw the effect of ball, shell and canister on the horses and men. Here and there some officers attempted to steady their men. Some of the horsemen were sabring the gunners while others, amazingly, were still charging. Did they want to get to Paris?

As I rode south, I saw a huge Life Guard to the west of Hougoumont. I later discovered his name was John Shaw. His sword was broken but he was swinging his helmet at the French infantry who were before him. The first of the lancers rode from Belle Alliance and I saw a handful of them ride towards this giant maniac. Even though I saw him speared by a lance he continued to lay about him with his helmet, felling three of them before they transfixed him with their weapons.

147

To a cavalryman such as me, this was heart-breaking. I saw a bugler from the Scots Greys. He looked dazed. He had been lucky for his horse had stopped. It looked like it had thrown a shoe. "Sound recall!" He looked at me as though I was speaking Russian. "Bugler, sound the recall! That is an order!"

I do not know if the tone of my voice did it or training, but he began to sound recall. "Keep blowing it until they come back!"

I rode forward. Although some were returning many had the blood lust upon them and were beyond obeying the bugle. I could see that many of the Gordon Highlanders had gone forward with their Scottish comrades and they were in an even worse position. I saw them as they reached the guns only to be ridden down by the French lancers who were waiting there.

I galloped across the rye filled field. I had to swerve and jump to avoid the dead and the dying. There were French and there were English. There were cavalrymen and there were infantry, horses and men. All had been caught up in this madness. There was no order to the cavalry ahead of me and although I could see them amongst the guns, I knew that Bonaparte was preparing to unleash cavalry upon them. The heavy horses had done well but they would be exhausted. The blades of the troopers had brought death and destruction but they were now blunt and broken. I had witnessed such a waste in the peninsula. The cavalry commanders had not learned the lesson.

I saw that the Life Guards and the Dragoon Guards were responding to the bugle call. They were the elite regiments. Some of them might be saved yet. The Inniskillings, those wild Irishmen, and the Scots Greys, even wilder Scotsmen, were just out of control and I galloped east to try to salvage as many of them as I could. As I passed, I shouted to the riders who were sat on wild and exhausted horses to return to the ridge. Some of them were as wild-eyed as their horses and that terrified me. I saw one or two move north. We would need every horseman who could be salvaged from this fiasco.

I was suddenly aware of shouts and the clamour of steel on steel. I looked up and saw that the Scots Greys and the Inniskillings were being attacked by lancers. Thankfully someone, I later discovered it was the Colonel, managed to order them into some sort of formation and they began to return across the battlefield. When the French guns began to fire again, I realised that in their attempts to wreak their revenge on the guns they had concentrated on slaughtering the gunners and failed to spike them. I saw grey horses and red-coated riders shredded by canister at point-blank range.

"Fall back! Fall back!"

It almost brought tears to my eyes as I watched the heavy horses struggling to cope with the rye covered mud over which they travelled. Wolf was finding life much easier and that, I believe, saved at least some of the Scots Greys as they headed back towards the ridge, using the path I had taken.

I saw half a troop riding obliquely across my front, back to the safety of Mont St. Jean. I recognised Captain Macgregor. Sergeant Ewart had taken his eagle back to Waterloo but my cousin was doing what a good officer should do, he was trying to keep his men together. In numbers lay strength and hope. Sadly, the lancers, on smaller, fresher horses, were catching the gallant greys. I drew two pistols. Wolf was a Chasseur's horse, and I rode him with my knees. I saw the trooper at the rear speared by an exultant lancer. I was approaching rapidly, and I fired both pistols. One of the balls hit the second lancer. I holstered those two and then took out my second pair. This time I was but thirty paces from the lancers who were busy concentrating on the greys. I fired and one lancer fell from his mount whilst the other clutched his arm, dropping his lance in the process.

The rest had now caught the Scots Greys who were looking desperately over their shoulders. Their mounts were labouring in the difficult terrain. The sergeant of the lancers had also recognised the danger which I represented and three of them turned and made for me. I did not mind for it meant less to attack my cousin and his men. I tugged my reins as I drew my sword and I did the opposite of what they expected, I rode towards them. The move took me away from the first lance and I slashed at the second lancer. I almost severed his arm. My sword was sharp having yet to be used that day.

I saw the sergeant as he brought his arm back to stab me with his lance. I let go of the reins and, as he punched forward with the weapon, I grabbed the lance and jerked it towards me. He failed to let go and I hacked across his face with my sword as he hurtled towards me. It ripped into his mouth and nose. He fell backwards. If he lived, he would be disfigured for life.

I gripped my reins and pulled Wolf to the left. I was now on the same side of the third lancer as his lance and he could not strike me; I was too close and it was too long. I whipped the sword around and hit him in the chest. He too fell backwards.

Ahead of me, I saw that the lancers had caught my cousin. His horse lay dead and he was defending himself with a broken lance. I took the reins of the nearest riderless horse and urged Wolf on. The lancers must have heard my hooves and mistaken me for one of their comrades. My sword hacked across the back of one of them as my cousin swung the broken lance and knocked another from his saddle.

"Captain, get on this horse now!"

I turned and parried the lancer who had drawn his sword now that his lance was useless. He was no swordsman and with a flick of my wrist I was inside his guard and my blade pierced his throat.

The Scots Greys were great horsemen and my cousin threw himself in the saddle. We began to catch the other Scots Greys who were still being pursued by lancers. Our fresher horses meant we caught them. The swords we wielded made short work of unprotected backs. A lancer with his back to a sword was a dead man. I saw that the sunken ditch was just a hundred yards ahead and I reined Wolf in. The survivors turned, "Just ride! I still have work to do."

David Macgregor turned and raised his hand in salute. He had lost his fur cap and there was a slight wound to his forehead but he had survived. "Thank you, cousin. Pray, visit with us when this is over. I owe you my life and the family would be pleased to see a distant relative."

I nodded, "If I come through this then I will do so. Take care."

I turned to survey the field. Those who would survive were close to me now. The bugler waved a salute as he passed me. The rifles had returned to the sandpit and were picking off the lancers and Chasseurs who pursued the survivors. The Heavy Brigade troopers who had survived the debacle were coming back at a walk. Some were walking horses and others were slumped over their saddles; their wounds testimony to their foolish courage. They were bloodied and they would not charge again that day. They had, however, returned. They were the few who had heeded the recall.

As I walked a weary Wolf back to Sir Arthur he nodded, "Thank you, Colonel. We may have a couple of troops should we need them later. What a waste." He threw a disgusted look at a shamefaced Earl of Uxbridge. The commander of the cavalry showed that the seven years since he had last commanded had taken the edge away from his skill. This was not the man I had admired on the retreat to Corunna!

There was a slight lull as both sides recovered from the slaughter of the last hour. The wounded closest to our lines were taken to safety. To our right, we still heard the pop and crack of muskets around the Chateau. I saw one of Sir Arthur's aides being carried away. His left arm hung uselessly by his side. It was dangerous being so close to Sir Arthur who was always closest to wherever the danger was. He might have been a cold man but no one could doubt his courage.

As I was reloading my pistols Sharp arrived with the spare horses. We changed saddles. We tied the two tired mounts by the elm tree. As I led Pierre back to Sir Arthur, I wondered about the wisdom of that. It was hardly the safest part of the battlefield to leave a pair of horses.

"Now that you have a fresh mount, Colonel, go with your fellow and see how the colonel fares at the Chateau. Tell him he must hold at all costs." He waved to the east. "My other aides are still communicating with the Prussians." He gestured for me to go closer to him. "Let me know of the Crown Prince's dispositions. I shall ginger up the regiments here. I fear we will be the focus of Bonaparte's attention again."

"Sir."

We rode along the ridge. Sir Arthur and his entourage rode in the opposite direction. I could hear the sergeants as they shouted a warning to their men, "Stand to, here comes Old Nosey!"

I saw the Crown Prince with his staff. They were further from the front than Sir Arthur. It was no surprise. As I passed the Nassau regiment, Major Von Normann waved cheerily at me. So far he had managed to avoid having his regiment slaughtered as so many others had been. He and his battalion were now supporting the rear of the Chateau and a battery of Dutch guns gave them some protection.

We dismounted some fifty yards from the Chateau of Hougoumont and led our horses down the path to the rear gate. The French were lobbing howitzer shells into the interior. I saw that parts of the building were on fire and I heard the screams of men who were burning to death. There was no one to fight the fire; they were all fighting the French. Steady streams of wounded men were trudging away from the chateau. I left Sharp with the horses at the rear gate of the chateau. There they could shelter from the musket and artillery fire. I ducked under the lintel and ran in to yet another scene of death and destruction.

I saw Nassauers and Coldstream Guards intermixed. The loopholes we had cut earlier were being put to good use. I grabbed a Coldstream's arm. "Where is Colonel Macdonell?"

The Guard pointed to the yard. "In there, sir."

As I entered the yard, I saw that the French had broken in. There was a group of Frenchmen already in the yard. Thankfully, there were only a few but more were threatening to enter. The gate was open and the Sous-lieutenant who led them was wielding an axe. He looked like some ancient warrior. He was a giant. Even as I watched I saw his axe take the head from a Dutchman. I turned to a sergeant who, like me was watching the scene. "Get half a dozen men and form a line behind me." His look questioned me. "Do it sergeant! I am Colonel Matthews from Sir Arthur's staff and we do not have long to remedy this situation." He nodded and ran.

I saw that the French were being attacked individually and they were dealing with each attack easily. I wondered if the colonel had been killed and then I saw him and a group of his soldiers trying to bar the gate. That made sense. He had to stop more men from getting in.

"Here sir!"

I turned and saw that the sergeant had found six men. "Prepare!" I raised my pistol. "Fire!" We all fired at once and a wall of smoke filled the space between us and the French. "Reload." As they reloaded, I drew my second pistol. "Fire!" We had the same effect, but we could hardly see the French for the smoke was so thick and the howitzer shells were still dropping. "Reload!" Our lead balls had ploughed into the French men who were now wreathed in smoke. "Fire!" As the seven muskets barked out for the third time, I drew my sword. "Coldstreams! Charge! Give them the bayonet and send them to hell!"

The seven of them gave a hurrah and we plunged into the smoke. The soldier on my right had his musket chopped in two by the mighty Frenchman. The force was so powerful that the Guard fell to the cobbled yard his musket broken. As the axe was raised to give the coup de grace I lunged forward and my Austrian sword sank into the officer's middle. He was a tough man and he turned to swing the axe at me. I ducked as I withdrew my sword. My hat was knocked from my head. The swing of the axe opened up the Frenchman and this time I whipped my sword across his throat. I watched the life go from his eyes as the axe fell from his hands and he slumped to the cobbles of the yard.

Other Guards had surrounded the Frenchmen who were being bayoneted to death. Suddenly I spied the French drummer boy as a wild-eyed private was about to despatch him. I knocked aside the musket and shouted, "Hold! He is a boy!" The man stared at me and then nodding, picked the boy up by his epaulettes and hauled him away.

The colonel ran over to me. I saw blood dripping from a wound on his face and his hands showed where he had been struck whilst closing the gate. "Well done, Matthews, that was a little hairy!" He looked down at the giant. "My God, what do they feed them on?"

I shook my head, "He is the biggest Frenchman I have ever seen that is for sure. Sir Arthur's compliments, how are things going?"

"Fine so long as the Young Frog stays clear, but we are short of ammunition."

"I will send some."

"Sergeant Graham, take some men and clear away these bodies."

"Sir."

The colonel wiped his forehead, "How are things going elsewhere?"

"General Picton is dead but we repulsed their first attack and the Heavy Brigade slaughtered them."

He cocked his head to one side, "Please tell me that the cavalry obeyed orders and returned in one piece." I shook my head. "It is always the same." Someone shouted for the colonel and he shook my hand, "Thank you for your intervention and now I must go."

When I reached Sharp the howitzers had eased momentarily and I could actually hear him. "A little rough eh, sir?"

"You could say that. Now, I fear, we must go and speak with the Crown Prince."

When I reached the Crown Prince he was viewing the battlefield through his telescope.

"Sir, Colonel Macdonell and his men are running short of ammunition."

He looked at me with a look of pure disgust upon his face. "Do I look like a shopkeeper? I have the battle to win and the Colonel must make do with what he has."

I felt my hand going to my pistol. I could just draw it and shoot the man! Major General Rebecque caught my eye and shook his head. "Come with me, Colonel Matthews." When we were out of earshot he said. "You are a fine officer but you must learn to be more diplomatic. There are ammunition carts yonder, sir." He pointed to an area about half a mile from the staff officers.

"Then why have they not been ordered forward?"

He shrugged. I knew that he was a good man but this was inexcusable. I jerked Pierre's head around in anger and rode to the carters. All of them were civilians.

"I need one of you to go to the chateau and replenish their powder and ball." They stared at me and then ignored me. I repeated my words in French in case they could not understand me. They remained silent. Eventually one of them said, "A man could get killed going down there. We will wait until it quietens down a little."

"By then it will be too late for they will all be dead."

The man shrugged. I pulled my pistol. "Perhaps if I used this then you might comply."

The man did not seem bothered. "If you use that then I will be dead and who will take it down then?"

I cocked the pistol and said, "I can drive a wagon. And it will be lighter without your dead body upon it."

His eyes widened in fear. "Very well but this is unfair. I am no soldier."

I took out a shilling and flipped it to him. "Then for the next hour, you are. Here is the King's shilling and when you return with an empty wagon then there will be another waiting for you."

Greed got the better of him and he drove his cargo down the slope into the chateau. It must have been frightening for shells were being fired once more and he had both ball and powder in his cart. Twenty minutes later he reappeared and held out his hand. I gave him the coin and he grinned as he drove his vehicle north. "That is me empty then. I shall have to go back to get some more and by then I have a feeling that this will be over, one way or the other."

I assiduously avoided the Crown Prince and his officers as I made my way back to the elm. Instead, I rode through the 3rd Netherlands division who were resting on the reverse slope. There were still wounded soldiers heading for the surgeons who were waiting at Waterloo. Disconcertingly I also saw fit and healthy soldiers skulking away too. I wondered why for there had been a lull in the French attack then I heard the pounding begin again. The lost French gunners had been replaced and the twelve-pound cannons were beginning to belch forth once more. We hurried to Sir Arthur. The French would be moving again soon.

Chapter 14

I saw Copenhagen under the elm tree once more and Sir Arthur seated alone. Around him, the various aides were taking the opportunity to rest. Sir Arthur never rested. Nor did he seem to need either food or drink. I reported what I had seen at the Chateau. He nodded as though not surprised.

"Sir, I should also report that many healthy men are retreating north too."

"Just so long as the majority hold where they are then we have a chance. Blucher is coming. We just have to hold on and now, gentlemen, we had better prepare for Bonaparte's next onslaught."

He pointed across the valley where the French guns began to fire along their length. This was the Grand Battery. The few which had been damaged in the charge of the Heavy Brigade had not diminished their power. Now that the ground had dried out a little some of the balls were bouncing, as their gunners intended, and taking out files of men. Fortunately, Sir Arthur had them in a two-deep line but as they continued to bounce and run down the reverse slope so they continued to cause carnage.

A stray ball flew towards us and we both ducked. I heard a shout and saw Fitzroy Somerset clutch the stump of his arm. "Take him to the surgeon now!" Sir Arthur was rattled for Somerset was a good friend. He turned to me and urgency was written across his face. "Ride to the 5th Division and tell them to retire beyond the ridge. There is little point in them suffering casualties to no good purpose. Have the Hanoverians do the same."

I galloped the few hundred yards to the left of our line. "The general wishes you to retire in good order from the ridge but maintain your lines."

Now that Sir Thomas was dead Sir James Kempt was in command. He too was calm under fire and in his precarious position that was vital. "Thank you, Colonel Matthews. It was getting dashed hot here."

He turned and ordered his men to turn and march one hundred yards to the rear. The Hanoverians did the same. All along the front the regiments and battalions retired to the reverse slope to take shelter from the ninety odd balls which flew towards them. Long after the battle was over, I thought of the effect that must have had on the French. All they would have seen would have been British and Hanoverian soldiers retreating. They must have thought that it signified victory. Certainly, it was the only explanation of what they did next. I saw cuirassiers lining up and preparing to charge. Sir Arthur saw them at the same time.

"Good God, have they gone mad? Are they going to attack us using cavalry without artillery support?"

"I think so, my lord."

"Tell the regiments to form square! This will be dicey Matthews! But if the fellows hold their nerve then we may be able to give these vaunted horsemen a good thrashing."

"Yes sir." It did not take much urging for the soldiers to get into square. All it needed was my shout of "Cavalry! Ware your front" and the ranks formed. Some of the smaller regiments who had suffered at Quatre Bras looked pitifully weak whilst the biggest regiment, the 52nd was so big it formed two squares. As at Quatre Bras, the brave gunners would wait until the last minute before flinging themselves beneath the protective umbrella of the bayonets of the front rank.

You could not see the valley, but we heard the thunder of the hooves and the crash of the artillery. I rode back to the ridge. The sight almost took my breath away. The whole of the valley was filled from Hougoumont to La Haie Sainte by cavalry. There appeared to be no space between them. This was the French version of our fateful charge. The difference was that this was not a few hundred, this was a few thousands. I even saw regiments from the Imperial Guard joining in. It was like a sea of horsemen, but the ground did not suit them. They were hardly charging at a gallop. At best they managed a fast trot. There was tough rye and sticky mud to contend with; there was the steep slope. Finally, there was the detritus of the earlier attacks. There were the dead and dying horses and men. For all of them, death would come soon as they were trampled beneath thirty thousand hooves.

I heard Sharp's urgent appeal. "Colonel Matthews, get in a square or you will die!"

He was, of course, correct and I turned to seek shelter. The heavy rye and the mud were slowing down the cavalry and by the time they cleared the ridge then they would be at the walk, but I felt that they would surely overwhelm us. I saw my old friends, the 69th. "Gentlemen, have you room within?"

The colour sergeant, who had a huge scar on his face from the encounter at Quatre Bras said, "Your more'n welcome sir. I saw you the other day. You are right handy in a fight and if yon fellow is as good then we might survive."

They opened the front ranks and we entered. Sharp had brought the spare horses. We dismounted and Sharp held their reins behind the colours. I took my pistols from my saddle and we waited.

One of the 69th looked up at the sky. "Sarge, is that thunder?"

"No son. That is heavy cavalry."

We heard the screams and shouts of the dying horsemen as they were raked with canister. When the gunners came racing back then we knew what was coming. Although we could see nothing, we could picture the horsemen galloping towards us with swords drawn and lances levelled. I knew more than any just what was coming for I had been the last to leave the ridge. All that the poor 69th could hear was the drumming of the hooves and the ground shaking.

"Hold your fire until I give the command!"

One of the gunners was laughing as he hurled himself beneath the bayonets. "Dozy bastards didn't know there was a sunken lane! The first ranks are lying there now with broken legs!"

Another one said, "That just leaves eight thousand of them then."

Their officer shouted, "Carpenter, shut up!"

"Sir!"

It was like a wave of steel that rose over the top of the ridge. We saw their plumed helmets and swords first and then the shiny breastplates. They were the cuirassiers. I felt some relief that it was not the dreaded lancers. They seemed to rise over the ridge like a wave breaking upon the sand. I have heard that in the far Pacific they have enormous waves called Tsunami. It is like being struck by a wall of water that sweeps all before it. That is what this felt like. We were about to be swept away by a wall of horses and metal. I found myself willing the Major to command his men to fire. The horsemen were almost on top of us and all that we could see before us was a solid mass of horse and men. Finally, and to my great relief, when they were forty yards from our front rank the order was given. "Front rank fire!"

Even as we saw horsemen and horses falling and the sound of the pinging of balls on breastplates we heard, "Second rank fire!"

It was the same result.

"Third rank fire!"

It was like a constant popping as each rank fired and reloaded. Inevitably the rate slackened off, but I had never witnessed so many lead balls all flying at the same time. No one needed to be given the order to reload. It was automatic. I realised that the horsemen had no scabbards. It was a bad sign; it meant they had no intention of sheathing their swords. In the French cavalry, it meant Death or Glory! I wondered how the cavalry could survive for they were so close that the muskets could not miss. I knew that the Dutch and Belgian regiments would fire too high at first but there were enough squares of British and Hanoverian veterans in this giant chessboard to ensure that the French cavalry would be hit many times over.

One cuirassier had his horse shot from beneath him and he ran to the front rank and hacked down at a private. The man was bayoneted to death but the soldier he had hit lay screaming. The captain shouted, "Be a good fellow and crawl to the colour party and do not shout so loudly. Bear it like a man. "

The man said, "Sorry sir." And he crawled with a bleeding arm to the drummer boys and bandsmen who would dress his wound.

I saw a cuirassier who had survived the volleys and he reared his horse as he tried to bring its hooves down onto the front ranks. It was the only way to break a square. It inevitably meant a dead horse and often a dead horseman. It was a brave act. The horseman's face was less than thirty feet from me. I aimed at his face and fired my pistol. As his horse was rearing, he was killed and his death grip pulled the horse back. The artillery officer darted forward and hacked across the throat of the horse with his sabre. Had he not done so then the flailing hooves might have injured more men. Instead of breaking the front rank and integrity of the square, the horse formed a barrier ten feet from the front rank. Such were the tiny margins between living and dying.

The volleys rippled on. They were gradually becoming more ragged as some muskets misfired. I saw soldiers hurriedly cleaning out their muskets. Other soldiers stepped forward to take the places of those killed in the front ranks. Some of the cuirassiers got through despite the barrage of lead.

The cuirassiers swept around us, and behind them, I saw the gold breastplates of the carabiniers. There were just two regiments of these in the whole French army and they thought of themselves as the Imperial Guard. They were arrogant butchers. Their riders were leaning forward, eager to use their sabres. Some of the cuirassiers who were swarming around us now used their own pistols to fire at point-blank range. They were inaccurate but one or two balls struck home. Sharp's horse, the one we had bought back in Antibes began to thrash around. He was in danger of hurting the colour party with his flailing hooves. "Sharp! Shoot him!"

I knew he would hate to do it, but I also knew that Sharp was a consummate soldier. He handed the reins of the other three horses to the three drummer boys. He held the reins tightly while he lifted the pistol, held it to the horse's head and pulled the trigger. We had killed horses before and Sharp killed it instantly. He jerked the head of the dead animal so that it fell away from the colour party. I saw the cost of his action written on his tormented face.

The carabiniers were furiously hacking down at the front rank. One of the sergeants jerked his pike forward. There was a hook on it. He hooked the corner of the carabinier's breastplate and pulled hard. The surprised horseman flew into the square where the sergeant deftly twisted the pike and plunged the spike into the throat of the horseman. I ran forward and pointed my pistol into the face of another horseman. He was just six feet away and his head almost disappeared when the huge ball hit him. I used another pistol to fire at the horse which was attempting to jump into the square. The flash and the ball made it veer to the side where four bayonets hacked into it making another barrier.

There were red coats dying all around me. Horse's hooves, sabres, musket balls all took their toll. However, there was also a wall of French dead which was preventing them from getting any closer to us. We were suffering but we were also surviving and that surprised the French cavalry. They had come to sweep us back to the sea and now they were the ones drowning in a sea of blood.

And now it was the turn of the Dragoons. Their horses were not as big as those of the cuirassiers, but they had musketoons. I knew that they would rather use their swords but if they were ordered to fire then it could be the end of the square. They would not be able to miss such a huge target. I emptied my two pistols and began to reload. It was like a scene from hell. Horses and men were screaming. Wounded men crawled or were dragged to the colour party and the little succour they offered. The air was filled with the smell of powder. You could barely see twenty feet from the square such was the pall of smoke that lay across the ridge like early morning fog. The ground was slippery with blood and we were completely surrounded by enemy cavalry. We knew there were other squares, but we could not see them. It was like fighting in a fog of powder. The enemy became darkened shadows that loomed up to bring death to the redcoats whose numbers were shrinking as the day went on.

159

After an hour the pressure diminished, and the smoke began to clear as the horsemen withdrew back down the hill. I ran to mount Pierre. "Stay here Sharp." As the gunners ran back to their guns I shouted, "Open up if you please." There were still dragoons before me limping away. I struck two with my sword and then I reached the top of the ridge where I could see the French cavalry. They had not gone far. They had not fled; they had fallen back to regroup. We had not defeated them and this was merely a respite. I saw the regiments dressing ranks while the gunners, returning to their nine pounders, began to fire into them. Turning I saw that some squares were now triangles and all that I could see were Hanoverian and British squares. There appeared to be no Dutch within sight, perhaps they were further west. I learned later that the ordeal had been too much for these inexperienced soldiers and they had run. Sir Arthur's army was becoming smaller by the minute.

I went back to the square. They opened for me. "Colonel, they are reforming. They will be here again soon. I would give the men any water that you have."

"Already done, Colonel Matthews, and we only have enough left now for the wounded." He looked around at the proud regiment. It had half the numbers it had had when it arrived in Flanders. "And the men are down to ten balls each."

"I think, Colonel, that it is time to rob the dead. Those Dragoons and Cuirassiers have pistols and muskets."

He nodded. "Sergeant Major, have the men take the balls from the dead French!"

"Sir! Come on. You ten men, come with me."

The men worked feverishly. The wounded were dragged into the centre, and the ranks made whole. We were much fewer than we had been. The regiment which had marched to Quatre Bras was now a shadow of their full complement. I knew that there were other regiments that would have suffered even more casualties.

I reloaded my guns and went over to Alan. "It had to be done, Alan."

"I know sir. The other three are fine. They are used to gunfire but…"

"I know."

We both avoided looking at the dead horse. After the day's battle, its fate would be the same as many horses. Starving soldiers loved horsemeat.

The gunners racing back told us what was about to be unleashed. The sergeant-major roared to his scavengers, "Back inside the square!"

This time there were fewer of the French cavalrymen and they were not knee to knee. However, this time there were fewer muskets ready or able to fire at them. I used my pistols judiciously. The French listened for the commands and tried to charge the square between volleys. I took the opportunity to fire in the gap. Like the 69th I had limited ammunition and I too ran out. How long could this go on? I had thought it bad enough at Quatre Bras but there I had endured it for less than thirty minutes. We had been in square for more than an hour and the charges showed no sign of stopping. I took some heart from the fact that the French horses looked exhausted. Horses are brave, sometimes too brave and will keep going until they drop down dead. These horses had negotiated the sapping slope and the sunken lane twice. Their riders might be willing but there was a limit to what the beasts could do.

The cuirassiers were having some success. Their long blades found gaps in the wall of bayonets. The volleys were fewer, and they could hack with impunity. I picked up a discarded musket and bayonet and ran to the left front corner. The cuirassiers had killed three of the men there and it was in imminent danger of collapsing. I jabbed the bayonet forward and skewered the arm of the cuirassier who had raised his sword to hack at a wounded corporal. He dropped his sword, and I twisted the bayonet as I pulled. He flew from his saddle towards me. I smashed the butt of the musket into his face as he landed at my feet. It became a bloody pulp.

I sensed a movement above me and I put up the musket as a dragoon hurled himself from his horse. The bayonet went into his chest, but the weight of his body flung me to the ground. The sergeant, who had let me in the square initially, picked up the body with one hand and threw it to one side. "They don't like you do they, Colonel?"

"I can't think why." I took the cartridge pouch from the dead dragoon and gave it to the sergeant. "Can you give these a good home sergeant?"

"I think so, sir."

The French horses were weakening. At about five o'clock they finally left. Once again, I mounted my horse and galloped towards the ridge. I could see that this time they were fleeing although that suggests a speed which they did not have. They trudged and they limped towards la Belle Alliance. Many horses had to be led by riders who did not have the heart to put their brave horses out of their misery. Other horses carried riders who would die before the day was out. It was a sad sight for a horseman, any horseman, to witness. The redcoat squares had held. But at what cost? The three deep squares now contained almost as many wounded as manned the sides. The gun crews had returned to their guns and the rifles had scurried from the security of the squares to line the sunken road once more.

I held my telescope to my eye, and I looked at the departing French. My heart sank when I saw another two columns preparing to march towards us, except that this time they had horse artillery and cavalry with them. These were the light cavalry, the Chasseurs, Hussars, and Chevau-Léger. When they next came the cavalry would hold the regiments in square while their infantry and their artillery battered us. As the weary troops headed back to the ridge, I saw the exhaustion and I saw the holes in the ranks. How could these soldiers stand another attack?

I rode, with Alan, to Sir Arthur and pointed south. "It looks like another attack, sir, except that this time it is all three arms. They mean business."

He gave me a wry smile, "Which begs the question, Matthews, what in God's name have they been doing so far?"

I laughed, "I think he means to push you off the ridge."

Pointing to the east he said, "Those guns we hear are our only hope. That is Blucher. It has cost me three young aides, but I have the news I hoped for. He is coming and he will be here by nightfall at the latest. We need to hold them here for a little while longer." He shouted to his remaining junior lieutenant, "Brown, have ammunition distributed to all the regiments and any water also."

Sharp had ridden up with Wolf during our talk while Sir Arthur scanned the field with his telescope he asked. "Sir, should I get a bite of something to eat for us?"

"I think that is a good idea and something to drink. If you can get some water for the horses too then that would help."

Sir Arthur smiled as Sharp rode away. "I had a fellow like him in India. Thought of all the things I did not."

"What happened to him, sir?"

He waved a vague hand, "No idea. I left him in India when I got the colonelcy of the 33rd."

Just when you thought that you were getting to know him the Marquess of Wellington had this ability to leave you no more the wiser.

The Earl of Uxbridge and De Lancey arrived from the squares in which they had been sheltering. The Marquess pointed to La Haie Sainte. "I hope that Prince William has garrisoned that well."

I looked at the Earl and shook my head. De Lancey said, "I fear not, my lord, and it looks to me as though it might be too late already. Look!"

The French were advancing, and the fire of the artillery was now focussed on the small garrison of La Haie Sainte. Bonaparte had realised that if he was to drive us from the ridge then he had to clear away this small obstacle.

"We are in for a hard pounding, gentlemen. Let us see who can pound the longest. De Lancey, direct the guns to fire at the column and have Mercer's battery move up to support the men in the farmhouse."

It was little enough and I knew that it would merely delay the inevitable. The Hanoverians and the Rifles who garrisoned the farm would now be sacrificed because of an incompetent commander.

The range was four hundred yards, and we were doing serious damage to the advancing column which came along the east side of the farm but a cloud of Tirailleurs raced up the hill and began to pepper the gunners who were exposed. They began to fall, and the fire of the guns diminished.

"Matthews, order some of those riflemen to deal with the skirmishers."

They were close enough to shout to, but I rode the short distance. "Captain Blaine, take some of your men and discourage those skirmishers if you please."

"Right sir. Come on lads. You don't want to live forever do you?"

As they clambered out from behind their improvised defences, I saw that one of them couldn't follow as his leg was bandaged. I handed him Pierre's reins and picked up the rifle from a dead colleague. "Watch him for me eh, rifleman?"

"They all say you are a mad bugger, sir and I can see they are right. I'll watch your horse for you." He threw me a cartridge pouch from a pile in front of him."

I crouched and ran after the pairs of riflemen. I saw that the officer was alone and so I joined him. He looked at me in surprise. "Can you use one of those?"

"I learned how to on the retreat to Corunna."

Nodding he dropped to one knee. "Ready?" I nodded. "I'll fire and then run. You cover me. When I fire then you follow."

"Righto."

The rifles had been cleared from the sandpit and the French skirmishers were using it. They had the shelter the 95th had just enjoyed. Fortunately, we were out of their effective range. The French musket was accurate to eighty yards on a good day and we had a range of two hundred yards on a bad day. I aimed at a sergeant who was directing the men at the western end of the pit. Captain Blaine's rifle barked, and a skirmisher fell. As he ran, I squeezed the trigger. I had forgotten what the kick was like. The sergeant fell and I ran towards the captain. "Good shot, Colonel."

I began to reload. I did it properly by using the special rammer. I knew that the riflemen often just rammed the bullet in like a musket ball but I wanted the accuracy and I did not want to damage the rifle. The captain fired and ran. I lifted the rifle and pointed it at the skirmisher who was aiming at my partner. I think I hit his musket and the missile then pinged off and hit him in the eye. He fell backwards.

When I reached the captain, he was just a hundred yards from the French. They could hit us with a lucky shot but any closer and we would be in great danger. There were too few of us for that.

"Let's stay here, Colonel, and see what we can do eh?"

We lay down and began to pick off the skirmishers. I saw, whilst I was reloading, that the farmhouse was now on fire and I watched as the defenders fled the building. We were now trying to limit the damage. We had lost the farmhouse, but the cannons could now rake the column. The French skirmishers were forced from the sandpit but then the light infantry which had just retaken the farmhouse began to stream north to attack the gunners on the ridge.

Captain Blaine knew his business. "Ninety-fifth! Into the sandpit."

We all ran and occupied the sandpit which had been recently vacated by the French. Not all of the French had fled, and the captain and I had to draw our swords. When two of the men left within had fallen the others ran south. Those riflemen who still had loaded guns fired at them as they fled. "Save your ammunition for the others. They are running! We have to hit the skirmishers."

We were not enough to do more than irritate the skirmishers for it was now a whole light infantry regiment that was sniping at the gunners. Unlike the French, we had a limited number of gunners and could not afford to lose them. Suddenly a line of infantry appeared on the ridge and I saw Sir Arthur himself appear behind them and order them to fire. The skirmishers fell, almost to a man but then the French guns which had been brought up began to fire at the infantry. Miraculously although many of the redcoats fell Sir Arthur remained unharmed.

"Captain, there is your new target." I had seen the French bringing up cannon. Now that the farmhouse had been cleared, they could move to within a couple of hundred yards of the ridge. There they could clear the defenders. Bonaparte was about to win.

"Rifles! To the other side of the sandpit."

Although a column of infantry was marching north to the ridge it was the artillery gunners that we had to target. They could do far more damage than the infantry. We kept firing until the gunners were forced to lie down behind their wheels and limbers. They could not fire so long as we remained in the pit. Even then the rifles cleverly used the metal of the barrels to send their missiles around corners. They fired to ricochet bullets. There was no hiding place. What was important was that the gunners could not fire while we were there. When I heard the controlled volleys from the ridge, I knew that the line of infantry had unleashed a devastating volley. The brigade broke and fled down the hill. The gunners tried to unlimber amidst fierce fire from the rifles. They did not manage it and the depleted crews took their precious guns back down the slope to the safety of the French lines.

When, at last, they had gone I stood. "I had better get back to my duties." I held out the rifle.

"No, Colonel, you have earned it. It is rare to find a staff officer who actually knows how to shoot."

I shook hands, "Farewell Captain, take care."

I scampered back up the hill to the ridge. Although the fighting to the east of La Haie Sainte had died down I could see it continuing ferociously to the west of the farmhouse. There they did not have the luxury of a sandpit. I grabbed Pierre's reins. The wounded rifleman nodded proudly to me. "You can always rely on the Rifles to get things done!"

"You can indeed."

When I reached Sir Arthur, I saw that Wolf was tied to the elm tree. Sir Arthur nodded to me; he was alone. "I had to send your fellow to the Crown Prince to ask why he was not supporting the farmhouse." He pointed east. "I think our friend Blucher is closing with us now if we can only hold on for an hour or so."

"Yes sir." I was distracted for I saw a Hanoverian regiment heading down the western side of La Haie Sainte. They were only four hundred yards from me. Behind them, I saw the Crown Prince and, waiting behind, Sharp. As the Luneburg regiment marched down the hill, I remembered the cavalry. I had seen French cuirassiers supporting the infantry. If I had seen them then surely the Dutch must have. Where were the cavalry? I had a sinking feeling in my gut.

As the Hanoverians neared the chateau I saw the Crown Prince shout something. He gestured down the hill and Sharp began to trot down the hill. I knew disaster was about to strike. Ignoring Sir Arthur's protests I spurred Pierre and he responded magnificently. I rode diagonally towards the Luneburgers who were desperately trying to form square. They were not going to make it in time. I realised at the moment that neither was I. The French heavy, armoured horsemen tore into the Hanoverian regiment which was in the process of forming square. A few managed to get off musket shots but most did not. Some just stood there and were skewered, dying with a puzzled look upon their faces.

I saw Alan as he drew a pistol to fire at close range. The horseman before him fell. I was willing my friend to retreat but there was too much noise. General Alten had sent the King's German Legion, belatedly, to the aid of the beleaguered Luneburgers but it would be too late for most. I was not concerned with the Hanoverians. My old friend was in the greatest of danger and it was all Slender Billy's fault. I drew my pistol and my sword. I watched as Sharp discharged a second pistol and then drew his sword as he was surrounded by four cuirassiers. I fired my pistol when I was only ten yards from one of them. The ball went into his neck and he fell from his horse.

Alan had managed to injure another but a blow from a heavy French sabre struck him. I saw blood spurt from his arm and then his sword fall. Pierre clattered into the back of one of the cuirassiers as I brought my Austrian sword like a club at the side of the head of the man who had just struck Sharp. Both the cuirassier and Sharp slid to the ground at the same time. I brought my sword around in a wide sweep. It hacked into the neck and almost severed the head of the last French horseman. The King's German Legion was engaging the rest.

I flung myself from my saddle. The sword thrust had almost severed Sharp's left arm. I took my silk scarf and tied it tightly around his upper arm. I knew how to make a tourniquet.

"Alan, stay with me. Look at me, it is Robbie!"

He opened his eyes. "That butcher just sent those poor lads in without any support. I couldn't let them go on their own. I tried to get them into square." He shook his head, "I'm sorry sir, I didn't know the words. Why did he do it, sir? Why?"

"Forget him. Now let's get you on your horse." It was strange for we were in the middle of a slaughterhouse and yet I was able to lift Sharp onto his horse. Half of the French horsemen were fighting the Kings German Legion while the other half were finishing off the Luneburgers. We were ignored. "Hold on to the saddle and I will lead him."

Once on the back of Pierre, I walked slowly north. I did not want to risk Alan falling. I glared at the Crown Prince as I passed. He stared impassively ahead. Alten's men had cleared the infantry and the Dutch horsemen were chasing away the cuirassiers. The front had been stabilised but no thanks to Slender Billy. The Crown Prince was a menace and he needed dealing with. I would take Sharp to the surgeon and then I would save some lives.

Chapter 15

I rode directly to Waterloo and the surgeon. My presence on the battlefield and my proximity to Sir Arthur afforded me some courtesy and men moved aside. When I reached the medical tent, I helped a semi-conscious Sharp down from the horse. The interior of the tent was terrifying. Blood lay in puddles on the floor and orderlies casually tossed mangled limbs aside like unwanted food. In the tent, I saw the surgeon as he sawed through a rifleman's leg. Suddenly the rifleman became still and the surgeon said. "Damn! He is dead. Next!"

Before his orderly could fetch one from outside, I shouted, "Doctor! This wound is fresh, and the man can be saved."

"The man is a civilian, Colonel Matthews."

"This is an officer, Lieutenant Sharp, and he is one of Sir Arthur's aides. He is next."

I must have shown my determination by the expression on my face for he nodded, "Very well." The orderlies put him on the trestle table they were using. "And you, sir, are now unnecessary. Go back to Sir Arthur where you can do some good."

I nodded and left. I led Sharp's horse back to Sir Arthur and tied it to a tree. Who knew if I might lose my own horse. De Lancey and Uxbridge had returned along with Baron von Muffling. Sir Arthur said nothing but narrowed his eyes as he looked at me. The French guns were still harvesting soldiers. The Earl pointed down the hill. "Those damn guns have almost destroyed the regiments, look."

I saw that the 30th and the 14th were so depleted in numbers that they were sending their colours to the rear. That was a sure sign that they thought they were about to be destroyed. The depot battalions would take the colours and remember the dead of Waterloo. Sir Arthur shaded his eyes as he looked into the sky. "We have less than two hours until nightfall. Baron, will Marshal Blucher reach us in time?"

"Our men are in Plancenoit already. The French have had to send in the Young Guard. He will be here. He gave you his word."

"You fellows go and reassure the regiments that we will hold. I will find some reinforcements!" He dug his heels in and Copenhagen leapt away towards the rear.

The Earl laughed, "Where from? Is he a bloody magician! Anyway, it is safer away from here."

As I rode towards the ridge I saw that the area around the elm tree was littered with dead horses and soldiers. Yet Sir Arthur and Copenhagen had not a mark on either of them. It was remarkable.

I rode to the 30th Foot. "Steady gentlemen. Sir Arthur is bringing more troops to your aid."

A young ensign said, "Sir, let us charge those guns and be done with it!"

I saw the guns which looked tantalisingly close. They were just four hundred yards away. I took out my sabre and pointed lower down the hill where the brigade of Chasseurs waited. "And if you did, young man, then those horsemen would have you for breakfast."

"But sir, at least we could fight then. It is hard to bear to stand here and watch fine fellows be cut down by ball and canister and not have the opportunity to reply."

"Endure it for but a little while."

He was right of course. Even as I turned a cannonball struck three men. Two would never rise again. It was a waste. As I headed back to the tree, I saw a howitzer shell as it landed, fizzing, close to the 23rd which was in the relative safety of the reverse slope. I watched a young private walk towards it. He picked it up and hurled it a prodigious distance away from his regiment where it exploded harmlessly.

I saw that Sir Arthur had stiffened the line with the last of our reserves. He had steadied the line but to our right, we could see the Guards Division. They were in square for fear of being attacked by the French cavalry which waited ominously in charge range. As a result, they were being cut to pieces by the French artillery and the skirmishers who swarmed around them. If they fell then the whole of our centre would collapse.

General Wellesley saw it too and he gestured to me, "Matthews! Come with me!"

When we reached the Guards he said, "Be so good as to ask Colonel Colborne to chase those skirmishers away."

The 52nd was one of our largest regiments and Sir John Colborne one of our most popular leaders. I had served with him in Spain and Portugal. As I rode towards them, I heard Sir Arthur giving commands to the Guards Division. "Guards, form a four-deep line!" The well-disciplined soldiers obeyed instantly despite continuing to take casualties.

Sir John Colborne was on his horse. As the cannonballs flew over, his men were bobbing their heads up and down to avoid the shot which screamed overhead. "You fellows, stop ducking. The Guards will think you are the second battalion."

It was a joke and everyone laughed. "Sir John, Sir Arthur requests that you clear the skirmishers away from the slope. They are causing too many casualties." I pointed along the ridge where the Guards gave their first volley.

"Anything is better than standing here and taking it. Form two lines." The men were in their lines almost instantly. "Forward, muskets at the ready." They reached the top of the ridge, halted and, as the sword swung down, the whole battalion fired. Normally skirmishers are hard to hit but with a large battalion, it was like firing a shotgun. The few who remained, fled. Another crisis had been averted. The 52nd fired at the flank of the gunners who were forced to move a little further down the slope and out of range of the battalion.

We had bought some time and I returned to the elm tree. I had just reached it when there was another cannonade from a battery across the valley. The constant firing had made them even more inaccurate but Sir William de Lancey fell to the ground even as I approached. Sir Arthur and I went directly to his side. We saw that a cannonball had struck him a glancing blow. I carefully undid his tunic and lifted his shirt. The skin was not broken but there was an enormous bruise close to his ribs.

The man I had followed for almost ten years looked at me with, for the first time that day, a troubled face. Sir William was a good friend of his. "Matthews, take him to the surgeon, I beg of you."

"Yes, sir."

We helped him to his horse. I could see the pain that he was in. Through gritted teeth, he said, "I can manage on my own, Sir Arthur. You need Matthews here."

"Nonsense this is nearly over now. It will be dark in an hour or two." It was the lie a friend tells another.

I led Sir William's horse back as gently as I could. This time the orderlies recognised the uniform of a senior officer and they rushed to help him.

"He was struck by a cannonball. The skin is not broken."

"Thank you, sir, you can leave him with us."

I glanced in the tent next to the one where the surgeon was operating. I saw that Sharp was lying on a blanket, seemingly asleep. He had had his left arm removed. I went towards him and an orderly said, "He's sleeping, sir. The surgeon gave him some laudanum. He'll recover right

enough, and sleep is the best medicine. I promise you that he will live,"
He shook his head, "He is better off than most of the poor buggers who
came through here." I nodded. "How is the battle going, sir? The reason I
ask is that we are getting more wounded, not less. Are we losing? Are the
French coming? I don't fancy being a prisoner."

"No, but the outcome is still in doubt. Don't worry, Sir Arthur knows
his business." As I rode back to the front I wondered if I was telling him
a lie to make things easier for, as I neared the ridge, I saw my worst
nightmare materialise; the Imperial Guard was preparing to attack. We
were already weakened, and all our reserves had been used. How could
we stand an attack from the best soldiers the French had? They had never
been defeated and we were already almost spent and on our knees. They
had more men in their elite ranks than there were British soldiers on the
battlefield. They had taken no casualties and had not moved all day.
They would be fresh and eager to destroy this annoying little army that
clung for dear life to a little ridge in Flanders.

As I reached Sir Arthur and the Earl of Uxbridge, I pointed across to
La Belle Alliance. Sir Arthur smiled, sadly, "I have seen already,
Matthews. It seems that this Bonaparte is a gambler."

"It is more likely that he has already used the last of his reserves."

"You may be right, Matthews. We will do what we can to hang on
until the Prussians arrive. Ride to Sir Hussey Vivian and ask him to bring
his light brigade to the centre of the line. We shall have need of him."

There were many troops protecting our western flank and Sir Arthur
was now bringing in the better of them to bolster our depleted line. I
spurred Pierre on for the brigade was a mile or two to the west. To my
surprise and delight, I discovered them just half a mile from the Dutch
Corps. The Major General smiled, "I thought that Sir Arthur might need
my fellows. They have been sitting on their arses all day."

"If you would place your brigade behind the 33rd and the 69th. "I
leaned in. "I fear that both regiments have suffered badly this day and
your presence behind them will be of great help."

He nodded, "I know. Today has seen a great slaughter of cavalry. Do
not worry, my chaps are solid enough."

"Let us hope that the waste is over." I thought of the men that Slender
Billy had sent unnecessarily to their deaths. Now Sharp was crippled. I
eased my pistol from its holster and cocked it. There was so much noise
and fire from skirmishers and cannon that it was almost impossible to
hear anything else. I had something to do. I suspected I would be dead by

the end of the day. I might as well die for something worthwhile rather than be struck by a random cannonball. The smoke drifted across the battlefield and it was hard to make out figures. The thought came to me that if I were to wound this disaster of a general then I would be saving men's lives. I pulled back the hammer on my pistol as I contemplated the unthinkable. Even as the thought entered my mind, albeit briefly, it was as though someone had answered my prayers for there was a flurry of shots from some Tirailleurs who had closed with the group of horsemen unseen. The Crown Prince pitched from his horse. The aides fired their pistols at the skirmishers and nearby Dutch regiments drove them off. Then the Prince's staff raced to their leader. Sadly, he was not killed but when he was taken to the rear for the wound was not trivial, I breathed a sigh of relief. He would kill no more allied soldiers that day. I eased the hammer of my pistol back down. I would not need to risk my name and my honour.

When I reached Sir Arthur, he was looking tired. "Well?"

"He was already on his way sir and he and his men are right behind me. The Crown Prince has been wounded."

"Has he? Senior officers are falling like flies today." He saw General Halkett prowling along the rear line of his brigade. "Things will get hot here soon, Halkett. Make sure your chaps have plenty of ball and powder."

General Halkett came over on his horse so that he would not have to shout. "It is those damned cannon which are causing the problem, sir. Can we not retire behind the ridge?"

"Very well but just behind and have your men lie down. I need them in action the moment I give the command."

I understood both men. The four regiments had taken a huge battering over the last three days. Already some of the Dutch and some of the Belgian regiments had broken. Although they had been reformed, they were well behind our lines. They would have to be kept as a reserve; if we advanced then they would be used and that would only happen if we beat Bonaparte.

The Earl of Uxbridge appeared next to us. "Sir Arthur, I have gathered every cavalry squadron I could manage to find. We have four brigades of light cavalry and I have cobbled together the survivors of the Union brigade. It is little enough, but they are there." He pointed just behind us where I saw a mix of Scots Greys, Inniskillings, Life Guards and

Dragoon Guards. There were barely four squadrons left from four regiments.

"Thank you, Uxbridge."

At that moment the Grand Battery belched its fire across the valley. It was like a scene from hell. The sky had already darkened as dusk approached but storm clouds were also gathering. The swirling cloud of smoke from the guns was also ever-present. I could not get the taste of the powder from my throat no matter how much water I drank. We looked as though we would have to fight on into the night.

The general pulled his hat down a little tighter as the wind gusted. I was still bareheaded. "Well, gentlemen, the game is afoot. I believe the French are to attack again. Any sign of the Prussians?"

The Earl said, "They are in the woods yonder, but the Young Guard is holding them up somewhat."

"Then we only have to endure this for a short time. Here it comes!"

It sounded like the wind as the cannonballs screamed towards us. There was little accuracy now. Every cannon on both sides needed cleaning. Many would need a rebore. The windage added to the accumulation of unburned powder meant that some balls ploughed into the hillside, others flew overhead but some managed to strike horses, guns and men; it was a lottery. There was little skill now. If you were hit then it was fate rather than an enemy which decided it.

I was on one side of the Earl and I felt the wind pass between us. Copenhagen reared a little and both the Earl and I looked at Sir Arthur in case he had been wounded. Then the Earl looked down and said, "By God, sir, I have lost my leg."

Sir Arthur looked down and said, "By God sir, so you have."

I reached over and grabbed the reins of the Earl's horse. Then I stepped down holding the reins of both horses in my right hand. Sir Arthur dismounted too. The ball had taken the leg off cleanly at the knee. I handed the reins of the horses to Sir Arthur and took a cravat from a dead officer whose body was close by. I tied it tightly around the thigh. It was my second tourniquet of the day. "Hang on, sir, and I shall take you to the surgeon."

I leapt onto Pierre's back and, grabbing the reins from Sir Arthur led the Earl back to Waterloo and the overworked surgeons. As I rode, I kept looking anxiously over my shoulder to see that he was still on his horse. The Earl was a superlative horseman and wounded or not he was not going to fall. "Nearly there, sir."

"Dashed kind of you Matthews. You are a good fellow."

His voice sounded slurred as though he was drunk. I shouted to the orderlies as we approached, "It is the Earl of Uxbridge! He has lost his leg. Lend a hand there you chaps."

Two big orderlies ran over to me. One had been there when I had brought Sharp. "You don't need to keep bringing us fresh ones, Colonel. We have more than enough to be going on with."

The other put his arm behind the Earl's back. "Just let yourself go, sir; I promise we won't drop you." As they laid him on the stretcher they said, "You can leave him with us, sir. It is a clean wound. It just needs cauterizing and stitching."

I left the Earl's horse to his own devices. I suspect the animal was as shocked as the humans had been. I noticed that Sir Arthur had brought up the troops from behind the ridge once more to face the guns. The French bombardment was a prelude to an attack.

When I reached the ridge there was just myself and Sir Arthur who were left. He gave me a wry smile. "We are becoming a smaller target, Matthews. Let us hope that at least one of us sees the outcome of the battle. I should hate to die and not know how it turns out." I don't know why but that made me laugh.

"Come let us rally the men." General Halkett's men were in square and they were suffering. We stood by the rear wall of the square. I saw at least two colonels lying wounded and General Halkett himself came over to us. "For the love of God, Sir Arthur, either let us withdraw or reinforce us!

Sir Arthur's face showed no emotion. "Every Englishman on the field must now stay where he stands and, if necessary, die on the spot we occupy!" As he turned his horse's head away, he shouted, "Hold fast, General. It will be over before too long." We headed back to the tree. "I shall go to Maitland and the Guards. Bring the 3rd Netherlands Light Cavalry Division and place them behind General Halkett. Perhaps their horses will stop them running." It was cold but it was necessary.

As I galloped the hundred yards or so Pierre had to step carefully to avoid riding over corpses of men and carcasses of horses. The ground was littered with them.

The light horse regiments looked to be a larger number than they actually were; their horses helped with the illusion. They followed me back and formed two lines behind the shaken division. When I reached

General Halkett I said, "The general says you may go in line now if you wish, sir."

It was a lie, of course. The General wanted them in square in case the French cavalry appeared again but they would suffer fewer casualties that way and with the Light Horse behind them then the threat of French cavalry was diminished.

The French army, and especially the Imperial Guard, like drama and we heard the pas de charge. The Imperial Guard were coming. The drums seemed to be the sound of our doom as they echoed across the valley. Occasionally the cannon would drown out the noise but then it would be there again as it came up the slope in waves. It was like a heartbeat. It was the heartbeat of the French army. I found myself alone under the elm tree. I checked my watch. It was shortly before seven-thirty in the evening of a very long day. Normally battles peter out but not this one. It was like two bare-knuckle fighters. Both are spent but neither will give in. The blows are weaker but still hurt. We were like that. We were trading blows and we were bleeding.

I watched the Middle Guard as they marched towards us. Shell and ball still flew overhead, and men still fell but every eye was fixed on the steady march of the five columns. Each column represented a battalion of very experienced soldiers. There were Chasseurs and there were Grenadiers. Both were fine soldiers. These men would not run after five solid volleys. They would trade punches and bayonets. The troops who marched were the most fanatical and the most loyal of the Emperor's troops. Behind them, I saw the Old Guard and the Guard cavalry. Should this blow not deliver the knockout then more fresh troops would do the job. It seemed hopeless.

I found myself looking over my shoulder. I wondered how Sharp was. I was resigned to dying beneath that elm tree, but I wanted Sharp to survive. He would be able to go back to the D'Alpini estate and enjoy a well-earned retirement. I would lie with the others here. I would remain with my comrades, French, and English.

Chapter 16

I realised that Sir Arthur had not returned and I was his only aide. I galloped a rested Pierre towards General Maitland and the Guards Division. Sir Arthur frowned when I rode up, "What's the matter, Matthews? Having a rest?"

"No sir."

"Good." He pointed to his right. "Join Sir John Colborne and the 52nd. This will be hot soon. If he is able, I want his men to fire along the flank of this end column. He should be able to enfilade them."

"Sir!"

That was Wellington's way. The General of that Division was General Adam, but Sir Arthur liked to use regiments. He knew that the 52nd was one of the largest regiments we had left and they had suffered less than most. I did not have far to ride. They were lying down in the field. "Sir John, his lordship would like you to try to enfilade the French column if you get the chance."

"Right, Colonel."

I left the highly competent Colborne to complete Sir Arthur's orders and rode back to the elm tree and Sir Arthur. "I think, Matthews, that you will be needed by General Halkett. His men have done well over the last three days, but they have taken a hard pounding." He hesitated and then put his mouth closer to my ear. The noise of shot and shell was deafening but I think he did not wish to shout. "If I fall..."

"Sir, you are a rock and you will not fall. You cannot for you are the heart of this army."

"Nevertheless, I have seen too many good friends fall. I think we can win today. We can hold them here but to win we need Bonaparte's Guards destroying. Choose your moment and send in the cavalry if you believe they can tip the balance."

"Sir, that is a great responsibility! I am but a Colonel."

"Matthews, you are the most dependable officer I have ever met. You are calm and you have a military mind. Use those abilities for your country. I trust you. Battles are won and lost on such tight margins and decisions. If things go as I plan and hope, then when I wave my hat three times that will be the signal to advance. Make sure that the cavalry is kept in good order." Then he turned and rode behind the Guards.

The French were now less than four hundred yards from our front line. The guns we had left were carving lines in their files but the Grenadiers and Chasseurs merely closed ranks. I placed Pierre next to Sir Colin. "The marquess sent me here, General. He thought I might be of some assistance."

"Glad to have you. These fellows are all but done in. If they were a horse, then we would have shot them already." He looked at the Brigade. They looked to have had the heart ripped from them. The shells were still exploding and the cannonballs still tearing holes in their ranks. The only consolation was that the hits were more random and haphazard.

General Halkett turned and faced the depleted and spent brigade. Despite the firing around him, he made his voice heard. "You have done all that can be asked of you lads, but I am going to ask you to do more. Boney is sending his best men here to test them against us. I think we are better. We will give them a few volleys and then stick the bayonet to them. What do you say?"

The sound of the guns was drowned out by a chorus of 'Huzzahs!'

I felt proud and terrified at the same time. The French were bringing horse artillery with them this time. We would have to endure both musket and cannon fire. We would have to stand against volleys from muskets that were as yet unfired. Our men had been firing for almost seven hours. I had seen veterans making water down the barrels to both cool and clean them!

As the huge moustachioed Guards approached, their bearskins wavering from side to side as they stepped and then passed over bodies and the undulating ground, I braced myself for the fierce fire and storm which would soon be coming my way. I did spy a kind of hope as I saw the French Grenadiers before us trying to deploy into line. They had to do so or else they would have only had a handful of muskets able to fire. The Grenadiers were the tallest men in the Guard and with their bearskins, they towered over us. It seemed as though we were being attacked by giants.

One of the privates suddenly said, "By but these are big buggers! At least we cannot miss them."

A sergeant roared, "That man! Quiet in the ranks!"

General Halkett saw the Imperial Guard appear at the same time as I did and he shouted. "Present! Fire!"

It was as though a fog had descended in the middle of a thunderstorm. The French Grenadiers disappeared as every musket was discharged and the black smoke rolled towards the French. The brigade got off a second volley before the French Grenadiers returned fire. I felt the wind from their musket balls. They were more ragged than I had expected. General Halkett's prompt command had given us a marginal advantage. Redcoats began to fall but still their discipline held, and they fired a third and then a fourth volley.

Out of the fog, a sea of bearskins emerged. They were less than twenty yards from us. The fifth volley made them disappear once more. I braced myself for another fusillade but instead, there was nothing in reply and then the cannonballs began to rip into the flanks of the French line.

I thought that we had won and then I saw that our soldiers were starting to move back. Halkett's brigade which had come within a whisker of victory now seemed ready to flee. They were falling back to the reverse slope. This was not a rout. They were retiring away from the enemy who seemed ready to push them back. Halkett's Brigade just turned and began to move back down the reverse slope.

From the back of Pierre, I could see that the French Grenadiers had halted. We had stunned them. They were trying to regroup. Officers were down and there was a hiatus as order was restored to the Middle Guard. We had to move forward. Now was the moment when the Imperial Guard could be driven from the field. I could not see Sir Colin. Officers and sergeants were looking to me for I was the only officer on a horse that they could see. I remembered Sir Arthur's words about margins. The French were overbalancing; one more push and they might fall and so I shouted, "The 5th Brigade will halt. About face!"

This was a crucial moment. To my immense relief, I heard the sergeants and officers who remained repeating the order. Sir Colin appeared at my side. I could see that he must have taken a tumble from his horse. He held the colours of the 33rd aloft and waved it. He nodded towards me as he moved forward still holding the flag. "The 5th Brigade will advance! Forward!"

The Brigade began to move towards the French Grenadiers. The 95th were peppering the horse battery with their rifles and the cannon fire had diminished somewhat. I put my heels to Pierre and drew my sword. A gap in the 69th's lines appeared and I hurtled through it. The young officer in command of the gun saw me when I was just ten yards from him. He was brave but the artillerymen of the French had only a short hangar sword with which to defend themselves. I had a long blade and I speared him with it. I withdrew it and was already reining Pierre in. I

178

wheeled my mount around and sliced across the head of the sergeant who tried to fend me off with his rammer. He was too slow and the edge of my sword ripped across his throat. I laid about me with my sword. Even if I did not strike them then I stopped them from firing.

Some of the 69th had followed me and they butchered the gunners where they stood. Soon the whole battery was silent, and our tormentors were dead. I allowed Pierre and myself to gather our breath. I saw the Imperial Grenadiers as they hesitated. The 5th had given them a bayonet charge and they had fallen back but they were trying to reform.

General Halkett shouted. "Prepare muskets! Fire!" At the same time, the gunners began to pour canister into the already thinning ranks. We had few guns close by, but they did serious damage to the Grenadiers. We had stopped our column. They had had to move down the slope. They were still trying to form a line but General Halkett continued to order volleys so that our firepower was superior to theirs.

I suddenly realised that we had borne the brunt of the first attack and that, to my right, the second column was about to strike the Foot Guards, our strongest regiments. The slope had been easier facing us. The French there had made better time. I saluted General Halkett with my sword as he continued to fire volley after volley into the shattered column. The French before us were still standing but all fight had gone from them. They were dead men walking. Their courage stopped them from retreating and the battered 5th Division stopped them from advancing. They would die where they stood. I had done what was needed and I would be needed elsewhere.

I walked Pierre to Sir Arthur who had also joined the Guards and the 52nd as they prepared to fire on the Chasseurs. General Maitland was watching Sir Arthur. The French advanced confidently. The smoke and the noise had hidden the fate of their Grenadiers from them. They did not know that a fifth of their force was gone. These were two big columns; one of Chasseurs and one of Grenadiers. They were attempting to deploy into line, much as the other column had done. Sir Arthur waited until they were just sixty yards from the bayonets before he shouted, "Now Maitland! Now's your time! Up Guards!" The muskets were all raised.

"Fire!"

The Guards Brigade was not a brigade that had suffered massive casualties like the 5th Division. These had not endured attack after attack. These were the elite of the British army and they would not miss. Over three hundred Frenchmen fell in that first volley.

179

Maitland took over and the Guards repeatedly raised and fired their muskets into the heart of the columns. The two columns, like the French Grenadiers we had destroyed, faltered. They were brave men but it is hard to advance into a wall of lead. It was made even harder by the fact that they had to march uphill and clamber over the bodies of their comrades who lay before them. They formed lines and fired a ragged volley but the iron discipline of the British Guards held.

I saw Marshal Ney exhorting these Guards who had never recoiled before to greater deeds of glory although, in truth, I did not see what else they could do. They were trying to march uphill into a storm of lead. The cannons at Belle Alliance were now silent for fear of hitting blue uniforms. I watched as Ney's horse was hit by a ball from the British guns. He jumped to his feet and clambered onto the horse given to him by his aide. The aide paid the price when a rifleman targeted him. He crumpled to the ground.

And still, the Chasseurs and Grenadiers tried to advance. Sir Arthur shouted, "The Guards will advance!" It was a bold move for the Imperial Guard were not yet beaten.

The resolute Foot Guards began to march down the slope. I waved my sword in the air and General Halkett saw my action. He must have thought that Sir Arthur had ordered them forward. Miraculously the battered 5th Division did advance and then another miracle happened. It was something I thought I would never have seen, the Grenadiers and the Chasseurs of the French Imperial Middle Guard began to fall back. The whole right-hand side of the French advance had been halted and was now being driven back. They were moving back down the hill. They were still in good order, but they were moving back.

The terrain and the slope meant that the last column, the largest one, the 4th Chasseurs was only now arriving at the ridge. Thanks to Sir Arthur's instructions Sir John Colborne had half of his huge brigade at right angles to the column. I heard the order to fire and almost jumped at the sound of the volley. The whole column disappeared in a cloud of black and acrid smoke. The volleys rolled around the valley. The artillery battered them. With the Guards, the 52nd and the 73rd all pouring volley after volley into them they broke, and they ran. This was not a withdrawal, it was a rout. When they ran the other two columns who had been retreating in the face of our onslaught also began to run.

This was the moment when I saw the exhaustion on the faces of my countrymen. They could not pursue. As much as they might want to, their bodies would not allow them. The guns and the muskets fired into the backs of the Middle Guard as they retired.

I knew that I had to find Sir Arthur; if he still lived. The last that I had seen of him he had been amongst the Foot Guards wreathed in a blanket of smoke. I raised my sword in salute. "My lord, they are withdrawing down the hill. There are still three battalions of Imperial Guards there but they cannot do anything."

He smiled. "Aye well, Matthews, it is nearly done but that is not enough. It must be done properly. In for a penny in for a pound eh?"

He took off his hat and I knew what was coming. I moved out of the way as he pulled back on Copenhagen's reins to raise the horse from the ground. He stood in the stirrups and raised his hat. Suddenly the thick clouds above us parted and a single shaft of evening sunshine caught Sir Arthur as he waved his hat three times. Sir Arthur shouted, "The Army will advance!" The cry was taken up by officers along the whole British line.

As the hooves of Copenhagen struck the ground he said, "Now, Matthews. The cavalry!"

I rode along the line of the Light Horse Brigades yelling as I went. "The army will advance. Drive the French from the field!"

Below me, the infantry advanced. It was not a line. There were too few men left for a solid line. It was pockets of a hundred men or so moving relentlessly down the slope towards the defeated French. The ones who marched were the ones who still had some strength left. Sometimes they were led by a mere ensign and colour party or a sergeant but still, they advanced.

I reached the Heavy Brigade. It was a shadow of the force which had bravely galloped down the hill that morning. I saw that there were but a handful of white horses left. "The army will advance." I waved my sword towards La Belle Alliance. "Let us finish what we started this morning."

The lines began to advance down the hill. This time there were no infantrymen to negotiate, just the dead and the dying. I saw my cousin. I nudged Pierre next to him. "I shall ride with my cousin, I think! The Macgregors will end this together."

"And I shall be proud to ride alongside such an illustrious countryman."

We trotted down the hill. Pierre was dwarfed by the greys, but he trotted proudly for all that. We gradually overtook the infantry who cheered us as we went by. I watched then as they bayoneted the wounded and then began to strip the bodies of valuables. Such was war and this would be my last. I would not have to either endure such torment or watch such barbarity anymore.

As I looked around me I saw that I was the most senior officer remaining although having no uniform only I knew that. The captains, lieutenants and the sergeant who had survived the morning debacle needed neither orders nor instructions. This was what they had been trained for their whole lives. They were about to swoop on a defeated and demoralised enemy who was retreating. The French had their backs to us and this time there would be no cavalry to come to their aid. The only thing which might save them would be nightfall.

As we rode down the trodden field of rye I saw that some of the advancing infantry had been wounded or were too exhausted to carry on. Bizarrely they waved cheerily, giving us a 'Huzzah!' as we passed and I saw them chewing the rye which had been threshed by feet and hooves.

The survivors of the Household division broke up into the composite squadrons. I rode with the Greys as we chased the grenadiers of the Middle Guard. They heard the hooves, and some tried to turn. None had reloaded and they only had a bayonet to fend off our sabres. I leaned forward as the sergeant who had lost his bearskin jabbed at Pierre with his bayonet. I flicked the bayonet aside with ease and then lunged with the tip. It entered his eye and, as it tore into his skull, he fell to the floor dead. Twisting my sword to remove it I looked for my next victim. They were victims but I knew that I could not relent. Bonaparte had inspired these men to return to the colours once. He could do so again. We had to destroy his Imperial Guard. Without them, he could never again threaten the peace of Europe. Our progress down the slope became slower as we had to despatch the Frenchmen who turned to face us. Soon it became hard to negotiate the slope for there were so many bodies.

It was now no longer the Guard who were before us. It was also the other infantry and even the cavalry who had joined in the rout and were fleeing the field. There was courage still in the French and some of the horsemen hearing cavalry approach turned to face us. It was a matter of honour. I saw some dragoons in their green uniforms. Their muskets were long gone and their swords were blunted but they turned and tried to charge uphill towards us. It was their horses that inspired pity in me. They were exhausted almost to the point of death and yet they still tried to carry their riders back up the hill. A squadron of them charged us and it was a hectic skirmish that ensued. I was buffeted and struck from all sides but we had the slope with us and we forced our way through them. I riposted the first sword and pushed the dragoon from his horse with the tip of my blade. A lieutenant like me without a hat tried to hack down at me. I blocked his sword which shattered. He tried to wheel away but a Scots Grey skewered him.

I saw French soldiers raising their hands and shouting, "Vive le Roi!" It made no difference to the British infantry who had advanced. They were in no mood for mercy. They had suffered at the hands of ball, powder, lance, and bayonet. They were intent on revenge. The French were slaughtered by redcoats with the blood lust upon them. We moved inexorably down the slope and then up towards La Belle Alliance. Napoleon's Headquarters was some four hundred yards up the slope. It was then that I saw the three squares of the Old Guard waiting resolutely for us halfway up the slope which led to the road south. Their presence told me that Emperor Napoleon Bonaparte had, along with most of his generals, already left the battlefield. These had not advanced with the rest of the Imperial Guards and they were not only intact, but they were also the best of the best the French had left.

I suddenly found myself alone. I reined Pierre in to ascertain where the rest of the Union Brigade had got to. I was suddenly aware of a blue uniform hurtling towards me. I just managed to duck as a sabre whizzed over my head. It was a Horse Grenadier of the Imperial Guard. As the rider reined his horse around, I recognised it as Major Armand, it was Colonel Hougon's cousin. He had come for revenge. I was at a distinct disadvantage: he had a bigger fresher horse.

He cursed at me, "We may have lost this battle, murderer, but I shall have the satisfaction of avenging my cousin." He charged at me.

I whipped Pierre's head to the right to avoid the sword which came towards my head. My nimbler horse easily evaded the huge black beast which the major rode. It was impossible for him to bring his sword down on me; I was on the wrong side of his mount. I continued to wheel around so that I came up behind the Major. As he turned his horse, he back slashed at me and I blocked it with my sword. I twisted as I did so. My sword had a straight, long blade. The Grenadier had a sabre. He lost control of the blade and I lunged at him. My sword sliced along his side. It came away red. He hacked down and I deflected the sabre, but it struck my leg. It felt suddenly numb.

"Coward! Face me like a man!"

I ignored his words and concentrated on his sword and his eyes. He tried to make his horse rear and clatter Pierre with his hooves. As the horse's head came up I had no compunction in slicing across the horse's neck with my sword. It ripped through the horse's jugular and I, along with Pierre, was sprayed with its blood. It was an enormous horse and the major clung on to the reins. The Horse Grenadier fell to the ground and then the huge dead horse fell upon him. I heard the crack as his back broke. Major Armand was dead.

I had no time to reflect. Muskets were still popping, and the battle still raged. Sir Arthur would be upon the ridge. For all that I knew I was the most senior officer on the battlefield, and I could not just sit and admire the scenery. I saw the Scots Greys close by. They were enjoying the chase and pursuing pockets of fleeing horsemen.

I shouted to David, "Captain Macgregor! Halt your men. They need to rest and those Grenadiers are fresh."

The Old Guard battalions were marching back slowly towards the ridge in square. It takes the most disciplined of soldiers to do this and the ones before us were just that. It was not volley fire they were enduring but they were being struck. As gaps appeared in their ranks they were closed up. I watched as dismounted French horsemen, artillerymen and infantry tried to get inside the square. They believed it was the safest place on the battlefield for a Frenchman. Despite the fact that they were French soldiers, they were killed by the Imperial Guard. If there had been any order to the allied formations, then volley fire would have decimated the squares. As it was the squares were being nibbled to death.

David looked down at me, "Sir, your leg. You have been wounded." I remembered the blow from the Dragoon and the one from Major Armand. Which one had given me the wound? "Trooper Menteith, see to him."

I looked down and saw that I had had my overalls sliced through from the knee to the thigh and I had a wound there. I had not noticed it. "It is nothing."

Trooper Menteith jumped down and took a neckcloth from a dead Frenchman who lay nearby. "You are bleeding, sir. We can't have that!" David waved him over and he gave him a bottle which was in my cousin's saddlebag. He poured some over the wound. It burned and numbed at the same time. He handed the bottle to me. "Whisky, sir. The water of life, have a drink. It is a shame to waste it all on a wound."

I swallowed the peaty spirit. It was like drinking smoky fire. I had not eaten since before the battle started and I wondered what effect the neat spirits would have upon me.

The trooper nodded, "There that is the best I can do, sir but I would see a surgeon as soon as you can."

Some Inniskillings joined us as we dressed our ranks, rested our horses, and watched the French Grenadiers slaughter all who came close to them, French and allied alike.

One of the Inniskillings asked, "Sir, why are they killing their own men? It's daft sure enough."

"These men of the Imperial Guard know that if they open their square then we will be in too. These are ruthless men. These are the men who marched back with Marshal Ney in a Russian winter fighting off Cossacks and wolves. These men are not afraid to die. They just want to take as many of us as they can with them. Do not be in a hurry to oblige them. We will let our horses recover and then when they reach the top of the ridge we will surround them and invite them to surrender."

David looked at me. "Do you think they will?"

I gave a rueful smile, "Not one chance in a thousand but it would be polite to ask."

As they neared the top of the ridge, I led the Union Cavalry Brigade I now commanded around them to block off their escape. The Life Guards and the Rifles joined me. The infantry and other cavalry units joined in so that we had them surrounded and they could retreat no more.

It was there we saw the 10th Hussars, a newly arrived regiment, decide to end it. I recognised Major Howard, the commanding officer. He was the son of the Earl of Carlisle. I knew him to be charismatic but incredibly reckless. He raised his sword, "Come on 10th Hussars. Let us show these Frenchies that we are not afraid of the bearskins and their moustaches! We will drive them all the way back to Paris!"

I watched in horror as they charged the square. The Old Guard raised their muskets. The order was given to fire. These did not fire high; they fired into the horses and the middle of the horsemen. They had the best French muskets on the battlefield and they could fire almost as quickly as an English regiment. The Hussars disappeared in the foul black smoke from poor French powder. All that we could see were the flashes of their muzzles. When they ceased firing and the smoke cleared, the 10th as a regiment had ceased to exist.

I saw Major Howard, who amazingly was still alive and laying about him with his sword, clutch his head as he was struck a glancing blow from a pistol ball and he fell at the feet of the front rank. He was not dead and he tried to rise. He staggered to his knees and he held his head. A Grenadier stepped forward and beat the colonel's head with the butt of his musket until it was unrecognisable as a human skull.

I had had enough. "Heavy Brigade, form a line. Draw sabres." I recognised the 71st Foot. They had reasonable numbers left still. "Captain, have your men form two lines before me here." The officer saluted and hurried to obey. I saw an abandoned French gun pointing forlornly at our lines. "You fellows, turn that gun around if you please and aim it at the square."

A colour sergeant who had a heavily bandaged head shouted, "You heard that officer. Make sure it is loaded and stick some more balls down the barrel. These bastards need wiping from the face of the earth."

There were few recognisable regiments now. But there were companies, platoons and troops who had come to surround the Old Guard and witness their death. There were many muskets and pistols levelled at their blue ranks. Many more had joined us since we had surrounded them. When the square was surrounded I rode forward. I recognised General Cambronne on his horse in the middle of the largest square. He was an unpleasant butcher. I had known him in Italy where he had been a captain. Even in those days, he had been ruthless and renowned for his toughness.

I felt I owed it to him to give him the chance to surrender although I knew that it was hopeless, "General Cambronne, you are surrounded. There is no dishonour in surrendering. You have served your Emperor well and he has gone. Do not waste your lives."

"I know you! You were in the Chasseurs. Have you changed sides?"

"Yes, General, for my mother was Scottish but hear me, my regiment was abandoned and slaughtered in Egypt. Your Emperor has abandoned you. These are brave men. Do not let them die for nothing!"

"I know," he said, "but buggers like us do not surrender. Do your worst!"

The whole square cheered and levelled their muskets. They were about to fire. I rode back to the 71st and the Rifles. Some of the officers had understood what I was saying but the men had no idea. "I asked them to surrender, they declined. Captain, you may fire!"

The muskets and the rifles fired before the cannon. I saw the general knocked from his horse in the first volley. He was later captured by a Hanoverian officer. When the cannon fired it swept through all four sides of the square. It had been filled to capacity and death went everywhere. The muskets fired and kept firing. I saw, through the smoke and in the light of the musket fire, the squares shrink and then join and then become triangles. Finally, the captain turned to me and said, "Sir, we are out of ammunition." I could see that there were still guardsmen who stood defiantly. This could not go on indefinitely.

I drew my sword, "Then let us end it here. Charge!" Charge was an exaggeration for it sounds like we moved with speed. We did not. We lurched towards them but the sight of the horses and the bayonets was too much and the French Guards finally fled down the road towards the crossroads at Quatre Bras where it had all begun days earlier. The battle the French called Mont St. Jean and the Prussians called La Belle Alliance was over but it is remembered by the name the Duke of Wellington gave it, after his final promotion, the battle of Waterloo.

Chapter 17

If I thought my war was over then I was wrong. I rode back across the battlefield which was still littered with the dead, the dying and the wounded towards Waterloo. The only hope for the wounded was that their comrades would come and find them and take them home. The ones who were abandoned would have their throats slit and their bodies robbed in the dark by locals and other soldiers alike. The vultures would gather in the night and they would be human. I saw the 71st doing just that, they carried off all their friends who had fallen. Others would lie on the field for another three days. Many would die before then as they had their lives ended by locals who could not wait for them to die. The price for fighting on their land was that the dead lost their valuables, their clothes and even their teeth. It was macabre. Many years later I was offered a set of false teeth on a visit to Paris. The seller took great delight in telling me that they were Waterloo teeth.

When we reached the camp of the Scots Greys, Captain David Macgregor, greeted me warmly. "I hope to see you in more peaceful circumstances, Captain. Come to Messina and visit with me on my estate."

"And you, sir, must come to Scotland and visit your ancestral home. My family will wish to thank you for your services not only to our country but to me."

"Perhaps, perhaps." We shook hands. His troop all saluted and gave three 'Huzzahs'. I know not if they were for me or for their survival. I waved as cheerily as I could for I was aching, tired and the whisky had worn off. My leg hurt.

I found Wolf still tied forlornly to the elm tree. I changed horses. Poor Pierre was beyond exhaustion. I made my weary way to Sir Arthur's headquarters leading my proud Pierre behind me. It was almost midnight when I reached it.

The sentry outside was almost asleep and he jumped to attention as I dismounted. "Sorry Colonel Matthews, it has been a long day."

"I know." My left leg hurt as I stepped down onto it for the first time. I led my horses into the stables. There was just Copenhagen there. Goodness only knows where the others had gone. I unsaddled both of my horses. I rubbed them down and gave them grain and water. They had both deserved it.

I entered the hotel and found Sir Arthur writing his report. He looked up when I entered and I saw him smile; a rare occurrence. "Matthews, you survived!" He saw the red bandage around my leg. "You are hurt, sir! You must see a surgeon!"

"I believe they will have more pressing matters than the leg of a colonel, sir. I will go in the morning." He nodded and returned to his writing. "Well, it is over with, sir. I can go back to Sicily and my family now."

He put his pen down. "Not quite yet, Matthews. It seems the Prussians want Bonaparte executed. Damned barbaric if you ask me. It is not civilised. We have to get to him before they do."

I smiled. He made the war and the battle sound like a game of cricket.

"We can't have generals being executed for losing a battle. I want you and Selkirk to take some cavalry tomorrow morning and find him. You know the man and you know the country. Find him and put him on a Royal Navy ship. Selkirk will know what to do." My face must have fallen for he said, "I know it is an imposition and you have done so much already for your country but Selkirk told me that you once served this man. It seems to me that Fate has marked you out for this job. You are the only aide who has survived, almost intact, today. This was meant to be."

I looked up from the fire, startled. Colonel Selkirk had told me my secret was safe.

"I have known for years but your secret is safe with me. As I said, you served him. Would you like him placed in front of a firing squad?"

To be honest, I did not know but I shook my head. It was the answer he wanted.

"Good, then get a good night's sleep and in the morning, when your wound is dressed you can find Bonaparte before the Prussians!"

I saw two pallets on the floor and I collapsed onto one of them. I was too tired to argue. I was asleep almost instantly.

I awoke well before dawn which meant I had had less than three hours of sleep. I noticed that I had been covered by a blanket. That must have been Sir Arthur. It was the only act of humanity I can remember receiving from him. A shooting pain in my leg had woken me. I looked at the next pallet and saw Sir Arthur asleep. I would not be able to drop off again and so I left the hotel. The surgeon and his orderlies were just half a mile away and I decided to walk there. I say walk but my gait was a stiff-legged limp.

From the crowds, it was more like the middle of the day rather than the middle of the night. Wounded soldiers were being helped from the battlefield by unwounded comrades. I even saw one soldier from the 69th, who was clearly dead, being carried by two of his comrades. There was little point in my saying anything. They had already walked a long way. I would have turned around rather than add to the surgeon's burden had not the wound been so painful. I could barely stand on the leg. If I was to hunt Bonaparte, then I needed to be as fit as possible.

It was a nightmarish scene that greeted me when I reached the surgeon's tent. Outside was a pile of discarded limbs. It looked like a factory for making body parts there were so many of them. Each one represented a life ruined if not ended. Oil lamps lit the interior of the makeshift operating theatre. I heard the sound of a saw on bone as I entered what looked like a scene from Hades. The soldier who was losing his leg was being held down by four orderlies and the wood he held in his mouth prevented his cries from being too loud. His back strained as the saw bit through bone and nerve. Mercifully the Coldstream Guard passed out before it was finished and the surgeon completed his work. He handed the saw to an orderly and he saw me. He was the surgeon I had seen each time.

"Finish him up, Jones. What can I do for you, Colonel? Have you got more business for me?"

I pointed to my leg. "Just this, doctor. I wouldn't have worried you, but Sir Arthur needs me to be able to ride this morning."

He took the cigar he had just lit from his mouth and held a light to the leg. "Austen, over here." Another orderly came over. "Cut the bandage and overall away. Let's see what lies beneath."

I realised I would need spare trousers. I almost laughed. There were so many dead horsemen on the battlefield that I should be able to take my pick. There would be all shapes, sizes and styles to choose from.

The bandage and overalls removed, the surgeon lowered the lamp to inspect the wound. "It has been cleaned well enough but it will need stitching. Clean it up, Austen, and put in a few stitches. Colonel Matthews has done well today by all accounts so try to make them neat ones eh?" Another soldier was brought in on a stretcher and the surgeon threw away his cigar. "Duty calls. Your friend is in the next tent. He is doing well." He looked at the soldier with the mangled legs who had just been brought in and shrugged, "He has survived, at least."

When Austen had finished, he handed me a better pair of overalls. He said nothing but he shrugged. The owner was dead and would no longer need them. I would don them later. I left hell and went in search of Alan.

I peered in the next tent. There were cots that were tightly packed against each other. Sharp was at the end and, surprisingly, considering the hour, he was awake. "Now then Alan, how are things?" I saw that the surgeon had taken his arm off just above the elbow. I frowned as I wondered how he would cope with everyday things like eating, lighting a pipe...

In typical fashion, he deflected the attention to me. He saw the bare leg and the bandage. "Sir, what happened?"

"A scratch, nothing for either of us to worry about." I pointed to his stump. "How is the arm?"

"It's strange, sir, it feels like it is still there. It felt like I could wiggle my fingers before but how can I? I have no hand!"

"I do not understand anything about the body, Alan. Today I have seen men fight beyond pain and disfigurement as though the loss of a limb did not bother them."

He nodded, "The orderlies said it was over and we won." I nodded, "Looking at the men coming in I don't know how."

"If I tell you that we just surrounded and blasted away three battalions of the Imperial Guard then you might understand the scale of death this day."

"Then we can go home, sir? Back to Sicily?"

"You can but I am afraid I have one more task to perform for Sir Arthur and Colonel Selkirk."

"Sir, haven't you done enough for them? For England? They have had their pound of flesh and no mistake!"

I almost smiled at the outrage in Sharp's voice. It was not for himself but for me. "Never mind, it will not take long. I do not think that the Emperor will be able to hide. That will give you the chance to recover."

Just then an orderly came past us. "Sir, he can go now. The doctor can do no more. The stump just has to heal." He leaned in. "Between you and I sir, we need the bed. I can't see us clearing the casualties this side of Christmas, Colonel Matthews."

Sharp was almost out of the bed as the orderly spoke the words. "Very well Alan but I will get you a room at the inn and pick you up when I have finished my mission."

He grinned, "That's not a problem, sir."

As we left and passed the pile of limbs I noticed, on a table, seemingly discarded, were various pieces of equipment. I found some hats. After trying on a number I found one which suited me. Sharp laughed. "Let's hope it lasts longer than the French one I found for you, sir."

Dawn was breaking as we walked back to the stables. Sharp had left our bags in the hayloft. They were still there. All modesty was cast aside as we changed. It was pitiful for with our wounds we had to help each other to dress. Sharp laughed. "Your leg will heal sir, but I am going to have to learn how to live with just one hand."

"It is not a problem Alan, I can hire a servant to give you a hand!"

I punned deliberately to see his reaction. I need not have worried he laughed and said, "That will come in handy sir! However, I won't be able to keep my fingers in as many pies!" We both laughed until the tears rolled down our faces. The tears were of laughter and relief. We had survived. Many others had not.

We had not seen Sharp's horse where I had left it; someone must have made off with it. "I fear you have lost your horse, Alan. You will have to make do with Wolf."

He nodded. "We shall have a few days to become accustomed to one another."

Sir Arthur was up and writing as we entered. I saw Doctor Hume leaving. He was the chief surgeon. Sir Arthur's face looked tear-stained. I felt embarrassed. He held up the paper, "Next to a battle lost, the greatest misery is a battle won! This is the butcher's bill." He seemed to see Sharp for the first time. It was as though his wound and disfigurement had made him visible. "Lieutenant Sharp has suffered as poor Fitzroy has, he has lost an arm."

I was astounded. I did not know that Sir Arthur was aware of either Sharp's rank or name. "There is a pot of tea there. Help yourselves to it while I write an order out for you. The colonel should be here shortly."

Sir Arthur's servant John appeared and held a seat out for Alan. "You have done enough for us, Lieutenant Sharp. You sit down and I shall see to the tea." He flashed an irritated look at Sir Arthur.

"I will see the owner and arrange for a room for you, Alan."

By the time I had concluded my business Sir Arthur had finished with my orders. "You will need to requisition some cavalry to aid you. I suspect you will choose good ones. You seem a good judge of both men and horseflesh."

"Sir."

He stood and held his hat under his left arm. He put forward his right hand. "I would like to shake your hand, Colonel Matthews. Despite an inauspicious beginning, you have consistently performed to my exacting standards. That is a rare thing. Enjoy your sojourn in Sicily. I envy you but I fear that I will never be able to enjoy retirement. The Government should do something for you. You deserve it. I shall see what I can do should I get back to England any time soon."

"Thank you, sir. It has been my privilege to serve the man who has saved Great Britain."

He shook his head and waved his arm towards Mont St. John. "The dead and the dying are the ones who should be thanked. They have given their lives for their country. I merely gave my time and my mind." He turned to shake Sharp's hand, "And you Lieutenant Sharp..."

He looked embarrassed at Sharp's missing hand. Alan shook Sir Arthur's hand. "It is lucky it was my left arm, sir. I can still write and I daresay I can get the blacksmith to make me something to attach to the end. We'll see."

The general shook his head. "That is why we won, Matthews because we had soldiers like Sharp here. Nothing gets them down. Not even losing an arm. So long as she has them then England need never fear."

Chapter 18

While we waited for Colonel Selkirk I found someone with a grindstone and had my sword sharpened. I had a feeling that I would need it again. I then cleaned my four pistols. I asked one of the junior aides who appeared, searching for General Somerset's writing case, to have a look around outside for ball and powder for me. He found both in abundance. Now that we no longer needed them there were seemingly unlimited quantities of them. Sharp insisted on helping me to pack. I disagreed and forbade him to move. He could not use his left arm but he could sit in the chair vacated by Sir Arthur and he advised me what I might need.

It was noon when the Colonel arrived. He had been in Brussels during the whole battle. I got the impression that he had not suffered at all. He barely glanced at Alan or his wound. I had not expected him to. Neither mattered to him. He was single-minded in that regard. "Robbie, we have a great opportunity here! Have you found the horsemen yet?"

"No, sir, we were waiting for you." I could not help but smile to myself. Colonel James Selkirk was going to get the shock of his life over the next days as he lived a life in a saddle and under the stars. His days of soft beds and fine meals were a thing of the past. I had seen, when I had rescued him from Antibes, that he was not a man who endured hardship well.

"Hmm. Well, we had better get moving. Bonaparte has a head start on us, you know!"

He was beginning to get under my skin already. I knew exactly how much of a lead he had for I had been at the battle and not skulking in Brussels. I held my tongue. There was little point in losing my temper with him this early in the mission. "We will catch him. Never fear."

"You seem damned confident..."

"Colonel, you said time was of the essence. Let us get this monster caught and then I can get back to Sicily." I turned to Alan. "You have plenty of money Alan. I will return here and..."

"Sir, why don't I meet you in Calais? I think I can ride, and it means I might be able to contact Captain Robinson and get a ship for us."

"Are you certain?"

He laughed, "It is better than sitting on my backside doing nothing here, sir. Besides, it will give me the chance to get to know Wolf. I will take it easy, I promise."

"Very well then. I shall meet you in Calais. Come along Colonel. Time is wasting!"

I mounted quickly. I did it partly to get things started but I wanted to surprise my injured leg. It worked. It did not hurt half as much as I had expected. I knew where the cavalrymen were bivouacked and I was anxious to get there before they left for Paris. The Colonel was not a great rider and he struggled to keep pace with me. I almost laughed; I had been wounded and yet I was more mobile than this desk-bound officer who fought his wars from the comfort of an office and through the eyes and arms of young officers. I remembered the trouble I had put up with when I had rescued him from Antibes.

"Steady on, Robbie."

"I need to find the squadron before they leave, sir. The best will be sent first."

"The best?"

"The best light cavalry!"

"Any will do, you know. Boney is beaten. We have to catch him before he goes to ground."

"Which shows how little you know both him and his men. They will still be with him and he does not know he is beaten yet. He still thinks he can win this war." I saw from the colonel's face that he disagreed.

I headed for the camp of the 10th Hussars. I knew that they would be keen to avenge the loss of their commanding officer and I had liked the way that they followed him even though they knew that it was futile. I had served with them in Spain and they knew me. We rode into a sombre camp. I knew that many would be sleeping but those who were up and about were like the walking dead. They moved listlessly and there was none of the happy banter you normally found amongst the troopers of Light Horse. I found the senior troop sergeant. "Where is the new commanding officer?"

"New sir?" His eyes narrowed and then he stood ramrod straight and saluted. "Sorry, sir. I didn't recognise you. You were the officer who was there when..."

"Yes quite."

"Come with me, sir. We haven't yet got used to the loss of the Colonel. He was a popular man."

"I am sorry too, sergeant. That was a little insensitive of me. My apologies."

He led us to a large tent. There were half a dozen officers lounging within. The air was thick with cigar smoke. All but two of the officers looked to be carrying wounds. Colonel Selkirk was, like me, out of uniform but they recognised me. The captain with his arm in a sling said, "Colonel Matthews, of the 11th Light Dragoons, isn't it?" I nodded, "You were the Johnny who was giving orders last night; Wellington's aide."

"Yes, Captain. I witnessed your heroic charge."

He downed his drink in one. "Yes, it wasn't the brightest thing we have ever done. The trouble was we had been sat on our arses all day watching everyone else do something brave and glorious and Major Howard was determined to show them that we were made of the right stuff too!" He banged his glass down hard onto the table.

"There is little point in lamenting what you cannot change, Captain. I daresay your regiment will be moving with the army first but I am here on Sir Arthur's orders." Everyone suddenly became interested. "This is Colonel Selkirk and he and I have been charged with a delicate mission. I need a troop for a task, I know it will not have a full complement of troopers, but they need to be sound fellows." I paused, "They will be under my command."

I glanced and saw the outraged look Colonel Selkirk gave me. I would speak to him later. No matter what he said or thought this would be my mission. He was a desk officer. I would command for I had been leading men into action for twenty years. My career had ended the moment the battle had. This was personal. This was the end of my story. The colonel would be useful but that was all.

The young officers all jumped up.

"Captain, a word in private." Once outside the tent, I said, "I need a reliable officer to lead the troop and the best sergeant you have left. I do not want a glory hunter. It can be an ensign or a cornet if you wish. But the troop sergeant and the men must be the most dependable that you have." I lowered my voice. "We are going to capture Boney!"

His face lit up. "Damn this arm. I would love to be there to capture the beast!"

"However you can't so who would be a good substitute for you?"

"Lieutenant Howard." I gave him a quizzical look. He nodded, "Yes, the Major's younger brother," he held up a hand. "Before you say anything, George is my first choice. He is not a glory hunter and the men would follow him to hell and back. Besides his troop has the most troopers on roll. I told you he is sound. He salvaged more of his men last night than any of us. Perhaps that tells you more of his composure. You were there. You saw."

"Then he is my man. Would you like to tell him?"

"Yes sir. Er, how long will they be detached?"

"Just until we catch Bonaparte."

He put his head in, "Johnny, I have a task for you." He put his head close to the Lieutenant's and I saw the beaming smile on the officer's face as he was told that he was to be detached.

The young officer before me looked like a younger version of the man whose head had been caved in the night before. I held out my hand, "Pleased to meet you. Get your troop. We will be living rough so make sure you have spares of anything we might need but we will be travelling fast. You will need sound horses. If you think any might be carrying injuries, then change them."

He nodded and his face was calm. At that moment I knew that he was the right choice. "Do you mind me asking the mission, sir?"

"When we are on the road then I will tell you."

Colonel Selkirk finally boiled, "For God's sake hurry up man! We have wasted enough time here already. We have no time for pleasantries!"

I nodded to the Lieutenant who scurried off. The captain gave me a smile and said, "I look forward to hearing Johnny's stories when he returns." He shook my hand, "Glad to have met you, Colonel. And thank you for what you did last night and," he nodded at the departing Lieutenant, "now. It will help everyone."

I put my arm around the colonel and led him out of earshot, "Matthews, what the hell are you doing?"

"Let us get one thing clear Colonel, I am in command. You may think that you outrank me, but we are going into dangerous places and your experience is sending others to do your dirty work. I am the cavalryman, and I will command. I am not going to jeopardise young Howard and his men for you. You have no hold over me any longer. I have ended the lives of enough people on your command. It is easy killing senior officers."

He paled, "Robbie! Is that a threat?"

"Colonel I thought you knew me. I do not threaten, I act. I am the dog that you trained. Perhaps you regret it now?"

He shook his head, "No, I have sown the breeze and now I must harvest the whirlwind. You are right Robbie. You do not even need me."

"Yes, I do for when I capture him, I hand him over to you and then I go home. That instant! I have wasted enough of my life either fighting for him or against him. I want to make sure he is sent somewhere where he can do no more harm."

We returned to our horses and mounted. We did not have long to wait. There were eighteen troopers and a troop sergeant. Lieutenant Howard said, "All the men have the supplies they need and they have carbines, powder and ball." I nodded my approval. "This is Troop Sergeant Joe Gargery."

"Good to have you with us, Sergeant. This is Colonel Selkirk and I am Lieutenant Colonel Matthews. When we get on the road I will brief you, but this is a delicate task; at the moment that is all that you need to know..."

We rode down towards Mont St. Jean. The battlefield was still filled with the wounded who had yet to be collected and there were some of the locals scavenging already. I waited until we were at La Belle Alliance before I spoke. The dead horses of their regiment were still there as well as the dead Imperial Guards. I wanted them in their mind when I spoke. "Gather round in a circle."

When they had done so I looked at each of them in turn, studying the faces of the men I would be leading for the next few days. I needed to rely on them as I would not have the luxury of growing to know them. I would have to take the Captain's word on trust. "We are going after Napoleon Bonaparte." I was pleased with the lack of histrionics from them although I saw that they were both surprised and pleased. "It seems that the Prussians want him too but the Marquess of Wellington has charged us with his capture. We want him alive and the Prussians want him dead." I turned to Colonel Selkirk. "And the Colonel here is with us to ensure that he goes where Sir Arthur intends."

He nodded. He gave one of his dramatic pauses. "He is to be sent to a remote island in the middle of the Atlantic."

"So you can see that this is important. He has a start on us, but we will find him. He will head to Paris first. That may be dangerous. We are still at war with France but your uniforms look vaguely French. It is one of the many reasons I chose your regiment. We need to be on our guard. Listen for my commands. If I say run, then do not hesitate. If I say fight, then do so as though your life depended upon it. It probably will."

Lieutenant Howard asked, "And if the Prussians object to what we intend?"

I paused and, after looking at the Colonel said, "Then I will deal with them. You need not fear for your career, Lieutenant, you will be acting under my orders and the Colonel here will see that no blame is attached to any of you. Now we have a long way to go. Let us ride."

I avoided Genappe. It was a town with narrow streets and the road was already thronged with refugees and retreating soldiers. I led the troop across country. When the colonel saw that I intended to ford the river he paled. The young troopers smiled as he went into the water gingerly. I held my pistols up as we crossed. I did not want wet powder. Luckily, it was both shallow and narrow. The horse did not even have to swim. I remembered swimming the Douro. That was hairy!

The crossroads at Quatre Bras was a depressing scene. The fields were still covered in bodies. It was hard to tell if they were French, Dutch or British for they were all naked. The locals had fallen upon them as though they were carrion. Now that the humans had finished then the crows, magpies, rats, and foxes were feasting. They scattered as we clattered along the cobbles. It had a sobering effect on both the colonel and the troopers. I think the sergeant had seen it all before. I just said, "The aftermath of war is even worse than the participation." We rode hard and were well south of Laon when I ordered a camp.

Troop Sergeant Gargery was as efficient as I had expected him to be and the camp was laid out in fifteen minutes. We had shunned tents. They were too much weight. We would sleep beneath our heavy cloaks and hope that it did not rain. While the designated troopers cooked, I went to Pierre and groomed him and then gave him an apple. The sergeant found me there.

"This is rare sir, an officer who looks after his own horse."

"Do not let my rank and my clothes fool you, sergeant. I grew up on a farm and I was a working lad."

"I have heard of you, Colonel Matthews. You were the officer attached to Sir Moore during the retreat to Corunna. You were there when the 15th held the Ebro." I nodded. "And I saw you at the battle yesterday when the major was murdered. You are not an ordinary officer are you, sir?"

"Is anyone an ordinary officer? I think everyone from the privates to the generals showed yesterday that they were capable of the most extraordinary things."

"Well, sir, I am proud to serve with you and you can rely on me and the lads." He leaned in, "By the way, sir, Lieutenant Howard is the best officer in the regiment and that included his brother, the Major. Just so you know."

We set piquets for we knew that there were bands of soldiers wandering the countryside. Our horses were as valuable as gold. I rolled into my cloak. After just three hours of sleep the night before I needed no inducement to drift into the arms of Morpheus. Just before I closed my eyes I smiled as I watched the Colonel trying to get comfortable on the hard ground. This was not what the spymaster was used to. It made my sleep even better knowing that he was suffering although my leg complained before it allowed me to drift off.

The sergeant woke me with a mug of hot black tea. "We have no milk, sir."

"Not to worry, sergeant, this will do. I think we will all have to get used to even shorter rations than hitherto."

The troopers were up and about. This was what they did every day and was their routine. The Colonel lay on his back, snoring. Lieutenant Howard joined me with his own mug of tea. He nodded to the colonel. "I take it the colonel is not used to this sort of thing, sir?"

I smiled, "No, Colonel Selkirk normally conducts his war from Whitehall. "

He nodded and I led us towards the horses which were being saddled even as we approached. "How are we going to pull this off, Colonel? I am not afraid of what we are going to do, I am excited but every French soldier is going to try to be as close to the Emperor as he can get. How can we even get past them and survive? I mean we are going into Paris. It is the French capital."

"Confidence."

"Confidence?"

"You and the troop must act as though you are French and have every right to be there."

"But we are English Hussars!"

I chuckled, "You will not believe the number of times French and English cavalry have been mistaken for one another. I told you that was the main reason I chose your regiment. You have the Colpack. Your facings are blue. You look like the elite company of the French 6th Hussars. When we ride through the streets of Paris your men will ride ramrod straight and not even think of speaking. Anyone who sees them will assume that you are a martinet and a good officer."

"But what if someone speaks to us?"

"Then I will answer. Do not worry, Lieutenant, I have done this sort of thing before. Normally I did it alone or with one companion so having such fine troopers around me is even better. What I will do is teach you a few words in French and you can teach your men. "He cocked his head. "Just the commands. It will add to the illusion."

"We were taught a little French at school, sir."

"Excellent then this will be easy." I threw away the dregs of my tea. "Come, let us awaken the sleeping beauty."

The troopers liked the idea of masquerading as French soldiers. I did not like to tell them that their lack of pigtails and moustaches made them look a little less like the French than they might have hoped.

Whenever we spied other horsemen in the distance, we left the road and rode across country. That was where the colonel became useful. He had brought maps of the area with him and we used smaller back lanes and tracks to avoid horsemen. Frequently it saved us time. We were now catching up with those who had fled the field first. These were not the wounded and maimed we had seen at Genappe and Charleroi. These were fit men who had broken. The battalions we did not see were the Imperial Guards. I knew that Bonaparte would still have any of the Polish Lancers and the Chasseur à Cheval of the Guard who survived around him. They would be the problem we would have to overcome.

As evening on the second day, the 21st of June approached, I knew that we were not far from Paris. We left the road and found an abandoned farm. There were many such buildings in France. Bonaparte's conscription had decimated the land and whole families had perished. The men had been taken by war and the women had been forced to the cities to make a living there.

It meant that we had a roof over our heads. While the food was being prepared Lieutenant Howard and Colonel Selkirk sat around the table with me and we studied the map. My leg was aching from the ride and I stretched it out to the side.

The colonel lit a cigar and sat back in his chair. "Robbie, you know Bonaparte better than anyone, what will he do?"

I saw Lieutenant Howard's raised eyebrows. When this was over, I might tell him but for the present, we all needed to focus on getting inside the mind of Bonaparte.

"He will think he can still fight. He always believes that he can defeat anyone. He was certain that he could defeat Sir Arthur. What he doesn't know is exactly how many men are coming for him. Do you, Colonel?"

He nodded, "Roughly? Yes. The Russians are bringing over a hundred and fifty thousand men. The Austrians have another hundred thousand. The British and the Prussians even with the losses at Waterloo can muster at least sixty thousand. "

"And Boney will only have the hundred and fifty thousand National Guard in addition to any remnants he can scour from those who survived the slaughter. It will take him no more than a couple of days to discover that." Colonel Selkirk, for all that he was an annoying man, had a mind like a steel trap.

I leaned back and closed my eyes. What would he do then? When he had been in Egypt, he had been able to flee back to France when he was in danger. Where would he go now?

"Surely, sir, he will just give himself up."

I opened my eyes, "In normal circumstances, Lieutenant, he would. He would return to Elba and dream and plot of glory again, but the Prussians have said that they want him dead. He will be hoping to return again as he did from Elba. He cannot do that if he is dead." I looked at the map. "Fontainebleau. He will go there."

The colonel gave me a curious look. "Why?"

"Because it is to the south-west of Paris and on the way to the coast. He stayed there first when he came north. It gives him the chance to head for a port and take ship somewhere."

Colonel Selkirk smiled, "Of course. You spotted him there!"

The young lieutenant looked mystified, "But where will he go?"

"The world is wide and there are French colonies with garrisons upon them. Any one of them might give him a safe haven. His problem will be a ship."

The colonel was on his feet. This was his kind of game. He liked getting into the mind of an opponent. He waved a hand across the Channel ports. "We can rule those out."

"I agree they would be too close to us and, more importantly, the Prussians." I jabbed my finger at the map. "The Vendee. He has sent an army there to suppress the Royalists and there are a couple of ports, La Rochelle and Rochefort. If he can lay his hands on some transports, he could even take many of the men with him."

"And there is always Ireland."

The colonel was correct. There was always a threat of a French landing in Ireland. The Irish did not like their English landlords and would jump at the chance to join the Emperor and drive them from their land.

I was satisfied, "Then we miss out Paris. You ride around to Fontainebleau and wait for him there."

The colonel's eyes narrowed, "You said '*you*' Robbie. What do you intend?"

"I will go to Paris and see what I can discover. Travelling alone I can go faster and be unobserved." I smiled at the colonel. "I am sure that the two of you can read a map, eh colonel?"

Chapter 19

I left before dawn and joined the trail of other soldiers heading for Paris. I had told the colonel and the lieutenant of the abandoned farmhouse close to Fontainebleau. I was confident that they would be able to hide there safely until I arrived. Once on the road, I just listened. I kept my head down and listened to the grumblings and the gossip. Bonaparte was not far ahead of me and was heading for Paris. I heard rumours of allies coming from across the sea; America would come to aid France. The Turks would attack Russia and become France's allies. All of them were false. The rumour that he was calling to arms every able-bodied man to fight the tyranny of the invader, however, was true. That was a reality. The Emperor had not given up. The lie that the invader was doing so to conquer France was typical of the hypocrite that was Bonaparte.

The press of men and horses on the road meant that it took me all day to reach Paris. If I had pushed my way through, then I would have attracted a great deal of attention. I needed anonymity. There were soldiers in amongst the refugees heading south and they might remember Wellington's aide for I had been in the thick of the action all day. It was a journey of only a few miles but it seemed to take forever.

I made directly for the inn which was close to the British embassy. I counted on the fact that I had paid the owner well and he might remember the Italian businessman. He did and I was able to stable my horse. Of course, the prices had gone up dramatically. I would have expected no less but it mattered not. The hunt was almost up. My prey was close by.

As I wandered the gossip-filled streets I wondered if the Prussians were not right. Perhaps an execution might solve the problem for the world. So long as Napoleon lived then the threat of war would remain. It came to me as I passed the old Louvre Palace. It would not be an execution but an assassination. I would kill the Emperor. All that I needed to do was to get close to him. It was possible that I might even survive but I doubted it. There would be fanatics around him who would fall upon me when the deed was done but I knew that I could get close. I had done so before. My death would be insignificant and would not affect the world. My affairs were in order. My wife and son would inherit my ships and my money. Alan and Cesar would both become richer men.

That gave me satisfaction. I had a reason to live. I had a wife and a family. There would be a new child soon and I had done enough in my time on earth of which I could be proud. That would be my legacy. Most of the men with whom I had fought were now dead. Perhaps Captain Macgregor, Monique and Julian might shed a tear but few others would remember me. Thus resolved I headed back for the hotel. All that I needed was to find the Emperor and then stalk him until a suitable opportunity for assassination arose. Of course, I would be disobeying my orders and doing the opposite of what Sir Arthur intended but I owed it to the dead.

I woke early on the 22nd of June and headed into the streets of Paris. I knew that Bonaparte could be anywhere. I was not looking for him. I was looking for his Guards. I headed for the Louvre. There were National Guardsmen on duty and the tricolour still flew but it was not the Imperial Guard who watched there. He was not present. I headed to the Seine following a crowd who seemed to be making for the Chamber of Deputies. I saw a huge crowd outside the Chamber of Deputies, a flash of red, lances with guidons and horses. The Lancers were there.

I made my way to the left bank of the mighty Seine. There were many civilians in the huge crowd but there were even more who wore uniforms. The Lancers and the Chasseur à Cheval of the Guard formed a cordon at the foot of the steps. No one could approach any closer. I joined the throng and listened. It soon became obvious that Bonaparte was trying to get the Deputies to back his demand for conscription. It was as I had feared. He was keen to continue the war. The views of the crowd were mixed. The old soldiers wanted war but the civilians had had enough. They wanted peace and prosperity even if it meant a return to the Bourbons. I suspected that it would be the same inside. Bonaparte was a powerful orator, he might be able to swing the politicians to his side.

I felt a tap on my shoulder. My left hand was on my stiletto even as I turned. It was Pierre-Francois. He smiled, "A little jumpy, Robbie. I see you survived the battle then?"

I tapped my left leg, "Just. And what brings you here? No students today?"

"They are all here. They would be the ones conscripted if Bonaparte has his way. I had no work and I thought I would come to hear the lies of the Little Corporal!"

A grenadier of the line turned aggressively with a bunched fist ready, "Do not disparage the Emperor!"

I stepped between them and stared into his eyes. "This man lost an arm fighting for the Emperor I think that gives him the right to be familiar."

The old soldier saw that Pierre-Francois had but one arm. He turned his attention and wrath on me. "You seem healthy enough! Why do you not fight!"

I pulled my coat back to reveal my pistols. "I can fight when I choose and I too fought for the Emperor. Go away now before I decide to do something about it. The world will not miss one less loudmouth."

He leaned forward and he glowered at me. I had dressed down aggressive soldiers before and I continued my stare. He must have recognised that I meant what I said, and he snorted, "You are probably a donkey walloper anyway and I will not waste my time with you." He stormed off.

Pierre-Francois laughed, "I see you are still as belligerent as ever."

"Only when I need to be. So, what do you make of this?"

"The Emperor is finished. There is no appetite for war. Do you know he had a victory speech printed out stating that he was in Brussels before he even left to fight his battles? Arrogance! He has no credibility. He had skills in war once but no more and the Deputies will refuse his request. He will leave."

I lowered my voice, "And what will he do next? Go to Versailles? Fontainebleau?"

"No, my friend. If he fails today, then he will have to hide." He pondered the question I had posed. I waited patiently. Pierre-Francois had a mind like a steel trap, and he was sifting through all that he had heard over the past few days since the news of the battle had reached Paris. "He will probably go to Malmaison."

"Malmaison?"

"The house he gave to Josephine. She died last year, and the house has been empty ever since. It is on the western side of Paris and he could flee to the west if the Prussians we hear are hunting him come to Paris." He smiled at me and said quietly, "If I were a gambling man..."

"But you are Pierre-Francois!"

He laughed, "True. Then I would bet a few golden Louis that he would go to America. They still like him I think. He has never ruled them. He just sold them half of their country. Yes, he might go there. Who knows that might solve the world's problems. He could try to become President!"

But first, he will find somewhere here in France to plan and to organise. Malmaison, Robbie."

That made perfect sense and I had sent my troopers fifty miles south of there. I pointed to the doors, they were opened, and Bonaparte stormed out. "I am thinking he did not get what he wanted."

"No, and if he heads west then he is going to Malmaison." He gave me a perceptive look. "Where you will follow him."

"Where I will follow him." I knew then that my fantasy of ending his life was gone, evaporated like a morning fog. There were simply too many men around him to contemplate such an action.

"Your destinies were ever entwined. I wish you luck but more than that I wish you a long life. You deserve it." I shook his good hand. As the escort and the Emperor clattered northwest Pierre-Francois nodded. "See."

Just then a group of politicians came out. They held their hands up and gradually the crowd was silenced. One of them held up a piece of paper. He shouted, "Emperor Napoleon Bonaparte has abdicated in favour of...."

We heard no more for the crowd heard the keywords; the Emperor had abdicated. There was joy unabated for those who wanted no war and despair for the old soldiers who wanted the war to continue. For me, it meant I had to hurry. The Emperor was slipping away.

"Farewell, my friend. I must ride once more."

I almost ran back through the crowds which thronged the bridges. It took me longer than I had hoped. Upon reaching the hotel I paid my bill and galloped south. I prayed that I could get to the others quickly and we would be in time to find Bonaparte. I knew where Bonaparte was heading now but if he left Malmaison before I returned it would be like looking for a needle in a haystack.

I reached the forest and dismounted to lead a weary Pierre to the farmhouse. My horse had ridden nonstop. It was almost dark, and I did not wish to risk my exhausted horse breaking a leg. It also gave me time to think. Malmaison was just outside Paris. In many ways, it would be easier to take the Emperor there for it was small. Fontainebleau was a huge palace. However, there would be nowhere for my troopers to hide and watch. It was a puzzle. Perhaps I would need Colonel Selkirk's advice and I knew that would please him.

I had always been able to move quietly. Even with a painful and aching leg, I could manage it. I smelled the smoke of the clay pipe before

I saw the trooper. They had found the farmhouse and set sentries. Sadly the two troopers were facing the wrong direction. I drew a pistol and walked up to the two Hussars whose backs were to me. I pushed the pistol in the back of one of them and said, in French, "Hands up!"

They both turned, startled. Relief flooded their faces when they recognised me. "Oh, it's you, sir. You fair gave us both a turn then."

I holstered my pistol. "If you are on watch then watch." I pointed into the forest. "That way!"

"Sir!"

Sergeant Gargery had observed the last part of the conversation. He shook his head, "Dozy lumps! I'll have a word." He waved his hand at the farmhouse. "Nice little billet this. How did you come across it, sir?"

I smiled enigmatically, "By accident. But don't get too attached to it, Sergeant. We leave in the morning and we are heading north."

"Righto, sir. Thanks for telling me."

I filled in the Colonel and the Lieutenant. "So, Colonel Selkirk, any ideas about how we can spirit Bonaparte away from his two squadrons of bodyguards?"

He lit a cigar. "How many did you say there were?"

"I counted twenty Lancers and twenty-five Chasseurs. But we don't know how many were guarding his house."

"It doesn't matter. Those are the forty-five we have to deal with." He glanced at Lieutenant Howard. "Your men may be good, Howard, but I can't see them taking twice their number of Imperial Guard, can you?"

The young officer showed his worth as he shook his head. "No sir."

I went to the pot and ladled some of the stew into a bowl. I was starving. "Then we will have to resort to subterfuge. We will need to whittle down their numbers."

While we ate, we pored over the maps that the colonel had brought. He was proving more useful than I had anticipated. "Look, Robbie. There is a forest here and it is within a few hundred yards of the village. We could hide there."

"Colonel Selkirk is right, sir. It is worth a look anyway."

It took most of the next day to reach the north-western outskirts of Paris. We could not risk riding through Paris, and we went the long way round. Paris proper was a few miles away, but a straggle of houses lined the road which led from Porte Dauphin to Malmaison. The Bois de Boulogne was to the east and the Forest of Malmaison to the south. After a cursory inspection, we chose the latter for our base. It was close enough to watch the house and yet large enough to hide twenty odd men and horses.

Leaving Troop Sergeant Gargery to set up a camp I rode with my two colleagues to scout out the house. It was dark as we rode along the main street. I only knew, vaguely, where it was. Bonaparte had bought it and given it to Josephine for romantic trysts. It was large enough to suit his ego and discreet enough to be away from prying eyes. The two Imperial Chasseurs whom we saw outside the largest house in the village were a good indicator of where Bonaparte was living. We found a side street and we dismounted. The house itself was isolated. Bonaparte had made sure that his neighbours were far from his fences. "Lieutenant, you watch the horses." I was about to turn away and then I said, "Have a primed pistol ready."

"Sir."

He looked guilty and I said, "Load it now, Lieutenant, and always keep a loaded pistol. I am guessing that the men's carbines are also not kept loaded?"

"No sir. My brother preferred us to use our sabres."

That explained a great deal and was not unusual. "When we get back have them clean and load their weapons. We will be needing them."

Colonel Selkirk smiled as we began to stroll down the tree-lined street. "This is the first time I have seen you command, Robbie. Impressive. You are born to it. You ought to stay in the service."

"No, thank you, Colonel. I have seen enough death to last me two lifetimes. And now we speak in French, or Italian; whichever you prefer."

He began to speak in Italian. "What do we do?"

"Walk down the street as though we have every right to be here. We are Italian businessmen visiting the city with a view to trading and this looks like a nice place to buy a house."

He nodded, "And what are we doing here?"

"Not only do we wish a home here we are also curious about the home of the fabulously beautiful Josephine Beauharnais and we will be surprised at the guards for we thought the Emperor was at one of his palaces and that the house was deserted."

"Can we speak French?"

"I can but they will hear your Scottish accent. You stick to Italian."

I was observing the house surreptitiously all the way along the street. I saw the two guards cocking their carbines as we approached. They stared at us as we approached. It was natural and to be expected. I detected a strong smell of horse manure. The mounts of the Imperial Guard were nearby. As I could not see them then I assumed that they were at the rear. That might prove a vital piece of information.

As we neared them and I saw their musketoons rise I began to jabber in Italian. "Which is her house do you think?"

It took a moment or two for the Colonel to realise what I was doing and then he pointed and said, "It must be the large one."

The Brigadier levelled his musketoon at me. I feigned shock. "This is a prohibited area." The Colonel excelled himself. He gave no sign that he had understood their words. He just looked confused.

I looked around as though seeking a sign and I spoke in French, "Prohibited? I thought this was the home of Josephine, the former wife of the Emperor."

The Chasseur relaxed a little and the barrel lowered to aim at my knee. "It was but it is now prohibited to all civilians. Go away!"

I turned to the Colonel and spoke in Italian, "He says we cannot go beyond this house."

"What a pity."

I smiled at the Chasseur. "Is it permitted for us to walk along the other side of the street? We are walking off a rather fine dinner."

He shrugged and gestured for us to cross the street. I heard him say to his friend, "Damned Italians! Not worth piss in a fight!"

We continued our walk and our inane chatter which would confirm the Chasseur's view of us. All the time I was looking at the house. Our scrutiny would now be understood by the Guards and they would not be suspicious of two curious visitors. I saw that the shutters were closed. The large double gate which led to the rear was also closed. He would need to use that for his carriage. It was as if no one was in the house. However, I did glimpse, between the trees and the bushes, red and green in the light from the torches burning at the rear. The Guards had a camp there. I could hear horses and I caught the faint whiff of pipe tobacco. I guessed that there would be guards behind the doors too. This would be tricky.

We took a street to walk down to the river and then back along so that we would not have to pass the house again. It took us almost an hour to return to the Lieutenant. I sensed his relief when he saw us. "I thought you had been captured."

"No, but we learned much. And you? Did you have to try your French?"

"Just *'Good Evening'* when two men rode along the road."

We mounted and rode back to the forest. The next morning I cantered down the street towards the river. I had a feeling that they would be different sentries, but I changed my jacket in case I had been described. It was the same as the previous night: the shutters and the doors were closed. However, I could see smoke rising from the chimney which confirmed that there were people in the house. It had to be Bonaparte although at the back of my mind was a nagging doubt that he was elsewhere. We needed more intelligence. If he was not inside, then we were wasting our time. I was going on Pierre-Francois' word and the presence of Chasseurs. They may have been decoys.

I made a decision at lunchtime. "The Colonel and I need to go into Paris again and see if there is any news. We need information."

The Lieutenant asked, "Could we not break into the grounds? We could confirm his presence."

"That is a possibility however it might scare Bonaparte away and we need him to move while we are watching. We will leave that as a last resort. I think he will stay there yet. While I am gone, lieutenant, find out if any of your men have experience of hunting."

"Hunting?"

"Yes Lieutenant, I have an idea of how we can keep a closer watch on our prey."

We did not travel into the heart of Paris. We found a bar close to the Porte de Dauphin. We sat outside at an end table. Once we spoke in Italian we were ignored, and we heard little snippets of information. After an hour we were able to return to the camp. We had one stop to make at a shop which sold working men's clothes.

I gathered all of the men, save for the sentries, around us. They needed as much information as we had. "Bonaparte has abdicated in favour of his son. I am not certain that makes a great deal of difference. There is a rumour that he is either at Malmaison or he has left the country. I do not think it is the latter. The bad news is that the Prussians are rushing towards Paris and they have sent Hussars to look for and apprehend the Emperor. We cannot allow that to happen." I saw them digesting the information and then nodding. "Now then, Lieutenant, any hunters amongst your troopers?"

211

"Yes sir, Troop Sergeant Gargery and Trooper Jennings were both countrymen."

I looked at the two of them, "Poachers or gamekeepers?"

Trooper Jennings spat, "Gamekeepers indeed!"

The other troopers laughed.

"Then you have answered me. Tomorrow night the three of us will enter the grounds of Malmaison. However, to make sure we do so without arousing suspicion, I have brought some clothes to use as disguises. In the morning I want you, lieutenant, to take one of your men and walk from here to the river. Walk on the opposite side of the road from the house. Look as though you are heading back to the country having failed to find work in the city. Trudge! You will find the river if you walk far enough and you just loop around. If they ask you are both looking for work. You can wear your overalls which will show them that you were soldiers once. We saw many old soldiers either looking for work or begging. I do not think that they will question you. Keep your head down and if they speak to you then avoid eye contact." I watched his face as I asked, "Is that all right with you?"

He grinned, "I'll say. This is more fun than piquet duty."

"Yes, but a damned sight more dangerous." I turned to the others. "If any of you sees or hears the Prussians then the Colonel and I need to know immediately! If they are here, then we will not have the luxury of time. We will need to act quickly and decisively and that may mean we will have to bloody our hands. Do not hesitate!"

The next morning I was aware that Lieutenant Howard was becoming increasingly nervous. I took him to one side. "Be confident, Johnny. Do not put yourself in danger. If there are no guards then come directly back. Look for smoke from the chimney. See if the shutters are open or closed. You are looking for little details."

He nodded, "Yes sir. I am not afraid it is just, well I don't want to let you or the chaps down."

"You won't."

They were back by eleven and they looked relieved. "There were two Polish Lancers on duty, sir, and smoke was coming from the chimney. The shutters were closed."

"Good, anything else?"

The trooper said, "Yes sir. Horse shit! It stunk! There are horses there all right. And I think I caught a glimpse of a carriage. I can't be certain though. It might just have been a posh wagon." The faint whiff I had had was now confirmed and the presence of a carriage meant that I was now certain that the Emperor was within.

The sergeant and the trooper who were to come with me were ready before dark. None of us wore jackets. They had both fashioned themselves a club. I had told them to leave guns behind. I did not want a gun going off as we clambered through the undergrowth. We were going to observe. I also told them to leave their swords. They would only get in the way. I had my stiletto with me, and my leather pouch filled with sand. It had never let me down. As we left, I suddenly missed Sharp. I had no doubt that these were both fine fellows, but I did not know them. I was used to Alan watching my back. Would they hesitate? Would I hesitate for fear of a mistake they might make? Only time would tell.

Before we left, I asked, "Trooper Jennings, what is your name?"

He looked confused, "Your first name, you dozy man!" Joe Gargery shook his head.

"Tom sir."

"Right then tonight if we have to talk then we use first names. I am Robbie. I don't want them to know we are soldiers. A 'sir' gives it away. Ideally, we will not talk. But if we have to then do not use rank. Watch my hands and I will signal what I want you to do. You two are here to watch my back!"

I had noticed that there was a high wall all around Malmaison. It explained why they concentrated the guards on the front. The high walls secured the rest of the grounds. We entered from the house to the right. While the trooper held his hands for my foot I sprang to the top of the high wall. I reached down and pulled Joe Gargery up. The two of us were able to pull Tom, who was a big man, up to the top.

I took the time to scan the gardens and the grounds. I could see the horse lines. There were just thirty-five horses. That, in itself, was interesting. They had a couple of Chasseurs with musketoons patrolling the interior walls, but it looked to be a token gesture.

We slipped down into the bushes and the undergrowth. They had been planted for aesthetic reasons but the grounds looked to have been neglected since the death of Josephine and they were somewhat overgrown. I moved forward about twenty paces and checked that there were no guards in the vicinity and then I waved the other two forward. I had my stiletto ready but there was no apparent danger. There was a large lawn and I headed for the edge of it. The grounds were lit by burning torches. We were hidden by the overgrown bushes and shrubs. I waved the other two to lie down as I did. I saw a group sat around a table close to the house. There were candles and oil lamps lighting it. I recognised a couple of generals, but Ney was not present and I saw no one of the rank of Marshal. I wondered if the Emperor had been abandoned or had the Marshals who had followed him been taken. It was largely irrelevant. Without the head of the snake, the beast was impotent. We now knew the numbers. I still had the nagging fear that Bonaparte had gone elsewhere. I waited.

I felt relief as I watched Napoleon Bonaparte emerge from the house. He seemed shrunken somehow. That may have been because of the tall lancers who flanked him. He was still here. He had not fled. That, however, did not help me for there were far too many guards and senior officers present. I would not sacrifice the 10th Hussars in a vain attempt to capture him; he was not worth one of their lives.

He sat at the table and I saw but could not hear the heated debate which ensued. One of the officers, I think it was Count Pajol the cavalryman, suddenly stood and stormed off. I could see others imploring him to come back but he mounted his horse and left. I saw that he left through another gate at the rear. That was a vital piece of information. There was a second entrance to the house. We had not known that, and I had assumed that he would leave by the front. We would need to find out where the rear gate was.

I had seen enough. I waved the other two back towards the wall. They were both halfway to the wall when the two guards stepped out with muskets levelled. They told the sergeant and Tom to halt and I realised that they had not seen me. My two companions raised their hands. I shouted, in French, "Hit them!" Of course, neither man understood me but the two Chasseurs turned to look in the direction of the noise. Joe and Tom swung their clubs and the two guards fell to the ground. They turned to look at me and I waved them to the wall. I let them move knowing that the other guards would rush towards them.

I felt a movement from my right and instinctively, I swung my hand with the stiletto. I felt the hot blood flood across my hand as the jugular of the Frenchman was severed. I waited, for the guards operated in pairs. Sure enough, the other guard came to look for his friend. He saw the body and, at the same time, sensed me. I smacked my sand-filled leather blackjack against the side of his head and then ran to the wall. The two Hussars pulled me up as a fusillade of muskets rattled through the trees and into the wall. I rolled over the side and ran after the other two towards the forest. When we reached the eaves, we stopped to catch our breath.

Joe's shoulders shook as he laughed, "By, Colonel, but you are a rum 'un and no mistake. You know how to handle yourself."

I shrugged and clapped them both on the back, "It is how I have survived for so long. But you two did well. I could not fault your actions."

In the camp, everyone was keen to know what had happened. They had heard the shots and worried about us until we emerged from the trees. I addressed my comments to the two officers but all of them listened. They now knew they were involved. "There are four or five generals with him. There are just the thirty odd Guards although a couple less after tonight."

"Sir, why did you shout in French?"

"I wanted them to think that we were French robbers. It is why we wore rough French clothes. The Guards who survived will also tell them that. We used clubs, knives, and a blackjack. They are not the weapons of either Prussian or British soldiers. They might increase their vigilance, but they will not be worried by a couple of robbers. Now if they thought that we were English then the Emperor might flee."

When everyone had dispersed Colonel Selkirk approached me. He nodded towards an empty part of the camp where we could talk in private.

"You could go and see the Emperor yourself, Robbie. He still likes you. After all, he let you go when he could have had you killed. You might be able to persuade him to give himself up."

I shook my head. "He is now like a cornered rat and he is more likely to lash out at anyone. I have a feeling that Pajol is not the only one who has had words with him. For the first time in a long time, he can no longer just make decisions. He has to persuade people to do his bidding. He prefers to order. He will not like this. We can only hope that he has more desertions and then we have the chance to grab him."

I saw the disappointment on the Colonel's face, "I thought that we might end it sooner rather than later."

I laughed, "Tired of sleeping on the ground eh, Colonel?"

"You and the others are used to it. This life is not for me."

"When this is over will you retire too?"

He shook his head, "No, I shall go back to my cubby hole. There are always enemies. I shall continue to fight them."

Chapter 20

We continued to watch for a crack in the defences of Malmaison. Over the next two days, we took it in turns to monitor the comings and goings of the occupants of Bonaparte's last refuge. So long as the large doors which led to the interior remained closed and the Chasseurs remained on guard then we knew that the Emperor had not left.

It was late on the afternoon of the final day in June when we heard the fusillade. We were close enough to the house to know that there was a battle going on there.

"Fetch your carbines. Sergeant, leave two men to watch the camp. I want every horse saddling in case we have to leave in a hurry. Colonel, you had better stay here with the two sentries. Use your maps to find us a route to the coast. It may come in handy"

I thought he might argue but then he looked at the young troopers eagerly preparing for war and he knew that he would only be a hindrance. "I can help them to saddle the horses, at least."

It took us just six minutes to run down the familiar trails to reach the road. When we emerged from the forest we saw that it was the Prussians who had found the Emperor and were attacking the house. The front of the house was wreathed in the smoke of muskets and pistols. We could hear the clash of steel on steel and the cries of those who were struck. I saw horses and guessed that this was a small troop such as we.

"Lieutenant, form a skirmish line. Try to avoid actually killing any of our allies but I want none of your troopers hurt."

"You heard the Colonel!"

Troop Sergeant Gargery growled, "And any man as gets himself killed will have me to answer to!"

"Sergeant, deal with the horse holders!"

There were four horse holders and they were busy watching the house. All four were clubbed unconscious to the ground. "Disarm them and send their horses away."

The horses' rumps were slapped, and the horses raced along the street. They would reach the river and stop to drink. It was in the nature of the beast.

I waved my sword and led the troopers towards the front of the house. They fanned out on either side of me. The two Chasseurs who guarded the door lay dead along with four dead and wounded Prussians. One of the wounded Prussians looked up at me and asked, "Who are you?"

I answered in German, "Friends!" It was a lie, but I was beyond worrying about the morality of lies. He lay back looking relieved.

There was a cacophony of noise from inside the house. The doors leading to the interior yard were open. Again the yard was littered with the dead and those who were not long for this world. We raced through and out to the rear of the house. There was a battle going on. The Prussians had their backs to us. Ahead I could see that the French had mounted their horses. I heard a French command. It was the charge.

"Take cover!"

The troopers ducked and hid behind anything which would protect them. The lancers charged the Prussians. There were only a handful but they knew their business. I risked standing. The charge had cleared the smoke, and, to my dismay, I saw blue uniforms surrounding the carriage of the Emperor as they left by the rear exit. The Chasseurs who remained formed a rearguard and they were gone.

I turned to the Lieutenant, "Back to the horses. The Emperor has fled. There is little point in staying here. We must follow!"

I saw his mouth open with a question and then he thought better of it. "Sir! Right lads, Move!"

The troopers ran out. The last lancer was being hauled from his horse and butchered as I turned. The distraction allowed me to slip into the house unseen. I had to see if there were any maps or documents which might indicate where Bonaparte was heading.

I ran into the house stepping over the bodies of four slaughtered servants. The Prussians had been ruthless. There were signs of a struggle in the rooms but no papers. I ran upstairs. I found the room the Emperor had used. I recognised the writing case and the spartan, functional travelling desk. This was where he had been working. There was a map and Rochefort was circled. I grabbed the map. I saw another map and this one was of America. The other papers I also stuffed into my jacket. I knew where he was going. I had what I came for and I turned.

"Where are you going?" The voice came from a Prussian officer, although he was speaking French. He had a sword in his hand. "Did your Emperor forget something?" He took me for one of Bonaparte's men. "Tell me where he is going, and you may live or I could just kill you and take the map from your hand."

I drew my sword and answered, with a flourish, "You will have to rip it from my dead fingers."

He smiled, "That will not be a problem. Your famed red lancers all died and a clerk, even one with an Austrian sword, will not be a problem."

I had to end this quickly. I had no idea how many other Prussians remained in the house. I could not afford to delay. Already Bonaparte had a head start. Each moment I wasted took him further from us. It was the Prussian officer's confidence that was his undoing. In his mind, the Prussian was already standing over my dead body and reading the map. He lunged at me and I flicked the tip away and then slashed to my left. The edge ripped across his arm and I saw blood.

"That was either lucky or you are not a clerk." He frowned and doubt crossed his face.

I remained silent and I feinted towards his injured arm. He brought his own sword across to riposte me. His sabre struck empty air and my longer, Austrian sword, sliced across his side. Once more I drew blood and I saw fear cross his face. He began to swing wildly at me and I heard shouts from downstairs. I did the unexpected. I dived inside one of his wild swings and punched him with the hilt of my sword. His eyes glazed over and he fell in a heap.

I stood behind the door and shouted, in German, "Get the horses! I have the map!"

I was answered, "Yes sir!"

I stepped out of the room and headed down the stairs. Not all of the Prussians had obeyed their orders. Two remained and were coming up the stairs. Fortunately neither had drawn weapons. My shout had made them relax. I ran down the stairs and punched with my sword hilt at the trooper to my right. The soldier to my left tried to draw his sword and I shoulder charged him. He tumbled over the side of the staircase and I was past him. He lay in a crumpled heap in the hallway.

I ran out of the front door, aware that I could be pursued. I turned and, drawing a pistol, fired into the hall. I wanted them to be wary of me. Then I ran. There were only a few of the Prussian Hussars remaining and they were seeking their horses. A single civilian running down the street was not a threat. I managed, somehow, to escape unseen.

I saw anxious faces when I reached the others. Lieutenant Howard said, "Are you hurt, sir?"

"Me? No"

"There is blood!"

I laughed. "Then it is not mine." I mounted Pierre. Holding the map triumphantly I shouted. "He is heading to Rochefort. We must get there before he has time to board a ship. He is heading for America."

Colonel Selkirk asked, "Is this a gamble, Robbie?"

I held up the maps again before thrusting them into my saddlebags. "The maps tell all. He left by the rear gate. We have no way of knowing which road he might take. We have no choice. We have to get ahead of him." I shrugged, "It is my decision, Colonel."

He nodded, "Your instincts are normally impeccable. Let us ride and get this finished."

We rode until dark. There was little point in killing our horses. I also knew that, so long as Bonaparte rode in his carriage, we would be faster. In the old days, he would have had relays of horses to enable him to travel huge distances without stopping. In those days he could ride whole squadrons of escorts into the ground. That was no longer the case. He was leaving incognito and discretion was all. As we lay beneath the trees, we speculated on what the Emperor would do.

"He will have allies along the roads. I have no doubt that he would have used scouts to prepare his way. He will be protected when he rests and that will be infrequently."

"Aye, Robbie but how many men will he have left?"

"I think, sir, that there will not be many. The Colonel and I saw many dead Imperial Guards in the house."

I shook my head, "Lieutenant, no matter how many are left they are the best. Do not underestimate the Chasseurs. You do not join the Imperial Guard, you are selected. Their troopers are the sergeants of other regiments. Every guardsman outranks every other soldier. They are fiercely loyal and will happily give their lives for Bonaparte. You saw the Lancers and how they sacrificed themselves for him?"

"Yes sir, and I remember the Old Guard at Waterloo." The young lieutenant shook his head, "What a waste. Why would a man give away his life like that? It was a pointless gesture."

"Not quite how they would view it. They were fanatics. They stopped our pursuit of their Emperor so that he would be able to raise another army and return to glory."

"Except there was no glory and no new army." The Lieutenant was growing up on this mission.

"They didn't know that. When I was in Paris there were many old soldiers who were unhappy about all talk of peace."

Colonel Selkirk clearly saw the importance of what we were doing, "Then it is a damned good thing that we are going to stick him on a little rock in the middle of the Atlantic. We don't need him raising his standard again."

"Amen to that, Colonel. I am keen to get back to Sicily."

"You mean you do not wish to carry on being an officer, sir?"

"I know that you lost many friends as well as your brother at Waterloo. Imagine that but tenfold. That is how many of my friends I have lost. When I sleep at night, I am haunted by their deaths over and over again. I am just grateful that none of your troopers has been either hurt or injured. I could not bear to have them join the cohorts in my nightmares."

The Colonel stretched as he prepared to sleep, "And that is why you are unusual, Robbie. Most officers do not worry about the deaths of others. Goodnight, although I suspect we will be on the road again in a ridiculously short time." He had not become used to the ardours of camping.

We rode almost a hundred miles. It was far too many. I was worried about the horses. Apart from the few restful days at Malmaison, these animals had been kept on the go for almost four weeks. Consequently, we stopped just outside Vendome. We had thirty more miles to Tours but I was not certain what we would meet there. We might have pushed on, there was still light, but I was worried about this vital crossing of the River Cher.

Typically Colonel Selkirk was all for pushing on. The Lieutenant sided with me. "I think that the Colonel is right, sir. It would be foolish to ride these animals into the ground."

"But Bonaparte is within our grasp! We can't lose him now all for a few horses."

I saw the look of shock on Lieutenant Howard's face and I shook my head. "And we will not. He can go no faster than us. If he attempts to do so then his horses will die and thanks to his war there are precious few remounts left. Besides, Colonel, I worry about Tours. We have to get across the Cher and we have no idea who is holding that town. Are they Royalist sympathisers or part of the Corps Bonaparte sent to quell opposition hereabouts? I want our horses as fresh as they can be when we reach that bridge. We must be prepared for anything."

I also knew that the troopers needed a rest. A tired man was a liability. He could make errors of judgement which could cost lives. I went to the sergeant and the lieutenant to check the horse lines and so that I could give them instructions, out of earshot of the colonel.

"Tomorrow may be difficult. I have come to know you and your men. You are quick to learn and we shall need that attribute before this is over. The further we get from Paris the less we can predict the situation. I will be ahead of you tomorrow. I shall be alone except for Jones, the bugler. He is a good man I believe?"

Troop Sergeant Gargery nodded, "He is, sir. I would have him back me in a tricky situation."

"Good. I want you to assign two of your troopers to watch over the colonel. He is no longer young, and it is many years since he had to do anything as strenuous as this. He will need protection."

"You think there could be trouble tomorrow, sir?"

"I think we have been extremely lucky so far. We need to get across that bridge. It is the last barrier before the coast. Once we are over the Cher then we can make good time to Rochefort. We still have the River Loire to cross but Tours controls the Cher. If the bugler sounds '*charge*' then you will need to draw your sabres and ride as though the devil himself was behind you. If I sound '*forward*' then it will be safe and we just cross as though we were in Hyde Park!"

"I'll have a word with the chaps tonight sir, and I will assign two troopers."

"Thank you, sergeant."

"Thank you, sir. It is good to be taken into your confidence."

He strode off leaving me with the lieutenant. "He is right you know, sir. I have noticed that your style of command is totally different from my brother's. Oh don't get me wrong; he was a damned fine officer and a great leader, but he just expected all of us to follow him regardless of the situation. We didn't know what was in his head. Well, you saw that when he charged the square."

"The difference is, Johnny, that I came through the ranks. I was the shit shoveller who became a sergeant and then an officer. It gives me a different perspective." As I left him, I saw he was reflecting upon my words.

Tours had once been a hugely important town but that was before the revolution. Now it was a backwater. The castle dominated the town, but it was the bridge that I worried about. I saw that the tricolour was still

221

flying above the castle. That was a disturbing sign. "Jones, keep your bugle handy and listen for my command. Until I give it, I will be speaking French. Do not worry about that. I am going to try to trick any French we might encounter."

"Yes sir. I'll be listening."

There were not only National Guardsmen at the bridge there was a barrier. As we approached the officer ordered his men behind the barrier. There were just eight of them but they had muskets levelled at us. I noticed that they had not fitted their bayonets.

"Halt. What is your business?"

"I am Major Boucher of the 6th Hussars and I have a message to deliver to La Rochelle."

"Where is your authorisation?"

I stared at him. "I can see that you were not at Quatre Bras. Nor were you with us when we charged the roast beefs at Mont St. Jean." I pointed to Jones. "We are on important business, now raise this barrier."

He looked a little less confident. He noticed the rest of the troop approaching in the distance. It seemed to confirm my identity. "You could be anyone!"

"I am on the Emperor's business."

I knew I had made a mistake when his hand went to his sword and he shouted triumphantly. "He said nothing when he passed through this morning, but he warned us about Prussians! Kill them!"

I drew and cocked my pistol as I shouted, "Sound the charge!"

My pistol discharging into the officer's face drowned out the strident sound of the bugle. I urged Pierre forward and drew a second pistol. "Move the barrier, Jones. I'll deal with these!"

I fired my second pistol and hit a National Guardsman in the shoulder. Drawing my sword I rode at the remaining soldiers. Had they had bayonets fitted then I should have been dead. As it was, I saw them raise their muskets to fire at me and I was able to duck. These were not experienced soldiers and they fired high as I had expected them to. The musket always kicks up when you fire, and you need to aim lower to guarantee a hit. Once they had discharged their weapons they were as good as defenceless. The barrier was hurled into the river and I spurred Pierre on whilst waving my sword at them. They jumped, to a man, into the Cher. I heard the hooves of the troop's horses as they clattered over the cobbles.

"Straight over. Well done, Jones!"

Troop Sergeant Gargery's voice called out. "Ride, Colonel Matthews, we will cover you."

I joined the troop as we thundered over the bridge. There were half a dozen Guardsmen at the other end, but they discharged their muskets prematurely and were then forced from the bridge by Lieutenant Howard and his troopers who were eager to emulate my deeds. We did not halt until we were three miles outside of Tours. While the horses rested, I held a meeting with the sergeant, the colonel and the lieutenant.

"Boney is ahead of us!"

"Damn it Matthews! I warned you! He has escaped us!"

"No, he has not. We now know where he is. We can steal a march on him."

"How?"

He will have to cross the River Vienne at Chinon. He is in a carriage. We can cut through the forest south of Azay-le-Rideau. We can ford the river and get ahead of him. This time we know for certain where he will be."

The colonel seemed mollified while Lieutenant Howard shook his head, "I can see why Sir Arthur wanted you for this, sir. You know this area like the back of your hand."

"No, lieutenant, but I can read a map and that helps."

We camped just to the south of the forest which adjoined the river. I did not want to risk fording the river at night. I had done it many times, but I was not certain about either the colonel or the troopers.

The colonel had calmed somewhat since his outburst. He came over to me and offered me one of his precious cigars. "That was damned brave of you, Robbie, stupid but damned brave. I see now why you have been so successful over the years." I lit the cigar from a burning twig. "Can you be sure that we will be ahead of him?"

"He is travelling in a coach and if you look at the map it is a longer route by the bridge. Once we have crossed the Vienne then we can rejoin the road. I will wager you a gold piece that we reach Rochefort before he does."

He grinned and held out his hand. "Done!"

The river was not wide and there was a mud bank halfway across, but it was fairly fast flowing. "Troop Sergeant, have you and your men crossed a deep ford before?"

"I have, just the once but the lads haven't. "

"Then you and I will cross first. If we go downstream, we can catch any chicks who fall from the nest." I turned to the others, "This is easy, at least it is for the horses. However, they are more intelligent than the troopers who ride them!" I was pleased that they laughed. "When you enter the water slip your feet from your stirrups and try to lie flat. It will be easier for the horse. They will swim but talk to them and keep talking to them. It is reassuring for them. Colonel Selkirk, I want you to go in the middle and Lieutenant Howard at the rear. The sergeant and I will go first. Do not, under any circumstances, stop once you are in the river. That would be fatal!"

I spurred Pierre to the water's edge. Surprisingly, he stepped in straight away. After drinking a little his head came up and I slapped his rump. He began to walk. Within a few steps, the bottom had disappeared and he began to swim. I shouted, "This part is deep. Remember that!" Lying flat on his back I glanced over my shoulder and saw that the sergeant was also in the water. When we reached the mud bank Pierre clambered across it. The other side was narrower, and he did not need to swim as far. Once ashore I jumped down and allowed Pierre to shake himself like a dog. The sergeant had slipped from the saddle and lost the reins but he was hanging on to the saddle with one hand. I ran into the shallows and began to call for the horse. His hooves found purchase and I grabbed the reins and pulled the horse's head. He made it ashore.

The sergeant looked annoyed with himself. "Thanks, sir. If one of the lads had done that, he would have had a bollocking!"

"Well, at least you can tell them how to avoid it eh? Next pair!"

I think that the troopers took some comfort in the sergeant's slip and the next four made it without difficulty. When it was the colonel's turn my heart was in my mouth. "Joe, take two of the troopers and go downstream in case the colonel slips."

"Righto, sir. There are some rocks down there. That might be a good spot." Picking up a fallen branch of a tree they ran downstream.

The colonel did the hard part. He negotiated the deep water and then the sandbank. I think he must have become overconfident for I saw him smiling. He lost his grip on the reins and unlike the sergeant, he did not manage to grab the saddle. He was swept downstream. Freed from the burden of a rider the horse made the shore and clambered up the bank.

"Next pair!"

I kept one eye on the colonel. I saw that one of the troopers was leaning out and holding the eight-foot branch while Joe and the other trooper held his belt tightly. Four more troopers crossed before the colonel managed to arrest his voyage of discovery by grabbing the branch. I was relieved. I did not want to lose anyone on this, my last mission.

By the time the four of them had returned, the whole troop was across. "We have no time to waste. Mount up. We will dry as we ride."

We were so close to our destination that I risked our horses and we pushed on. We reached the outskirts of Niort before midnight. We had, according to the road marker, just fourteen miles to go. I risked a longer rest. The men had not eaten all day and were dead on their feet. We did not even make a camp; the men collapsed next to their horses. I went with Troop Sergeant Gargery to the road. We were the only two still awake.

"You ought to sleep, sir. We will be needing you tomorrow I daresay."

I shook my head. "I can sleep when all of this is over. I have much to finish first."

This is personal isn't it, sir? You and Bonaparte, I mean."

"Yes, sergeant."

He shook his head. "He ruled half the world, and you knew him and Old Nosey too!"

"They are both just men, Joe."

"No sir, I can't believe that. Old Nosey, he is special. We all know that if he is in command, sat on Copenhagen all calm as you like then we have a good chance of winning. We know that some won't survive. That is in the nature of fighting but a soldier likes to win. I reckon that is why Boney is so popular too. He always won."

"Until he met Sir Arthur."

"You are right there, sir. He met Sir Arthur, and he met his match." He shook his head and left, "Goodnight sir."

I did not sleep. The game was almost over. I could sleep then. I woke them all before dawn. The Lieutenant was unhappy, "You let me sleep sir, you should have woken me."

"When you get older, Johnny, you do not need as much sleep. You and your troopers will need to be as sharp as tacks today. Do not underestimate the Imperial Guard. They are good." I paused, "I know for once I was one of them."

His jaw actually dropped open, "You were one of Bonaparte's Guards?"

I smiled; now that it was almost over there was no need for secrets. "When we have time, I shall tell you all. I want no more deaths, either French or English. Stay sharp."

"I will, sir, you can rely on me!"

We reached Rochefort by nine o'clock and we saw neither carriage nor ship. We had beaten Bonaparte to the port. Once we arrived then Colonel Selkirk came into his own. "Well done Robbie! I never doubted you! I shall find out about the proximity of Royal Naval vessels." He looked over to the Customs House and then back at me. I knew what he was thinking.

"Troop Sergeant Gargery, "Two troopers to watch the Colonel's back if you please."

"Yes sir!"

My old spymaster smiled and patted my arm, "You are reading my mind. I shall miss you, you know." He strode off with his escort.

It was almost as if it was over and I knew that it wasn't. "Lieutenant Howard, I want every horse out of sight. There should be no sign of us."

"Sir!"

I waved Sergeant Gargery over. "We need to be able to surround this harbour and stop anyone leaving."

He nodded. "Four men over there, sir, two on either side of that road. It is the only way in and out."

"I want you there then, Sergeant. When the Emperor arrives, I don't want him running away. Have someone watching the road so that we get a warning. Just whistle and wave your arm as a signal that the carriage is coming."

He nodded and scanned the harbour. "There is a wagon there. I shall commandeer it. When he enters, I'll block the road." He smiled, "The lads'll have their pistols and carbines loaded this time, sir."

"You are a good man, troop sergeant."

He shook his head, "Let's just say that I am learning and getting better at it." He shouted, "Oi, you three follow me."

I saw four National Guardsmen coming towards me. Lieutenant Howard and the rest of the troop were coming from the opposite direction. I knew that this could be a tricky situation and I was determined to handle it calmly. I had no need for deception. I was there legitimately. I had yet to use Wellington's authorisation, but I would if I needed to.

It was a sergeant with three men. "Who are you and what are you doing here?"

I sensed confusion rather than anger. "I am Colonel Matthews attached to Sir \Arthur Wellesley's staff and I am here to apprehend Napoleon Bonaparte. He is to be arrested." I spoke slowly and clearly so that there could be no mistake. "You know that the Emperor has abdicated." He nodded, "And that there are four armies who are here to ensure the war is over." Again he nodded. I saw that the muskets were no longer levelled as they had been. "There is no need for useless heroics. You have done your duty." They all nodded, and their guns were lowered. These were not front-line soldiers and the twenty horsemen were a large enough threat. I did not need to say anything else. "Have you seen any warships?"

"There was a British ship which entered the harbour and then left. That was yesterday."

"Good. I would keep you and your men away from here. I want no trouble, but he has Chasseurs with him. Enough have died already."

"Yes sir." He saluted. "It is over then?"

"It is over, sergeant."

He led the men away. I saw them go into a small bar. Their brazier still burned away; the evidence of their nighttime diligence.

I turned to the Lieutenant. "I want you and your men hidden around here." I waved around the dock area. There were many places where the troopers could hide. "The sergeant has the entrance covered. I want the Chasseurs to have weapons aimed at them when they arrive but listen for my command. I need you and your men to be both calm and controlled. If they are calm and committed, then the Chasseurs will be less belligerent. Take your lead from me."

"Yes sir. We will be ready."

The colonel hurried over to us. "Good news. H.M.S. Bellerophon is in the estuary. The customs fellow was very helpful," he smiled wryly, "once I had greased his palm. They are loaning me the pilot's cutter and I am going out to bring her in. Are you happy to be left here?"

"Do not worry, Colonel Selkirk, I can manage. Bonaparte will not escape."

I watched him descend into the small ship and it sailed down the river towards the sea. There was a small wooden hut next to a pile of ropes at the end of the jetty and I chose that as my seat. I found the tobacco Sharp and I had purchased in Mauberge a lifetime ago. I filled the pipe I occasionally used and wandered over to the brazier. There were some tapers close by and I used one to light my pipe. I returned to the rope and sat there.

It was actually quite peaceful. Perhaps it might have been noisier had we arrived earlier, but most people had concluded their business and left. The puddles on the pavement showed where the fish had been sold but they too had gone. Our presence, threatening as it was, had cleared the harbour. There was danger coming and the people of Rochefort had learned to keep their heads down.

Suddenly the peace was shattered by a whistle. I looked up and saw Troop Sergeant Gargery waving his arm. Bonaparte was coming. I kept my head down so that my face was hidden and smoked the last of the tobacco. I heard the clatter of the horses and the rumble of the wheels as the carriage and Chasseurs approached. Still keeping my head down I stood and tapped out the spent ash from my pipe on the heel of my boot. The carriage horses were less than ten feet away.

I raised my head and saw that there were just six Chasseurs who remained. Three were wounded but they all held pistols which were pointed in my direction. I held my hands out to the side. The driver and the carriage guard jumped down and, while one put the step down, the other opened the door.

A very crumpled figure in a green coat with the familiar hat stepped down. He looked into my eyes. He actually smiled, although it was a sad smile "So Robbie, it comes full circle. You were there at the start and you are here at the end." He strode over to me and I saw the excitement in his face. "Now you can join me. The Americans are not my enemies. I sold them our lands in that wilderness of theirs and I will make a home there. When my men join me, we will build up our army once more and this time it will have all the resources of the New World to hand. We might even take Canada as a new empire. Come, this will be a great adventure."

I shook my head. "It is over, sir. The Prussians want you dead. They would have a public execution. None of us wants that do we?"

"If I am in America then they cannot reach me."

"And unless you can walk on water then you cannot reach America. The Marquess of Wellington would not have you executed but he would have you imprisoned. He cannot have you begin another war. It is over, sir. I am here to secure you."

The six pistols were all ominously cocked. Bonaparte looked around and said mockingly, "On your own? You have courage my friend, but these soldiers will blast you where you stand."

I nodded. "Lieutenant Howard!" Suddenly the troop of Hussars appeared. The Chasseurs saw immediately that they were surrounded. They had me covered but that made them easy to contain. They looked at the road down which they had travelled and saw that the sergeant had blocked it with a wagon. They were trapped. My plan had worked.

The lieutenant of Chasseurs looked to the Emperor who waved his hands indicating that they were to lower their guns. They did so.

I nodded, "A wise move, lieutenant. Have your men dismount. There is a water trough over there I am certain your horses will be thirsty." He nodded, "Troop Sergeant Gargery, I have told them to water their horses. Watch them please."

Lieutenant Howard joined me. I could see that he was curious about this most famous of men. Bonaparte came and linked his arm in mine. "Let us walk, Robbie, and you can tell me about this prison." I began to walk, and he suddenly said, "It was you and these men at Malmaison! It was not robbers as I was told. I should have known. It had your style all over it."

"And we would be there yet if the Prussians had not come."

"You drove away their horses?"

I nodded, "My orders were to secure you. I did not wish to fight my former allies." He stopped. We were at the edge of the river and I wondered if he considered jumping in and ending it. Then I realised that this was Napoleon Bonaparte. He would still be planning his return.

"So then, where is my new home to be? Elba again?"

"You are to be taken to St. Helena."

"St. Helena? Is that close to Italy?"

"No, it is in the middle of the Atlantic. You will be a prisoner but in a gilded cage."

His shoulders slumped. "Then this is over. When will I be taken there?" I pointed to the mouth of the estuary. There were the sails of the Bellerophon in the distance. She was tacking her way closer to us. "That soon?"

"It is better that way. The Prussians want revenge. We can protect you there. We still rule the waves."

"You do," he said bitterly, "your Nelson saw to that. I was within a whisker of invading!"

I remembered Nelson. He, like Sir John Moore, had been a charismatic leader and like Sir John, he too had given his life for his country. "You could never have invaded England. It was a dream. You understand the land but not the sea."

"Wisdom too. But you are probably right." He suddenly looked to sea. "The Bellerophon you say? She was at the Nile. That ship has dogged me for many years." He laughed wryly, "An appropriate end." He looked at me and seemed to study my face. "Your Marquess of Wellington is an interesting commander. He sits on his backside to fight a battle yet his men do not run. How did he do that? I was certain that my horsemen would sweep your redcoats and the ragtag army from the ridge, but they did not."

"He is a good general. You two are very similar. And those ragtag soldiers might have been inexperienced, but they were fighting to defend their land." I felt a little sorry for this man. He did not yet understand his own victories. "Tell me, sir, where were your greatest victories?"

"Why Italy of course! Marengo was a magnificent achievement!"

"And there you were giving hope to the Italians for they wished to be freed from the yoke of Austria. The same is true at Austerlitz. But Spain and Portugal were your undoing were they not? They did not want what you offered and then you tried to defeat nature in Russia. No, General Bonaparte, you forgot that people do not want to have one tyrant replace one they already had."

"Philosophy too. I should never have let you go." We both turned as we heard the commands given aboard the seventy-four gunship which was ghosting into the harbour wall. He turned to his driver, "Get my bags. These will be my last steps in France. May I speak with my Chasseurs?"

"Of course but do not try anything silly. I would hate to have to shoot you. You would not be dead merely crippled and retirement with a whole body might be better eh?"

"Wise and cruel. Did I make you what you have become?"

"No, sir, the war did that." Lieutenant Howard stepped closer to me. "Did you get all that Johnny?"

"Most of it sir." He shook his head. "I shall dine out on these stories in London. I was within a few feet of the most powerful man in Europe."

"And at the end, Johnny, he commands eight men. Look at your troop. I know that they would follow you against the whole Prussian army. Who has more, you or him?"

The gangplank was lowered as Bonaparte came back. "I have told my Chasseurs to return home. Let them go eh, Robbie, for old times' sake?"

I nodded, "Of course. They were just doing their duty. And these two?"

"They will be with me. They are loyal servants and they would serve me yet."

"Lieutenant, go and tell the Chasseurs that they are free to go."

Colonel Selkirk, Captain Maitland and six marines walked from the ship towards us. The Emperor turned to me and, grasping my shoulders, kissed me on both cheeks. "I should have made sure you stayed close to me, Scotsman. Your advice was ever sage. Will you visit me on my rock?"

"No sir. My war ends here. You were the last task I undertook." I detected sadness on his face when I said that.

"Well done, Colonel Matthews. I'll take it from here." The colonel was back in his comfort zone. He would take charge now.

And that was the last I saw of either the Emperor or Colonel Selkirk. They boarded the ship which left before the tide turned. Neither even waved but why should they? I was no one important. I had served them both and helped both men get what they wanted.

"What do we do about this carriage sir?"

"Well, Troop Sergeant Gargery, I put this under the spoils of war category. I would suggest that you and the other troopers sell it and share the proceeds."

The sergeant looked at the Lieutenant who nodded and then back at me, "Is that an order, Colonel Matthews?"

"It is my last order, Troop Sergeant Gargery!"

Epilogue

D'Alpini estate 1821

Alan and I were sipping the new wine when young Charles, now grown and able to read, ran in with the newspaper. "Napoleon is dead! He has died on the island of St. Helena!"

I looked at Alan, "Well, it is finally over. I always wondered if he would find some way to come back and start again."

Alan tapped the newspaper with his good hand. "Well, there is plenty of unrest in France."

"And England too. Remember when the cavalry charged those protesters in Manchester a couple of years ago."

"Aye, they called it Peterloo!"

"By newspapermen who were nowhere near the real battle." I downed the wine. "Yes Alan, Bonaparte was born too early. He would have worldwide followers now. Look at Sir Arthur. He is now a politician and he is repressing the very soldiers who fought for him."

Alan stood and stretched, "But we are happy enough, sir. We have all of this."

"You are right, Alan. Somehow we came through the horrors of war and not only survived but prospered."

Sir Arthur had kept his word. He had promised me a reward for my services. I had expected a Waterloo medal, but he had shown that he appreciated what I had done for him. Perhaps it was for the dead he could not reward. He had me knighted. Alan and I took our families to London where King George bestowed that honour upon me. All those who lived on our farm by the Tottenham Court came to see me when I emerged. It was an honorary title but I think it might have pleased my mother and, I hope, my father. He had been a French aristocrat and understood the importance of titles. To me, it meant little save that my wife was now a lady. Titles had never been important to me. It was the man who held the title who was important, and I hoped that I had never changed. Of course, I knew that I had. War did that to a man. It was like a circle; I had begun life as the son of a lord, albeit an illegitimate one and I would end my life as a lord. It did not change me. I was still the same man I had ever been. All that had changed me had been war and the title would not make me different.

Alan was right and we had a more than prosperous life. Our business had gone from strength to strength. Our ships now plied the world's seas. My wife and I had another two children, young Emily and Robert, a lively two-year-old who needed at least two servants to watch him! Matthew Dinsdale ran the empire we had created from London. He and the Fortnum family had done well out of the association. We had almost nothing to do. Captain Robinson now ran a small fleet of ships that plied their trade all over Europe. One day we might even begin to sail to the Americas and the Indies. We received our income without having to work. My home in England provided a healthy income for all those who had served me and retired from the army. Money was not an issue and our life was a good one. I was pleased that I had been able to help my friends in France too. I had sent money to both Monique and Pierre-Francois. The *'Chasseur'* was now a successful enterprise and my old friend was now a teacher at the Sorbonne; he taught politics.

Already Charles and my two younger children, as well as Alan's, constantly pestered me to tell them the stories from the war. So far, I had declined to do so but one day the time would be right, and I would be able to view the battles and deaths a little more dispassionately. Then I could tell then the adventures that I had had as the Napoleonic horseman.

The End

Glossary

Fictional characters are in italics

Cesar Alpini- Robbie's cousin and the head of the Sicilian branch of the family

Sergeant/lieutenant Alan Sharp- Robbie's servant

Colonel Robbie (Macgregor) Matthews-illegitimate son of the *Count of Breteuil*

Captain David Macgregor- Royal Scots Greys

Colonel James Selkirk- War department

Colpack-fur hat worn by the guards and elite companies

Crack- from the Irish 'craich', good fun, enjoyable

Joseph Fouché- Napoleon's Chief of Police and Spy catcher

Laid up in ordinary-Royal naval vessels which were still serviceable but no longer commissioned

Old moustache-a veteran of Napoleon's army (slang)

Paget Carbine- Light Cavalry weapon

pichet- a small jug for wine in France

Pierre Boucher-Ex-Trooper/Brigadier 17th Chasseurs

Pompey- naval slang for Portsmouth

Rooking- cheating a customer

Snotty- naval slang for a raw lieutenant

Windage- the gap between the ball and the wall of the cannon which means the ball does not fire true.

Historical note

The books I used for reference were:

- Bayonne and Toulouse-Lipscombe
- Napoleon's Line Chasseurs- Bukhari/Macbride
- The Napoleonic Source Book- Philip Haythornthwaite,
- Wellington's Military Machine- Philip J Haythornthwaite
- The Peninsular War- Roger Parkinson
- The History of the Napoleonic Wars-Richard Holmes,
- The Greenhill Napoleonic Wars Data book- Digby Smith,
- The Napoleonic Wars Vol 1 & 2- Liliane and Fred Funcken
- The Napoleonic Wars- Michael Glover
- The Waterloo Campaign- Albert A Nofi
- Waterloo- Bernard Cornwell
- Waterloo 1815 (Quatre Bras)- John Franklin
- Waterloo 1815 (Ligny)- John Franklin
- Waterloo 1815 (Mont St Jean and Wavre) John Franklin
- Waterloo The Battle of Three Armies- Lord Chalfont
- Wellington's Regiments- Ian Fletcher.
- Wellington's Light Cavalry- Bryan Fosten
- Wellington's Heavy Cavalry- Bryan Fosten

The best of these by far both in terms of readability and content is the Bernard Cornwell book. If you only read one of them then it should be that one. The maps and illustrations are excellent and help someone who has not been to the battlefield visualise what it was like. The battlefield itself is well worth a visit. I went there as part of my research. Despite Slender Billy's ridiculous monument, you can still see what a tiny killing ground it must have been. The whole field is the same size as Hastings where a much smaller battle took place.

I have used Robbie rather like the Captain Shepherd character in the film, *'Sink the Bismarck'*. He is a tool to enable me to tell the story of the whole battle. It is not to make him seem more heroic for the real heroes of Waterloo were the rank and file who died for both generals.

Napoleon escaped Elba when his gaoler went to Italy to visit his mistress. He did disguise his ship as an English brig.

Wherever possible I have tried to use the words spoken by the key players. General Cambronne's words were what he said he spoke when invited to surrender. He survived the battle. I used Robbie Matthews to show the battle from as many places as possible. He could not have been where he actually went and survived. That is fiction. I have only shown the battle from the English/Dutch perspective as it is done in the first person. The Prussians were important (see below) but their actions are only reported; not seen.

Martha Deacon was the wife of a wounded ensign. She was nine months pregnant and had three young children. After failing to find her husband on the field of battle she walked the 22 miles to Brussels through a rainstorm which Wellington himself said was worse than an Indian Monsoon. Remarkably she made it in two days, found her husband and had her baby the day after the battle. He was called Waterloo Deacon. Women appeared to be tough in those days; even the wives of young ensigns.

The John Shaw story is also true. He had been a prizefighter and was a huge tough man. The thought of someone using his helmet as a weapon is frightening and shows that there was a little of the Viking Berserker in him.

The buying and selling of commissions was, unless there was a war, the only way to gain promotion. It explains the quotation that 'the Battle of Waterloo was won on the playing fields of Eton'. The officers all came from a moneyed background. The expression cashiered meant that an officer had had to sell his commission. The promoted sergeants were rare and had to have to do something which in modern times would have resulted in a Victoria Cross or a grave!

Colonel Selkirk is based on a real spy James Robertson. Wellington also relied very heavily on his Exploring Officers who ranged far behind the enemy lines gathering information. At Waterloo many of these were unavailable. It might explain why Wellington appeared to be outwitted by Bonaparte's sudden early moves in the Waterloo campaign.

Much has been made of Marshal Ney and his mistakes. He did delay at Quatre Bras and he did countermand Bonaparte's orders and had D'Erlon marching ineffectually between the battlefields. However, at Waterloo itself, Bonaparte was on the field of battle and could have overridden any of Ney's poor decisions. The fact was that the 18th of June was not a good day for Bonaparte. Grouchy let him down and Ney let him down but Bonaparte was the biggest architect of his own downfall.

236

He was, unusually for him, unimaginative and did exactly what Wellington wanted him to do. He tried a frontal assault after a battering from his guns. When the battle is refought with model soldiers the French always win. Even Wellington was surprised by his victory. It speaks much of the bravery and resilience of his men and in the Prussians who did what Blucher promised, they came to Wellington's aid. This was despite senior Prussian officers begging him not to. Had Blucher not ignored them then the battle would have had a different ending. The Young Guard would not have been wasted attacking Plancenoit, they would have attacked Wellington's left flank.

The attack on Hougoumont was supposed to be a feint to draw in the allies but his young brother wanted glory and he ended up drawing invaluable troops who could have been used elsewhere. The disastrous cavalry charge was originally supposed to use just 900 cuirassiers but a combination of Ney and cavalry commanders eager for a glorious charge meant that over 6,000 horsemen were used. Neither cavalry forces did what their commanders wanted.

The incident with Sous Lieutenant Legros, 'The Enforcer', happened very much as I described. The French broke into Hougoumont and the Lieutenant Colonel did not try to kill the ones who had entered but closed the gates instead. The whole party was killed with the exception of the drummer boy who was captured. The Marquess of Wellington singled out the Colonel and Sergeant Graham for an annuity after the war.

Whenever possible I have used the actual words spoken at the battle. I realise the story of the comments surrounding Uxbridge's leg may be apocryphal but it is a good interchange and I have included it.

The Crown Prince was shot by a mysterious ball. In Sharp's Waterloo, it is a rifleman who does it. I had Robbie considering it. The man was such a disaster that I think it is highly likely to have been one of his own men who did. It certainly saved many lives. He proved to be a better king than a general but his monument at the battlefield totally ruined the aspect of the site.

Bonaparte fled to Paris and attempted to raise another army. The deputies refused and he abdicated. He went to Malmaison and then tried to take a ship to America. I have used my imagination for the area around Malmaison. Paris has grown a great deal in the last 200 years. Apologies if anyone who was there remembers it differently!

The Prussians did, indeed, want him executed but I have found no evidence to suggest that they sent hussars to capture him. Nor was there a firefight at the house. That part of my story is pure fiction and the product of my imagination. Bonaparte fled to Rochefort where he gave himself up to Captain Maitland and he was taken immediately to St. Helena. That part of my story is true.

Waterloo

The battle is much debated. I have read most of the books which debate it. I have war-gamed it more times than I care to remember. I have used my opinions throughout the book but I have studied both generals and armies extensively. This was the last battle which either general fought and was the only time they opposed each other. It was also a decisive battle. It was the last battle when the French and the British were on opposite sides. The peace in Europe lasted until 1870 when the Prussians and French fought. Indeed the next war in which the whole of Europe became embroiled was 99 years later! The battle saw the beginning of the end of the Austrian Empire as well as the rise of Italy and Germany.

Both generals and their subordinates made mistakes. Here is my list of the mistakes and the key moments in the battle.

- Wellington underestimated the speed at which Napoleon could move and was in Brussels at a ball when he should have been closer to the front.
- Bonaparte and Ney both wasted D'Erlon's Corps which spent a whole day marching, rather like the Grand Old Duke of York, between Quatre Bras and contributing nothing to either battle.
- The Crown Prince caused more allied deaths than the Old Guard! It is hard to find a decision he made that was correct. He constantly sent battalions in line when there was cavalry close by.
- Ney dallied too long at Quatre Bras and sent his troops in piecemeal. He exacerbated the problem by delaying the day after too although Bonaparte was equally guilty as he gloated over his victory at Ligny.
- The orders given to Grouchy were incredibly vague and Grouchy managed to totally misinterpret them. Both he and Bonaparte were to blame. Had his 30000 men been available at Waterloo then the French would have won.

- Prince Jerome committed too many men on what was supposed to be a diversion. That too could be said to be Bonaparte's mistake as he allowed his brother to call on other troops and waste them.
- The Earl of Uxbridge and all the cavalry commanders were totally guilty of not controlling their men. The loss of the Heavy Brigade could have been catastrophic.
- Both Ney and Bonaparte were guilty of sending cavalry in without horse artillery in support. Had they done so then the French would have won for they would have blasted the squares apart. They barely held against just the cavalry.
- The Prussians were crucial. Their advance meant that the Young Guard was not available to Bonaparte. Had they advanced against the ridge alongside the Middle Guard then who knows what the outcome would have been.
- Finally, the age-old problem of changing from column to line was one of the key reasons the French failed. The British had the confidence to use a two-deep line and bring the maximum muskets to bear. As the threat of the skirmishers was eliminated by the rifles it meant that the British with up to five volleys a minute could outgun any French column which, even if in line could only manage three volleys a minute. Every French infantry attack during the day advanced in column and took too long to get in line. The British infantry won the day for Wellington: The Guards and the 52nd ended the last threat when they decimated the vaunted Middle Guard.

I do not subscribe to the theory which has recently been resurrected that the battle was won by the Prussians. It seems fashionable these days to try to diminish what was done in the past. I hate it when people try to rewrite history. The fact is that without the Prussians then Wellington might not have won but the Imperial Guard and the French cavalry attacked Wellington, the Dutch and the Hanoverians. They sent their best to beat the allies. In the end, it was a damned near-run thing. It could have gone either way. And I wonder what would have happened had Bonaparte made it to America. Would he have been welcomed? Would he have become involved in American politics? Could he have become President? I give that outline to any other writer who wonders...what if...?

Griff Hosker April 2021

Other books by Griff Hosker

If you enjoyed reading this book, then why not read another one by the author?

Ancient History

The Sword of Cartimandua Series
(Germania and Britannia 50 A.D. – 128 A.D.)
Ulpius Felix- Roman Warrior (prequel)
The Sword of Cartimandua
The Horse Warriors
Invasion Caledonia
Roman Retreat
Revolt of the Red Witch
Druid's Gold
Trajan's Hunters
The Last Frontier
Hero of Rome
Roman Hawk
Roman Treachery
Roman Wall
Roman Courage

The Wolf Warrior series
(Britain in the late 6th Century)
Saxon Dawn
Saxon Revenge
Saxon England
Saxon Blood
Saxon Slayer
Saxon Slaughter
Saxon Bane
Saxon Fall: Rise of the Warlord
Saxon Throne
Saxon Sword

Medieval History

The Dragon Heart Series
Viking Slave
Viking Warrior
Viking Jarl
Viking Kingdom
Viking Wolf
Viking War
Viking Sword
Viking Wrath
Viking Raid
Viking Legend
Viking Vengeance
Viking Dragon
Viking Treasure
Viking Enemy
Viking Witch
Viking Blood
Viking Weregeld
Viking Storm
Viking Warband
Viking Shadow
Viking Legacy
Viking Clan
Viking Bravery

The Norman Genesis Series
Hrolf the Viking
Horseman
The Battle for a Home
Revenge of the Franks
The Land of the Northmen
Ragnvald Hrolfsson
Brothers in Blood
Lord of Rouen
Drekar in the Seine
Duke of Normandy
The Duke and the King

242

New World Series
Blood on the Blade
Across the Seas
The Savage Wilderness
The Bear and the Wolf
Erik the Navigator (April 2021)

The Vengeance Trail

The Danelaw Saga
The Dragon Sword

The Reconquista Chronicles
Castilian Knight
El Campeador
The Lord of Valencia

The Aelfraed Series
(Britain and Byzantium 1050 A.D. - 1085 A.D.)
Housecarl
Outlaw
Varangian

**The Anarchy Series England
1120-1180**
English Knight
Knight of the Empress
Northern Knight
Baron of the North
Earl
King Henry's Champion
The King is Dead
Warlord of the North
Enemy at the Gate
The Fallen Crown
Warlord's War
Kingmaker
Henry II

Crusader
The Welsh Marches
Irish War
Poisonous Plots
The Princes' Revolt
Earl Marshal

Border Knight
1182-1300
Sword for Hire
Return of the Knight
Baron's War
Magna Carta
Welsh Wars
Henry III
The Bloody Border
Baron's Crusade
Sentinel of the North
War in the West
Debt of Honour (May 2021)

Sir John Hawkwood Series
France and Italy 1339- 1387
Crécy: The Age of the Archer
Man at Arms
The White Company (July 2021)

Lord Edward's Archer
Lord Edward's Archer
King in Waiting
An Archer's Crusade
Targets of Treachery (Due out August 2021)

Struggle for a Crown
1360- 1485
Blood on the Crown
To Murder A King
The Throne
King Henry IV

The Road to Agincourt
St Crispin's Day
The Battle for France

Tales from the Sword I

Conquistador
England and America in the 16th Century
Conquistador (Coming in 2021)

Modern History

The Napoleonic Horseman Series
Chasseur à Cheval
Napoleon's Guard
British Light Dragoon
Soldier Spy
1808: The Road to Coruña
Talavera
The Lines of Torres Vedras
Bloody Badajoz
The Road to France

The Lucky Jack American Civil War series
Rebel Raiders
Confederate Rangers
The Road to Gettysburg

The British Ace Series
1914
1915 Fokker Scourge
1916 Angels over the Somme
1917 Eagles Fall
1918 We will remember them
From Arctic Snow to Desert Sand
Wings over Persia

Combined Operations series

1940-1945
Commando
Raider
Behind Enemy Lines
Dieppe
Toehold in Europe
Sword Beach
Breakout
The Battle for Antwerp
King Tiger
Beyond the Rhine
Korea
Korean Winter

Tales from the Sword Book 2

Other Books
Great Granny's Ghost (Aimed at 9-14-year-old young people)

For more information on all of the books then please visit the author's website at www.griffhosker.com where there is a link to contact him or visit his Facebook page: GriffHosker at Sword Books